31472400139931

A DROP OF
CHINESE
BLOOD

Also by James Church

A DROP OF
CHINESE
BLOOD

JAMES CHURCH

MINOTAUR BOOKS
A THOMAS DUNNE BOOK
NEW YORK

This is a work of fiction. All of the characters, organizations, and events portrayed in this novel are either products of the author's imagination or are used fictitiously.

A THOMAS DUNNE BOOK FOR MINOTAUR BOOKS.
An imprint of St. Martin's Publishing Group.

A DROP OF CHINESE BLOOD. Copyright © 2012 by James Church. All rights reserved. Printed in the United States of America. For information, address St. Martin's Press, 175 Fifth Avenue, New York, N.Y. 10010.

www.thomasdunnebooks.com
www.minotaurbooks.com
Maps by Paul J. Pugliese

Library of Congress Cataloging-in-Publication Data

Church, James, 1947–
    A drop of Chinese blood / James Church.—1st U.S. ed.
        p. cm.
    ISBN 978-0-312-55063-9 (hardcover)
    ISBN 978-1-250-01792-5 (e-book)
    1. National security—Korea (North)—Fiction.   2. National security—China—Fiction.   3. Missing persons—Fiction.   4. Suspense fiction.
5. Mystery fiction.   I. Title.
    PS3603.H88D76 2012
    813'.6—dc23

                                                    2012033780

First Edition: November 2012

10 9 8 7 6 5 4 3 2 1

For my mother,
who likes a good mystery

Acknowledgments

This book was written thanks to the initial and persistent nudging of David Straub, who finally convinced me that although James Church and Rex Stout certainly never met, Inspector O and Nero Wolfe might well have.

Deep thanks as well to the gracious people I met during my stays in Mongolia. They are rightly proud of their country, and bravely looking to the future at a time when the rest of us are shaking in our boots.

SEOUL, JULY 13 (YONHAP)—A Seoul appellate court on Wednesday sentenced a fraudulent seal maker to three years in prison for defrauding the government in a project to make the nation's newest state seal.

. . . The state seal scandal has jolted the nation for months after a police probe revealed that the craftsman had embezzled gold from the state seal project and did not have traditional skills as he had claimed while producing the state seal.

. . . The state seal is used by the president on official documents and national certificates, for proclaiming constitutional amendments, and for ratifying international agreements.

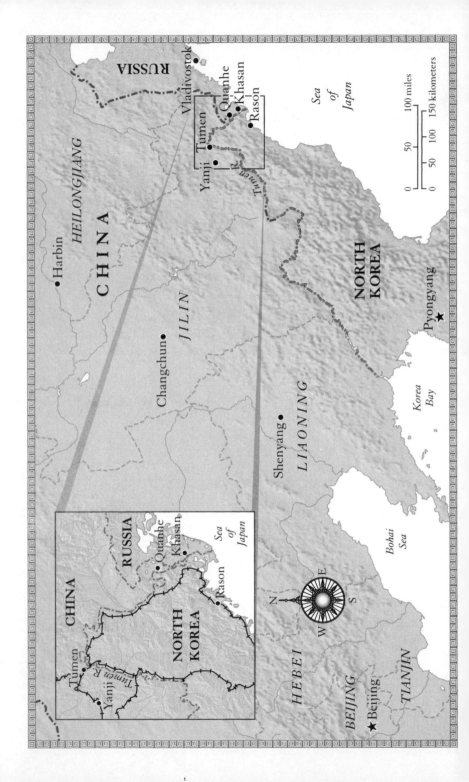

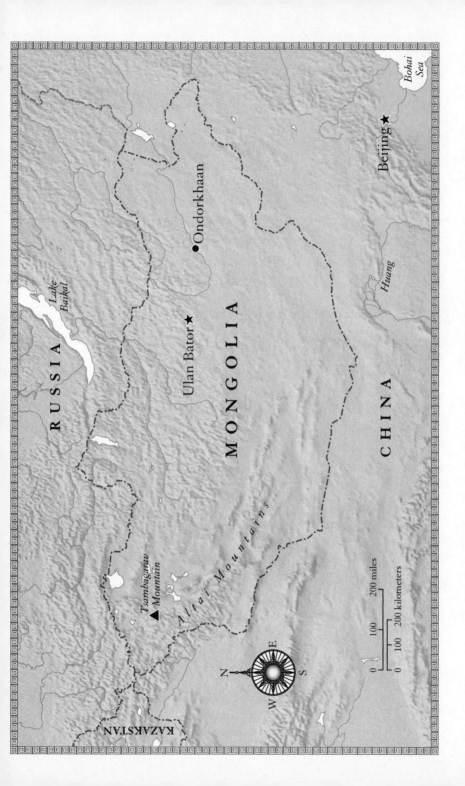

PART I

Chapter One

Fang Mei-lin was the most beautiful woman in the world, and for weeks rumors had been flying around that she might show up in our neighborhood. Naturally, there was a pool at Gao's on who would spot her first. The bet doubled on when the first sighting would be. It tripled on the location. That meant there was a lot of money in the pool, but no one bet that she'd show up on my doorstep on Tuesday, the day I always stay home to make lunch for Uncle O. You would have been crazy to make a bet like that; too bad I didn't.

Since no one collected, Old Gao took the money for the house. There was no grumbling. Everyone knows that Gao runs the most serious gambling establishment in northeast China, and he makes the rules. He's also very careful about the sort of betting that goes on in his place.

"No can do," he says if I offer odds on something he considers unusual. Then he frowns and puffs on one of his awful cigarettes, an Egyptian. Boxes of them show up at his door a few times a year, payment for a bet someone lost long ago. The tobacco smells like a large animal died, but Gao doesn't care. His only concern is making sure nothing interferes with the cash flow—in.

Given whom you can bump into at Gao's—which is to say, a surprising number of high-level officials from the better stations in life—the place isn't much to look at, just a shabby, one-story building off an alley in Yanji, a barely awake city thirty kilometers from the North Korean border. On the inside, Gao's is even less impressive—three tiny rooms, each with a beat-up round table and five or six folding chairs. The walls used to be red. They still might be, but no one can tell because the old man doesn't believe in paying a lot for electricity. Even when all three rooms are full, the place has the noise level of a tomb. People who come to Gao's are serious about losing money, which they almost all do. Gao makes sure the experience has nothing to recommend it—no drinks, no snacks, no music, no women. You come in, you lose what you're going to lose, and you leave. Anyone who wins keeps his mouth shut.

The iron house rule is that the betting stays simple—only horses, dogs, or cards. A sign taped to the wall spells it out for newcomers: NOTHING ELEGANT, NOTHING WEIRD. A week ago, I ignored the sign and tried to convince Gao to give me odds on something out of the ordinary. He snorted. "I don't take money from children or idiots. Go away, Bingo. If I need your pathetic savings, I'll come knocking."

That might be why when there was a knock on the door Tuesday around noon, I assumed it was Gao, though I didn't figure he wanted my money. More likely, I thought, he wanted to tell me a sad story about how Ping Man-ho, a lowlife with a taste for expensive Hong Kong suits, had stiffed him again. But when I opened the door, there was no fog of Egyptian tobacco. Instead, a delicate cloud of perfume enveloped me, followed by an eyeful of the most beautiful woman I'd ever seen. My nervous system figured it out before my brain delivered the news.

2

If Fang Mei-lin was on my doorstep, that meant she was in my territory, referred to in official Ministry of State Security correspondence as YS/SB, shorthand for Yanji Sector/Special Bureau. YS/SB doesn't look like much on the map. It doesn't cover a lot of real estate. It's just a strip of mostly empty land, twenty to thirty kilometers wide, that starts at the flyblown town of Tumen perched on the narrow, winding river of the same name. From there the sector heads north and east along the river, which loops aimlessly a few times like an adolescent dragon before finally making up its mind, turning south and east toward Russia and the East Sea. YS/SB stops at a raggedy place called Quanhe, the easternmost of China's bridge crossings into North Korea. From that crossing to the Russian border, barely twenty kilometers away, is another MSS sector chief's headache, usually someone junior and therefore unhappy.

Yanji Sector has been described as a bad dream spilling over onto 3,000 square kilometers. Sometimes, in especially bad times, it expands to 3,250 square kilometers. The exact configuration changes depending on who at Headquarters in Beijing has just looked at pins in the map and decided that rearranging sector responsibilities is urgent to prevent things along the border from getting worse than they already are. They are always already bad. Bad is the best they ever are.

When I was handed the assignment to head Yanji Bureau, the betting at Gao's was that I wouldn't last a year. MSS billets on the border with North Korea usually go up in flames for one of three reasons—stress, corruption, or, as true of my predecessor, unexplained and permanent disappearance. Yanji Bureau directors rarely last eighteen months. To everyone's surprise, this was my seventh year. I was becoming a legend in Headquarters, which meant I couldn't get a transfer out of Yanji no matter what I tried.

The population of Yanji City can fit into a few square blocks of apartments in Shanghai. What it lacks in size, though, Yanji makes up for in hyperactivity. Rumors constantly pour in, swirl around, and stream out. Paying attention to them is a good way to waste a lot of time chasing ghosts to nowhere. That's why it didn't mean much when my office suddenly started picking up the rumors that Fang

Mei-lin would be in northeast China. Some of these graduated from rumors to agent reports, unusually detailed about her travel plans. A few even listed Yanji as a probable destination. That gave us a good laugh. What would anyone like Fang Mei-lin want with a town like Yanji? I put a little in the betting pool at Gao's to be friendly, but otherwise I forgot about the rumors as quickly as they crossed my desk. There was plenty else to do at the time, and my mind was focused elsewhere. That's how I remember it, anyway.

A week or so after the rumors died down, Beijing sent out a barrage of flash messages, three of them in quick succession. Flash messages are considered very urgent on a scale of how rattled your teacup should get when one arrives. All three of them screamed at us that the lady was definitely in our neighborhood. We were to inform Headquarters immediately—immediately!—about potential threats to her safety. I did what I always do with flash messages, which is not much.

Ignoring high-priority Headquarters messages is not easy. They arrive via special couriers riding big, thundering motorcycles. The couriers all look like they're bred on a farm where they get a diet of good genes. They all wear the same outfit—high black boots, show-off leather gloves, and a helmet with a reflective visor they don't like to flip up so you rarely get to see their eyes. The only thing missing is trumpets when the courier walks into the office. In case motorcycles and boots don't get the requisite attention, every flash message comes in a special envelope, double wrapped with two thick black stripes around the middle. Across the flap is the best sealing tape money can buy. The tape has been specially designed by the Ministry's technical department to tear the hell out of any fingers careless or untutored in removing it.

In mid-May, three couriers showed up one right after another; three envelopes were signed for; three messages duly read. Then, as I said, I tossed them aside. I wouldn't say I ignored them; I just didn't focus.

Now, planted in my doorway, I was paying attention to nothing else. Slowly, I looked Fang Mei-lin over from head to toe, making sure there were no threats to her safety. I had gone crown to foot and was coming up the other way when she spoke. I'd heard sultry voices before, but hers was in a class by itself.

"May I come in? Or do you need to frisk me first?"

As she brushed past, her perfume hung in the air. It was the expensive stuff, and it took up all the space the little oxygen molecules are supposed to occupy. Even without oxygen, it registered that she had on a silk suit, pale blue, with matching high heels and a pearl necklace that must have cost plenty. The pearls were perfect against her skin. They were the sort of pearls that make you think oysters know what they're doing.

"I take it you are Bing Zong-yuan." She didn't wait for a response. "I need to see your uncle." Standing in the narrow hall, she looked like she owned the place and was thinking of tearing it down to build something better.

"Not possible," I said without having to give it a second thought, which was good because I was still breathing more perfume than air. As soon as the words were out I mentally lunged to take them back. It seemed a shame—a crime, actually—to say anything that might cause this image of perfection to turn and walk out the door. The problem was that I knew my uncle would see no one, not even a goddess from Shanghai, without an appointment. From the tilt of her chin, I knew that my fears were unfounded. She wasn't about to be brushed off so easily. In case she changed her mind, I went quickly to Plan B—a spoonful of honey.

"If you'll follow me into the library, we can discuss what this is about. Then we'll put our heads together"—I paused to let my heart recover from the image of her face close to mine—"and devise a request for him, my uncle, if you follow my meaning, to consider on an emergency basis. I can pull out all the stops when necessary."

"Don't be a fool." The sultry voice had been checked at the entrance, replaced by one with a good deal of brass. "Your uncle and I are old friends. Just tell him I'm here. I'll wait." She looked at me.

"Shall we close the front door? Or would you like *all* the flies to come in?"

I reached around her and pulled the door shut.

"Have it your way," I said, smiling to show how I wasn't nonplussed in the company of women like her. Actually, it was the first time I'd been in the company of a woman like her, and I had the feeling that if I didn't watch my step it might be the last. "This may take a while," I said as I led her down the hall. "Maybe you should come in and count rose petals while I go explain the situation to him."

Wrong approach. Her jaw was too delicate to clench, but the sparks from her eyes made it clear that I was treading dangerously. I'm smart enough to know when quiet is good, so I played dumb the rest of the way to the room we used for business. It wasn't much of an office, more like a sitting alcove with two small desks, two upholstered chairs for clients, and numerous bookcases of various shapes that my uncle churned out on a regular basis. There weren't many books on the shelves, mostly papers in untidy stacks, and a vase or two filled with long-forgotten flowers. Some people called them dried. I called them dead.

I pointed to a red velvet chair against the wall. "Why don't you sit there? It's the most comfortable seat in the place. I'll try to find some tea. Today is the maid's day off."

This was an approximation of the truth, but I didn't think she'd mind. There had been a maid at one time, but I couldn't pay her after my wife took all the cash—including what had been buried in the backyard—and skipped town with a Japanese pastry chef. The maid left for Beijing a week later, hard on the heels of one final, noisy argument with my uncle and considerable slamming of doors. Shortly before she disappeared, she announced to the neighborhood at the top of her lungs that if she had to stay in the northeast for one more day, it was a good bet she would die of boredom assuming that she didn't end up in jail for throttling my uncle first. The two of them had hissed at each other on first sight. I never figured out what it was; chemistry maybe, the sort of thing that makes one king toss another into boiling oil.

After locating a teapot and a clean cup, I left Fang Mei-lin in the office, walked down the back hall to a side door, crossed the tiny courtyard filled with squash vines, and entered an annex building through a low entrance that my uncle had made into his workshop. Scraps of wood were everywhere, nails and screws of different descriptions, rasps, hammers of varying sizes, a saw from Turkey of all places, a giant metal T-square leaning against the wall, and pots of varnish huddled together on a shelf. Bookcases in varying stages of completion occupied three of the four corners.

"You couldn't just tell her to leave. You felt compelled to invite her in." My uncle did not appear impressed or surprised when I explained who was waiting in the library. He was on a bench raised a few centimeters by wooden blocks under each of the legs, allowing him to sit while at his workbench. "The beauty of the flesh is fleeting, you know, or maybe you don't. On the other hand, this"—he held up a length of dark wood—"will be beautiful for a very long time. It's from a rain forest somewhere, but don't ask me where. All I know is what they told me at the lumberyard in Harbin, and for once I believe them. It's hard wood, dense, completely resistant to rot, unlike this so-called beauty that has made you gasp like a mudfish in summer. Those bandits in Harbin charged me an arm and a leg for it. I'm saving it for the right project."

I didn't think Fang Mei-lin's beauty could be described as so-called, but this was no time to argue. When I didn't give my uncle the satisfaction of a reaction, he continued. "She might have caused hearts to flutter once, mine included, but that didn't last long and anyway it was years ago. This, however, is not fleeting. With this you could knock someone out for a week, maybe even permanently." He tapped the piece of wood lightly on his head. "Want to try?"

"Possibly a good use for it," I said, "but let's perform the test later. I'll make things simple. Yes or no. Do you or do you not want to see her?"

"I don't suppose you have a rain forest in this grand country of yours?"

This caught me a little off guard. "What?"

"We used to have a map around here." He looked at the walls, which had waybills and receipts tacked to them in no particular order. "It was one of those elaborate things, with different colors for vegetation, forests, grasslands, and I don't know what. Did you take it down?"

"Me? I haven't touched anything in your workshop. I never do. Everything is sacred. I'm surprised we don't perform sacrifices to the gods in here."

"My jade knife is out being sharpened." Uncle O pointed to a half-finished chair. "Sit down if you want to talk. Talking like this is uneven, with me sitting and you standing. It makes you fidget. Don't fidget, sit."

"Thank you, I will." I sat.

"Don't lean back! The back isn't attached."

I leaned forward. "We don't need an involved conversation, uncle. This isn't a complicated issue." Conversations with my uncle were rarely simple. There was a lot of bobbing and weaving. He did not see the utility in getting straight to the point. In fact, he was sure it could lead to nothing good. I sometimes worried that trait was beginning to rub off on me.

"Then go ahead and explain," my uncle said. "Why are we dancing around the fort while the enemy is without?"

"This woman doesn't have an appointment, and I know that normally means you won't see her, but I couldn't simply tell her to go away, could I? First of all, she's gorgeous." That was also second of all, and maybe third. "She said you were old friends. It crossed my mind that she could be making this up in order to get a meeting, but somehow I wasn't sure, so I thought I should check with you before I booted her out. By the way, how does she know my name?" That I would never have booted out Fang Mei-lin we both understood without saying.

"Admit it," my uncle said, "the real problem is she's so tough you couldn't tell her to leave even if you wanted to. You turned into a puddle as soon as you opened the front door." He snorted. "She's not even fifty, I don't think. We never established exactly." He smiled to himself. "How could we be old friends? And you'd better realize right now, she does her homework. She probably knows your sock size."

I stood. "Actually, I would have bet she was quite a bit younger than fifty."

That drew the hint of a frown. "Gambling rots the mind, I've told you that. Even as a figure of speech, it's debilitating."

By now I knew enough not to take that barbed hook. He didn't like my gambling, and he made it a point to say so regularly. "I have to get back to work, so after she's out the door, I'll fix you some noodles for lunch and be on my way."

"You think you can get rid of her that easily?"

That should have been warning enough, but I passed it off with a wave of the hand. "I'll tell her you are indisposed, something to do with your bowels, and to make an appointment for tomorrow or the next day. She won't be happy, that's pretty plain. She seems to have an iron will."

"More like titanium." He turned to the pile of tools on his workbench. "Why is there never a file around when you need it?"

When I returned to the office, the red velvet chair was empty, and Miss Fang was standing near the window. In silhouette, she had the look of a Tang princess wondering whom to poison next. Very tough, I told myself, beneath those pearls. What was she doing here? Why did she need to see my uncle? And nagging atop everything: How did they know each other?

"Your uncle is on his way?" She turned away from the window, so the light from the back created the hint of a halo around her head. "May I suggest you don't want to be in the room when he gets here. He and I have a few things to discuss." She made "a few things" sound like rubies and pearls rolling across the naked backside of a five-hundred-yuan hooker on Dooran Street.

"Actually, he's not available." I sat down at the desk that I used when we had clients and pulled an appointment calendar from the bottom drawer. "He has a full schedule today." I made a show of studying the pages and then brightened as if I'd found good news. "There is time tomorrow morning, though. Shall we say ten o'clock?"

"Oh, come now," she said and fingered her pearls with a hint of annoyance. "Let me be direct." She glided to the desk and leaned over. "I'm told being direct is one of my most attractive features."

Some might quibble over what was her most attractive feature. I shrugged noncommittally.

"I must see your uncle today, within the hour." She looked at the watch on her wrist. The watch was expensive; I didn't think it was a copy of anything. The wrist was beautiful, leading to a graceful hand and long, slim fingers. She waved the fingers in my direction. "It's not a question of choice. I wouldn't be here otherwise. This is urgent. So, why don't you trot back to his workshop, which I'm sure is where he's sitting at this moment, and tell him to pull his nose out of those boards and get in here." She smiled at me, a ravishing smile that would paralyze a racehorse heading for the finish line. "You can do that for me, can't you?"

3

My uncle made her wait twenty minutes, in the polite range but on the edge of irritating. When I told him what she had said, he gave me a hard look. "Lucky for you I'm not paying you a salary, or you'd be fired. Never mind, I knew you couldn't do it. Don't feel bad. No one could. She's implacable when she wants to be." He shook his head. "That and insatiable."

I coughed.

"All right, all right. She says it's urgent. We'll accept it is urgent because she's not one to exaggerate. Don't call her Miss Fang to her face, though. It will only flatter her. She's Madame Fang to you."

"Are you going to meet her like that?" I pointed at his trousers, which were covered with sawdust, and his shirt, with spots of dried glue down the front.

"She's seen me in worse."

"Not in less, I hope."

He smiled faintly. "Hope crosses many rivers," he said and brushed the sawdust from his pants. "You go in first and tell her I'll be right there. Then sit and keep quiet. Don't engage in chitchat. Don't hum a happy tune. Just sit."

"Is she married?"

"Why, are you going to propose while you're waiting? She'd eat you alive and then look around for dessert. Keep your distance. Didn't you learn anything from your former wife?"

I winced twice, once at the mention of dessert, and again at the reference to my wife. "That wasn't called for," I said. "I'm assuming you won't drag out this meeting too long." I looked at the clock on the wall. It was from the Harbin lumberyard my uncle visited occasionally. Two pine trees served as the hands, with the face of the clock a slightly blurry photo of the forests of Changbai Mountain. Fortunately, they hadn't done anything cute with the numbers or it would have been completely unreadable. "I'll take notes, but don't forget, I have to be back at my office by two o'clock. If I'm reading those pine branches right, I don't have much time."

4

There was no danger of chitchat. While we waited, Madame Fang sat and looked out the window as if I did not exist. Around one forty my uncle came through the door. He had changed his shirt and pants and combed his hair.

"Fang Mei-lin," he said and extended his hand. It was scrubbed clean. "No less beautiful than the last time we met."

The woman remained seated. "I am less beautiful, but much richer, and I didn't come here for your honeyed tongue." She put out her own hand and touched his lightly. I could see her palm was sweating.

"You said it was urgent?" My uncle cocked his head slightly when he said the last word. It was his way of seeming temporarily to cede ground. "A problem, perhaps? You've already met my nephew, Major Bing."

"We've met." She glanced in my direction and then focused back on my uncle. "I have a few things to discuss, things that are urgent and extremely private. And don't cock your head around me."

My uncle smiled in an ingratiating way that he hadn't demonstrated in the nearly two years he'd been in my house. "Whatever you say to me you say to my nephew. He does most of the work, so he has to know all the details. That's the way we handle things. If you can't accept it, then I'm afraid we can't do business."

I held my breath while I waited to see how Madame Fang would react to such a direct challenge.

"Goodness, who said anything about business?" She smiled back, the ravishing one directed at my uncle and then another, less lustrous, at me. "I don't need a private detective. I need advice, that's all, another viewpoint. I thought yours might be valuable. If your nephew has learned anything from you, perhaps his views might be interesting, too. Of course, I'll pay."

I looked at the small clock on my desk. I'd won it in a bet with the man who eventually ran away with my wife. Charming fellow, smooth as they come, superb at making desserts with tiny flowered vines made of green sugar climbing walls of chocolate bricks. He made tiny chocolate bricks! What a bastard! Why didn't I smash the clock with one of my uncle's hammers, and scatter the pieces up and down the river for a hundred kilometers? Why didn't I?

The hands on the clock were climbing toward two o'clock, and my office was near Renmin Road, a half hour away by bicycle. It took less than that by car, but my wife and her brick-making paramour had taken the car with them.

"I'm sorry to say that I can't stay to watch this reunion unfurl," I said. "One of us has to earn steady money." I put the emphasis on "steady." "I'm sure we'll meet again, Madame Fang." My bow in her direction seemed inadequate; I should have been groveling at her feet. I turned to my uncle. "There's a pack of instant noodles on the table near the stove. The cabbage is in the sink, if you want to throw some in. You can boil the water yourself?"

The woman looked out the window and smiled faintly.

I stopped at the door. "Dinner will be at the usual time, uncle, unless you have other plans."

My uncle gazed for a moment at Madame Fang, the tide of memory tugging at him. "No, I'm sure there will be no other plans."

Chapter Two

Your uncle called." The officer on duty pushed aside a magazine he was reading and consulted the logbook as I approached the front desk. "He said to tell you that he wouldn't be home for dinner."

"He called the duty office number to tell me that?"

"If there's trouble, I'll send someone over right away to check on him." This was a new officer, transferred from Shanghai and already painfully eager not to stay any longer than necessary here in the backwaters of the northeast. After reviewing his personnel file, which had appeared suddenly a few days ago, I had come away with a feeling that he was too close to the chief of the Shanghai office. That put him in a deep hole right from the start as far as I was concerned. I tolerate most human failings, but being close to the Shanghai office chief is a bridge too far, broken in the middle, and burning at both ends.

"Your name is Jang." I leaned toward him, lowering my voice in order to give our exchange an air of intrigue.

He observed me closely.

"Well, Little Jang, we can't send someone if we don't know where to send them, can we? And for your information, my uncle isn't in trouble. My uncle can take care of himself. He probably just wanted it on the record that he was going out to dinner with a beautiful woman, possibly the most beautiful woman in the world, eh?" I gave him a quick smile.

Instantly, Jang took on the mien of a tiny palace dog sensing a favored eunuch up to no good. His face twitched; he looked to be calculating whether to bite me or to run barking an alarm to the emperor.

"I didn't know, sir," he said at last, having decided to do nothing. "I'm pleased to learn that everything is all right."

"If my uncle happens to call on your line again, put him through to my office right away, will you?"

Jang made a note in the logbook.

"How do you like it here in our fair city of Yanji, Jang? Quite a change from the bright lights of Shanghai, isn't it?"

"I'm sure I'll get used to it, sir. Part of a well-rounded Ministry career. The Second Bureau has to be ready to serve wherever the need is greatest. That's what they say."

I recoiled slightly. "They say that in Shanghai, do they? It's the sort of thing that would roll off their silver tongues."

"Yes, sir." Jang looked concerned, worried that he'd said something to set me off.

"Well, here we're right on the border, busy guarding the frontier, not spending our time shopping at swank stores."

"I've noticed, sir."

"Good, keep noticing." I picked up the magazine he'd been reading and threw it into a trash can across the room. "Who are you assigned to work with?"

Jang looked quickly at the trash can, his eyes smoldering for an instant before he pulled himself under control. "Next week I'm paired with a Lieutenant Fu Bin, according to the roster. I haven't met him yet. He's on temporary assignment, apparently; no one knows where."

"No one knows where? Has anyone asked? He's in Changchun. It's not a secret, for heaven's sake. Have you been to Changchun?"

"Once or twice." I sensed his internal GPS shouting at him to recalculate. "I mean, only briefly, when the train stopped."

"Lieutenant Fu goes there to see a girl, maybe two girls. He can do that. You can't. Don't forget, Jang."

"No, sir, I won't forget."

I waited to see from his eyes if I'd lit a fuse I'd have to worry about later. There was nothing. "And take that call from my uncle out of the logbook."

"I can't, sir."

"Sure you can, I just told you to do it."

"It's in pen."

2

On my desk was a folder stamped READ ONLY. This was a new stamp. It had been sprung on us a few weeks ago, and the explanatory instructions still hadn't made their way here to the outer reaches of the empire. That meant none of us in the office was sure exactly what it meant. Were we not to nibble on the paper? Not to mark on it? No duplicating? Not act on it operationally? Not forward it to anyone else? Not use it as down payment on a car? Not sell it to a foreign service? No one knew. Maybe they had already figured out READ ONLY in Shanghai, but here in the forgotten northeast we remained in the dark. That was normal. Yanji was an afterthought, in a section of the country that hadn't been part of the ancient core of the central kingdom. In fact, the northeast had joined the empire late in the game and, worse, had for centuries been home to barbarian tribes, one of which had marched into Beijing and stayed for a few hundred years. It wasn't as if we were being punished for old sins, but Beijing had not forgotten or, I sometimes suspected, forgiven.

The folder itself consisted of a few pages of anodyne observations by what appeared to be a low-level source based in Tumen.

From the summary on the cover sheet, I saw that the source had little credibility and access to even less, but was paid regularly—too much, in my view—in hopes that one day he might stumble onto something worthwhile. Cutting away this flotsam was nearly impossible. No one wanted to authorize letting an agent go in case someday before the sun burned out, it might be discovered that a terminated agent had been connected to someone who knew something.

This agent was code-named "Handout." Code names were assigned from a central office, supposedly at random. In this case, it seemed too apt to be random.

Handout, according to the file, had recently made a trip across the river into North Korea and seen the usual: people here, cars there, thus and such number of trains crawling in this or that direction, the price of shoes at one market below what similar shoes cost at another market. He had made the acquaintance of a certain "K" who was engaged in moving "things" across the border. What these "things" were was not explained in the report. The unstated—but glaringly obvious—subtext was that giving a good deal more money to Handout would help us get in better with K, though why we should want to be in bed with K was left to our imagination.

I reached for the phone on my desk and punched a button. "Li, I've had enough. Get Handout off our rolls. Immediately. Yesterday. I'm going to start trimming the fat."

Li Bo-ting was my deputy. He was levelheaded and knew how to get things done. He had spent most of his career in this region, had a map in his head of every back alley in every town in our sector, and could move around without leaving a trace when he had to. As the deputy in the office, Li handled personnel matters, assignments, most of the evaluations, and almost all the annoying instructions from Headquarters. I made final decisions if there were any to be made. Otherwise, I was supposed to supervise from a cloud, watching for dangerous trends along the border. It wasn't how MSS had always done business, but Headquarters thought it needed a new management style, and someone decided this let-the-banana-peel-itself-approach was just the ticket.

Li laughed. "You want him off the rolls? I hope your luck is better than mine. We can't seem to get rid of him. Believe me, it's been tried. He must be joined at an important body part to someone in Beijing."

This was news to me, but then again, Li was aware that I didn't always want to know everything he learned, at least not right away. In the new management theory this worked the other way, too, though it was rare I knew anything before my deputy did. "There's a Headquarters reference to Xiang Feng Bao in this file," I said. "Any idea what that is?"

"No."

"Well, scratch around. Maybe Handout is in trouble. If not, we'll have to find something, manufacture something, doesn't matter which. It hints on the cover sheet that he likes to live beyond his means." I thought of the mountain of bills on my desk at home. "Apparently he floats around sipping nectar from the flowers. He's waving another one of those worthless sources in front of us, and he's holding us up for a lot of cash."

"Believe me, he's not alone." Li paused. "If it's a he."

The possibility hadn't occurred to me. For some reason, I'd pictured Handout as a short man, sticking to the shadows, quick-footed with a ready, slippery smile.

"Whichever," I said, "he or she, a little finesse would be nice occasionally from an agent. We pay them enough, don't we?" Li knew this was a rhetorical question. He let me continue. "Who's going out to debrief Handout? Have them take a farewell envelope and a medal of appreciation, shake whatever sort of limp hand it is, and tell the owner of it to get lost. Who is in charge of Handout these days?" I flipped through the pages. "It isn't in the file. In fact, the entire contact sheet is gone. That leaves an awfully thin record for all the money we've probably shoveled out. If there is an audit, how are we supposed to explain the expenses?"

"Handout has been Fu Bin's agent for the past four years. It must be noted in the file somewhere." There was a longish silence.

"You still there, Li? A problem with these phones again?"

"No and yes. No, I'm here. Yes, there's a problem, but it's not the phones this time. Fu Bin is gone."

"He's not gone. How many times do I have to tell people? Fu Bin is in Changchun visiting a woman. Two women, maybe, if he can afford it. Maybe he's been dipping into the payments to Handout."

"That's what you're supposed to think."

"That he's been running around on Handout's money?"

"No, that he's in Changchun with a woman. That's what you're supposed to think."

"Oh?"

"He's working for the Third Bureau, actually. I only found out by mistake."

Of course by mistake. No one finds out about what the Third Bureau is doing on purpose. Not even the Third Bureau. Their job is to make sure those of us in the lesser sections of the Ministry of State Security are not working for the "other side," haven't been bought off by the triads, haven't fallen into sloughs of chicanery or forms of corruption not officially approved and relabeled as acceptable. If Third Bureau rats cannot find anything, they lure the unsuspecting into traps; if they cannot lure, they embellish whatever might turn up from under long-discarded rocks.

It would have been better if I'd stumbled on the truth of Fu Bin's real job by myself and much earlier, of course, but Li knew I hadn't, which meant there was no sense pretending I was ahead of him on this. Still, I wasn't trailing that far back. As soon as Li told me, odd pieces tumbled into place, pieces that should have jumped up and pulled my nose long before this. Fu Bin had always walked more softly than anyone else in the office, almost on tiptoe. His desk was always clean, but he was always months behind on his paperwork. He went to the best restaurants and loved to take photographs with the fanciest new camera.

Usually, Third Bureau officers sent out to localities were easy to spot, that's why they rarely stayed more than a few months. Other than his curious walk, though, Fu Bin hadn't stood out. By itself, that should have tipped me off. People who don't have obvious quirks, have all the rough edges smoothed off, fit in like shadows on a peaceful summer afternoon, they're the ones who need the most careful watching.

Fu Bin had been in Yanji, supposedly under my supervision, for four years. Four years in one place for someone from the Third Bureau was a long assignment, too long, and that did not bode well. There were a lot of possible explanations, but the most likely one was that a decision had been made to clamp the jaws of internal investigation on my office—or my throat, to be accurate—and not let go. Why? What had I done? No one followed all the rules all the time; otherwise we'd never get anything accomplished. Gambling wasn't encouraged, but I didn't use anyone else's money, and I wasn't in debt to any shady characters. All right, I had been a little lucky, once, but that wouldn't keep a Third Bureau rat hanging around for four years.

That Fu Bin had operated so long without my noticing might also lead some at Headquarters to say that I didn't have a sense of my own people. It was the sort of charge that would be easy enough to refute if someone brought it up to my face, but this sort of low-frequency criticism tends to get slipped into a part of the personnel file that we weren't allowed to see. It could rumble for years, and you'd never be able to locate the source. In retrospect, I realized that Fu Bin's regular trips to a "girlfriend" were probably bogus. They must have been concocted in order to file reports and compare notes at the Third Bureau's regional office, which was rumored to be disguised as an old age home on the outskirts of Changchun.

Then again, maybe he did have a girlfriend or two there. Fu Bin was a ladies' man, I would have bet on that.

"When will he be back?" I asked.

"He won't. It's a permanent move, rather sudden apparently. He didn't clean out his desk drawers or even pay his final month's apartment rent. I've been tidying up after him. Headquarters won't want bad press about MSS not paying its rent."

"Don't use office funds! Let the Third Bureau pay for whatever he owes." I fell to light brooding. "You didn't bother to tell me sooner? I don't live on Mars, you know. I am reachable at all times by phone."

"Don't worry, you were going to learn about it as soon as orders arrived tomorrow from Headquarters for you to take over his agents. I mean, his agent, Handout. He only had one."

"He only had one. In all these years?"

"I'm afraid so."

"What was he doing the rest of the time? Never mind, I don't want to know. You handle personnel, I don't interfere. That's the way they want it, that's the way they get it."

"OK by me." There was a pause. "Listen, you'd better brace yourself. My information is that Headquarters is insistent that you pick up running Handout. I know you don't like running agents, but I don't think you can cut the cord right away. Maybe after a few months when things blow over. My advice is go ahead with a regular meeting, at least one or two for appearance's sake. Let's set up the contact, anyway. If Handout doesn't show, it's not your fault."

This made me sit up in my chair. First of all, I didn't like Li's casual reference to things "blowing over." What things? What's more, I hadn't run agents in a long time. Agents are often odd people, a little too psychologically needy for my taste. Besides which, it struck me as a bad idea to handle an agent who had been run by Fu Bin, especially one Fu Bin had supervised for so many years. Maybe working with Lieutenant Fu for that long explained why Handout was so annoying. Third Bureau traits could easily rub off on people; someone like Handout would soak up quirks like a sponge. Anyway, who could understand what the Third Bureau was up to half the time? Handout could be a Third Bureau–directed psychopath, a trained assassin for all I knew. Which raised another question. Since when did Headquarters assign local agents? Those of us on the scene were supposed to be the ones who knew the details of our local sea and the fish that swam in it. OK, maybe I didn't know a few details. Fu Bin had handled Handout and I hadn't known. So what? I was the office chief, wasn't I? There was always a delicate balance between knowing enough about operations and knowing too much, especially if something went wrong. My job was to stay on this tightrope and not fall off. So far, the annual inspection teams from Headquarters had been satisfied with my performance. Once in a while there was a little comment about the need for tighter supervision, but these sorts of complaints were always balanced in the next inspection by praise for the way operations were allowed to run "without excessive interference." I had long ago decided I couldn't please everyone, so I just kept doing what I did best. If they didn't like it, they'd pull me out and put me somewhere I could snooze with my feet on the desk.

Li Bo-ting waited, as always, while I mulled things over. Li was patient and efficient. Without him and his "sources" in Headquarters, I would constantly be hopping on hot coals.

"Fine," I said at last. "Good. You know how pleased I am when Headquarters sends me orders."

Now there was a new coal in the fire in the form of our latest arrival from Shanghai. It couldn't possibly be a coincidence that Jang appeared almost the same day that Fu Bin vanished. Come to think of it, Jang's use of the term "Second Bureau" in his conversation with me was very odd. The Second Bureau was where we sat on the MSS organization chart, but we never referred to ourselves that way. To top it off, why would anyone be so shifty about whether or not he had ever been to Changchun? When the question came up, Jang had changed directions like a cockroach on a noodle shop's steam table.

The thought that the Third Bureau had shuffled in a replacement so soon, right under my nose, was infuriating. Already Jang had shown he wasn't going to be as smooth as Fu Bin, but that didn't mean he wasn't as dangerous. Maybe the new officer was all the more dangerous for being so distasteful. It must be a deliberate effort to rattle me. I reined myself in. The Third Bureau loves paranoia; it bottles the stuff and hands it out for its operatives to sprinkle around. The best way to combat this is to stay calm. All right, I could be calm and rational. Jang had trotted up to us from Shanghai? That was reason enough to put ground glass in his food.

Li's patience finally ran out. "Talk to you later? I have a meeting outside."

"Hold it, Lieutenant, one more thing. There is still a formal complaint channel, isn't there?" It wouldn't do much good to file a complaint, more like spitting into a funeral pyre, but at least it would show the Third Bureau I knew their game. "Can't we use it? The forms are around somewhere. In the vault, I think."

"No."

"How about a tiny, informal complaint next time I'm in Beijing?"

Silence.

"Anyone know about this but you?"

"You mean in our office? No, of course not."

"Well, keep it that way." I hung up the phone.

3

It was early the next morning, right before dawn, when my uncle came back to the house.

"Everything all right?" I called out as he passed our client office, treading as softly as a seventy-year-old knew how. On nights I stayed up late, reading the newspaper or going over bills, I often fell asleep in my chair. It wasn't that comfortable, and I wasn't that asleep.

"Don't worry about me," he said. "You have problems of your own."

"What is that supposed to mean?"

"It means we'll talk later. Go back to sleep."

Around ten o'clock, my uncle was in his workshop, eyes bright, humming a Korean folk song, not so much carrying the tune as pushing it in a wheelbarrow over rocky ground. He didn't look up when I came through the door.

"Good morning, uncle. That's a song my mother used to sing to me, if I'm not mistaken. Rather melancholy verses about two lovers who become distant stars. Have you eaten?"

"Don't be coy, nephew. It never pays off. You're not interested in folk songs or astronomy. You want to know what happened last night."

"In that case, what happened last night?"

"Nothing. Not a thing. Disappointing, isn't it?"

"Madame Fang didn't have anything to say?"

"Perhaps she did, but I don't know what it was. We had arranged to meet at some bar she said was very swank and discreet. She never showed up. I sat around until all hours. The bar girls in this town seem to be all Koreans and Russians, have you noticed?"

Instantly, foreboding slapped me on the back of the head. Madame Fang had appeared in my sector. Worse than that, she'd been in my house. Not the general vicinity, not a few streets over, not even just passing by outside, but within my flimsy four walls. As far as Headquarters was concerned, that made her my personal responsibility. I didn't like the idea of her going to a lot of trouble to arrange a rendezvous with my uncle and then not showing up. Headquarters wouldn't like it either. You didn't have to be very suspicious to smell a problem here.

"Did she leave a note? Give a reason?" I was hoping there was still a net that might break my fall. "And if she didn't show up, why were you so late getting home?"

"My goodness, aren't you the concerned one."

"Not at all." I feigned unconcern, but it was useless, not much better than being coy. My uncle could read me like a banner head-line in the newspaper. It was uncanny, and ever since he moved in, it had been getting to be more annoying.

He shook his head. "It can't be genetic. It must be something in your upbringing. That my nephew should be the sole completely scrutable Chinese official in the long history of this peacock-strutting empire is unbelievable. The fact that you are half—more than half—Korean makes it all the more bizarre. Maybe it's some-thing to do with the schools, I don't know." He picked up his favorite screwdriver from the workbench and started to twirl it in his fingers. "What's your worry? Do you have instructions to keep an eye on Mei-lin?"

"I'll be blunt. If anything happens to her, my next duty station will be checking zombie caravans on the Silk Route. It isn't the transfer I've been hoping for. You'll be with me, incidentally, and there's hardly any wood in that part of the country. People cook with dried cow dung."

"Charming. In that case, better pack your bags. Apparently, she did leave a note."

"Nothing good, I take it."

"The note apparently said she had gone across the river, planned to stay for a week or so, and promised to be in contact when she got back."

Normally, I would have picked up right away that he said "ap-parently" twice, but I was too busy mentally bracing for the flam-ing rocket that would arrive any minute from Headquarters ordering my immediate transfer to the toughest, ugliest, most remote post they could find.

"Sichuan is pleasant in the spring." I sat down on the chair

with the bad back. "That's assuming they don't shoot me first."
Fang Mei-lin had gone across the river—probably on that damned
narrow stupid excuse for a bridge in Tumen. The most beautiful
woman in the world, the subject of numerous twin-stripe envelopes with special tape, had walked out of my house and into North
Korea. I looked around the workshop for the dense, dark wood.
Maybe I could brain myself with it.

"Don't worry." My uncle's voice poked through the despair.
"She'll show up again. She's more than a match for any of them."
He flipped the screwdriver once in the air and caught it right be-
fore it hit the workbench. "Besides, she's been there before."

This snagged my attention. "You dealt with her in Pyongyang?"

"Who I dealt with and who I didn't is off-limits to you, and
anyway it isn't the question. The question is, what is she doing there
now? Maybe there's a second question, too: Why was she in such a
crashing hurry to get over the border? None of it matters to me,
since none of this is my problem. But you might want to consider
such questions, because they seem about to fall onto your desk."

"Thank you. I know what I might want to consider, and I know
what's on my desk. I am, you sometimes seem to forget, director of
a special bureau in charge of the border, part of it, anyway. I flatter
myself into believing that means there is a certain competence I
am judged to have, even if you don't happen to think so. The border is considered a sensitive area, and I'm considered tough enough
to handle it." I held out my hand. "The note. I need it."

I was met with a blank look, tinged with the innocence of babes
and old men.

"She left a note; those were your words. Let me see it."

"Yes, those were my words. They still are. She left a note. I
didn't say she left it with me."

Even in the morning, or maybe especially in the morning, he
could be infuriating. I looked around more intently for that piece
of hard, dark wood.

"I'm not playing games with you on this, uncle. Beijing will demand to know what happened to her, and the inquiry won't arrive wrapped in a silk kerchief. The dragons at Headquarters will roar; they will breathe fire and lash their tails. They'll find out about the note within twenty-four hours, assuming they haven't already received a report from one of their informants. They'll want to know if I saw the note, and if not, why the hell not. So, let me ask: Whom did she leave it with if not you? Because if I tell them I don't have it and can't get it, they won't be happy. Believe me on this, it's not good when MSS Headquarters is unhappy."

"Whom did she leave it with, you ask? I would imagine with whomever she intends to contact when she gets back."

"And that would be?" I expected Li Bo-ting to call any minute with news that an urgent message had arrived from Beijing, the motorcycle courier waiting impatiently in the reception room for me to show up and sign for the package personally, allowing the motorcycle to roar back into life and unsettle things at the next stop. Little Jang's suspicious eyes would take in the whole show. I slowed my breathing and said to my uncle very carefully so as not to be misunderstood either in tone or in purpose, "Whom is she going to contact? Whom is she going to contact, and why?"

My uncle looked at me, half amused, his look of innocence put away for another day. "Very good. Exactly what I'd ask. That's the first thing—or rather, the first and second things—you want to figure out after you get us some breakfast. By the way"—he started arranging the tools on his workbench—"doesn't that crook Gao still owe us money?"

4

After a breakfast of noodles and dried fish, I left my uncle in his workshop. He was examining a long, twisted mulberry board. "Useless," he muttered as I closed the door to head off to work. "Might as well be a piece of crap pine in a Chinese whorehouse."

It was raining hard, making the traffic worse than usual. I arrived at the office late, soaked to the skin. The special branch occupies the first floor of a ramshackle former Imperial Japanese Army General Staff hotel off Hailan Road. For the past ten years, it has been wedged behind a new high-rise containing the Bank of China, a drugstore, and the corporate offices of a number of crooked trading companies. Originally, the hotel was considered an ideal location for the special branch because of its setback from the street and the screen of trees in front. When the new high-rise was built, it occupied every square centimeter of the lot in front of ours, blocking our main entrance. To compensate, a side door leading through the hotel's former kitchen was pressed into service. The kitchen was in the same state it had been in when the Japanese left hurriedly in the summer of 1945. The duty desk sat behind the big woodstove. The duty map, which showed our area of responsibility, shared a wall with a variety of old, wicked-looking Japanese kitchen implements. A special secure vault for files had been installed in the billiards room. Two of the high-ceilinged parlors where officers entertained guests and wrote letters home had been converted into interrogation rooms. It wasn't very effective, trying to interrogate suspects in rooms with elaborate woodwork and chandeliers; we needed people to feel intimidated, and instead they put on airs like they had been invited to a ball. We had three bathrooms, all with cracked, elaborate fixtures; two of them had deep bathtubs with ornate French taps. Overall, we had more space than we needed, so the broad, curved stairway to the second-floor rooms was sealed off.

Our entrance was always locked, and the storm had knocked out our new, highly secure entry system. I pressed the buzzer that was attached at the other end to the duty officer's desk. There was no response. Waving my arms in front of the security camera got me nowhere. The alternative was going through the bank and out a fire exit facing what had once been the hotel's front door. This door could be opened with a special key that I kept with me for emergencies. The bank didn't like it when we utilized this route, but by now I was too wet to care.

I kept a change of clothes at the office for just such emergencies. After I put on a dry pair of trousers and a shirt, I went through the overnight mail folder. There was nothing waiting from Headquarters, but under the folder was a lightly penciled message from Li Bo-ting saying he needed urgently to see me as soon as I got in.

Li's office was on the opposite side of the building from mine, with a large, high window that looked out on a pond surrounded by maple trees and filled with carp. Why the second in command had an office with such a lovely view while I had no windows at all, not even a small one, was a mystery. Some people said it had to do with security, but I didn't think so. The simple solution—trade offices—was impossible because mine had "special wiring" that only the chief of the special branch was supposed to know about. Getting the wires moved was a major undertaking involving high-paid cable technicians sent from Beijing. None of them liked the food in this part of the country, and they all had a list of excuses for never showing up.

Li's door was shut, which wasn't normal. I knocked and went in.

"Bo-ting, what's the problem?" If by some miracle he didn't know about Madame Fang yet, I wasn't going to tell him. If Li didn't know, then maybe Beijing didn't either. Unlikely, but maybe for once things were not that dire, at least not yet. Still, there was no reason to relax. If Li needed to see me urgently and his door was shut, something was wrong.

Lieutenant Li had a fair complexion, but this morning fair had turned to deathly pale. As soon as he saw me, he leaped from his chair. "Let's go for a stroll and enjoy the air. I want to stretch my legs." Bo-ting and I only went for a "stroll" in serious emergencies. Air had nothing to do with it.

"Can it wait a few minutes?" Going back outside into the rain was not something I wanted to do right away. "How about I have some tea first?" The closer I looked at Li, the more he resembled a corpse. It was unnerving. "You feel all right?"

"This country is full of tea," he said and waved his arms. "We can get some down the street."

"Yes, we can, but it's storming, you realize." His fishpond was full to overflowing, and the trees behind it were bending perilously in the wind. "The roads are flooded near the river. I got soaked on the way in; all the buses were throwing up sheets of water."

"Then don't go near the river! Stay on streets with no buses!" Li is always calm. I didn't like to see him in this exclamatory mode. "Rain is not our biggest concern right now, trust me. And this storm is nothing compared with what is coming up from the south. I'll meet you outside in two minutes. Get an umbrella."

Gloom enveloped me as I walked back to my office. I never should have let that woman into my house, pearls or no pearls. Umbrella in hand, I was on my way out, reaching for the doorknob when the new man, Jang, looked up. "Going somewhere, sir?"

"Where have you been, Jang? I rang before and you didn't buzz me in. Something wrong with the wiring?"

"I must have been in the bathroom. I'm sorry, sir, but I'm not used to the food up here. It's not like Shanghai."

"There's a drugstore in the building out front. Get yourself fixed up when you're on break."

"Thank you, sir. Are you going somewhere?"

"Out."

"Contact number? Is your cell phone on?"

"When I need a nanny, Jang, I'll put in for one."

"Yes, sir. Just trying to be helpful. It's standard procedure in Shanghai: Keep in touch. That way, if something comes up, there's no gap in communications. The chief there always wants to be in touch. By the way, the rain has picked up. You might consider wearing a hat. I don't think an umbrella will do much good in this wind. This is Shanghai weather." It was said smugly.

I turned around and walked back to the duty desk. "This is not Shanghai weather. This is our weather. Shanghai hasn't got a lock on the heavens. How things get done or from which direction the wind blows in Shanghai is of no interest to me. None. Nor is it of any interest to you as long as you are attached to this office. We have our own procedures here. They are effective. They are what we are comfortable with. Moreover, they suit our tastes. The chief in Shanghai can . . ."

Jang went on alert, his little dog nose twitching. I discarded what I felt like saying and fell back on less descriptive language.

". . . do whatever he wants." I despised the chief in Shanghai. The feeling was mutual, which didn't bother me. I knew that he had his hair done once a week in a beauty shop and that he owed his position to a relative. "I'm going. Period. I will be back. Period. Over and out. Am I clear?"

"Yes, sir, only one thing. Who's in charge in your absence? Lieutenant Li went out the door a minute ago. If you don't mind my saying so, he was wearing a hat."

"Give it a rest, Jang." New officers could be fussy, trying to prove their worth, but Jang was worse than normal. He was unusually worse, and if he was from the Third Bureau, it complicated the task of flushing him down the toilet. At least I was alert as to what I was up against, not like with Fu Bin. I made a mental note to put something nasty in Jang's file at the proper time. "There won't be any emergency for the next twenty or thirty minutes. We're in Yanji. It's quiet compared to the big cities. That's how we like it, and that's how we plan to keep it. Try to remember that."

When I stepped outside into a ferocious wind, Bo-ting was braced against the wall, holding on to his hat with one hand and looking at his watch impatiently. "We don't have much time," he said.

"Fine, we can talk as we sail over to the tea shop on Dooran Street."

5

The tea shop was one of Lieutenant Li's regular haunts. It wasn't actually on Dooran Street but tucked away in an alley nearby. The couple that ran it worked for us part-time. They were old and liked the extra money. It wasn't hard work, and it wasn't much money, but it gave them something to do beyond pouring tea. If someone odd wandered in and watched the door anxiously from a table in the back; if there was a long conversation between people who shouldn't be having a long conversation; if something didn't seem right about someone, Li heard about it when he stopped by. Mostly, the couple heard things from the girls who worked on Dooran Street. The girls were like little birds; they came in on cold evenings and huddled together, chirping and laughing about their customers before it was time to go out and work some more. They knew enough to tell the old couple if one of their customers let drop a piece of information that would interest us. We could have employed the girls directly, but that would have led to a lot of extra paperwork. This way worked fine, through the teahouse couple, so Li and I agreed we should just let it alone.

On the walk over, through the wind and the rain, Li gave me a quick summary of what he'd heard from his sources. There was a Headquarters operation in the works, he said, and it looked like it was going to be unusually ugly. He didn't actually have the order in hand yet. I listened and didn't ask any questions. How he knew what he knew, I had long since stopped wondering. His sources were his; if he trusted them, so did I. The main thing was that I knew Li wouldn't hold back. Whatever he told me would be everything he knew from his sources. Anything he didn't say was what he didn't know. There was no need for poking or prodding.

Once we were in the teahouse, we sat glumly, dripping and windblown, for a few minutes. After the tea arrived, Li came to life again and filled in the details. We were about to receive orders to launch a special crackdown—a "hard strike," as Headquarters likes to call these things in a dramatic flourish—in both Yanji and Tumen. In a break with normal practice, the bureau wasn't going to handle this one alone. Two, maybe three squads would show up suddenly—no date yet—from Headquarters with a list, and in the space of twenty-four hours, we were to assist them in rounding up everyone on it. Li said even his sources hadn't seen the final list, but as soon as they did, they'd pass it along.

Having Headquarters squads show up suddenly, without any notice, would complicate our lives. These squads were clumsy, and they smirked.

Li kept piling on the bad news. The list apparently would go beyond the normal quota of ten or fifteen officials suspected of taking money on the side, selling off state assets, or stepping too ostentatiously on people who had then not suffered in silence but complained so loudly it had reached the ears of outsiders, especially Western reporters.

"Bad," I said.

Li poured some tea into my cup. "Worse," he said. "The list includes Chinese or Korea-Chinese who have dealings with North Korea."

I groaned.

Li indicated there was more. "The order, it's numbered."

That was like a death sentence, only not as welcome. Numbered meant the order was part of a sequence. A number one meant there would be a number two, and then a number three. Maybe more. There was no way to cauterize this wound. We would be bleeding for months.

When he was done, Li looked at me numbly. Li didn't like hard strike operations of any type or size. They disrupted the rhythms he'd established, scrambled relationships, cut links painstakingly forged with people whose activities we needed to know about. It took months to put things in order again. This monster would set him back a year, at least. What neither of us said, but we both knew, was that the timing of this operation was ominous; nothing special was going on in Yanji, other than Madame Fang's appearance. Expanding things to include people with contacts across the river meant Headquarters knew something we didn't, and that meant we were goats.

Almost as an afterthought, Li added that he was working on my meeting with Handout. If he could, he said, he'd arrange it before the hard strike teams showed up so that Headquarters wouldn't be able to complain that we had overlooked a source that could have given us important information—even though both Li and I knew that Handout was the last person on the planet who had important information on anything.

I thanked Li, finished my tea, and left. He'd do whatever he had to do to warn his local contacts. My first thought was that I needed to get home and see if my uncle knew anything that might be helpful. Before that, I decided, I might as well stop at Gao's. It was on the way, and on top of everything, my uncle had reminded me that Gao owed us money. The debt was an old one. Not long after my uncle arrived unannounced at my door, Gao had appeared to ask his help in discovering the source of several threatening notes that had been wrapped around bricks and thrown through his windows. I hadn't told anyone that my uncle had once been a police detective in Pyongyang; after Gao left, I asked my uncle how word got out.

"Beats the hell out of me," he said.

The case turned out to be ridiculously simple. Uncle O had charged only for five days' expenses, but because he didn't like Gao—I didn't know why, and he wouldn't tell me—the expenses had been abnormally high. Gao had looked the bill over, taken a few puffs on the Cleopatra hanging from his lips, and said he would pay in a couple of weeks. "The man charges like Sholock Hams, Bingo," he said the next time I saw him, "but in this case, it's worth the money."

Apparently, it was so much worth the money to Gao that he neglected to pay the bill. I'd forgotten all about it, but a debt is a debt, especially one that was two years overdue. Other than our general lack of cash, I couldn't figure out what had sparked my uncle's interest in debt collection at this moment. At least it was a good sign that he was finally paying attention to our financial situation, which—as I kept trying to impress on him—was dire.

The rain had stopped, but the wind was not about to give up yet. It blew trash along the street, sending empty cans clattering and discarded broken umbrellas spinning down the sidewalks. I made my way to Gao's neighborhood, which is several notches below nondescript. The front door to the place was locked. That got my attention. Gao never took vacations, and if he was sick, he had his younger brother take care of the betting. One thing Gao didn't want was for customers to walk away because of a locked door, especially customers who made the trip in stormy weather, maybe especially those who particularly came in stormy weather because they didn't want anyone else to see them. I went around to the back door, which was slightly ajar.

"Gao," I called. "You in there?"

There was no answer, so I went up the steps and knocked. I heard a thud and then a groan. There wasn't time to call the police, and anyway Gao didn't like them nosing around. He didn't consider me the police, mostly because when I was there, I made it a point not to notice the other customers. If local officials walked in, they didn't see me and I didn't see them. I had a harder time ignoring provincial officials, but Gao kept the lights dim enough that it was possible to pretend. I listened for half a second, heard nothing else, and pushed the door open.

"Nobody move," I shouted. Since I wasn't armed, that seemed the safest thing to say at the moment.

"Don't worry, Bingo, I'm not going anywhere, OK?" Gao was on the floor, his face twisted in pain, like when some high-stakes gambler got lucky at his expense. He groaned as he raised himself up on his elbow. "Can you get me a cigarette? They're on the counter, next to the betting slips."

"What happened?"

"I slipped, OK? I think I hit my head on the way down."

"How come the front door was locked? You on strike?"

"What are you, a one-man interrogation bureau? I hit my head, I twisted my ankle, OK, and I need a smoke. If you don't want to help, get the hell out and come back tomorrow."

Gao wasn't known for his bonhomie, but I could see he was worried about more than his ankle. "You alone?" I glanced at the doorway into the next room.

"No, I'm not alone. There's a troupe of half-naked dancing girls in the front parlor drinking tea, OK, what do you think? Stop asking questions." He frowned and rubbed the back of his head. His hand came back with blood on it.

"I think you may have broken your ankle." I looked at the blood on his hand. "Let's take a look at your head, too, while we're at it."

"You're a doctor on top of being a lousy gambler? My head hurts, OK, more than my ankle. I told you, I slipped."

"You don't seem in a mood for company. Maybe I should leave you here on the floor."

"Maybe I owe you money."

"Yeah, you do, quite a bit. When I put on the interest for late payment, it's going to come to a nice package."

"I'll pay, OK, next week."

I thought about telling him he'd pay me right now, just to see how riled he would get, but I decided to let it go. "Fine."

"Your uncle sent you?"

That might have caught my attention if it hadn't miffed me. "My uncle doesn't send me places. I'm allowed to make my own decisions. I even have a decree from Headquarters giving me plenipotentiary powers in that regard. You know what plenipotentiary means? It means I can kick your tail all the way to Mount Tai if

I want to." I patted my pockets. "Damn, the paper must be in my other trousers. I'll bring it next time I'm in the neighborhood. You'll still be there on the floor, of course. Your ankle will have swollen to the size of a basketball." I turned to go. "You might even have gangrene. They amputate for gangrene. Not too many one-legged gambling shop operators, but it might increase business—you can never overestimate the novelty factor."

Gao looked at his ankle. Then he gave me a slippery smile. "Lucky you dropped by."

"Yeah, lucky. I was on my way home and remembered you owed us. I thought I'd stop in. It seemed like a good time to collect, but I guess not. See you around."

I was out the door and on the first step when Gao shouted, "Get back in here, OK? I got something to tell you."

6

"Uncle, we don't have time to waltz around each other." I was standing in the workshop, among the pots of glue.

"Good, we'll skip the dancing. You're welcome to sit, or are you in a crashing hurry, as usual?"

"I am, and I'm not."

"In that case, sit on the edge of the chair. That way you can spring up and leap out the door if necessary. Can I offer you refreshments? Tea?" He pointed to the brass teapot he kept on a hot plate near one of the glue pots.

"I wish you'd move either that hot plate or the glue. Sooner or later there's going to be a fire in here."

"So you say once a week. You mentioned you have a problem, and we can be sure it isn't how I arrange my workshop."

"The problem is a special order from Beijing."

"A special order." My uncle wasn't easily impressed. "You don't mind if I make some tea? Would you like a cup?"

"No, I don't want a cup. I want to talk about this order. It's numbered. When they number orders, that's a bad sign. It signifies a series, and that means the first one isn't the only arrow in the air."

"Go on."

"All of a sudden, they want me to come down hard on corruption in this sector. Not just a normal cleanup. Not the light dusting we do a couple of times a year. It's to be something thorough, a tough, hard strike, that sort of thing. They'll want quick prosecution followed by even speedier execution of several people—enough to scare the daylights out of the rest of the crooks for a good long time."

My uncle nodded. "Off with their heads."

"Let's hope they don't order me to raid Gao's place. Half the provincial government will be shot. He'll be furious, probably cut off my entrée for at least a few weeks. That is, if they don't shoot him, too."

"Did he pay up? If he's executed, I don't want him leaving this planet with what he owes us."

"He said he'd do it next week. Just before I arrived, I think, someone hit him on the head to keep him from talking, probably someone who knows about this corruption strike order. They might as well put these supersecret operations on billboards with flashing lights."

"Someone hit him on the head? What do you think they used?"

"A length of dark wood."

"It wasn't me, if that's what you're thinking. I wouldn't waste a good piece of lumber on his skull. That man must have a long list of enemies by now. All sorts of people owe him money, and for his part he probably owes some very bad people a pile. Look at how he's held off paying us."

"What do you have against Gao, other than the fact that he's stiffed us for so long?"

"What makes you think I have something against him?"

"When he came over here to ask your help that first time, I had the feeling you two already knew each other. Bad vibrations."

"Your tuning fork needs work. I never saw him before. Some people I dislike at first sight. I have good instincts, finely honed, in that regard."

"He told me he saw Madame Fang last night." I dropped this little bomb casually.

"Gao said that? Was that before or after you hit him in the mouth?"

"I don't hit people. I try not to, anyway."

"What would Mei-lin be doing in a low-class place like that?"

"I thought you could tell me."

"I don't have a tracking beacon on her fanny. Believe me, it's been tried."

"Maybe you were there with her."

"You interrogating me? I already told you, we didn't meet. Did Gao say he saw us together? If he did, he's lying. Him and his stinking Egyptian cigarettes."

This caught my attention. "How do you know they're Egyptian?"

"Was I once a police inspector?"

"You were, and a good one, too, from what I hear."

This stopped the conversation. I didn't praise my uncle to his face very often. He looked at the ceiling and then at the floor. "Never mind that," he said finally. "Did he say I was with her?"

"No, not exactly, but it occurred to me. Just a hunch."

"Good, I'm in favor of hunches. Nothing wrong with hunches, except that most of them turn out wrong. Maybe yours are better than mine used to be. When you go back tomorrow to get the money, ask him directly whom she was with. Don't let him slip around the question. If he doesn't change his story and insists she was there, did she show up to meet someone? Or was it that she simply wanted to make a bet?" He took the kettle of boiling water from the hot plate and poured some into a small celadon cup with a tiny bit of tea on the bottom. "That would be like her. She's been known to gamble a little. Maybe going into Gao's den appealed to her sense of adventure." He closed his eyes and took a sip of tea. "Now about this Headquarters order you mentioned. It's number one?"

"That's what I said. I shouldn't have even told you that much. You agreed when you moved in here that you wouldn't pry into my work."

"I wasn't prying, simply repeating. Or is that not allowed either?"

"What I meant to say was, *if* I received such an order."

My uncle moved a couple of awls to the side and found a pencil. "I must have missed the speculative part. My Chinese is fair, but it's not perfect. What is it that signifies the uncertainty, a verb ending? Some sort of particle at the end of the sentence? Here, write it down for me."

His Chinese was good enough to know what I meant. His Chinese was better than mine, sometimes. "It isn't about verb endings. Don't play games on this."

"All right, *if* you ever did receive such an order, and *if* you did happen to mention it to me, do you know what I would say? I would say 'so what?' Where's the problem? You want to find corruption? Stick a pan in the lake, and it comes out with fish, maybe one, maybe more, probably a whole school of them."

Away we go, I thought. I want to talk about corruption, my uncle talks fish.

"There's a lot of river between here and Quanhe, plenty of people trying to make a little extra money. I never blamed them." He took another sip of tea. "Are you sure you won't have some? Mei-lin gave it to me yesterday."

First fish, then tea. Sometimes I wondered why I even tried to have a normal conversation with him.

"Corruption is like carbon; life on earth couldn't exist without it. It might even be more widespread than we think." At least we were back on the main subject, though the biological origins of corruption weren't my concern at the moment. "Corruption in every corner of the universe, every life form, every stinking piece of algae—all corrupt. Ever considered that?"

"For some reason I was hoping your experience would do me some good on this. Crazy idea, thinking you might be helpful. They want me to get rid of corruption, not rationalize it!"

"If you don't like my solution, don't bring up the problem." Uncle O closed his eyes again. His voice took on a soothing lilt, all the more irritating and he knew it. "Do your job, and leave me out of it. That way there's no chance of my prying, as you put it."

"Nothing would please me more, but I'm afraid I can't leave you out of it this time."

"Is that so?"

"Yes, it's so, and I'll tell you why. Because there are additional concerns here, connections with your old friends to consider." I paused. Whenever I use the term "old friends" it almost always annoys him. As it did this time. His eyes flew open. I pretended not to notice. "How do I know there are connections? I can read between the lines."

Other than his eyes opening, my uncle maintained a posture of indifference, but I was sure it was just a facade. Sometimes he thought it useful to play dumb when we wandered onto the topic of North Korea. I decided not to hop around the cabbage patch on this anymore. "The current problem on this side of the river is tied to things on the other side. On your side, understand? We're not talking happenstance. We're not talking loosely connected, or hypothetical strings. We're not talking biology, or astronomy, or fish. What I'm talking about is events, people, actions, all linked together on this side and your side, linked with a steel chain." I didn't know how they were linked, or even if they were linked. Li's sources hadn't gotten into that, but it was pretty obvious that's what the target of this Headquarters operation was all about.

"Linked?" My uncle lifted the teacup close to his nose and breathed in the aroma. "Here and there? You don't say. What a surprise!"

Under the irony, I sensed a flare of genuine interest. The subject of connections across the river always made him perk up his ears.

He'd left North Korea in a hurry, under threat, but he still missed home. Though he pretended not to care, he devoured news from there, good news, bad news, anything to make it seem that he hadn't left for good and abandoned everything he knew.

"Nothing about that lousy border surprises me anymore," I said, "and it doesn't surprise you either." It was true. The border was a nightmare. There was never a twenty-four-hour period where something didn't go wrong. I had no control over the flow of people or things across it. I had no say in enhanced security measures, no say in better fences or more cameras. According to my job description, I was supposed to keep things quiet, and if they didn't stay quiet, it was my fault because I was supposed to collect information that would alert Beijing to a problem before it happened. That was the reason the special bureau had been formed; it was the theory that underpinned our continued existence. It was complete monkey crap, but it paid the bills, of which I had plenty.

"This isn't our normal sort of problem," I said, "not by a long shot. It's bigger than you might imagine." That didn't seem to get a reaction, so I upped the ante. "Much bigger."

My uncle grunted. "I hope there isn't a verb ending in all of this that I'm missing."

"You mentioned fish." I couldn't tell my uncle exactly what the problem was. Headquarters was holding its cards close for fear something would leak. Li might be able to come up with some more in a day or so, but meantime I had to work with what I had. Anyway, sharing operational information with my uncle was a bad idea; it could put him in jeopardy. Nobody could get in trouble talking about fish, though. "Let's start there, that's a good image."

My uncle understood discretion, but he didn't like it when I was so obvious. He frowned slightly, but I stayed on track. "We both know that some fish are expendable. Some are not. Some fish swim upstream to where they were born, some fish don't."

My uncle nodded slowly, so as not to dislodge the frown.

"Some fish are less tasty than others. Some have too many bones."

At this my uncle gave me a sideways glance. "Bones," he said. "Bones stick in the throat."

Something had caught his attention, or maybe it had just snagged on an old memory.

"Have you eaten those little fish from Lake Geneva?" He moved the pot of shellac a couple of millimeters away from the hot plate. "They were full of bones. That's what they were, all bones. I wouldn't go near them again."

Still not the advice I was hoping for. "I'm not concerned with little fish," I said, "and we're not talking about Geneva."

"Why not? Little fish feed big fish. It's nature." He waved a rasp at me. "Let's stop for a moment and review what you've just said, hidden as it is behind a veil of discretion so thick that you're lucky we both haven't smothered in it."

"Go ahead, review if you want to."

"You don't have any idea which fish you are supposed to catch or which to throw back as unpalatable, possibly poisonous. It could be your bosses don't know, or they don't want to let on that they know and intend for you to stumble around. Either way, it's clear that your hind end is the one closest to the fire." He moved the shellac back to where it had been. "Something goes wrong, you're the one who gets burned."

This was the sort of challenge I couldn't let go unanswered. "You think I don't know my territory? Actually, I have a pretty good idea about the fish on my side. I have files. I have subfiles. I have data files, personality files, grouped files, and computerized linkage files. If any two of these fish scratch their noses on the same day, it gets noted. I could bring in a half dozen of them before lunch. Don't worry, I know my fish."

My uncle smiled slightly. "I'm half inclined to believe that you could. In that case, if you know so much, where's the problem?"

"The problem, as I've been trying to make clear, rests not on my side of the river but on yours. Yours. That's where it always is. Always on your side we get ourselves in the muck. Simply by wading halfway across, everything becomes suddenly delicate. Heaven forbid I should offend anyone's exquisite sensibilities! Your old friends can commit all sorts of mayhem over here, and I'm supposed to do what? Buy them dinner and a night with the girls on Dooran Street!"

"You were saying . . ."

I forced myself to calm down. "Via channels—never mind which or whose—it was intimated to me that I'm supposed to haul in some fish from your side, but if I hook the wrong one, we both know that the situation will get messy. And this mess, as we are both aware, will lap at my feet."

"Don't mince words, nephew, come out and say it. You'll be drowning in shit at that point. That's why you want my advice."

Tied to me by blood or not, the man was exasperating beyond measure. Wasn't it obvious why I was asking his advice? "You understand how things work over there, uncle. I need to know where to step and where not to step."

"No, no. How many times have I tried to tell you? I don't know how things work over there, not anymore. I did, once, up to a point, anyway." He held up his hand to keep me from interrupting. "That's wrong. Let me restate the obvious. I never knew how anything worked. Nobody did. Sometimes I thought not even the Center knew how things worked. Clarity was not our strong point. We did not fuss much with transparency."

"Then why is the damn place still there? Someone must know how to keep it spinning."

"Inertia. Gravity. Water running downhill, except when it was running uphill. I don't have knowledge, if that's what you're looking for. All I have is experience, and some people will tell you even that falls on the wrong side of history."

"All experience falls on the wrong side of history," I said a little pompously, but it must have meant something to him, because I saw it register in his eyes. "Without going into detail," I continued, "in order to deal with this problem, one particular . . ." I fumbled for the right word. ". . . concept is being studied at the moment."

"Concept." He repeated the word as if it had landed from another planet. "What happened to the fish?"

"A loose thread has appeared. We may pull on it." Handout was the loose thread. If he had anything at all about new sources of payments from the North that were creating holes in the border around Tumen City, it would give us something to use against the smirkers from Headquarters. If he didn't know anything, at least we could say we checked. Either way, it would cost me some operational funds, which I couldn't spare.

My uncle shook his head. "Pah. Too many images. No wonder you're drowning. My grandfather used to say that precision in thought is all that keeps the world in order. He was particularly suspicious of any idea too enthusiastically embraced, or the tendency on the part of some people to blurt things out. It's one reason he was so disappointed with your father."

Here we go again, I thought, plunging into the swamp of the past. "This isn't about my father, and it isn't about your father."

"You mean my grandfather," he said quietly. "My father died in the war, or have you forgotten? Is it so far away for you? He would have been your grandfather. Maybe it would have done you good to know him. Maybe you would have learned something."

"Maybe."

Whenever the subject of the family reared its head, it always brought on a pitched battle, with one of us throwing spears and swinging a club at the other's head. This time, though, he wasn't in a fighting mood. I wondered if seeing Madame Fang again had done him some good.

"Where were we?" He put his hand to his forehead. He seemed tired suddenly, weary. When he'd first come to live with me, he had been full of fire. Over the past year, I sensed it dying down, little by little. That would have been to the good, but as his died down, mine seemed to flare up. He was my father's brother, about the only family I had left, and so I felt, at first, an obligation to give way to him and his eccentricities. That only led to resentment, though, and at the wrong times, I said what I shouldn't have, usually in the worst possible way. It was taking more and more conscious effort on my part to keep myself in check. Every time it happened, I resolved not to let it happen again.

"Images," I said, softly.

"Ah, yes. Pick an image, any image. I don't care what it is. It doesn't matter. But after you pick one, stick with it religiously. If you tell me we're dealing in fish, and then you tell me that there has been a nibble on the hook, and then you add because of that you pulled on the line, there's no doubt in my mind what you mean. At that point, we'll know where we are and where we need to go next. Yet suddenly we find ourselves faced with a loose thread? Where did that come from? Was the fish wearing an old sweater? It isn't a minor detail. It's a question of being systematic. Or is that no longer considered worth anything, being systematic? That's the problem with your gambling. It leads to sloppy thinking, leaning on chance."

No, seeing Madame Fang hadn't changed him. If anything, things were worse. Now he was using guerrilla tactics on me, seeming to retreat from the fight, only to attack from behind. Like every fire, this one could flare up suddenly.

"My imagery is fine," I said. "We pulled on a thread. When I say a thread, I mean exactly that, a thread." I kept my voice as even as I could.

My uncle sat lost in thought. Finally, he said in Korean, "Don't clench your teeth when we talk, even mentally. And you don't have to go on about this thread. You pulled on it, and now you wish you hadn't. That is usually the case with thread pulling. It's one thing experience taught me."

When he spoke to me in Korean, it meant we were on the verge of his retreating into himself, indicating I should leave him alone in his workshop. That isolation could last a day or a week. I never knew how long it would be. This was a bad time for him to disappear down his rabbit hole. I needed him to stay engaged, much as I hated to admit it.

I tried a quick smile to lighten the mood. "It's complicated, that's all I'm saying. Complicated in this case means dangerous, ready to blow up in someone's face, probably mine, exactly as you said." It was not much of a nod in his direction, but it was the limit of what I could stand to dole out at the moment. "If the whole thing didn't slop over onto your side of the river, I wouldn't be bothering you, uncle. When you showed up here, we made an agreement, remember? I would never involve you in my official duties, and you would use me strictly during nonduty hours to help out in your private detective service." I stopped myself from saying what I wanted to add, which was that he hadn't taken a case in so long it wasn't much of a bargain anymore.

"A bargain is a bargain, whatever its current state, and I will abide by it, don't worry." He was reading my mind. At least he'd switched back to Chinese. "If I don't stick to our bargain, I'll be up to my neck chasing fish, or pulling threads, or stepping around ill-considered concepts in defense of your imperial court."

"It's not an imperial court! We are still a socialist country, which is more than you have across the river." It was a stupid remark to make now or anytime in his presence, something I knew even before the words were out of my mouth. He could criticize what went on over there. I could not.

My uncle fell silent again and closed his eyes. When he spoke, he was back to using Korean. "We aren't going to argue about politics right now, or we will never get out of this workshop in one piece. We will go at each other hammer and tong, and I know where both the hammers and tongs are located, whereas you don't, which puts me at a clear advantage."

I searched around for a good exit line. "Why don't we move to the library? That's more neutral territory. We both need to cool off."

He opened his eyes and looked at me sadly. "I know where the tongs are there, too. However, what you want to discuss is depressingly official, and staying here will upset the atmosphere in my workshop, so let's move. These tools have no use for politics."

I stood up and bowed to the T-square. "Please forgive my transgressions, O holy one," I said.

"They don't react any better to sarcasm than I do to imprecision," my uncle said as he slid off his stool. His mood seemed to improve as his feet touched ground. "Lead the way, nephew. With banners flying and cymbals crashing we will proceed to more propitious surroundings and maybe even a bowl of noodles. It's nearly lunchtime, my stomach tells me."

After we were settled in the library, my uncle picked up a notebook from his desk, opened to a blank page, and began sketching plans for yet another bookcase. He had notebooks full of those sketches piled on the floor of his workshop, but there was always need for one more. I let him draw for a few minutes without interruption. The silence would do us good.

"I'm on a journey of discovery," he said at last. "I'm going to discover the perfect form, pure harmony. This is the sort of bookshelf they might have in Plato's Republic. Whether it can be built, I don't know, but at least it needs to be put on paper. Your great-grandfather never made a sketch of anything. Did you know that? Just built things from images in his head. Times were simpler then, not as much crowding the brain, no microwaves or cell phones upsetting the air."

"Ah, the peace of the past." I sighed dramatically. It was bunkum, and he knew it. There was no sense arguing. "Unfortunately, we don't live in such times anymore. That's what I keep trying to tell you." I thought over what he had said. "Where did you hear about Plato?"

I was at my own desk going through the drawers looking for a pen. There was none in the first drawer. The second drawer was filled with stacks of wood chips. Whenever we got into a case, which hadn't been in a while, my uncle would call for a wood chip, but not just any chip. He'd want something specific. "Elm," he'd say. "We need to empty our minds, and this time of year there is nothing more vacuous in the forest than elm." Later on, he'd call for something else, depending on where he thought things stood. "Oak," he might say. "Very straightforward tree, nothing devious about it."

When we set up the office, a month or so after my uncle arrived, the drawer was a jumble of chips he'd brought in his suitcase. On our very first case together, the maiden voyage, things went badly. He had called for birch; that sticks in my mind for some reason. I handed him the first chip I found. He took it, closed his eyes, and sat back in his chair, swirling the wood with his fingers. Suddenly his eyes popped open. "When I say birch, I mean birch." He had glared at me, his jaws working furiously. "This is Siberian elm, and I won't have it."

For several nights after that, I sat up late sorting through the pile of wood chips and arranging them in stacks, doing my best to make sure they were labeled as correctly as I could manage, given that I didn't know one type of tree from another. Trees had branches, and birds sat on them—that much I knew. In the end, there were eight stacks, plus a few exotic loners, gathered from whatever was in his workshop. If something new came in, I made arrangements.

Now, searching for a pen, it occurred to me that I didn't have chips from the new hardwood my uncle had brandished when Madame Fang came to call. If I'd had a pen, I would have made myself a note to remember.

My uncle carefully drew lines on the paper in front of him, ignoring me. Finally he looked up. "I read Plato after I read Kafka. When I was on the mountain, the year after I quit my Ministry job, there was plenty of time to read. A doctor came up to visit occasionally. He brought books sometimes. Nice man. Your father visited once, too. Did you know?"

"You hadn't mentioned it."

"He did. He seemed distressed by my living arrangements. He thought they were too crude; I had a one-room cabin I built myself. I think he was trying to tell me that he had intervened on my behalf, but we ended up arguing, as we always did. It was the last time I saw him."

I didn't say anything.

My uncle pushed the paper aside. "Begin at the beginning, or don't begin at all. I can't offer advice on how to get out of a box unless I know how you got into it."

"Box?" I went on alert, sensing a possible breach in his defenses. "Box? I thought we needed to be consistent. What about the fish?"

"Flopping at the bottom of the box." He closed his eyes and sat back in his chair. "I'm listening."

7

I glided through what Li had told me, which I had to admit was moderately fuzzy. Whatever I told my uncle had to be even fuzzier so I couldn't be accused of leaking sensitive information, even if I really didn't have much of an idea what it was. The main thing was to put just enough clarity into what I said to indicate where things were headed. My uncle had a finely honed sense of danger; it wouldn't take much for him to realize how dangerous things were about to become. Everything was complicated by the fact that when I came right down to it, I didn't know whether my uncle had severed all ties with his former colleagues across the river. Some discreet checking after he moved in led me in that direction, but it still wouldn't be a surprise to learn he had a few links left. I wouldn't have blamed him if he did, but in that case, I would also have an unpleasant time explaining to Headquarters what I was doing with a still-active North Korean security type living in my house, uncle or no uncle.

When I finished, my uncle looked up from the bookcase plans he'd been reviewing the whole time. Unusually, he hadn't interrupted, hadn't raised something extraneous, hadn't even cocked an eyebrow.

"It's late," was all he said, before giving me a bland look and going off down the hall to bed.

I sat in the library for about ten minutes, then got up and went to the kitchen, where I fixed myself a bowl of noodles, read the paper, and tried not to think about fish or threads. The image of the hard strike operation—a lot of doors broken in and people chased down alleyways in their underwear—seemed even worse late at night, when everything was quiet. Two special squads from Headquarters would cause a lot of headaches, but that was nothing compared with what would happen if I pulled in the wrong visiting North Korean. It would help if someone would give us a list of people to stay away from, but no one would do that, not even Li's sources. If a paper like that got into the wrong hands in Beijing, there would be too many questions about who was on the list and why. I thought about how Madame Fang had materialized at my front door, and then about her perfume. For some reason, that led me straight to tiny chocolate bricks. This was going nowhere good, so I gave up, walked softly to my bedroom, and fell asleep as soon as my head hit the pillow.

Chapter Three

The phone rang the next morning, well before seven o'clock. I had climbed out of bed early, as usual, and after a cup of tea was sitting in our office reception room library scrutinizing the newest collection of unpaid bills. In a grim attempt at humor, I was separating them into piles: to be paid soon; to be paid eventually; to be paid if the creditor could figure out how to reach me in the grave. When I picked up the receiver, a woman's voice, trembling softly and betraying a slight touch of the Yunnan backcountry, inquired whether I was Inspector O.

"I am not."

"May I speak to him?"

My uncle did not accept calls unless I screened them. "I'm afraid he is unavailable at the moment." Actually, he was sleeping, and there was no way I was going to wake him. He said he'd been up early his whole life, and that all it ever did was increase the amount of time during the day something could go wrong. When he moved to the mountain, he said, the birds woke him at dawn; there was no way to ignore the chatter of a bird in a pine tree. The only thing worse, he said, was two birds in a pine tree. "If you tell me what this is about, I'll pass on the message. He'll call you back later today or tomorrow at the latest."

"This is not something that can be discussed over the phone.

I need an appointment. It has to be today. I can do it this evening, it doesn't matter how late."

"Today is not good, I'm afraid."

"I'll pay. Will fifteen thousand yuan get me in the door?"

"For fifteen thousand yuan, you get to take the door home. Let's say two o'clock."

"I'll be there."

At ten in the morning, I walked down the hall, out the side door, through the courtyard, and into my uncle's workshop. By ten o'clock he was always dressed, in his workshop, looking at plans for bookshelves. If there was a chance of catching him in a decent mood, this was it.

"Good morning, uncle. You have a two o'clock appointment. We're selling the front door for fifteen thousand yuan."

That got his attention. "A client? What do they want? Maybe I won't take the case. I'm busy these days. Tell them I'm sick of blackmail cases."

If he was busy, I was the sultan of Brunei. "No, you're not busy, and we're about to starve unless you take this one. Don't even contemplate passing it up."

"Why? You've lost your job? I knew it would happen sooner or later."

"No, I haven't lost my job." The image of Fu Bin tiptoeing into the file room flashed before my eyes. The Third Bureau front office must have told him to try everything possible to get me: malfeasance, dereliction of duty, abuse of office, excessive spitting. It was a matter of pride. The more they looked and couldn't find anything, the more frustrated they must have become. That explained why Fu Bin kept poking around, treating other officers to drinks, undoubtedly trying to wheedle complaints out of them about me. Why he didn't get me for spending time at Gao's was a mystery, now that I thought about it. I never saw him at Gao's, also a little odd. Everyone drifted there sooner or later. There wasn't a lot else to do in Yanji.

"Good," my uncle said with obvious satisfaction as if he'd won an argument. "You're still employed. Then tell the client to go away."

"Not on your life. We have debts. Our debts have debts. If we don't start paying them off, we'll be on the street. Us and all of these tools."

Before leaving with the cream puff prince, my wife had run up an enormous phone bill with calls to every capital city in the world, mostly to Bern. We didn't know anyone in Bern, at least I didn't. Later I found out that the prince was there at a swank hotel getting refresher training in wedding cake design. The phone bill wouldn't have been that bad, but she also cleaned out my bank account and sold the house—without access to any sort of legal proof of ownership—to a real estate developer who had plans to knock down all the buildings in the neighborhood and build a condominium complex called Happy Meadows. The sale was illegal, and the developer knew it. He also knew people in high places who didn't care about legal title or proof of ownership. It was costing me plenty of time and effort to keep the bulldozers at bay. I didn't have the money to bribe anyone back to my side again. A nice gambling win would have helped, but that was a question of the odds, and my luck was running the wrong way lately.

My uncle couldn't understand why MSS Headquarters didn't weigh in on my side. "All they have to do is send someone over to the developer's office to break a piece or two of furniture," he said whenever the subject came up. "Your people have forgotten how to break furniture?"

He also didn't understand how my wife had been able to rob me blind, but he knew it was a sensitive issue and rarely raised the subject. As it happened, he chose this moment to do so. "You let her lead you around by the nose, and all the while she was playing with someone else's pastry?"

"I was preoccupied."

"So it seems," he said.

"It's pointless to talk about that now. What's done is done. Water down the drain. She's gone. Good riddance. Anyway, it's only money." It was a lot of money, some of it won during a rare lucky streak at Old Gao's but most of it from a trip to Macau many years ago. I had kept it at home, since laundering it would have raised flags I didn't want raised. I had thought a lot about what to do with the money; having my wife take it with her hadn't been on my list of options.

"Only money." My uncle ran his fingers across the teeth of his Turkish saw. "Well, it's your business, you'll figure it out." He didn't think I'd figure it out; that much was obvious by his tone of voice. He cleared his throat. "You're right. Money brings nothing but unhappiness. The worst cases I ever had to handle were about money. Sex came in a close second."

"What about this case?"

"This case?" He picked up a pencil and prepared to redraw an old set of plans for bookcases with vertical shelves. "I don't like the sound of it."

"What sound? The only sound so far is fifteen thousand yuan rustling in an envelope."

"Even so, I might not take it."

Take it or I'll break your arm, I thought. I picked up a crowbar from against the wall and hefted it in my hand. Aloud I said pleasantly, "We'll see. At least you can give her a hearing."

"Her? Where is she from?"

"I don't know. She didn't give anything away over the phone. From her voice, I'd say she is from Yunnan."

My uncle groaned. "Kunming," he said more to himself than to me. "A woman from Kunming." He groaned again.

"Something happen to you in Kunming?"

"Another time. Fix up the office so it's less of a dump. If she has drug money, we'll know soon enough. Drug people are fussy about room hygiene. Can't you hang up next time?"

At two o'clock, there was a knock on the front door. My uncle was at his desk in the office, reviewing drawings for three pairs of rolling bamboo bookshelves. They were part of a contract for an open-air library to be built on Hainan Island. He insisted that he couldn't work under contract, but I had finally convinced him at least to submit a bid.

I opened the door to a young woman, fashionably dressed, holding an embroidered handkerchief to her nose.

"I didn't realize you lived in an industrial area," she said. The accent was even lighter in person than it was over the phone. "I hope you keep the windows closed. It smells like there is a rendering plant next door. Surely that's illegal."

"Industrial area? You must mean the neighbors. They are fond of piglets, at least the husband is. He thinks they are good for his vitality. It leads to a lot of squealing."

The woman lowered the handkerchief and gave me a determined frown, though it didn't detract from her many good features. "I've heard this neighborhood is up for redevelopment. It can't happen too soon." She put the handkerchief back over her nose, which was small, like a button. Her mouth, by contrast, was wide, with the result that the lower half of her face was mostly occupied. Her lips were the color of cherries—I'm no fan of clichés, but that's what they were, the color of ripe cherries—and full. She was wearing a hat that made her look taller than she was, though I wouldn't want to call her short even in her bare feet. Not that her feet were bare at the moment. They were in expensive shoes, probably handmade, probably from leather that could double as butter. Though it was a warm afternoon, she had on a long coat that must have cost multiples of what she had agreed to pay just to step into the house. The coat matched the color of her lips. A sudden craving for fruit came over me.

"Are we going to do this interview on the front step?" This put a bit more of Yunnan in the air, but not much.

"No, of course not." For the second time in a week I had nearly left a beautiful woman standing outside. It was a bad habit that needed breaking. "Please, come in. May I take your coat?"

Underneath she had on a short-sleeve bright yellow sheath, with a small gold brooch pinned on the left. The hemline was slightly above her knees, which were pretty good for knees. I'm trained to observe, and I can't help doing it even off duty at my front door, looking at a beautiful woman. Other than the brooch, I noticed, she wasn't wearing jewelry—no earrings, no necklace, no bracelet, and no rings. She didn't need anything flashy, and she knew it.

"If you'll follow me to the office," I said.

My uncle was complaining to himself when we appeared at the door. "I doubt they even know how to read on Hainan," he said, staring at the bid tender. "No one in his right mind makes bookcases out of split bamboo. What the hell sort of book sits on a bamboo shelf?"

I knocked twice. "This is . . ." It dawned on me that I didn't have a name to go with the lips.

"Du Hwa," the woman said. "I take it you are Inspector O." She stepped into the room, which instantly improved the color scheme.

"Please sit." My uncle smiled at her. In a heartbeat, I was worried. He never smiled at clients right away, especially not women. I was only moderately reassured when he fell back into his regular client face. He once told me he put on that face at the beginning of a client meeting in order to communicate total control of the situation, whatever the situation was. This time, though, I sensed something was missing. The look on his face wasn't that of a veteran investigator. The effect was more one of resignation, like a sea bass on realizing it has landed on a large plate covered in Kunming black bean sauce and scallions.

The woman sat in the chair indicated. From outside the window there was a shriek and a brief squeal.

"Our neighbor." My uncle smiled again.

"Was that the wife?" Miss Du looked vaguely alarmed.

"No, that was the piglets," I said, hoping to put things back on track. "The wife has a lower register."

The woman looked around the cluttered shelves. Her gaze lingered for a moment on the dead flowers. "Let's dispense with further pleasantries, shall we?" From her purse she took a white envelope. "Here is the fee that we agreed would start the soup simmering."

I took this as some quaint Yunnan saying. Either that or she was planning to stay for lunch.

"Very well, my nephew will count it later." My uncle flashed me a count-it-twice look. "Now, Miss Du, why don't you tell me the nature of your problem? Start at the beginning. Just be yourself; don't try to sound like a police report. We'll fill in the details once we establish the overall picture."

The woman sat demurely in the chair. Her lips held a cherrylike look of satisfaction. I had the feeling she recognized an old sea bass when she saw one.

2

"My father is in pieces."

There followed a prolonged silence. My uncle gave no hint that he was prepared to speak. Miss Du looked as if she might shed a tear—two at the outside—for effect. I put the envelope with the fifteen thousand yuan on my desk and sat down.

"He's in pieces in my brother's restaurant freezer."

Another silence, broken by a brief squeal from next door. This seemed to jar loose a thought from my uncle.

"What sort of restaurant is it?"

Miss Du stood up. "I'm sorry I came. If you think this is funny, I don't."

"Funny? Why would I think that? I assume you want to know what happened and who is behind this. To find out, I'll need to know a lot of things that will make you uncomfortable. I'll need to know how long the process of your receiving the pieces, or whatever they were, continued." My uncle sounded annoyed, which I recognized as merely an act to get the upper hand. "Sit down, Miss Du. We can't talk with you standing there. First of all, I need to know who your father was."

"You're assuming he is dead?"

"Ah, good for you. You are sensitive to verb tenses. Well, I don't know at this point whether he is dead or not. How could I? It will depend on the details."

No, I thought to myself, it will depend on whether or not he is dead.

"For example," my uncle charged ahead, "at some point I will no doubt ask if the pieces arrived in any particular order."

Miss Du gasped and sat down heavily on the red velvet chair. She composed herself quickly, though. I gave her extra points for that. Her next question was completely on target. "Should I assume that these details you've mentioned determine the price of your services? I imagine a murder investigation must cost more than a missing persons case."

"But this isn't a missing persons case."

"Why do you say that, Inspector? You just told me you didn't know what it was. Now you say you do. Am I supposed to be impressed with how quickly you jump to conclusions?" She had clearly regained her composure and then some.

My uncle was unfazed. "Actually, Miss Du, I'm not jumping at all. Your father cannot be described as missing. If what you say turns out to be true, then we already know where he is, in so many words."

I thought Miss Du would spring up again, but she merely nodded. "What's the fee?"

"I'm not sure I want to take this case."

The envelope with the fifteen thousand yuan fell quietly off my desk into the open top drawer.

My uncle sat upright in his chair, a dangerous sign that he was reaching the wrong conclusion about what to do next. "You seem to be hiding something, Miss Du, and I don't work with clients who hide things. Are you?"

"No, nothing."

"Then I'll ask again, who was your father?"

"Du Hua-son." She leaned toward my uncle, and her eyes sparked. "You may have heard of him."

From the way my uncle looked at me, I sensed he had dropped his reluctance about the case. Even so, I used my knee to nudge shut the drawer with the envelope.

"Du Hua-son," he said slowly, "the master forger?"

"Forger?" Miss Du jumped from her chair again, her face flushed. I was out of my chair a split second before she could lunge across the desk at my uncle. I had my hand lightly on her shoulder, careful not to wrinkle the fabric.

"Forger? My father was a world-famous sculptor. He had pieces in the top museums of Europe and Asia. How dare you call him a forger!" She shook off my hand. "If your nephew touches me again, he'll sing soprano in the karaoke bar."

"Sit down, Miss Du, and don't be a fool," my uncle said firmly. "I don't know anything about your father's artistic side. That may be what it may be. I knew him as a master forger and counterfeiter without peer. You can be proud of him. He was the best." My uncle saluted, albeit from a seated position. "The very best. I'm saddened to learn of his passing." This was said in a somber tone, as if the man had died intact after a long illness. In the same tone, and with barely a pause, my uncle continued. "A murder investigation is 135,000 yuan plus expenses, which I warn you can be considerable. If I don't solve the case in forty-five days, however, I return half the fee."

This was all fabricated on the spot, completely made up. We didn't have a fee schedule, none, not even close, and we had never charged anything like 135,000 yuan, for anything. It seemed to me to be overreaching—135,000 yuan is a lot of money; maybe not in Beijing or Kunming, but it is in Yanji.

"Very well." The cherries returned to Miss Du's lips. "I'll have the money for you by tomorrow morning. I take it the fifteen thousand in that drawer is a down payment?"

"That will be fine," my uncle said. "Before you leave, so I can get started with this right away, I need to ask—please don't be angry—how do you know the body parts belonged to your father?"

"I suppose I don't," she said calmly.

"In that case, we'll have to do some testing. That will cost more than a little, I expect. These laboratories are nothing but crooks. We'll try fingerprints first. I assume there were fingers."

Once again the cherries fled with the rest of her color. I felt sorry for her. My uncle stood up and walked around the desk to where she stood gulping deep breaths. He patted her hand gently. "Again, let me say I knew your father. Admired him."

"A sculptor," she said between gasps.

"We'll speak in more detail tomorrow. Meanwhile, go home and get some rest."

Don't forget to swing by the bank while you're at it, I added silently.

"My nephew will see you to the door. Do you have a car waiting?"

"Thank you, yes."

The chauffeur was leaning against the front bumper. He gave me a sour face as I opened the rear door. As she climbed in the backseat, Miss Du looked into my eyes.

"I'm sure you have a lovely baritone," she said. "Try not to lose it."

Chapter Four

Do you want the long or the short version? They lead in different directions, and I couldn't tell you at this moment which one ends up in the right place." We were sitting in the office after Miss Du's departure. "I didn't give you the whole story yesterday, but something about what we just heard makes me think there is a bigger fish out there than I first thought."

My uncle nodded slightly. He was awake, I could tell, though his eyes were closed and his breathing was shallow. There was no sense waiting for an answer beyond the nod. There wouldn't be one.

"Good, go ahead and maintain radio silence," I said. "I'll give you the short version, because, frankly, it's the one I'm more comfortable with for now."

No change in breathing patterns.

"Since you'll notice anyway, let me admit at the outset that I'm going to have to blur some of the detail." Actually, I'd seen dead men breathe more deeply than he was doing now. "To save time, I may also skip over a few secondary points. The essence is as follows: Someone on this side of the river supplied, for a considerable sum of money, a phony state seal, which was somehow transported somewhere. Exactly where, unknown. Purpose? Unknown. But it was definitely forged, and that apparently has Beijing worried. Counterfeit state seals rolling around unchecked are not good for buttressing central authority, apparently."

This, more or less, was the rest of what Li Bo-ting told me on our rain-battered walk to the tea shop on Dooran Street. Li had apologized deeply that he hadn't been able to write down verbatim what had been relayed to him, explaining that was because there would be a READ ONLY/NO FILE note attached to the official message conveying this information once it arrived. Nevertheless, he'd scribbled down a few notes, and he passed them over furtively once we were in the tea shop. As usual, I didn't ask how he knew this stuff or whom he talked to. Maybe he rubbed a lamp, I didn't care.

As our tea brewed, Li said that while waiting for me to arrive at the office, he'd made a few quick, discreet enquiries. He'd been told that the seal was considered extremely important and that it needed to be found at all costs. When he pressed, the answers were sketchy and evasive, but he'd extracted the fact that this was an excellent copy of a specially made seal fabricated with a new casting method meant to ensure it could not be counterfeited. This superseal, as one of his sources called it, was intended to authenticate particularly important documents and agreements. Li told me he had rarely encountered so much difficulty getting details out of his network. When he complained, his sources suddenly remembered they were due in meetings and hung up.

In any case, I now knew that our office would soon be secretly tasked to locate and/or retrieve this phony seal. Locating it would be considered good work, but retrieving it would be looked on with highest regard. Much praise, albeit discreetly bestowed, would come our way. There was a strong suspicion, Li said softly, that one of the seals—whether the real one or the phony one was not clear—was on the North Korean side of the river. This grabbed my attention. Anything the North Koreans had that we wanted and managed to wrest away from them was considered a Class A operation. Whether the North Koreans were witting or their territory was being used as a parking place by another party wasn't yet known, nor did it seem to matter. Getting the seal out of the North and back to China without an embarrassing incident would be a major undertaking. A successful Class A operation meant more than a vaguely worded plaque on the wall. It meant a bonus and a promotion, almost always to a post in a nice place with good weather and very little crime, or at least not the sort of crime that needed our attention.

I included none of this detail in the version I gave my uncle. These were threads he would pull on later, but he didn't need to know about them at this point. If I even hinted at these additional angles, he would come to life in his chair and lift off like a firecracker, a state of agitation I couldn't handle right now.

"That's it," I said briskly, "the short version."

My uncle opened his eyes and raised his head. "Terrifying."

"How about saving the snappy repartee for your dates with Madame Fang."

"You related the version you said you're comfortable with. I just meant I'd hate to hear the one that makes you uncomfortable."

"In that case, your advice is what?" My uncle, I knew, was risk averse. This was a protective coloring he'd adopted in the course of his career, though it was clear from what he said occasionally and what I'd gleaned from questioning the few high-level North Korean defectors who crossed over in my sector that he wasn't a coward. My father, who had risen through the ranks of the North Korean Communist Party, had hinted to me on a few occasions that his younger brother was exasperating. I tried but could never get a fuller explanation during the short visits he paid my mother and me once a year when he came to China on some official business he'd concocted in order to see us.

"You want my advice?" My uncle sounded a little surprised. I made a silent bet that he'd tell me to stay away from the whole thing. In his world, crisis avoidance was essential. Shifting your gaze, taking the long way around the park, meant survival. That wasn't possible here anymore, or was it? Lots of people still thought it was an approach that worked fairly well. That's how most everyone in Headquarters got there—avoiding trouble. Class A operations were fine for freaks who loved kicking in doors or jumping off cliffs. I didn't enjoy either. There were plenty of exit ramps out of this problem. With no more than normal concentration, surely I could pass the case off to another district office. If need be, Li and I could choreograph a ballet to dance the whole mess to the Harbin Bureau, or better, maybe even down to Shenyang. The MSS office in Shenyang thought of itself as the queen bee of the northeast. Well, let them make honey out of this piece of paska.

"Nephew! Are you with us?"

"Sorry, uncle, I was thinking."

"My advice is to stick this problem on someone else, your worst enemy if possible."

Uncanny! The man had a knack for hitting the bull's-eye when he wanted to. Forget Shenyang. What I really needed to do was to hang this around Shanghai's neck. I barely had a moment to savor the notion before a dose of reality slunk into my fantasy.

"All of a sudden I have a sinking feeling," I said, thinking aloud, "that this purloined, apparently phony government seal is connected somehow to the crackdown on corruption I'm supposed to engineer. It has that you-can't-have-one-without-the-other feel to it. No evidence, just a hunch." Actually, it was a little more than a hunch. The seal and the crackdown were part of the same conversation Li Bo-ting had with me, though he hadn't directly connected the two, and neither had I at the time. "Anyway, let's face it." More reality flooded into the fantasy. "I can't run away from this. Neither can you."

My uncle looked at me with disbelief. "You have just enough integrity to get yourself killed. Where did that come from? Surely not from your father."

Where my father was discreet in talking about his brother, my uncle was less so. At first it had bothered me, but gradually I realized he couldn't help himself. The two of them had had a serious falling-out at some point, over what I didn't know, and they never reconciled. Quite by accident, I'd first met Uncle O at the gravesite, a year after my father's death. My uncle hadn't known of my existence, and in the shock of meeting me, he made an effort to avoid criticizing my father. Even after moving in with me, he generally kept the poison in his heart to himself. From time to time, though, it overflowed.

"Let's stick to the crisis at hand," I said. "We can engage in relative bashing any old time."

"All right." He seemed momentarily subdued. "Go on, I'm listening."

"Go on where? That's all I have, the whole thing, soup to noodles."

"No names? No clues as to official positions—because officials are surely implicated? Nothing on how much money was involved, how the money was transmitted, what bank it ended up in, and most important, whose account?"

"I've already thought of that. You know I couldn't give you such information even if I had it, which I can say with a straight face because I don't have any answers yet. A lot of questions, but no answers. It was a considerable sum, that's all I've been told, and I'm willing to bet that's an accurate estimate. If it hasn't already been taken out and laundered, it will be soon." If it was in a Swiss bank, I was determined to refuse to go there to get it back. I had no desire to be on the same continent with the cream puff prince.

"No need to bet how much it's worth. A state seal like the one you described is worth plenty, even if it's phony. Especially if it's phony. And your source?"

"Meaning?"

"You have one, obviously. "

"I don't know what I have." The only source I had was Li Bo-ting, and I wasn't about to give him away, not even to my uncle. Bo-ting did not deal in half-truths or whispered innuendo in dark alleys. Somehow, his information was always good.

"You don't know the source? Hopeless." This was just needling to get me mad enough to defend myself. It was standard interrogation procedure, and for once I was ahead of him. I smiled. He looked at his watch. "How about a bite to eat? Have we made progress on getting a new cook? Sooner or later, we need something beside noodles."

My uncle knows detective work, and he knows his noodles. What the connection is, I have yet to figure out. He knows noodles no matter the shape or size, noodles with chicken, noodles with beef, noodles with pork, and noodles with shrimp although he turns up his nose at the latter. He knows rice noodles, wheat noodles, long noodles, and short noodles. He is particular about noodles and fussy when he is around them, probably because he eats them all the time. He told me once that in his career he had learned a lot of tactical intelligence sitting in noodle shops. People let down their guard around noodles, he said.

"Since when don't you like my cooking?"

"In a perfect world, I'd turn up my nose at it, but you've kept us alive this long, so I'm not complaining. That maid of yours was insufferable, but her noodles were not all bad."

We had a drawer filled with scraps of paper containing the names and phone numbers of prospective cooks. We had interviewed several, but all had been unsatisfactory. "They cannot cook," my uncle growled after watching each one walk out the door. "I can tell, just by looking at them, the way they slouch and pick their teeth. They aren't cooks, I don't care what they call themselves."

2

At work the next afternoon, I slouched at my desk and let ideas chase each other around the room. None of them were particularly good, but I had to try something. I picked up the phone.

"Get me all the reports from Handout."

"They won't tell you very much." The woman in charge of the files in the converted billiards room always said that. She had no faith in the vast amount of paper she collected, collated, registered, and found eternal resting places for in the floor-to-ceiling shelves of our Certified Level 1 vault. She had one of the two keys to the special lock on the heavy steel door. I had the other.

"I appreciate your optimism. Bring them in here, and bring a pot of tea from the kitchen, too."

Half an hour later, Mrs. Zhou wheeled in a basket piled high with folders. "These are everything on Handout in the vault. They go back fifteen years, more or less. The gold leaf from the ceiling is starting to flake onto the files, incidentally. It isn't good for the paper."

"Fifteen years. Amazing." The whole damned building was falling apart. Gold leaf from the ceiling wasn't so terrible. Maybe we could sweep it up to sell for extra operating funds.

"There should be more folders in this case file. We're missing six years, something like that. They were checked out and never returned."

"By whom?"

"I don't know." Mrs. Zhou was in her late fifties. She was stooped, never smiled, and had speech patterns that set my teeth on edge. Her cadences didn't help things in that regard, nor did her voice, which crashed against the walls of the big rooms. To top it off, she had a Fujian accent. Even when she was all the way across the office, her voice carried like the ghost of a fishmonger loose in the old hotel. When she spoke, I shuddered.

Mrs. Zhou had been in charge of various MSS file rooms for thirty years. She was in place before I arrived, and would probably be there after I left—after we all left. She was a permanent fixture in the bureaucratic universe. On gloomy days, I concluded that when the world ceased and heaven blew to the other side of nowhere, Mrs. Zhou would make a file marked THE END, which she would put on the lowest shelf so she could reach it later.

Whenever Mrs. Zhou said, "I don't know," it was not a comment on the state of her knowledge. It was a declaration of complete certainty about uncertainty. When she said, "I don't know," it was like absolute zero; zero chance of ever finding out. Questioning her on missing files was like questioning why light disappeared into a black hole. Yes, there were unquestionably black holes, and six years of Handout's reports were somewhere in one of them. I was willing to accept that as a reasonable explanation if it meant not having to listen to Mrs. Zhou go on at length.

"I asked for tea, or has that disappeared, too?"

Mrs. Zhou pushed the basket of files against my desk. "They're in reverse chronological order, the newest ones on top. Don't get them out of order."

"My tea?"

"I'm in charge of files. Do I look like a tea lady? Besides which, I don't like that new officer, Jang, watching me in the kitchen. He has an evil eye."

Well, at least Jang couldn't recruit her. That cheered me up. "You do not, Mrs. Zhou, look like a tea lady. I simply asked, that's all. There's no harm in asking."

"Here's the checkout sheet." She held up a narrow piece of paper for me to see. "You have to sign for the files if you're going to read them in here."

"I realize that. It's procedure. We wouldn't want another six years of files to disappear, would we?"

"Are you suggesting I'm to blame? Because if you are, don't bother, it's not my fault. People treat these files like gum wrappers. I do my job, but I can't do it if I'm not here, can I? In 2003, I was detailed to the provincial office in Jilin. It was September. Very hot in those old offices; we didn't have any fans. This place is a palace compared to that one. I mean, the chief had a fan, but he kept his door shut. Bastard!" She spat the latter word out in Fujian dialect; it rattled the windows and crashed out the door into the waiting area. "You think I'm kidding? Take a gander at my personnel file."

"Not necessary. I'll take your word for it." If I'd ever known that Mrs. Zhou had been seconded for several years, I'd forgotten. Maybe the deal could be resurrected.

"Don't you want to know who was in charge of the files when all eight years of Handout documents disappeared?"

"Eight years? You mean we're missing more? A moment ago it was only six."

"Don't let it worry you. Files come and go. The sun doesn't rise or set differently depending on what we have or what we're missing. Think of it that way."

"Nicely philosophical, Mrs. Zhou." For a crazed fishmonger, I added silently.

"Are we done?" Mrs. Zhou looked at the clock on the wall behind my desk. It was always slow, probably because it doubled as the junction box for the special wiring. She made a mark on the accompanying checkout sheet. "Allowable checkout time for these sorts of files is three hours. Some of the files are four hours. These are three."

"Then what?"

"Then you have to turn them in and check them out again."

"No exceptions?"

"None." She shook her head firmly.

Going through Handout's files turned out to be a waste of the afternoon. I didn't learn much, or at least not what I needed to learn. Recruitment had been unusual. Handout had appeared one day at the old airport as the office director, my predecessor, was waiting for his driver. My predecessor—himself an open file, a running bureaucratic sore. Now, it turned out, he was also the fool who had recruited Handout.

"I have something you want." This was the sole and single quote from Handout in the entire file, reportedly what he said that day at the airport. Usually there are pages and pages of transcripts of conversations, but there were none here, unless they had been part of the six years, or was it eight, gone missing. No transcripts, no quotes, no way to figure out how Handout's mind worked. A whole basketful of files filled with indirect quotations, surmises, chits, phony receipts, and babble.

There were also no concrete indications that Handout had been vetted in the usual fashion, no background investigation, no full employment history or family register examination beyond the sparse facts on the cover sheet. Not even a complete date of birth, only the day and the month. It occurred to me that some, maybe all, of our older sources in the files were similarly thin on bona fides. Ascertaining that would mean asking Mrs. Zhou to find at least a dozen more files. Maybe another time.

* * *

(Summary sheet from Handout's personnel file)
READ ONLY

1 of 3 - Cover Sheet
CASE FILE: "HANDOUT"
ESTABLISHED: AUGUST 26, 2001
TRUE NAME: XXXX XXXXXX
DOB: APRIL 30 XXXX
POB: HANOI, DRV
FAMILY BACKGROUND (DETAILS IN HQ FILE 5255-B): FATHER SENT TO XXX COMMUNE, SICHUAN. DECEASED JUNE 1968. MOTHER AND CHILDREN LIVED WITH HER PARENTS IN SHENYANG. ONE BROTHER, DIED IN AUTO ACCIDENT MARCH 1997. MOTHER DECEASED 1998.
MARITAL STATUS: SINGLE
EDUCATION: SHENYANG INSTITUTE OF AERONAUTICAL ENGINEERING,
- GRADUATED 1991
TRAVEL: NO FOREIGN TRAVEL UNTIL 2001
- MAY 2001—SOUTH KOREA, TECHNICAL CONFERENCE ON MATHEMATICAL MODELS FOR CHEMICAL REAGENTS USED IN THE PETROLEUM INDUSTRY

READ ONLY

2 of 3 - Cover Sheet
EMPLOYMENT: L
DATE OF RECRUITMENT: MAY 24, 2001
PLACE OF RECRUITMENT: YANJI AIRPORT
METHOD: SELF-INITIATED
RELIABILITY: EXCELLENT FIRST YEAR
PAYMENTS: REGULAR - LINE 5
MOTIVATION: PSYCHOLOGICAL OBSERVATION INCONCLU-
SIVE
HQ COMMENTS: XIANG FENG BAO, BG special vetting *
OFFICERS IN CHARGE: (See p 3.)

3 of 3 – Cover Sheet
B L A N K

READ ONLY

*   *   *

I put the file back in the basket, on the top of the pile. From out on the street, I heard the roar of a big motorcycle. I braced myself for what would come next. The phone rang a minute later. It was the duty officer, young Mr. Jang.

"Special courier for you, sir. Shall I let him in?"

"No, Jang, keep him standing outside until he calls the army to bring around a tank to blast open the door. Yes, let him in, and tell him to come straight to my office."

Another minute, heavy boots on the floor, a knock. "Courier!"

"Enter and be made whole."

"What?" The door opened and a tall, fully decked-out courier stepped into my office, thick gloves tucked in a regulation belt, boots shined beyond the spectrum of visible light, helmet under one arm, and a large envelope with two stripes of special tape under the other.

"Sign." The courier stood at attention. They didn't like to hang around chatting.

I signed. "Want something to drink? Fine northeast tea?"

"Very kind." He handed over the envelope. "Not today." He stepped backward to the door. "Closed?"

"Yes, please."

As soon as he was gone, I retrieved a small knife from my desk and cut the tape in the approved manner. There was a single page inside. I read it twice, then lit a match and burned it in a vase I keep on the floor for that purpose.

3

Late that afternoon, as we sat in our library/office after I'd returned from work, I realized it was necessary to see if my uncle had any ideas about a particularly uncomfortable part of the puzzle—the disappearance and current circumstances of my predecessor. There was no easy way to wade into the subject, especially given the sensitivity that had been emphasized at least three times in the flash message I'd received earlier in the day. The best way, I decided, was a direct frontal approach against the ramparts. That gave me the benefit of surprise and thus a chance of shocking my uncle out of asking too many probing questions. He was unlikely to have any direct knowledge, I figured, but he might have heard this or that about the episode when he was still in North Korea. Word gets around, even when it sticks to the shadows and only crosses the street at night.

"I've got a question, if you don't mind," I said.

My uncle was fussing over a sketch he'd just completed. "I don't mind."

"I was wondering. My predecessor left work suddenly; perhaps you heard. He disappeared."

"Dead?" My uncle didn't lift his concentration from the sketch. Maybe he didn't know anything after all.

"Might as well be. He slipped away, and no one knows to where. At the time, it gave several people in Beijing whiplash. No one likes it when a bureau director vanishes." That was true, and hardly a blinding revelation. It didn't give anything away, but at least it might buy me a few seconds of my uncle's undivided attention.

"Impossible." My uncle looked up suddenly. "I don't care what anyone says. No one simply vanishes. There are always traces."

"Usually, yes, there are. Apparently not this time, though. The investigation was thorough, from what I hear. It was also kept very quiet, but rumors floated around. I was in another job at the time, on the other side of the country, and even I heard a little of this and that." I knew somewhat more than this or that, having received a cryptic briefing in Beijing in a special locked room shortly before being approved for my current assignment. Before I could get out of the room, paperwork had to be signed in two places swearing I wouldn't tell anyone what I'd been told—nobody, never. A few more tidbits, very few, had been thrown into this afternoon's message. It didn't add up to much, except that Headquarters knew what had happened to its bureau director, seemed to know he was still alive, and was not happy.

"Maybe someone snatched him." My uncle snorted. "The Americans? The Israelis? Did anyone ask?"

"You don't really think that's much of an explanation, do you? I never heard anyone suggest he was kidnapped. That would almost make it worse." The thought hadn't occurred to me. It was unnerving.

"Don't worry about it. I have a feeling that MSS bureau chiefs are on the do-not-snatch list of almost every foreign intelligence service of any competence. How do you know he's not dead?"

I hesitated for a fraction of a second. "I know."

At this my uncle paused. A flicker of surprise lit on his forehead before vanishing. "Do you also know where he is?" he asked carefully.

From this point on, I knew I had to tread with utmost caution. I could almost hear the range finder in his brain switch into operation as he sensed a target of interest. I'd been right the first time; he had heard something.

"After all these years, that may be the question—where is he now? If Beijing has dusted off the file, they must have something new to go on." If my uncle knew anything at all about this, the only way to get it out of him would be to dangle a little something. "They haven't exactly said anything yet, not to me, anyway, but I know they looked at the file again."

My uncle thought about that for a second, the range finder clicking softly. He was far too experienced to show even passing interest in how I knew Beijing had looked at the file.

"Very well," he said, "assume for the moment someone gets a bead on him, establishes contact. Then what?"

I shrugged. "We welcome him back."

This was ridiculous, and my uncle had no trouble figuring that out. It was so ridiculous he didn't pursue the point. Instead, he asked the next logical question. "What if he doesn't want to come back?"

"But what if he does? What if he does, but he's not sure how to go about it? After all this time away, we can imagine he's a little cautious about his reception."

"Gun-shy."

"You might say."

My uncle looked out the window at the setting sun. "It must be getting toward summer. I think the weather is changing. My joints ache."

"I'm just speculating here, but I'll guess that if we don't get him back from wherever he is, there will be an incident, something ugly." I made sure my next comment came out casually. "Some people seem to think he's living across the river." No response. "Already, there's talk of throwing out all of your friends again, like they did when he first disappeared. Even then they must have thought he went over to your side. Funny business."

My uncle looked at the ceiling. "Up to now, you haven't asked a real question. I assume this is it—do I remember anything?"

"I don't know. Do you?"

"Yes, it was a funny period. I remember people from our State Security Department racing around with worried looks on their faces when your side began rolling up their operations in retaliation. But what made anyone think your man came across the river to our side? All the traffic was going the other way at that time; it still is. And I wish you wouldn't refer to them as my friends. They're not my friends, not a single one of them. Except for a couple of times when I had no choice, I stayed away from their operations, especially anything on the border."

"Really? I heard that you tangled with an MSS colonel at some point. He was something special, outside channels. I never got the full story. He shot someone, on your side of the river is what I heard."

"You want the full story? He didn't belong on my side of the river, and I told him as much. The person he shot was standing right next to me. I don't like standing beside people who get shot, and I also made that clear."

"Interesting, but what matters is now, and now you're on a list that you don't want to be on."

My uncle finally looked up from the sketches on his desk. "A list? What list? I don't work for anyone. It wouldn't mean anything if they threw me out. No one would care. It would be like throwing a pebble at the Milky Way."

"Headquarters doesn't consider you a pebble. A sharp stone in their shoe, maybe. Be thankful they haven't hauled you in already."

"For what, may ask? I realize the what doesn't actually matter, but these things usually follow a certain dramatic line. They like to concoct a cause, if only to fill in that part of the form."

"You already know the what. You saw her before she went over there. They probably think you lured her."

He laughed until he started coughing. "Lured her?" he asked when he could speak again. "You saw Madame Fang. Do you think anyone could lure that woman?"

4

A few days later, Uncle O took the train to a lumberyard on the outskirts of Harbin, a twelve-hour trip on a hard seat. With the exception of winter, he'd taken that journey once each season since he moved in with me. The first December he'd made it known that he wanted to go but couldn't because if he slipped on an icy side-walk in Harbin, he would lie there until he froze to death. "Harbin people are callous," he'd said, "and don't tell me they're not."

"How do you know people would just walk over your body? I bet someone would stop and give you a hand."

He snorted. "Have you ever met anyone from Harbin? Don't make bets you might lose. Don't make bets, period."

"I know lots of people from Harbin."

"Name one."

"None leap to mind."

"When they do, you can call and tell me I'm wrong. Mean-while, I'm not going until spring. It gets muddy up there, but mud is less lethal than ice."

It was already late May, far into the safe zone by his calculation. "I'll see you in five or six days," he said. "If I'm not back in a week, send out a scouting party."

"We don't have scouting parties anymore. I'll call the MSS office in Harbin and tell them to keep an eye on you. The chief there will be delighted to have something to do."

My uncle picked up his small carry-bag. "Do you think I want a tail on me the whole time? Leave your boys in Harbin alone. I'll call when I get there to let you know I arrived."

"Take your cell phone."

"I will not use that thing. Throw it in the garbage."

There was no phone call, and four days later, my uncle returned, empty-handed.

"Nothing worth my time," he said when I opened the door. The train from Harbin is overnight, and he was yawning as he walked past me. "They had something they called 'fortune wood.' What is it about you Chinese with naming things? It was jumped-up pine, that's all it was. You think I couldn't tell? Fortune wood! That whole lumberyard is full of crooks. They would cover their mothers with creosote and sell them as fence posts if they could. What a country!"

"Promise me you'll never open a business where you have to deal with the public. Speaking of which, you must have scared away Miss Du. She never called us back."

"She'll call, don't worry. She's probably arguing with her brother right now about our fee and how to keep the body parts separate from his restaurant supplies."

"What makes you think she'll pay your price?"

"I'm tired. There's no way to sleep on that train. It's overheated and the windows won't open. A gang of kids ran up and down the aisles all night. Don't people control their children in this country?" He looked ready to fall asleep on his feet. "Have we got any noodles around here? I haven't eaten since I don't know when."

"How did I know you would get back this soon? I wasn't even sure you arrived there. For all I knew, you'd slipped in the mud and sunk in up to your ears. Anyway, I've been busy at work. No time for shopping. As a matter of fact, I was planning to get some dumplings at a place on Wenxue Hutong. It's dependable. I've never had a bad dumpling there."

"Dumplings? Why not go for noodles? You should try the noodle shop on Lanxiang Hutong."

"Is there one? I haven't seen it. Must be new. What makes you think it's any good?"

"One never knows until one tries, nephew."

"All right. You can join me if you like."

My uncle walked into the office and put his carry-bag on his desk. "You still have a job?"

I followed him in. "One of us has to earn money."

"You have your father's gift for gab, like a saw with a broken tooth."

I knew where we were heading—more comparisons with defective tools. "Never mind that. If you want noodles, I'm leaving in five minutes. Or you can go to sleep. Your choice."

Five minutes later, my uncle was at the front door. I was half surprised to see him. Usually after a trip to Harbin, he retreats into his workshop and stays there for days. He never likes to be interrupted after being away. He insists it is important to have quiet and calm in order to bring everything back into harmony.

"It's nothing mystical," he said when I told him he sounded like a religious zealot. "I'm not casting a spell or invoking spirits. It's simply a matter of settling in again, getting acquainted. All of us."

By that he meant the tools and the lumber against the wall, the unfinished bookshelves, everything but the shellac. He viewed shellac as something purely functional, outside his circle. I asked once why this was so.

He screwed up his face, as if summoning the spirits from the deep. "If you've ever worked with shellac, you'd know the answer," he said. "It might do you some good, as a matter of fact, getting acquainted with shellac. You need to know something other than pushing paper and padding files."

5

Noodles any time are a nonevent, but especially in the morning. As far as I am concerned, at that hour they are simply warm and filling. There is little else to be said for them, or around them for that matter. Soon after he moved in, my uncle made clear that conversation and noodles don't mix, certainly not in a noodle shop like the one we were in, where the din of other people slurping and smacking their lips makes it hard to hear anything else. It surprised me when he broke his iron rule and spoke.

"There's something wrong with these." He frowned into the bowl.

"Mine are fine," I said. I'd heard of a rat's head sometimes bobbing among the noodles. Noodle shop owners don't always care what goes in the pots in their kitchen as long as the cash register is working. I glanced nervously at his bowl.

"Then what is this?" My uncle held up several noodles and let them dangle from his chopsticks. "They have dried ends."

I realized right away there was going to be a problem. My uncle has no use for imperfect noodles. He pushed back his chair with a loud clatter and stood. A few customers looked up from their morning meal, annoyed at the interruption.

"It was your idea to come here." I kept my voice low. "I was in favor of dumplings. Are you leaving?"

"No, I'm going back to the kitchen."

"Don't, don't do that, uncle! They have large knives in kitchens, and they don't like customers poking around. We have been getting a lot of in-kitchen violence calls from these little eating places."

"Then they shouldn't serve garbage."

"Calm down. Let's call over the owner and discuss this rationally."

My uncle had no patience with half measures. A dimmer switch was not his idea of a sensible invention. "The owner? The man's a crook, one of many in this country. He'll only defend his noodles. Look at them!" As he pointed at the offending pasta, his voice cracked with emotion. "They are indefensible."

"Uncle, sit down, will you? I'll call him over. Maybe he'll offer you another bowl."

My uncle laughed grimly. "Why would I want another bowl of noodles in this place? I'm going to tell the cook he's an idiot." By now he was shouting. A few of the customers had grounded their chopsticks and were grinning.

"Lower your voice, would you? The whole place is looking at us. Calling the cook a name, what will that solve?"

"The goal is not to solve anything. I am not interested in pouring oil on bad noodles. Whoever made these is an idiot. The sooner that is made crystal clear, the better."

"Uncle, listen to me just once, will you? I can't have a scene here." In fact, we had already crossed that particular threshold, but I still held out hope of containing the damage.

"Why? You said you never heard of this place. Is this where you meet sources? Is the owner on your payroll? Do you take convicts here and execute them with a bowl of bad noodles?"

"You know what I mean. If there is a scene, the newspapers will jump on it. MSS doesn't like being in the news. Headquarters will be annoyed. I'll get cited and have to write a long report. Please."

"So, this abomination"—again he gestured at his bowl—"is to be perpetuated. Insanity!"

"What?"

"I said, insanity."

"Let's find another place if you feel so strongly."

"I'm not paying for this animal feed."

"Don't worry."

"And I forbid you to pay."

"I can't just walk out."

"Since when can't a security officer walk out of a restaurant without paying? What sort of bizarre social system have you created on the backs of the masses?"

"Let's not start a revolution over a few bad noodles, all right? We don't need a scene."

"Ah, a scene! I nearly forgot. You're worried about a scene. No wonder this country is about to come apart. It starts with bad noodles and escalates from there. I thought things were supposed to be different here. Streets paved in gold, everyone driving a Japanese car and sporting around in Italian underwear, that sort of thing."

"If you want to go, let's go. Quietly."

At that moment, a thickset man walked in the front door, followed by three more men each incrementally thicker, and somewhat shorter, than the previous one. I knew there was going to be trouble. This sort of thuggish *matryoshka* never spells anything else. The manager knew it, too. He turned the color of the scum floating on top of the large aquarium near the door.

"Nobody moves, nobody gets hurt," said the first man through. He turned to the manager. "You're late. It's two months in a row. I told you what would happen if you were late again." He had on a dirty brown suit that bagged at the heels. He also had a heavy Fujian accent. Extended kin of Mrs. Zhou's, I thought to myself.

The second man casually picked up a chair and smashed it against the aquarium. The tank fell to the floor; the fish inside scattered under the nearest tables.

The baggy suit laughed. "That's you next time." He took the manager by the scruff of the neck and shoved him against the wall. "Next time, you and your fishies get ground into little pellets for pig food. Nice fat pigs." He nodded to the trio behind him. "Go get the cook."

The three fell into line and disappeared into the kitchen. There was a crash of pots, dishes smashing onto the floor, then a howl of pain. One of the men emerged from the kitchen holding his left hand. It wasn't attached to anything.

"What happened to you?" the first man snapped.

"He's crazy. He cut off my hand with his fucking carving knife. What do I do now?"

My uncle looked deeply into his noodles.

"Put a towel on it or something." The baggy suit looked away. "I hate blood. Where's Wong?"

"The cook threw boiling water in his face. He can't see. I think he passed out."

The man put a dirty finger in the manager's chest. "You're dead, you get what I'm saying? You're as good as dead, and this place is gone by morning. A grease fire is bad, and yours is going to be the worst."

There was another scream from the kitchen. The cook appeared at the door. He stared hard at my uncle. "Someone got a complaint?"

My uncle stared back. "I want to talk to you about your noodles sometime," he said evenly, but more surprising to me, in Korean. "Meanwhile, if you need employment, let me know."

The manager used the moment to retreat behind his cash register. "We're closed," he shouted. "Everyone has to leave. Go away. You!" He pointed at the cook. "Go back where you came from. You people are nothing but trouble." He turned to me. "Nothing but trouble from these people. Why do you let them pour across the border? Put up a fence or something. Take a look at those fish! Cost me plenty! Do you think I can serve fish that have been on the floor?" He paused, and I could tell he was thinking about it.

I grabbed my uncle's arm and hurried him through the kitchen. We went past the cook without eye contact, out the back door, down the steps, and were already on the street when the first police showed up in front of the noodle shop. "Keep walking," I muttered to my uncle. "Nice and calm. Don't turn around, and don't look interested. Look dumb, if you can manage that."

Late that evening, as we sat in our library/office, I asked the obvious question. "How come you knew that cook in the noodle shop? How come you knew he spoke Korean?"

"Who said I know him?" My uncle was reading a book on trees. "It says here that the red sparrow tree was so rare in the Southern Sung Dynasty that the emperor used the wood from it for a marriage bed and then had the bed disassembled to reuse the boards for the imperial throne. The last red sparrow tree in China was cut down by the Red Guards in 1967." He put down the book. "Crazy bastards. Of course, without them, your mother wouldn't have met your father. Which would have left me with nowhere to go when the weather got unsettled in Pyongyang. Who do I thank? The Sung emperor, or the Red Guards?"

Since he'd arrived, my uncle rarely took the initiative in raising the situation in Pyongyang, and when he did, it was always indirectly. All he would say was that the weather there was "unsettled" and "unhealthy." On rare occasions, he elaborated and said it was "stormy" or "peculiarly humid."

Given my access to reporting from across the river, I knew he was talking about the political state of play, not the sun or the rain, and he knew that I knew. For the past few years, we'd been paying for rumors about jockeying in the leadership, sudden disappearances of key people and then, just as suddenly, their reappearance. None of this information was from Handout, of course; luckily we had other sources, all of varying degrees of reliability depending on individual quirks. Much of it came down to money. Personally, I didn't trust any of them very far. It seemed to me likely that several of them were working for my uncle's old outfit in Pyongyang, the Ministry of People's Security, or worse, its rival, the State Security Department, which ran many of the operations on my side of the river. Beijing kept emphasizing to me that it didn't want the North Koreans to think they had free reign on Chinese territory, so Yanji Bureau was supposed to spend a lot of time and manpower keeping track of them. Some of the North's operations we penetrated easily; some we sat back and watched; some we couldn't locate but knew were under way from the odd transmission or the stray body in an alley.

Beijing was modestly happy with my record of keeping Yanji as clean of North Korean operations as could be expected. The other bureaus in the northeast were told to send people a couple of times a year to learn from our technique. Li Bo-ting said it was no more complicated than swatting mosquitoes in August, but I never knew a mosquito that could handle a knife.

According to my uncle, he left the North because he could not stay. That's all he would say, but our sources had uncovered a little more. Three or four years ago, his former employer was put under investigation, reorganized, and purged as a result of apparently well-founded suspicions that its leadership was taking money (and possibly orders) from a foreign intelligence service. My uncle, who had retreated to a rural mountaintop to live after retirement, received a timely message from an anonymous friend—the best kind, he maintained—that his file was in the next batch to be examined, and that people with old scores to settle with him would likely use the opportunity to do exactly that.

At that point, things were particularly bad for veterans of the People's Security Ministry, especially those few like him who had personal experience with embarrassing events involving high-level personalities, information that no one wanted scattered around. He was a little safer living under my protection, but not much. His trips to Harbin were particularly worrisome to me. I didn't think there would be any attempts targeting him while he was in Yanji, but I couldn't keep him under lock and key. He knew enough to be careful, and he still knew how to watch his back. At home he affected a lazy image, but on the street, he was sharp and alert. I'd watched, as had Bo-ting, whom I sent out once in a while to tail him. Uncle O said he wasn't in contact with anyone across the river, and from all I could gather, he was telling the truth. That's what I thought until noodles suggested otherwise.

He obviously wasn't going to tell me what he knew about the cook, meaning I would have to find out on my own. Li Bo-ting could poke around; he would eventually come up with something.

Meanwhile, I might have to pull in the cook and talk to him directly. Cooks cutting off other people's hands, especially during business hours, could be a problem, though in this case I was willing to look the other way if I got some cooperation. It wasn't an ideal situation, but I hadn't bumped into anything ideal for a long time. It had reached the point that I probably wouldn't recognize ideal if it jumped into my arms and kissed me on both cheeks.

As my uncle read his book on red sparrow trees, I was totaling the week's new harvest of household bills, matching them against our income. Even with the infusion of cash from Miss Du, the numbers were not coming out well. They rarely did, though the problem had deteriorated over the past six months. It was time for a serious conversation with my uncle, something I knew would be difficult and would almost certainly end badly. It meant being brisk in tone, plain in meaning, and relentless in pushing home the main point. The main point was simple enough: We would soon be without money. If I applied Miss Du's advance to the pile of bills, it disappeared, a few raindrops sprinkled on the Gobi Desert. We would not just be low on funds; we would be completely without. We couldn't keep up the current, widening gap between income and expenses. We were, in the language of the street, peeling our last potato.

The opportunity to convey how close we were to the choice between robbing a branch of the Bank of China or eating once a month arose later the same evening. It was past midnight. We were both still in the library. I couldn't sleep and was going through the receipts one more time, hoping to discover lifesaving errors in subtraction. Uncle O was at his desk, refining plans for yet another bookcase.

"There are limits," I said aloud. To my ears this sounded brisk. My uncle didn't look up. "Limits," I said the word again and held up a handful of bills. "If we spend, we have to earn. Spend"—I waved the bills in one hand—"and earn." I held up the other hand, which was noticeably empty. I was pleased. This was the sort of clarity I'd hoped to convey.

My uncle put down his pencil. "There is an ideal relationship between the number of shelves and the length of the whole, did you know that? Theoretically, you could build a bookshelf so small that it would need no shelves at all, if you only knew the right ratio."

I jumped in before he could continue. "No, actually you could not. Just as you could not build one so big it would need no shelves. And do you know why? Because in another month, you won't be able to afford any lumber, none, not even a matchstick. We'll have to start selling the bookshelves you've already built. We'll have to take apart those unfinished ones—"

"Like the emperor of the Southern Sung," my uncle said neutrally.

"—and use the parts to finish others to sell so we can get enough cash to buy food. You think I'm kidding?"

"If things are so dire, why can't you take a little on the side, like everyone else in this sparkling land? You're a policeman! People need favors!"

"I don't do that."

"You don't? Why not? You haven't lost your job, have you?"

"No, not yet. Of course, when they come to arrest you, they'll probably take me away as well. At that point, it's a good bet my employment prospects will become shaky."

"Then don't worry. No one is going to arrest me. It would be too much trouble. I don't do well under arrest. I get cranky."

"That I have to see."

"Let's be clear, your job is to keep me out of trouble. My job, or so your headquarters seems to calculate, is to soak up your excess energy. We're supposed to balance each other. They're pleased to imagine we're even useful to them from time to time. Most ridiculous of all, they have convinced themselves that I keep you informed about what things are like over there."

"Ha! If only they knew."

My uncle stood up. "No one would buy a single one of these bookcases. No one understands them. They are not meant for the commercial market. If we have to live off the income from them, we'll be dead of starvation in a week."

The phone rang, an ominous sound at that late hour. "If it's for me," my uncle said as he disappeared out the door, "I'm not here."

I picked up the phone.

"You're needed at the office," a male voice said.

"Who is this?"

"Never mind who this is."

"Sorry, you hit the wrong buttons. We're closed."

"No, you're not. We're sending a car. It's black."

"I don't ride in black cars, especially at this time of night."

"It's not night, it's morning. And for this, you make an exception." The phone went dead. I dialed the office number.

"What's going on?" I looked at my watch. "All good children should be in their beds."

"A flying team flew in." It was Lieutenant Li. His voice was guarded and a little on the nervous side. "That's it, the sum total of my comment. See you soon."

"Someone said they were coming to get me in a black car."

"Yeah."

"You know who it was?"

There was a conversation offline. Bo-ting came back on. "It's busy here right now, like a train station. See you in a few minutes, huh?" He was pleading.

"If you say so." I hung up with a bad feeling in my stomach. Li didn't scare easily.

Chapter Five

Y ou may sit if you wish. This won't take long."

"That's good." I made myself comfortable behind my desk. It was obviously going to be a long night. The visitors had the air of people who were planning to stay for a while. A woman seated at a small table that had been moved into the office and placed near the door was taking notes. She'd laid out three extra pens neatly on the table. I figured she knew the drill.

The man doing the talking wore the brush haircut of someone from the old school of interrogation. I could tell he'd been around. The others, younger, lounged at each of the four compass points, ensuring I would never be without a reminder of who was running this meeting. They looked a little bored, but I knew they were on full alert. One of them fiddled with a cigarette, put it to his lips, and then took it away. His eyes darted around the room. I noticed they rested for a fraction on the woman. She ignored him.

"Don't tell me that we're all friends," I said, "because I don't think we are. My friends usually leave me alone at this hour."

"OK, we're not friends." The old man leaned against my desk. He seemed tired, not just from lack of sleep. Too many questions, too many furtive answers. I might have felt sorry for him if he wasn't in my office at one o'clock in the morning. "But we're acting friendly, we're talking friendly. I'm thinking friendly thoughts. How about you, Penguin?"

The one with the cigarette and the white vest nodded. He had a hotshot air about him, maybe because he appeared to be the youngest. "Yeah, I'm awash in friendship." He looked at the woman. "Never felt friendlier."

The old man glanced at the clock on the wall. "Is that time right? You're slow, but that's normal for this part of the country, right? Lucky for you, we have a convergence of interests. You want to get home, and I don't want this to drag on. I have a pain in my shoulder these days; questioning people who don't cooperate makes it worse. They get tense; I get tense. You know what I mean? We flew up here because those were our orders. Let's keep it simple, and maybe we can clear out of here in time to catch the morning flight. That will leave you the rest of the day free to annoy your staff, and I can get one of those Shanxi farm girls to walk on my back when I get home. Worth a shot?"

Well, at least we had established that they were thinking of no more than six hours for this session. Six hours I could handle.

"Good idea," I said. "Tell me what this is about. That's a friendly way to start, don't you think?"

"Sure. I'm going to jump the monkey, if it's all right with you. I probably know a few tricks you don't, but why bother?" He moved the pile of flash messages to the side and sat on the edge of my desk. "What do you know about a source named Handout?"

"Hand down?"

"Smart guy. You heard me right the first time."

"Sorry. I can't discuss some things with strangers unless I know they have authorization. You have authorization? A black car doesn't count."

"You're only going to stretch things out past tomorrow if you keep on like this. How about we don't pick at each other? It isn't a bad question, nothing tricky, no hidden agenda. Just a simple inquiry." He turned around and took a couple of papers off the table where the woman sat. "This is a flimsy of the Handout file. It's from Headquarters. You want to look at it? It's the same one you have." He put it on my desk in front of me. "Go ahead, take a look. I've got the time."

I didn't bother to look. I wasn't about to start taking advice from him. "OK, so you have a flimsy. Good for you. What do you want to know?"

"See, that's better. We're getting along already. I knew we could do it. I just wanted to know what you think of Handout. Good source?"

"All I know is what I read. I haven't picked him up yet. His old case officer left in a hurry; maybe you know something about that. I'm going to arrange a meeting as soon as I have time, when people aren't calling me into the office in the middle of the fucking night."

The man on the south wall let out a low whistle. "Angry sort."

The gray-haired man ignored him. "So, you were about to set up a meeting. Funny, I heard you were trying to get rid of him. Why would you want to do that, if you haven't met him yet? We spend a lot of money vetting sources and so forth. Why would we want to waste it, that's the question people are going to ask, don't you think?"

"You want Handout on your payroll? Go ahead, he's yours. Did you vet him? You might want to spend an extra ten yuan and do it again."

There was a low chuckle from the north end of the room, but not from the man in front of my desk. He studied me for a moment, then nodded in the direction of the woman at the table. She turned to a fresh page.

"OK," he said, "have it your way, leave that for now. We'll get back to it at some point. Let's go to something easy. Let's go over your career. You know the facts. I'm just reading from your file. Presumably, they are the same. If you hear something out of kilter, you'll let me know. Miss Bao over there will mark it for further study, and we can check the box. Meet with your approval?"

I shrugged.

"Sometimes that indicates yes, sometimes no. I'll take it as a yes." He put on his reading glasses. "Subject is chief of the Chinese State Security Ministry's (MSS) special bureau for the northeast tier, covering the border with North Korea along a particularly sensitive stretch, from Tumen to Quanhe. Subject assumed the post in late 2009, as part of Political Bureau decision to beef up security in tandem with a sharp acceleration and expansion of economic relations with the Korean Democratic People's Republic. Special note—" The man looked up. "Are you with me?"

I shrugged again.

"Special note: This bureau had gone without a chief officer for over a year previously because the last occupant of the office had defected to North Korea in early 2007. During this interim period, the deputy, Lieutenant Li Bo-ting, was in charge with circumscribed authority." He looked up. "How are we doing? Anything you think Ms. Bao should mark for correction?"

"No."

"What a relief. If you had shrugged three times in a row, we would have faced a serious problem." The man turned the page in the file. "Ah, here is something I want to run by you. It says here that you and your mother lived alone."

"It's all in the file. I don't think we need to go over it."

"You have friends?"

"Sure, the whole world is my friend. Isn't that where we started, being friends?"

"What about Ping Man-ho, he your friend?"

I rolled this around real fast in my brain. I hadn't talked to Ping Man-ho more than three or four times since being assigned to Yanji, all of them at Gao's. "Ping shows up once in a while. He's a sharp dresser, borrows money and doesn't pay it back, but that's not actually a crime. Bad upbringing, maybe, but not a crime."

"You know about his upbringing?"

"Nope. Just being chatty. You want us to open a file on him? I'll tell Mrs. Zhao to make room on the top shelf. I don't think we'll have to get to it very often."

"Maybe you should do a little digging, turn your hunting dog Lieutenant Li loose on the case and see what he comes up with."

"If you have something, why don't you just save me the time and hand it over? We're busy enough up here; I can't spare resources on vague hints. Better yet, you have a big team. Do it yourself, why don't you?"

"Why don't I? Because it's your bureau, that's why. It's your territory. You've built up a nice reputation; important people at Headquarters purr when your name comes up. I don't want to take anything away from you. I'm not in the business of subtracting from other people's fitness reports. I'm just giving you a tip, that's all. You decide what to do with it, OK?"

"Anything else?"

The man turned a couple of pages in the file. "I see you have an uncle."

"You're not interested in biology."

"No, what interests me is that he is a North Korea police detective."

"Retired." Now we were getting somewhere, though not anywhere I wanted to be.

"Retired from North Korea, or retired from the police?" The old man closed the file and looked at Miss Bao. She picked up a new pen. The man smiled at me. "About your uncle, what is he up to?"

"Up to?" That wasn't normal interrogation-speak. It was vague, left too much to the discretion of the person being grilled. "Up to? You mean right now?"

"Don't repeat my questions. It wastes time. Just answer them."

"Sure. Want to try being more specific?"

"Your uncle is still in touch with people across the river. How does he contact them?"

"Well, if I knew that the first part of your question was correct, I might have a clue how to answer the second part. As far as I know, he's not in contact."

"We've noticed funny people hanging around near your house."

"You have any photographs? That might help."

The old man nodded to Mr. Penguin, holding down the east flank of the office. "Show him the pictures."

2

By the time the questioning and answering was done, the morning flight had left. So had the one at two o'clock. It was already late afternoon. The session had not been friendly; it certainly had not been short. By the end, I was tired, hungry, and plenty mad. I don't like being badgered, especially for prolonged periods. If they weren't going to drag me away, then they could go to hell as far as I was concerned, sore shoulders and all. I told them that. They finally stopped and looked at the woman with the pens. She shook her head; they straightened their ties and told me to go home, so I did.

The house was quiet when I stepped inside, which meant my uncle was in his workshop, either dozing or contemplating plans for another bookcase. It turned out to be the latter. He had a pencil in his hand and a slight frown on his face.

"I can come back," I said. After being the object of a nightlong interrogation, I wasn't about to deal with his moods.

"You could. Or you could come in." He put down the pencil. "You have some sort of news or you wouldn't be home this time of day. You left in the middle of the night; now here you are. You've been cashiered?"

"I need to sit. May I?"

"Sit, by all means. Of course, sit." He pointed to a stool in the corner of the room. "Let's see if the new glue I tried this morning dries as fast as they say."

I sat gingerly. "First, if you see strange people hanging around the house with or without cameras, let me know, all right? Second, unknown quarters in MSS Headquarters filed an oversight complaint. That has worked its way up through channels, where it lodged in the brain of someone in charge of sending out special teams. One of those teams was in my office. That's where I've been."

My uncle picked up his pencil again and made a few marks on the bookcase plans. From what I could see, this one was to be built into a house with a fifteen-meter high ceiling. It actually looked like it might go well in Mrs. Zhou's file room.

"The complaint is against you," I said. "It is serious."

My uncle grunted. "The problem with lumber around here nowadays is that it dries out too quickly. Even if I go to Harbin, it's the same problem. You'd think good lumber would be easy to find at least somewhere in this country. You Chinese are buying up everyone's resources, but you can't import good lumber? If I'm going to build something fifteen meters high, the lumber has to be straight. Straight means straight, not curvy like that wall of yours in the front hall."

"Apparently, Headquarters held the complaint for a week while it was discussed at higher levels. The highest levels, actually. A decision was dropped back down with a great deal of sizzle attached two days ago, and the team was dispatched almost immediately."

"Your headquarters is nothing but trouble. It always was as far as we were concerned. When I was in the Ministry, we never liked going through Beijing on liaison trips. Too many of your people breathing down our necks. Moscow wasn't so great either, believe me, but it was tolerable. They treated us like germs."

"Germs?"

"They didn't want to catch us. Too much paperwork."

"There's never too much paperwork here. I think it has something to do with inbreeding at the court. Like those little dogs."

"Let's be realistic. Why would anyone complain about me?"

I stifled my first response.

"Don't stifle yourself, boy. What possible reason could they have? It wasn't for making a scene in a noodle restaurant."

"We've been through this already. You were among the last people to see Madame Fang before she disappeared, maybe the last. She must be close to someone in Shanghai who misses her pearls."

"She's been close to a lot of people, not all of whom miss her. She'd be the first to tell you. I can probably get a hundred testimonials to that effect, if you want."

"I don't want. I was told they have a bulging file of reports from people who say they saw her come here to meet you, and the next thing anyone knew, she was on the wrong side of the river."

"And this has what to do with me? We've already established I didn't lure her. Do they think I smuggled her across in a sack of rice?"

"They think you have connections." I didn't mention the pictures I'd been shown.

"Good for them. If I had connections, job one would be to get lumber that doesn't warp, not fool around with Madame Fang."

"Well, she came up here to see you, and that has a lot of people wondering why. The complaint recommends that you be brought in for questioning. 'Recommends' is a word you don't want to see in communications from Beijing. It's a nasty, explosive term."

"I must add it to my vocabulary cards someday. They want to ask questions? Fine, go ahead, ask. You can do it right here. You're authorized to ask questions, aren't you? Then you can sit down, write a report, send it by one of your jazzy special couriers back to the imperial censor."

"They don't want a piece of paper. They want flesh and blood, not necessarily in equal measure. No, you're to be brought to Beijing, unless . . ."

My uncle tapped the pencil on the worktable. "Go on."

"Unless you agree to work for MSS."

"Meaning they're desperate. Pah!"

"That's not all."

"Of course that's not all. They're threatening to drag you in if I don't cooperate, right? They think that's leverage? Complete fools, all of them."

"I suppose you did things differently in your day?"

"My day?" The voice became treacherously calm. "Let's leave my day out of this. That's the past, beyond anything you can understand. You don't know what my day was like. Or your father's, for that matter." It was the closest I'd ever heard him come to saying something kind about his brother.

"Forget I brought it up." The old interrogator had handed me a summary of the complaint just before things broke up. It had found its way into one of my pockets, though which one I couldn't recall. My uncle watched as I searched.

"You looking for something special, or is this a spring cleaning ritual? Try the back pocket."

It was in the back pocket. "This is what we have to deal with, here and now." I held it up for him to see. "To be clear, I'm not asking you to go to Beijing. I'm not ordering you to do it either."

"Good, because I'm not going. I travel to Harbin a few times a year. That's enough of a concession to the wider world at my age." He paused and drew a couple of lines on the plans. "I'll do this much, I'll meet them here." He erased a line and drew another.

"Here? In this house? You expect them to crawl to see you?"

"In this workshop, about where you are now, though they won't be sitting. And I won't meet with a pack of them. It has to be only one." He crumpled the plans and threw them in the corner along with the pile of his other ideas and dreams too bizarre or breathtaking to follow through to completion. "One or nothing at all," he said.

"Impossible. They don't do that sort of thing. Trust me."

3

The knock on the door at 10:00 A.M. wasn't crisp or authoritative. It was barely halfhearted. We were expecting a visit by an MSS Headquarters team at 10:30, so I needed to get rid of whoever was there. The last time I checked, about an hour earlier, my uncle was on his bench in the workshop, writing poetry. I had made sure there wasn't anything overly sharp within reach and then left him alone.

Outside the front door, for a change, wasn't a beautiful woman. There were three men. Two of them I didn't recognize, though I knew the type. The third was the cook from the noodle restaurant. From the way the others were standing, they had no doubt that he was in charge. He wasn't carrying a knife, not that I could see, anyway.

My uncle had offered him a job. Why he had asked two friends to come along on an interview struck me as a little odd. Maybe they were references; maybe he was insecure, though people who cut off other people's hands tend not to be. In any case, if he was here, it meant I wouldn't have to send Li Bo-ting out to find out who he was. I could take him back to my uncle for fifteen or twenty minutes, slip in some of my own questions, and then show him the door.

"Welcome," I said, not wanting to show surprise at seeing the cook again. I held the door half open. There was no chance I could keep all of them out if they charged in; there was no sense pretending I was going to slam the door. "Maybe your friends would like to wait outside. It's a nice day, they can watch the birds."

The heftiest man, with the neck of a bullock, hauled himself up to his full height, which wasn't all that much. There's going to be trouble, I thought and reached behind the door for a steel bar I keep handy.

The cook shook his head. "No need for anything physical. If my colleagues can wait inside, everything will be fine." Colleagues? This was a gaggle of noodle chefs?

I made a command decision. "They can wait in the office," which sounded more official than "the library."

The cook's eyebrows went up slightly. "And where is the royal audience to take place?"

"You'll see." I put the steel bar back against the wall and opened the door the rest of the way. The group followed me down the hall to the office/library. "You two amuse yourselves here. Those things on the shelves are books. None of them are cookbooks; otherwise you could find new ways to prepare bird's nest soup." The bullock scowled and occupied the red velvet chair. I closed the door and locked it from the outside.

"Won't do any good," said the cook evenly. "They're both pretty good with locks. You'll have noticed that Mr. Liang has a big right shoulder. Locked doors don't stand a chance."

We walked quickly down the hall and across the courtyard to the entrance of the workshop. At the doorway, the cook stopped suddenly. "Wait a minute. Is he here? Because if he's not here, you're going to be sorry."

I put my hands in my pockets. "Calm down. This is his workshop." I jerked my head in the right direction. "Lucky for you, he's in a good mood. Don't be nervous. He'll just ask a lot of questions about noodles. Keep your answers short."

As we entered, my uncle was pondering a sheet of paper. He

put a finger to his lips. "A moment, please, I'm on the edge of finding the right word." He concentrated again on the paper. "What I need is something that sounds like grass when the wind sweeps across a field."

He looked up and frowned when he saw the cook. "You wouldn't know anything like that, I suppose. Any language will do."

"Very sweet. You've taken up poetry in your old age, O?" The cook glanced around the room. He was speaking Korean. "Still stuck on wood, I see. Any of these finished?" He pointed at the bookshelves against the wall.

"It depends on what you mean. I consider them finished. They served their purpose. To you they may appear incomplete, but that's because you always had a bad habit of starting from the wrong place."

"It's never my starting point that has been the problem, it's where I've ended up. I'm not going to play around with you, O. No one is anymore."

I moved toward the door. If the man wanted a job, he was going about it the wrong way. The mood music didn't seem scored for sharing fond memories. "Time for me to check on your sous chefs," I said.

"They're fine." The cook took his eyes off my uncle and pinned them on me. "I want you here during the questioning. In fact, maybe you ought to make yourself useful and take notes."

"Notes?" I echoed. "For what?"

My uncle nodded. "Good idea. We need a record of this encounter." He sat back and smiled. "A complete record, nothing omitted. Nothing added afterward, either. I know how you make yourself look good in the reporting."

"All right, O," said the cook. "Let's get this over with." He took out a small notebook and flipped through several pages. "I'm going to ask a series of questions. They are perfectly clear, but I'm willing to repeat them once if you want to play your old games. Then you're going to answer each one of them, and for a change, you're not going to give me long, involved answers. I don't want to hear any tortured logic or elliptical phrasing. You're going to get to the point and stay on it. Don't build me a watch. Am I getting through?"

"Like a brick over the transom."

The cook smiled, only I didn't think he was happy. "We'll start with the obvious, and work from there."

"Let me ask you a question first, if that's allowed." My uncle was also speaking in Korean, but it was very clipped so I had a hard time following. "Since when do you work for the Chinese? Or should I ask, how long have you been on their payroll? You can't cook, by the way. You should be arrested for trying. You're not with the MSS, I take it."

"You can take it any way you want, O. My career path isn't under the microscope here. Yours is."

My uncle turned to me. "I want a verbatim record. Verbatim as in word for word. Even the pauses. Nothing left to the imagination. If you miss something, anything, just tell us to wait until you catch up. There's a pad of paper on the top shelf of that red lacquered bookshelf."

The cook moved quicker than I did. He lifted the pad from the shelf and fanned through the empty pages. "Nothing here you don't want me to see, is there? Maybe I should have the boys take apart this workshop. They'd enjoy that."

"Go ahead, try it." My uncle retrieved a long-handled chisel I'd missed from under the workbench. "You'll lose more than a hand if you do."

"Are you threatening me, old man? Because you don't want to do that."

"You said you had some questions. Why don't you ask them and leave aside the tough stuff?"

"Where is she?"

My uncle laughed. "That's the first question on your carefully composed list? No warm-up? No setting the stage? No priming the pump? What happened to foreplay?"

The cook grabbed a board from the floor and smashed it against the workbench. "There's your foreplay." My uncle didn't flinch. "Next time, it will be your head, Inspector, and if you don't think so, just try me."

"I'm no longer an inspector, and if you break another board you'll have to pay for it. That's red sparrow wood, very rare and expensive." He looked at me. "Make a note of it. We'll check the prices later."

"Yeah, and make a note of this, while you're at it. Inspector O refuses to cooperate."

"What the hell is this about?" I wasn't following very well.

My uncle tossed the paper and pen aside. The two of them glared at me. My uncle climbed down first. "All right. Let's start over." He picked up his pencil. "I still need a word that sounds like the wind sighing through the grass. That's where we were when you walked in."

The cook picked up one of the splintered pieces of wood. "You are either a prime suspect or an accomplice, O. That's the thinking in Beijing. This time you can't charm your way out of trouble. They're serious about bringing you in. And once they're done, they'll toss what's left of you out across the river. You don't want that, do you?"

"Meaning what? You're here to save me the trouble? You're finally going to do me a favor? One of several you still owe me."

"Me owe you?" The moment of calm had passed. "I owe you spit, and this is why. Drugs over the border. Money laundering. Illegal goods. Bribes. An occasional body floating down the river. Teams of agents crossing at night for completely forbidden operations, then racing back. Kidnapping. Prostitution. Gun running."

"That's it?" My uncle yawned.

"No, one more thing. Suborning an MSS officer." He whacked the broken piece of wood on the workbench.

My uncle glanced at me from the corner of his eye and then looked back at the cook. "He came over completely on his own. No photos. No tapes. We never even bought him a drink."

"The hell you didn't." Whack!

"What, you think there is money enough to buy someone to cross the river backward? Or enough embarrassment in a single heart? Be realistic for a change, will you? He jumped. We didn't push; we didn't pull. We didn't even know he was coming. One fine day I turned around and there he was. I told him to go back where he came from, spent most of an hour arguing with him. Might has well have been talking to a ginkgo tree. He insisted he was staying. Completely adamant, almost pleading."

"O, in your old age you can't carry it off anymore. Once you might have skated by with a story like that. Not anymore. It doesn't convince me, and it won't convince them in Beijing. They want to know what he told your people, what he brought with him. They need to know, and they're going to make sure you tell them."

"What if I wasn't in the debriefings?"

"You admit he was debriefed?"

"Admit?" My uncle snorted. "What's to admit? The director of the MSS office in Yanji skips out and turns up on the wrong side of the river. Show me someone dumb enough to think that he wouldn't be asked a lot of questions."

"Where is he now?" Whack.

"Now? Don't know. Really, I don't know. He disappeared. It wasn't my job to keep track of him. I wasn't appointed his babysitter. Not in my position description, and I checked. Maybe he settled down with some beauty in a big, drafty apartment and died of overfulfillment. I didn't enquire."

"We want him back. He says he wants to come home, and we want him back."

"We? Ha! Since when are you one of them? I wish you all the best. Every bit of all the best. Is this conversation done? I'm in the middle of a poem."

The cook threw the piece of wood on the floor. "I'm not authorized to pull you by the ears out of this house, O. Someone will be here later today for that. You might want to pack a bag." He turned to go and then turned back. "You are the most stubborn, infuriating person I've ever met. But I think you knew that already."

I would have bet my uncle would not take that as criticism, but I didn't expect him to smile so broadly. "Allow me one more question, will you?"

The cook frowned. "It's not your show—but go ahead; what the fuck do I care about anything these days?"

"Are you in communication with Fang?"

"Me?" For the first time, the cook laughed. It had a mean undertone to it, but it qualified as a laugh. "Are you kidding? Why would she have anything to do with me? I'm not her type."

"You're not, but you know what I mean. Is she sending reports out through you?"

"I don't have access to operational reporting. That's not what I do."

"No, you just make bad noodles. OK, never mind. It was worth asking, though."

After I had seen the cook and his friends out the door and locked it, I went back to my uncle's workshop. "Who the hell is he? What's going on?" I had a pretty good idea, but I wanted to hear it from my uncle.

"He's not one of yours? I thought he might be." My uncle looked at the dent in his workbench and the splintered wood on the floor. "In that case, he must belong to someone else in your system, which complicates things. How I'm not sure, and you don't want to make inquiries."

"Don't tell me when not to inquire! I heard what you said. I'd have to be in a coma not to realize that at some point in the past he worked with you, or for you, or some damned thing on your side. What the hell was he doing cooking noodles in Yanji?"

"That's what I'd like to figure out, once I clean this place up."

"Screw noodles, I don't care about noodles. I want to know who that guy is. He was here with a pair of thick friends. I would like it if they didn't come back to my house. Now, this minute, I need to know exactly who he is. I can't call to get protection unless I know whose orders are supposed to be countermanded, and even then I might not be able to do it." I picked up one of the pieces of broken wood. "See this? This is going to feel like goose down when they're through with us."

"You have that envelope with the money that Miss Du gave us?"

"Yes, it's in my desk."

"Where you parked his two plague rats? Why didn't you just hand them the cash wrapped in a red ribbon?"

He reached under a pile of wood and came up with another envelope. "Never mind. Here's the rest of it. She sent it over the next morning while you were at your office. That's 120,000 yuan. Even if we lost the down payment, there's plenty here for two plane tickets out of the country."

"Out of the country? Not a chance. How are we going to breeze past immigration, even if we get out our front door? And no, under no circumstances am I going across that damned river, like—" Then it hit me. I had to sit down. "This just got a lot worse than I thought."

He gave me a blank look. "A weather front. It will pass."

"Not this time. I think this time the consequences are deadly."

"Consequences? What would you know about consequences in this hothouse of a country? I'm not asking for your help, and I don't plan to stay here forever. I'll go back when the time is right. There is going to be a break in the clouds at some point. There always is."

"You're going to go back. Whenever you're ready. I'm not pushing you out, but I can't help either of us if I don't have a better idea what is going on. You think keeping things from me is going to make the road easier? Most of that conversation you had with the cook, or whoever he is, didn't make a lot of sense. "

"It wasn't supposed to make sense. I wanted to see how much he knew."

"So what did you find out?"

"It's lunchtime, isn't it? Let's not have noodles."

Chapter Six

Iit little profits that an idle king."

After dinner we were following our usual practice of sitting in the library. I looked up from the pile of bills on my desk. "If anyone would know about an idle king, you would."

"No need to be literal. It's poetry. Rings nicely, wouldn't you say?" He had a small book open in front of him.

"That wasn't your line, I take it."

My uncle had a dreamy quality in his eyes as he surveyed the room. I didn't like that look. I'd seen it before. Nothing good came from it.

"All art is shared," he said and waved his hand airily. "Like all ideas are shared. That goes for existence, too."

He didn't believe such a thing, not for an instant. I'd listened to him long enough to know that he believed life was solitary, each of us in our own cage. "Shared? I tell you what we need to have shared. Money. Maybe we can get someone with a lot of money to share a little with us, wouldn't that be something?"

"Why are you so obsessed with money? The grand crypto-capitalism that has infected this society seems to have only one thing on its mind—money. Getting, saving, keeping, spending, owing, or paying money. More money. Not enough money. Money just around the next corner. I see in the newspaper that prices of apartments in Shanghai have doubled in six months."

"Too bad we don't have an apartment in Shanghai."

"Yes, let's get an apartment and then spend every waking hour calculating how much will be lost if prices go down next week. Pah! Ridiculous. You don't even like that city."

"You're right. Forget money. We'll sit here and wait for food to appear magically at our door. A food fairy on a motor scooter will deliver it."

My uncle closed the book. "Fine, you have my full attention. I'm listening. What do you propose we do?"

I gathered my wits. Rarely was I asked for an opinion. It was a moment that called for supreme caution. The old man was always a step ahead of me, and he never left much room in the passing lane. The surest way to get in front was to hang back, not give him a chance to say no before I'd even prepared the battlefield. One false move, I knew, and we'd end up doing exactly what he wanted, no matter how much he painted it to look like my suggestion. I thought fast, but not fast enough.

"Very well." He jumped in ahead of me. "You contemplate the options, I'll review where things stand. Stop me any time you think I have something wrong."

I pushed the pile of bills into the drawer. "Go ahead."

"First, there is an odd current swirling around us, set off by the sudden appearance of Madame Fang. You never should have opened the door to that woman, but you did." He held up his hand before I could say anything. "Past is past. We can't fix that first fatal step, so we won't anguish about it."

"Second?"

"Second, two disappearances, Madame Fang and Lieutenant Fu."

I never discussed what went on at the office with him. I was sure I didn't talk about it in my sleep. How did he know about Lieutenant Fu? "Who told you anything about Fu?"

"It's not important. You have your sources. I have mine. Fu disappeared. I never liked him."

"You *knew* him?"

"Nephew, this is and is not a closed system we inhabit. The illusion is one of stark degrees of separation. Believe me, it is only that, an illusion. Yes, there may be a billion Chinese, but there are a very limited number that deal with your border up here, and from that an even more limited number moving back and forth across the river with doctored passports and an odd mincing walk. Fu Bin had a strange walk, you have to admit. Many Third Bureau people do."

"Oh, really?" What did my uncle know about how Third Bureau people walked? They weren't supposed to have anything to do with foreigners; even their existence was supposed to be kept secret from outsiders. The Third Bureau didn't even show up on the Ministry's internal organization charts. "Anything else I should understand about what you think you know about my ministry? How far do these hands of friendship across the border go?"

"You're the bureau director, I'm not telling you your business."

"Thank you." Third Bureau officers on the other side of the river? That was exactly my business. No Chinese official with operational knowledge was supposed to go into North Korea without approval from the local MSS bureau director. Lots of rules get bent, but not this one. This one was supposed to be ironclad. No exceptions. I hadn't given approval, not to Fu Bin or anyone else. All meetings with sources were supposed to take place in China; that way we could control the environment and avoid unpleasant surprises. Handout was a source, he could skip into North Korea anytime his heart desired, but not his handler. So what was this about? Was Fu Bin making extra cash to support his love life, or was the Third Bureau now running private operations? Either way it was bad. Another thread to pull.

"Did I say there were two disappearances?" My uncle rubbed his chin, which he did when he wanted to appear thoughtful.

"You know perfectly well what you said."

"I meant to say, three. The third one? Your cook."

"She didn't walk funny; I don't see a connection."

"Nor do I, actually. What a woman! She could annoy the scales off a snake!"

"Don't pick at old scabs. What does her leaving have to do with our problem?" I knew what he was doing. He was changing the subject.

"At this point," he said, "we're merely laying out points for agglutination."

"One of your fancy terms? I don't know what it means."

"Things sticking together. Like blood."

Full stop. "Whose?"

"That's to be seen." My uncle took a chip of wood from his desk drawer. "Do you know what this is?"

"It's a piece of wood. I think it's elm, and the reason I think so is because I put it in your desk a few days ago."

"Yes, it's elm, and that is exactly what I don't need right now. What else do you have?"

I opened the drawer of my desk and read off the labels. "Larch. Mulberry. Cedar. Oak. Walnut."

"Pitiful selection. Nothing worth a damn." He paused, brow furrowed. "All right, give me the walnut."

I picked out a piece of walnut and tossed it in front of him. "We're low on everything. Pretty soon, it will be a choice between buying wood chips or rice."

"No contest," he said.

"You were reviewing where things stand, I think."

"I was. I was marching through some of the coincidences. Let's move on to the happenstance. There is a scuffle at the noodle restaurant, and who should emerge from the kitchen but an old acquaintance of mine."

"At first you said you didn't know who he was."

"Surely you don't believe everything I say."

No, as a matter of fact, I didn't. "I take it from the discussion I witnessed that he is not a cook."

"Anyone eating his noodles would figure that out in an instant."

"You say he's not a cook, and I'd say he's not much of an interrogator. Who is he? How do you know him? What was he doing in a kitchen on Lanxiang Hutong?"

"You keep your secrets, I'll keep mine. We agreed. I'll tell you this much. Our paths crossed in odd ways over the years. We never had much use for each other. He skated in and out of your father's circles for a while. The last time, about thirty years ago in Romania, I saw him slumped in a chair in the Hotel Union with a bullet in his neck. Didn't fill me with remorse. I thought he was dead."

"He's not, apparently." I didn't want to pursue the sly mention of my father's "circles."

"Apparently. Now he seems to be working for your side, which doesn't surprise me. He's not one of yours?"

No, he wasn't one of mine.

"Whatever he's involved in"—my uncle let my silence speak for itself—"I'd guess from where we found him whatever he's part of has been in the planning for quite a while."

"And why is that?"

"Your people wouldn't try that ridiculous cover with someone they didn't trust, and they don't want it ripped open too easily. A North Korean pretending to be a North Korean on the Chinese border, cooking bad food in a restaurant run by the Fujian mob? That's not for everyone. It means it isn't part of a routine defector roundup operation either. They're not interested in trapping teenagers from Onsong with this snare. This is something special."

"You sound surprised." He also sounded like he had it figured out, a step ahead of me.

"Surprised? I suppose I am, which isn't good. On second thought, maybe it is. If he thinks I'm surprised, he'll think I'm vulnerable. Let him. The best way to deal with double agents like him is to leave them alone. Sooner or later, they hang themselves."

"An operational bromide, thank you. I'll file it when I have a chance." Next he'd tell me that this cook character and Fu Bin worked together, for whom, against whom, paid by whom not yet determined. "I have an idea, something straightforward. Let's focus on what's staring us in the face. How do we keep you from being shipped off to Beijing for a nasty bout of questioning? I know you think you can handle anything they dish out, but Headquarters has mood swings and can be very ugly about things when it wants to be. I may seem short-tempered with you, but you're my uncle, and I'd rather not have to come and claim your corpse."

"Very moving, nephew. I would do the same for you in similar circumstances. To prove it, I'm going to ask you a question. What do you know about your predecessor?"

"Excuse me?"

"Simple question. What do you know about your predecessor?"

"I can't talk about that. Keeping you from of a basement room filled with rats and bugs is one thing, but operational details? Completely out of bounds. I told you more the other night than I should have."

"Why, do you think it's a big secret? You heard what that phony cook and I talked about. Your predecessor not only defected, he practically jumped into my arms. Shall I tell you what he was wearing when he appeared? What he had in his wallet? The papers in his briefcase? You don't have to worry about his leaping out of the shadows and stealing your soul. For all I know, he really is dead and buried. Maybe dumped at sea."

I digested this. It was more than I knew before, more than the briefing in Beijing seven years ago had imparted, multiple times more than the message the courier had recently delivered. Other than those scraps, I'd never picked up anything from around the office here in Yanji, though I'd probed where I thought I could. The previous chief had disappeared, his file was locked securely and put away, and no one raised the subject. Even the bravest of souls ventured no more than that he had probably been executed in secret, but none of them claimed to know for sure. The post of bureau chief had been kept vacant while Headquarters sent out teams to scour all of the regional bureaus for other snakes in the grass, but eventually there was need for a replacement in Yanji. My name came up. I told them I didn't want the job. They said they weren't asking.

"No, he wasn't dumped anywhere." It was time to feed out a little more information to my uncle. He already seemed to know a lot more than I did anyway. "I told you, he's not dead. He wants to come back. That's definite." I narrowed my eyes. "And that's not to leave this room."

My uncle thought it over. "This would be the fish that will swim upstream to return home, I take it."

"Yes." I'd already stepped over the line, so it didn't matter if I threw in a few more facts. Even so, I wanted to keep things on the vague side. That wouldn't bother my uncle. He was comfortable with vagueness. Anything too precise made him nervous; anything tied up too neatly at the end made him suspicious. It was a sort of protective coloring, and he wasn't about to shed it this late in his life.

"Yes, and . . ." He was happy to leave things vague, unless he wasn't.

"And word is out that the fish has sent a message that he is ready to come back."

"You believe he would risk such a thing after all these years?" My uncle was as close to incredulous as I'd ever seen him. "Or that he'll be welcome after betraying his colleagues and his profession? What sort of deal could he possibly work out?"

"I don't know what deal he has or might get, and I haven't inquired." I didn't have to inquire. My instincts told me he would be eliminated, permanently, as soon as they had wrung from him everything he'd revealed to the North Koreans.

"In that case, I'd say, the subject is closed."

"Not quite. I'm supposed to figure out how to get him back over here."

"They want *you* to do it? His successor!" My uncle was stupefied. The concept seemed to strike him as coming from another universe, and not a parallel one. "Your people haven't already made other arrangements on their own, like meeting him halfway across the bridge in Tumen?"

"No. He's not being released, or traded, as far as I know."

This prompted a long pause while my uncle mulled over this piece of news. "So," he said finally, "it's to be a redefection. Not a lot of those, if you don't count triple agents."

"Call it whatever you want. From what little I'm privy to, the preferred formulation is that he's 'returning home.' Important noses will wrinkle if they ever hear the term 'redefect.'"

"What do you propose to do, if I may ask?"

"You may ask. You of all people may certainly ask, because I'm convinced that's why Beijing wants to see you. They want your advice on how to ease his passage back this way. Think about it. They know that Pyongyang isn't going to kiss him on both cheeks and send him sailing home, so they need someone who can devise the route. They gave me the job, but they know perfectly well I don't have any special insight into the solution. I don't, but someone with a workshop off the back of my house does."

My uncle snorted softly.

"They figure you can help, uncle, but can't admit to themselves that they are looking for your advice. That means they have to go through the motions of arresting you. It will be more than just motions. No doubt, there will be bright lights and very uncomfortable seating. You may not be able to sleep on a regular schedule for a week or two."

"Like hell I won't."

"They think you are still in touch with your friends, and that you could pull some strings."

"Of course, you know better."

"To be honest, I'm not sure." I still didn't want to say anything about the photographs. They weren't conclusive, and besides they were very grainy. "Until Madame Fang showed up, I thought maybe you really had cut off all your ties, but now, first with her and then with the visit by the noodle cook, I have begun to wonder. That's the nature of my job, I wonder about things. And if I've begun to wonder, imagine what is going through nimble minds in Beijing."

"You actually believe your fish wants to come home, it's as simple as that? First of all, he's not a fish. He's an eel, slippery and full of those bones that stick in your throat. He's up to something. His type always is."

"He's been away from his family." I was careful with my words. There was little sense saying that no Chinese in his right mind would want to live in Korea, north or south, for very long. "It can't be all that pleasant in his situation, no matter what sort of creature comforts he has."

"And his loyalties?"

"They're not an issue. He threw them away. No one doubts that. So, yes, he'll be kept at arm's length once he's back. They want him where they can see him, that's all. They may put him in a hole for a few months, but after that, he'll be allowed to walk around, on a long leash. They'll make sure he dies of boredom." If a bullet in the back of the neck could be called boredom.

"What will you do once he's back, if I might inquire?"

"Do? I'll do whatever it is that I do now."

"That's not what I mean."

"After he's safe and sound in whatever hands are groping for him, it's not my concern. He doesn't have any current knowledge of the office or of our operations over the past ten years." I stopped and gave the idea a moment to sink of its own weight. It didn't sink. It was too buoyant with possibilities. "You think he has been running people over here, using his knowledge of our procedures?"

"If not that, something like it had occurred to me. It hadn't occurred to you?"

"No, of course not, and I'll tell you why. Because that would be traitorous, and he's not a traitor." I didn't sound convincing, probably because I wasn't convinced.

"Ha! If what he did isn't traitorous, I'd like to see what is. He defected with two briefcases of documents."

I thought of Mrs. Zhou's missing files. "Names?"

"You mean to tell me you don't know for sure what he had? You haven't figured that out yet?"

I wasn't part of the investigation of his disappearance. I hadn't figured out anything. It wasn't my job. "Were they names?"

"No, numbers."

Code? Why numbers?

"He said they were his insurance. At first glance, I thought they might be bank records, maybe he had money stashed somewhere overseas. Then I thought, no, they were coded operational files—secrets to use to buy a safe harbor. I didn't have time to examine things very closely. After I gave up trying to convince him to go home, I called Headquarters. They arrived in a crashing hurry, and hustled him away in a big car, tailed by two other big cars. That was the last I saw of him."

"You never told me any of this. Not a peep. You've been here nearly two years, and you never told me anything. It didn't occur to you that it might be relevant? That word of your connection with his defection might have found its way over here and into a file—a very active file?"

"You never asked. No one else did either. Anyway, it was better you stayed in the dark."

"Beijing knows. They've probably known for a long time. Also with you here, they must have thought I knew all along, too. As far as they were concerned, I wasn't in the dark. So now I'm in their gun sights. Thank you."

"Sure, who knows? It might even be worse than that. Bad enough they think that you haven't told them that you knew. From where they sit, they might even think you're working with the other side. They're awfully suspicious in your headquarters, awfully suspi-

cious." He nodded thoughtfully. "Yes, it probably looks very bad."
He was thinking in the abstract, just tracing things out, like he
was tying a hangman's knot without reference to the fact that this
was the rope likely to end up around my neck.

Bad as it was, it explained a lot. It explained why Fu practically
took root in the office, beyond the normal tour of duty for a Third
Bureau mole. It might even explain what he was doing in North
Korea. Once my uncle showed up in Yanji, they couldn't believe
there was no evidence linking me to the whole defection affair. Fu
must have been ordered to keep searching. Maybe even Mrs. Zhou
had been recruited to help. I considered the idea for a moment and
then dropped it. Mrs. Zhou wasn't the type. Of course, Fu hadn't
seemed the type either.

My uncle was still measuring the noose he'd dropped around my
neck. "Yet they've left you alone. Just waited and watched. Extraor-
dinary system you have, very patient people. We wouldn't have
waited. You wouldn't be sitting here now." He looked at me thoughtfully, as if he might not see me again. "What did they think you
were going to do, I wonder?"

"Good question."

"If they suspect you, why would they put you in charge of getting him back, assuming they really want him? Two possibilities
come to mind. First, this is a test of your loyalty. Mine, too, I suppose, though how they can imagine I'm loyal to this place escapes
me. Do they think I'm grateful to be here?" He closed his eyes and
shuddered slightly. "They'll watch, and if something goes wrong
with the return, wherever and however it occurs, they'll conclude
one of us leaked the details to the North Koreans in order to prevent the homecoming." His eyes popped open. "Either that or he
has insisted on your involvement as a guarantee of his safety."

"My involvement? Or yours?"

"Mine? That wouldn't seem to be a point in our favor either,
but you can never tell about these things. Something like this has
the mechanics of a pinball machine. So many crazy angles, you

wouldn't want to bet on the outcome." He gave me a purposeful look.

"Right now, they seem to think I'm going to haul in a long-gone fish with your help."

"Back to fish. I never liked them. My grandfather knew how to cook fish, but I would only pick at them when he did. We went fishing once in a while. He was particular where we sat on the riverbank, how much sun came through the trees onto the water, what we packed for lunch and when we could stop to eat. All of that was fine. It was catching things I didn't like. They lie on the bank and look at you with those fish eyes. I wouldn't eat anything I caught. What if it had a family? Father fish goes out for a swim, never comes back, that sort of thing." He started to sink into the past. I needed to throw a life jacket at him, something to keep his head above water. Nothing was within reach.

"So you'll help?"

He floated back to the present. "I won't get in your way."

Chapter Seven

Two men were waiting for me at work the next morning. They were already in my office taking up chair space. That irked me. I don't like people walking in and making themselves at home. Neither one stood up when I came through the door. That annoyed me, too.

"Anything I can do for you?" I sat down behind my desk and made a show of getting comfortable. "Or are you just passing through? There's a map of the city on the wall in the reception area if you're lost. Nice big map, hard to miss. If you need help reading the symbols, Mrs. Zhou can assist you."

Both were sharp dressers, though I didn't pine after their ties. The first one, with a scarred face and close-cropped hair, had on a pale yellow shirt. The cuffs showed exactly the right amount from the sleeves of his coat, which was more or less tan. His partner was wearing a blue suit with a light pink shirt. Altogether, it made for a lot of color so early in the day.

We sat looking at each other. I made myself even more comfortable. They didn't move. Finally, one of them—the one in the blue suit—took a notebook from his breast pocket and opened it carefully, turning the pages slowly until he found a clean one. He took a pen from the same pocket and pointed it at me. "You think you're pretty smart, don't you?"

"I took a test once and did OK, but I never let it go to my head."

"You know who we are?"

"No idea. You might want to get some new ties, though."

The one in the yellow shirt glanced down at his. "This is fine," he said. "I picked it out this morning special for you." He looked up and smiled, a self-assured smile that had Beijing written all over it. "You want to see some ID?" He looked over at his partner. "Maybe we should show him some ID."

The blue suit nodded slightly. "Sure, why not?" He put his notebook down and stood up. "Which ID do you want to see?"

"The one that will make me shiver with admiration."

"I'll tell you what we're going to do. We're going to pretend we didn't get off to such a bad start. We're going to pretend that we knocked softly at your door, that you came over and let us in, shook hands real nice, offered us a seat, and called your tea lady to bring us some refreshments. How about we do that?"

"That's OK by me." I waved the blue suit back to his chair. "Do we need names, or do we just point pens at each other?"

"You're Bing."

"True."

"I'm not." The blue suit grinned.

"Neither am I." The yellow shirt smoothed his tie.

"Good." The blue suit beamed. "Now that we have that out of the way, we can get to business. You want to call your tea lady, or does she come in all by herself when you have company?"

"Mrs. Zhou?" I picked up the phone. "Mrs. Zhou, will you bring in some tea?"

A voice from outside battered the door. *"Tea? Do I look like a tea lady to you?"*

I put down the phone. "Nothing personal, she does that all the time, even to me. You had questions?"

"No, we don't have any questions."

"Ah." I paused and pondered the situation. "You're here to report a crime? You want to turn yourselves in?"

"We are going to relay orders."

"These couldn't come in the normal manner?"

"We understand you've lost some files. Paper seems to disappear from this office. So it was decided not to risk using paper. It was decided that we'd pay a visit and whisper in your ear."

"You each going to whisper in a separate ear, or do we go in order of seniority? The left ear is my bad one." I turned my head slightly. "The right one is better, but someone nibbled on it the other night so it might look a little red."

The yellow shirt cracked his knuckles. "You're cute."

"So I'm told. Why don't you finish your business and clear out? I have work to do."

The blue suit looked hurt. "Why, listen to him. He wants us out of here. Whatever shall we do?" He picked up the notebook again. Again he turned the pages slowly, smoothing them as he went.

"You said it wasn't on paper." I grinned.

"This? This is my menu for lunch, the dessert part. You like dessert?" He grinned back. So they knew that my wife ran away with a Japanese pastry chef and they were trying to pluck my strings? So what?

"I don't eat dessert. In fact, I don't even eat lunch these days. Why don't you both go back where you came from. Can I borrow your pen? I'll draw you a simple map of the road out of town. The one in the reception area might be a little complicated for you."

"Maybe you should just listen for a change. I'm going to speak real slow, the way you country people do up here, everything in simple sentences. Ready?"

I looked at the yellow shirt. "The tie isn't bad, but I think you'd look better with something natural on it. Rutting deer, maybe."

The blue suit motioned his partner to sit still. "Point one. You are to proceed immediately to Ulan Bator and make contact with"—he looked back at the notebook, searching for his place—"Mr. Ding."

Mongolia. There weren't too many reasons they'd send me there. My current job didn't call for a certificate in sheep shearing. This must be what my uncle had been speculating about the other night, a test to see how watertight the information channels were. "There's only one Mr. Ding in Mongolia? I assume you don't want me to put his name on a slip of paper as a reminder. I could make it look like a grocery list. Buy half doz Dings. That sort of thing."

"He'll be at a camp about forty kilometers east of the city. You rent a four-wheeled vehicle to get there. We own one of the clerks at the rental place, so it won't be a problem."

"What color?"

"If the owner is there, he'll insist on giving you a driver when you do the paperwork, but you tell him you don't need one. If you get a driver, we don't know who he's working for, you understand what I'm saying?"

"Perfectly."

"When you get to the camp, Ding will brief you on step two." He put away the notebook first, then the pen.

"That's it? It took a pair of you to deliver that?" If the North Koreans found out about any of this, either my uncle or I—or both of us—wouldn't be coming back. Or maybe that had already been decided, that's what my uncle would say.

"If for any reason Ding is not there, you go to the fallback."

"What if he's late? How long do I wait for him?"

"You want to know the fallback? Because if you don't, it's fine with me. Is it fine with you?" He turned to the yellow shirt.

"Yeah, sure, fine with me. Let him rot with all those sheep for all I care. Someone told me there are wolves." The partner gave me a toothy smile. "Wolves eat sheep, I hear."

"See? It's unanimous, we don't care if you know the fallback."

"But I bet it's on your little lunch menu," I said. "Why don't you tell me what it is and then get the hell out of here? You're wasting my time. I don't have all morning."

"You bet you don't. You have to pack, you and that uncle of yours."

"What's my uncle got to do with this?" That clinched it. My uncle was right; this was the loyalty test. "If you think he's going, too, you have another think coming. He doesn't travel well."

"Let me ask you a question. Strictly between you, me"—he nodded at the yellow shirt—"and the lamp post. You saw Fang Mei-lin a few days ago?"

"Says who?"

"Is she really hot?"

"You forgot something."

"No, we didn't forget anything." He turned to his partner. "Did we forget anything?"

The yellow shirt shook his head. "Nothing. We didn't forget nothing."

"See? Oh, wait, I know. You want to know the fallback." He turned to his partner. "Go on, tell him the fallback."

"There isn't one."

2

I put in the rest of the day at the office. Part of the time I pieced together what information I could find on Jang, the new Third Bureau rat. Around noon I went for a walk with Lieutenant Li to tell him about my two visitors. Halfway down Renmin Road, Li stopped to look in the window of a medical supply store.

"Looking for something special, Lieutenant?"

"A man and a woman. Twenty meters behind us." He pointed at a pair of crutches in the window. Anyone watching would have thought he was shopping.

"Should we lose them, or take them for a nice stroll?" I wasn't happy with the way things were trending. First I learn strange people are loitering around my house and other people are photographing them. Now this. People weren't supposed to tail me in my sector, certainly not two blocks from my office. "Anyone we know? The man doesn't have on a yellow shirt, does he?"

"The woman hangs around the Muslim Hotel. The man started working at a massage parlor on Fenghou Hutong a couple of weeks ago. He's wearing a dirty white shirt with a missing button. The slob doesn't even know how to tuck it in. I have a little file on him, but nothing on her other than that she's from out of town. How about we let them tag along? I need to see how good they are at this game."

Half an hour later, we were sitting in a dumpling shop near Taiping Street. "I say we invite them in for lunch," I said. "Maybe they'll treat."

"I did some research on that kid Jang."

"And?"

"And very blank. Lots of forms, all filled out in detail, all made up. Too normal, like they had come from a computer program. One thing checked out, though. You'll like it."

"I can't imagine anything about Jang that I'll like."

"He's related to the chief in Shanghai."

I called the waiter over. "Two bottles of beer, and make it snappy. We're celebrating."

Li picked up a dumpling and put it on my plate. "Not only that, but he was slipped into the Third Bureau through a side door. That's icing on the cake, right?"

He saw me frown.

"Sorry, wrong image in a dumpling joint." Li always covered his mistakes pretty well. When the beer arrived, he poured for me and then a glass for himself. "Got to look ahead," he said. He raised his glass. "To ridding the world of annoying people."

"You can say that again," I said and took a long swallow. "What do we know about Ping Man-ho?"

Li put down his beer glass rather oddly. "Ping Man-ho? Not much. He acts rich, he dresses sharp, and he does all right with the ladies. He travels now and then, nothing eye-catching. A few gaps in his trail, but those are normal. I was thinking of recruiting him a couple of years ago, so I ran a check. Nothing much of interest. When I tried to pitch him, he ran the other way. I guess he figured it would interfere with his lifestyle." Li poured some more beer for me. "Why do you ask?"

"Let's just say his name came up somewhere. There's nothing funny going around about him?"

"Other than Gao's complaints about never getting paid back, I haven't heard anything. I'll keep my ears open."

I shrugged. "Don't waste a lot of time on it."

"It's not my business," Li said, "but how are things between you and your uncle?"

"What brought that on?"

"Birds are singing and bees are buzzing all of a sudden. Some of it has to do with your uncle. So I just wondered if there was anything going on."

"You think that's why the man with the missing button is following me, something to do with my uncle?"

Li mixed a large amount of hot mustard with a drop of soy sauce. He dipped a pork dumpling into the mix, put it in his mouth, and instantly started to sweat. His eyes filled with tears. "Beer," he said. "Quick."

"Why do you do that, Li? I've told you a hundred times, that mustard is going to take off your stomach lining." I handed him the bottle that was full.

Li gulped half of it down and then took a deep breath. "Better than a bullet in the head." He grinned. "This is nothing. Back home we'd eat this mustard as candy." He grinned again and finished the beer. "If you don't want to talk about your uncle, it's OK with me. I shouldn't have asked. It's out of bounds."

"There's nothing special going on. He's as hardheaded as always and doesn't know how to back off. Still, he is my father's brother, and he needs a place to stay. There's plenty of room in the house, and besides, he knows what's what on the other side of the river. He pretends he doesn't, but if I provoke him enough, he gives me some interesting nuggets once in a while."

"He's not talking to the other side, I hope." Li mixed himself more mustard. This time he used a drop more soy sauce. "Maybe he'd be more comfortable someplace else."

This was Li's way of telling me he thought my uncle should move out of my house.

"You have reason to think he's still in touch?"

"Forget I raised it, OK?"

"You want the last pork dumpling? Or should we wrap it up and give it to the woman from the Muslim Hotel?"

3

After lunch, Li and I walked back to the office unaccompanied. The couple that had been tailing us was gone.

"They were better than they looked," Li said. "The man dresses like a slob, but he's no dope."

"Shut down that massage parlor," I said. "Let's see where he turns up next."

"What about the lady?"

"I can't close the Muslim Hotel, too much trouble. Send her picture around the region, see if anyone recognizes it."

"Do I mention why you want to know?"

"Say she lost her puppy, and we're trying to help out."

Li nodded. "I'll send it out right away."

It was early evening by the time I got home. From the moment I stepped into the house, I could tell my uncle had been into the kimchi. I opened the windows and let the breeze fight it out with the garlic.

My uncle was in his workshop, but he'd been alone all day so I didn't think he'd mind the company. "Good evening, uncle. Sorry to be back so late."

"Don't apologize." He was straightening up his worktable, putting the tools in some sort of order that made sense to him. "You don't have to worry about me so much. I can take care of myself."

"Can we talk?"

He indicated a newly built stool for me to sit on. "I had the pieces lying around for a couple weeks; let's see how they fit. Tell me if it feels solid."

I sat down. It felt solid. "I had some visitors at the office this morning."

"I'll probably put on a different seat. That one is made out of poplar, and I have a feeling it might itch."

When I finished the story of the visitors, my uncle looked at me without saying anything. Then he frowned. "You didn't see any ID. You don't know who they are. You don't know who this Ding character is. Yet you expect me to pack to go with you?"

"I asked someone whose knowledge about these things is impeccable." It had taken Li Bo-ting several phone calls to find the answer. "He told me exactly who they were, down to the yellow shirt and the tan jacket. They aren't too smart, but they're legitimate."

"Who are they, or are you going to dodge?"

I dodged. "Part of a unit attached to a hurriedly formed detail. It's complicated. This detail operates without links to anything else. The people who fund it don't know it exists, and they put their hands over their ears whenever someone tries to tell them."

"Well, I want to know. All of a sudden I'm a big fan of transparency. I've been through too many of these go-here-go-there-look-under-the-bed operations. Step one is that Mr. Ding will be at the camp, you're told. Oh, really? And will step two consist of our being buried where no one will ever find us once Mr. Ding carries out his orders?"

I had had a feeling my uncle would say that. "We'll take it slow and careful. Don't worry, no one is going to kill us."

"What makes you so sure?"

"They're not going to pay for air tickets to Mongolia just to do away with us there. It's cheaper to do here."

"Maybe." My uncle didn't sound convinced. "I'm still not going. You can if you want."

"It's not a question of want or not want."

He was back to rearranging his tools. "It would do you good to go. See something of the world. When was the last time you were out of China? If you're so sure about Ding, jump on the first plane to Mongolia."

"Sure, I'll see the world, and you'll be right beside me. For once, you don't have a choice." I was going to have to scale back on being deferential and pull rank. Normally around him I was willing to play the junior officer. It didn't cost me anything, other than a little extra enamel from grinding my teeth. This was different, though. "It's either go with me or get hog-tied and carried to a basement in an old building on the outskirts of Beijing. I'm warning you, you won't like it. It's not a broadening experience."

From the way he let a rasp drop on the workbench, I knew my uncle had picked up the change in my tone. "Maybe I could go back across the river. Maybe the weather's cleared up."

"Shall I wave good-bye from the front door?"

"Don't bother." He half-smiled, which hid plenty. "So, you are off on a merry chase, following clues to bring home your errant knight. As we both know perfectly well, this is the loyalty test I mentioned to you. It's more than that. They're dropping you into an operation without any preparation. We would never have done anything like this."

He was right, but I wasn't going to let him crow. "Don't pretend you know something if you don't, all right? It isn't helpful. That's how things get off on the wrong foot. Why should our fish be in Mongolia? How the hell did he even get there? Why would some state seal be rolling around with a bunch of sheep, anyway? Maybe you're right, but maybe not. Maybe it's something else entirely."

"Like what?"

"Give me a moment, I'll come up with something."

"You know what you lack? A hypothesis. If you don't have a hypothesis, how do you know which way you are going and where you'll end up? I'm reminded of the Blue Sparrow murders."

"The what?"

"The Blue Sparrow murders."

"I don't want to hear about blue sparrow murders. We don't have time for that now. Blue sparrows, red sparrows, birds of any type, color, wingspan, or mating habit, all immaterial."

"The case was quite a challenge. Every now and then I go over it in my mind." He folded his arms and looked innocently at me. "Not completely the same as what we have here, but instructive nonetheless."

It was obvious that he wasn't going to relent. We'd been through this sort of thing before, his raising "challenging cases" from the old days. I had learned the hard way that the more I objected, the more he would be determined to tell the tale. The best move was to feign interest. It saved time in the long run. "Why blue sparrows?"

"Did I say sparrows? I didn't say sparrows plural. I said sparrow singular—Blue Sparrow, as in one small, dully brown little bird. Only one. If there had been more than one, I might not be here."

"That's a thought."

"Blue Sparrow wasn't a bird, actually. It was a code name, or a recognition sign more likely. We never found out exactly. Fascinating." He nodded to himself. "Thoroughly fascinating case."

"I'm waiting." I pointed at my watch. "You are determined to tell me about it, so go ahead. I'll give you five minutes. Maybe just the summary and conclusion will be enough? Then we could get on with figuring out how to save our necks."

"Very well, a summary. Man meets woman. Woman disappears. Man turns up dead." He stopped. I thought he was just taking a breath, but he sat back and looked at his hands.

"That's it?"

"There's more, but you are in a hurry."

"How does Blue Sparrow figure in this?"

"That's not part of the summary. For that, you have to listen to part one."

I pointed at my watch again. "You have exactly ten minutes."

My uncle gave me a tight smile. "So fleet the feet of time. Five minutes extra? The fate of empires can be sealed in five minutes. Less, sometimes." He closed his eyes as if to convince me he was going into the inner reaches of his memory. "This was a complicated case. It twisted around itself. We never solved it completely." He held up his hand before I could say anything. "Not every case has a solution. Still, essence can be instructive. This was the most instructive case I ever encountered. Young as I was, it made an impression." He opened one eye, to make sure that I was listening. Assured, he continued. "Vice Minister J one afternoon—about three o'clock, we later determined—opened his door and found on his doorstep a note attached to a severed ear."

"There was no mention of an ear in the summary."

"That's why it was a summary."

"How about a basic question?"

"If you think it can't wait until the end."

"Who was Vice Minister J?"

This appeared to make him suspicious. "Why do you need to know?"

"Apart from idle curiosity? Perspective, I suppose. At some point, it had to come up whether the man or the office was the more important in determining the significance of the ear and his connection to it, assuming it wasn't dropped on the wrong doorstep, which sometimes happens. And if the office is more important than the man, perhaps it is connected to something going back many years. For all anyone could know at the outset, it had nothing to do with the vice minister himself but rather the ministry he represented."

"A little off track, but a fair point. A good point." He sounded pleased. "You have a quick mind, even if you don't always use it."

"Again, who was Vice Minister J?"

"Railways, the vice minister of railways."

"And the ear?"

"Aha! A woman's. Delicate, shell-like. Still had attached to it an earring of some beauty. A gold filigree cage in which hung a pearl of perfect luster."

A pearl. I thought back. No, Madame Fang had definitely been intact. "Left ear or right?"

"Very good. You had to ask. It was the right. We thought that would be important, but it turned out not to be. In any case, we were sure the vice minister didn't take the time to determine that fact. He panicked and called his chief of staff for advice."

"He didn't call the Ministry of People's Security right away? A little odd, wasn't it?"

"In those days we were still the Ministry of Public Security, but never mind. You haven't asked about the note."

"I was about to. I take it there was something in the note that caused him not to want to get mixed up in the whole affair, which is why he went to his chief of staff first."

"That could be." My uncle tapped his fingers on the desk. "Yes, that's what I wondered, too."

"So, what was in the note?"

"Never found out. Damn thing disappeared. There was some suspicion that the chief of staff destroyed it, though there was no way to prove anything. It was a windy day, might have just blown away. Not having that note hurt us for a while, kept us running in circles, but in the end it wasn't fatal to our work."

What work? The case was never solved. "When did he finally call the police?"

"He didn't. As I told you, he died."

I realized instinctively that asking the next question was a bad idea, but it could not be avoided. "Died of what?"

"Ah." My uncle smiled.

4

The next afternoon we were in the library, anxiously digesting after lunch. I was waiting for Li to call with news about the woman who had followed us the previous day to the dumpling restaurant. Maybe Li had been wrong, unlikely as that seemed. It wasn't impossible that she and her friend had been out for a walk that took them on our exact route. The odds were against it, but they probably weren't at zero.

My uncle looked at the clock just as the phone rang. He mimed that if it was for him, I was to say he was out of town. As a rule, detectives make poor mimes, so I was only half sure of what the rest of the excuse was supposed to be.

"Is this Inspector O?" It was Miss Du, and she didn't sound happy.

"No, I'm afraid not. He's gone away, duck hunting."

My uncle shook his head.

"Is that how he is spending all the money I gave him? I called to find out what sort of progress he's made in finding my father."

I indicated to my uncle that he should pick up the extension and listen in, which he did as standard procedure for phone calls that came when he was "out of town."

"I use the term 'duck hunting' loosely, Miss Du. In the criminal investigation world, it means that someone is on a case and moving toward a solution. It's jargon. I hope you'll understand."

"Apparently, someone is listening to the jargon on another extension. I can tell from a little electronic gadget my father had built for me before he disappeared. It turns red when someone is on the line who shouldn't be."

Naturally, MSS didn't have any such technology. Handy equipment like this always went first to the underworld, though I was loath to put Miss Du in that category.

"The phone in the kitchen must have been knocked off the hook," I said. "Sometime maybe you'll show me your gadget."

There was a very long silence.

"Miss Du? Did you have something you wanted to tell my uncle? I can get him a message."

"Tell your uncle that if he doesn't have a preliminary report to me in a week, he can expect a visit from my solicitor. Whether that is before or after my cousin's wrecking company's bulldozers pull up to your door I cannot be sure."

"I'm quite positive you'll have a report in short order. I'll give him your message."

The moment I hung up the phone, there was a knock at the front door.

"You don't suppose that's her cousin, do you?" my uncle asked. "At least they knocked. I was worried they might break down the door with one of those big machines. You want to let them in?"

"It's not Miss Du's cousin. It must be the taxi to the airport. When are we going to have time to send her a report? Have you packed, like I told you?"

He reached down and retrieved a red suitcase, a small four-wheeler, from beneath his desk. "I have packed, against my better judgment. Where are we going, by the way? Shanghai?"

"No, I already told you." It was a little worrisome. He was starting to forget things. "We're going to Mongolia."

"Really? You did tell me, but I was sure you were kidding. Well, I'll buy more there if I need it. Can you lend me a tie and a razor in the meantime?"

"We can take turns wearing the tie. As for the razor, get your own."

"You're squeamish, like your father."

The knocking became more insistent. "You'd better answer it," my uncle said. "Taxi drivers don't like to wait."

When I opened the door, two men and a woman looked at me. One of the men was sucking the knuckles on his right hand. "Damn! What is this door made of? Concrete?"

The woman rolled her eyes. "Give him a lump of sugar, will you, or he'll complain all afternoon."

I took a liking to her instantly. "Have we met?"

The second man rumbled ominously. "This isn't a pickup bar. You and your uncle ready? We need to get to the airport or you'll miss your plane." He started to push his way in, which left me no choice but to shut the door real fast and lock it. Taxis in Yanji were going upscale, but none of them had gotten to the stage of personal valets for each passenger. I didn't know who these people were, but I was pretty sure we didn't want to get into a car with them.

My uncle emerged from the office wearing an old jacket and rolling his red suitcase. "What are we waiting for? If we're going, let's go." For a moment he contemplated the closed front door through which angry shouts were getting louder by the minute. "On second thought, let's use the side door." He started off in the other direction. "I have a feeling this driver isn't in a welcoming mood."

We went out the side entrance, which led into a narrow alley with the smell of charred piglet trotters floating from the kitchen of the house next to ours, and emerged onto the street about thirty meters from our front door. The woman I had admired turned her head at that moment and saw us. I braced, waiting for her to give the alarm, but she only nodded toward a brown car parked across the street.

"Come on, uncle," I said. "There's our ride to the airport."

5

The first person we recognized at the air terminal was Jang. He was leaning against a pillar like rich people in Shanghai do in the slick picture magazines, scanning the departure hall. It was obvious he was looking for me. I stepped into a large tour group that from their attire seemed prepared to leave on a vacation to someplace warm, maneuvered my way behind the pillar, and tapped him on the shoulder.

"Little Jang, going on a trip? I didn't realize you had accumulated enough vacation time already."

If his legs had been up to it, he would have hit his head on the ceiling as he leaped like a rat that has suddenly discovered a cobra behind him.

"Nice surprise," he said when he could talk.

"Sure. I'm full of nice surprises. Aren't you supposed to be at the duty desk? Don't tell me you've left it unmanned again. Or isn't that where you are supposed to be anymore? Could someone have changed your orders and reassigned you to airport departures? Who would have done that?"

He gulped, recovered, and gave me a nasty stare. "Why would you think that, sir?"

"Let me ask you something. In Shanghai, when your splendid chief of office is about to go on a trip, does a mere duty officer scurry out to the airport to bid him farewell? Or is it a family tradition?"

"You must be mistaken, sir."

"Careful, little Jang, don't make me do what I want to do, which is exceedingly ugly and would attract a crowd. Let's try something else."

"Such as?" He was getting back a touch of verve.

"Such as, you go back to the office and fire off an immediate cable to whoever sent you here that you didn't see me. Yes, that would work, it would prevent a lot of needless violence creeping up on us at this very minute."

Jang's mouth opened and shut wordlessly. His verve had a short half-life.

"Something the matter?" I asked. "Because if you have a problem, you should speak up. Isn't that how things work in Shanghai? Free expression by all ranks! Let me ask you a mundane question, just to clarify things. Assuming you live that long, who is going to write your fitness report?"

"You?"

"Very good. Me. And if I write you a bad report, a very bad one—you know what I mean, subtly bad, nothing blatant, but filled with slow poison and rusty nails—do you think anyone else in the whole country will be interested when you put in for transfer? A young pup such as yourself may not know it, but every bureau in the Ministry lives by personnel evaluations. Trust me, if I put my mind to it, even your relatives will blanch when that report appears under their gilded front door. Veteran bureaucrats in the Headquarters review process will seek shelter lest you file an appeal and they have to soil their hands dealing with such an enormous piece of shit, as you will by then be known throughout the system. The tiniest, poorest village in Gansu will not even consider you fit to feed chemically adulterated grain to their half-crazed chickens. Am I clear, or would you like me to go on?"

"As it happens, I didn't see you," Jang said coolly. Watching him trot away, I wasn't sure what he'd do once he got back to the office. The odds were slightly against his loyalty to whoever sent him after me outweighing his desire to get out of Yanji as soon as he could. That was the sort of bet Old Gao would never take.

"He's a mouse turd." My uncle appeared from behind the pillar. "Whom does he work for?"

"I couldn't say."

"Because you don't know. Are you sure about your number two?"

"Lieutenant Li?" I laughed. "Sometimes, uncle, you have a lurid sense of reality. No, I don't think my number two is selling me out." It was ridiculous even to contemplate. Li and I had worked together for years. "He's solid, I trust him completely. If I can't rely on Li Bo-ting, then I can't rely on anyone."

"Good point. Keep it in mind."

The loudspeaker called our plane and gate.

"Can you get through the security scan, uncle? I hope you don't have anything odd in your suitcase. Maybe you should double-check. You may have something in there, nails or something, from your last trip to Harbin."

"If that nice lady with the white gloves gives me a good pat-down, they can confiscate everything in here for all I care. You should have been around when Mei-lin was going through security. She could have been carrying an atom bomb and they wouldn't have noticed. The boys were stepping on their tongues."

"You traveled with her? Someplace nice, I hope, with white sands and warm breezes."

He smiled to the woman at the security checkpoint as he passed through the metal detector. "No, I'm not taking off my belt," he said as she patted him down. "Nor am I going to remove the stainless steel rod in my leg."

When we were finally on the plane and safely airborne, I tapped him on the shoulder. "You never told me you had a stainless steel rod in your leg."

"I don't approve of all this probing and rooting around in my luggage."

"So you don't have a steel rod in your leg."

"Why would I?"

"Do you remember what the phony cook said the other day as he left?"

"That he wanted a cup of tea?"

"No, that you were the most annoying person in the world."

PART II

Chapter One

The airport at Ulan Bator had a rough-and-ready feel that I found instantly appealing. On the taxiway in to the terminal, we passed several biplanes sitting in high grass off the tarmac. My uncle nudged me as he looked over my shoulder. "Tell me we aren't going up in one of those."

"I can't tell you that because I don't know. It looks like it could be fun."

This seemed to fill him with gloom, but as soon as we stepped into the terminal building, he brightened noticeably.

"Just like home," he said, meaning the airport in Pyongyang. "It's what an airport should be, not so busy that you can't catch up with yourself when you get there." He looked around. "I like it."

Once through the immigration check, I picked up my bag. Then we ambled past a small crowd waiting for arriving passengers and headed out the door. My uncle breathed deeply as soon as he stepped outside.

"The first breath you take in a new place is the most important."

"I didn't know you were superstitious. Anything else we should do, sacrifice a bullock or something?"

He gave me a cold smile. "It's not superstition. It's ritual. They're not the same. You have to mark things off in life. Otherwise, every place blurs with every other place. There's nothing wrong with ritual, nephew. It's what keeps us sane as a species."

At least we were off to a good start.

2

As we stood around, searching the parking lot for whoever was supposed to drive us into town, a short man popped out from behind a knot of bushes at the edge of the asphalt and headed straight toward us. He moved like a torpedo propelled by an erratic engine shifting him slightly from side to side. His shoes were mud caked, trousers filthy, beard unkempt. He wore a hat that looked like a smaller version of what everyone wore in American cowboy movies. It looked so greasy that I was sure it would catch fire if it sat too long in the sun. The man stopped a whisker or two away. My uncle took a step back; the man took a step forward.

"Buy some postcards?" A packet of cards appeared from somewhere under a leather coat that no cow would want to claim. "Cheaper than in a hotel. Where you staying? Buy several. My house burned down yesterday."

"Terrible news," my uncle said. He seemed to be warming to the man. "Show me the cards."

"We're in a hurry, uncle," I shook my head. "Sorry about your house," I said to the man. "Tough luck."

"How about a map?" One appeared from somewhere else under the jacket. "Pretty good, 1:20,000 survey map, genuinely left by a Soviet army officer. Mine fields, everything."

"How much?" I took the map and started to unfold it.

"You! Leave them alone!" Another man emerged from the terminal and hurried over. He had a testy exchange with the postcard salesman in a language I took to be Mongolian. He turned to us. "I've told him over and over not to bother arriving guests. Are you Mr. O?" He looked from me to my uncle and then back again. "I apologize for being late, but the traffic is terrible. You got your bags already? What luck, not a moment to lose. Come, I've got to get you into town. You can talk in the car."

As we rode from the airport, I was amazed to see my uncle still enjoying himself. He smiled broadly as we drove along the bumpy, narrow road, past the smooth, low hills that formed one edge of the basin where the city of Ulan Bator had grown up. He smiled at the city's skyline in the distance, nothing more than a higgledy-piggledy collection of rooftops that barely rose above the dusty earth. He smiled at the round white tents dotting the landscape. Once we entered the city, he grinned at the clotted traffic, at the girls in their miniskirts, at the broken pavement, at anything and everything we passed.

To my disappointment, the light mood disappeared like duck fat in a furnace once we secured our car and were out of the city onto the empty plain that stretched as far as the eye could see under an enormous and perfectly blue sky.

"There's something about this landscape," my uncle said ominously.

"Yes, there is," I replied.

"It sets my teeth on edge."

"Unlike you, I can't find anything wrong with it," I said, rolling down my window and letting the air rush in. "It's a good change of scenery from Yanji. Very refreshing in its own way."

"In its own way," my uncle said firmly, "it's lifeless. There are no trees. The place is barren."

"Some might call it pastoral. Look at all the grass. And the air, when was the last time you could actually use the word 'pellucid' in a sentence?"

"It's barren." He closed his eyes tightly. "What can grass do but sough in the wind? That's it! The word I wanted—sough." He said it in English again. "Why can I never come up with the word I need when I need it?" He opened his eyes and stared mournfully out the window. "Barren."

I had to admit, the Mongolian landscape, at least in this part of the country, was not particularly well treed. There were rolling hills in the distance off to the north and west. Otherwise, as I will probably mention several more times, there was an abundance of sky; sky and little else. It was the sort of scene that greatly appeals to many people. My uncle wasn't one of them.

Scenery wasn't uppermost in my mind, however. In less than an hour, it would be dusk. From then until all traces of sunlight disappeared—probably into a moonless night with my luck—I figured it would take another twenty minutes. The darkness of an unfamiliar place was bearing down on us, and I didn't know where the hell we were or where we were headed. The map I lifted from the little man at the airport was useless. If we weren't at camp drinking some form of liquor with this Ding character pretty soon, my uncle would complain ceaselessly until we were. Already he was checking his watch every few minutes.

"Sunset isn't far off," he said. "Dusk might put a little color in the picture. A normal person can have too much of this." He waved his hand across the landscape. "I already do." From the corner of my eye, I could see he had sunk into thought. After a few minutes, he broke his silence, but only to say, "No wonder."

I waited for the rest of it, but there was no more. The trip had been long, and my shoulders had a dull ache from trying to keep us on a dirt track that kept disappearing in the fading light. Lack of judgment gets the jump on me at such times. "No wonder what?" I asked.

"I was thinking aloud. My grandfather would say a place without trees is a place that can't be read. I never understood what he meant. Now I do. Who knows what this place has in mind? Too much sky. Everything is so far apart, nothing has any idea how it relates to anything else. We might as well be on one of Jupiter's moons."

"Maybe not. There's a tree right up ahead. Look! You want me to pull over and let you admire it?" We were in a vividly red four-wheel-drive vehicle, a big clumsy thing that my uncle had refused at first to enter.

"Reminds me of a tank," he had said as the man at the rental agency pointed it out. "Why don't we get a tracked vehicle with a machine gun on the back? That way we can take care of bandits and terrain at the same time. Do you have something in an olive drab camouflage? This red will stand out as a target a kilometer away."

I had pulled him aside. "The orders are for us to rent a four-wheel-drive car. It's probably a good idea in case we get stuck. There aren't any bandits in this country. It's perfectly safe. Let's not worry about the color. Red is fine. I'd be more concerned about the roads. They didn't look all that good from the air. Did you notice as we were coming in for a landing, most of them aren't paved? Save your complaints. You'll need all of them for later."

Just as I'd been warned, the rental agency man said he couldn't let us drive by ourselves outside of the city and that he'd find us a driver. I told him my uncle didn't trust anyone to drive but me, which wasn't true, but no one in Mongolia could contradict me on the point, and for once, my uncle backed me up by nodding in agreement.

The streets getting out of the city were jammed. For a place in the middle of nowhere, there were lot of people who seemed to think they were needed somewhere else.

"This is ridiculous," my uncle said, though at that point he still seemed to be enjoying the scene. "These people drive like they are in camel caravans."

I almost said, "When were you ever in a camel caravan?" Except he might have been, and that would have ignited a story I didn't want to hear.

3

The tree was about five hundred meters away. It didn't look very big, but I didn't see why that made much difference. "You want me to get closer?"

"No, leave the poor thing to its misery. If it has survived this long in solitude it doesn't want any company, certainly not this flaming red car."

"That's fine with me. We'll keep going, unless you want to stop and stretch your legs."

"What you mean is that you want to stop and look at that worthless map. Let's get to Ding's camp. All we have to do is follow this so-called road; sooner or later it leads somewhere. All roads do."

The man's never heard of a dead end, I thought to myself.

"Even a dead end leads somewhere, nephew. Just not where most people want to go."

"As long as we seem to have some time, why don't we use it to mull over our problem? How do we handle Ding?"

"It's your problem. Think about it all you want. Just watch where you're going in the meantime."

"It's our problem, not only mine, otherwise you wouldn't be here. You want to figure out what's going on, though you won't admit it. Most of all, you want to know what has happened to Madame Fang, but you're not sure if this trip will shed any light. Tell me I'm wrong, I dare you."

"Over there, way, way over there!"

I braked suddenly. "What? Where?"

"A horse and a camel. Look at them. They're in a meeting of some sort, probably a conspiracy. Look how the horse is nodding. They've agreed on something. They don't mate, do they?"

Horse and camel were some distance away, and in the rapidly retreating light, I might not have noticed them. "I don't think so. Since when did your eyes improve so much?"

"There is nothing wrong with my eyes. Keep driving, and not so fast. How much farther is it to this place?"

I looked down at the map and pretended to trace the route. "Another sixty kilometers. We'll be there soon after sunset."

"It's already sunset, which means it will be pitch dark when we get there. The question is, will there be anything to eat? Do they have noodles in this country? They don't have trees," he said glumly, "they might not have noodles."

4

A minute later the sun dropped from sight. A big sky like this apparently didn't have to fool around with dusk. The one working headlight on the car revealed nothing but more dirt track. I made sure my aching shoulders were set confidently. There was nothing to be gained by letting my uncle realize we were lost.

"You may as well slow down before we drive over a cliff. Also, we might be better off not going in circles, which is what we started doing about twenty minutes ago." He squinted at his watch and then out the window. "Now that it's clear we're not arriving on time, maybe your friends will send out a search party. They know this country better than do you. The average goat knows this country better than you do. Pull over." He looked out the window. "What am I saying? There's no lane, no road. We're in the middle of nowhere. I don't think even the stars bother with this place. The moon obviously doesn't."

I stopped the car and turned off the ignition. "If there isn't anything to complain about, you invent something. Don't worry, there are plenty of stars around here. They'll be out in force soon. We can't be far from the camp," I said. "They're expecting us. By now, Ding must wonder where we are."

"We have no idea if Ding can even tell time!" He waved his watch arm in front of me. "We have to hope someone can and is wondering if we've been waylaid by bandits. Maybe they got drunk waiting for us. Maybe they've all gone to sleep already. Honk the horn."

"What?"

"I said, honk the horn. Out here the sound will carry forever. They'll hear it halfway to China. If they hear it in Gao's place, they'll put down bets on how long it is before we starve to death. Go ahead, honk the horn."

It didn't seem like such a bad idea. I honked the horn twice, two short bleats that the empty night swallowed whole. My uncle leaned over to the steering wheel.

"A pattern," he said. "Give it a pattern."

"A pattern?"

He leaned on the horn, three long blasts. "Like that."

Twenty minutes later, two men on small horses rode out of the darkness. I rolled down the window. "Looking for someone?"

"The camp is a half hour away. Follow us."

We set off at about five kilometers an hour. My uncle was silent the whole time. Thirty minutes later, we came to a gate across the road, which at this point wasn't even a dirt track. One of the horsemen dismounted, opened the gate, and motioned I should drive ahead.

"How did you know it was us?" I asked as we pulled abreast of him.

"The horn. First it was confusing, two bleats, like someone trying to clear the road of sheep. Then we heard the three long blasts— figured it was Morse for the letter *O*."

My uncle didn't bother to smile.

5

"I'm staying here." From the passenger's seat, my uncle surveyed the camp, or what was visible of it. What was visible wasn't much. A few traditional Mongolian gers on a hillside. Off to the right was a more substantial wood frame building of some sort; with no moon, it was too dark to be sure what it might be. Our guides' horses stood quietly. On the wind blowing from our backs was the smell of open country at night. No asphalt or tires, no garbage, no gasoline. Just a fragrance of vast silence, the grass, and maybe a camel or two.

"Come out of the car," I said to my uncle. "It's refreshing in the night air. You ought to stretch your legs."

"It's refreshing in here. Probably safer, too. My legs aren't complaining, and neither am I. Where is Ding?"

"I thought you liked it outdoors. Didn't you live on a mountaintop for several years?"

"The outdoors is fine. This place is beyond outdoors. You go do what you have to do."

"There aren't any wolves, if that's what you're afraid of."

"Wolves don't scare me, the only thing that does—"

A man emerged from the middle hut and shouted in a Beijing accent, "There's a storm coming. Better not stand around and yap." As soon as he ducked back in the hut, the wind picked up. A huge bank of clouds, glowing from within as if it carried its own light to see the way, swallowed the hills in front of us. It spilled down the slope, devoured the huts, and then the cloud light clicked off, turning the night black with rain.

"*Shut the windows,*" I yelled at my uncle and made a dash in the direction of the hut where the man had appeared. The rain was deafening; it sounded like it would beat the car roof into scrap. I started to turn back to see if my uncle was all right, but a hand grabbed my arm and pulled me into a large circular room with several iron-stead beds and brightly painted chests neatly arranged around the edge. One of the chests had a shrine with candles on it. The center of the room was occupied by a small iron stove, and beside it on a low red stool was a man with a face as round as a full moon. Unlike the moon, he also had hooded, dark eyes and a cruel mouth, as if he ate orphans. He stood up and stared at me.

"Actually," he said, "there are wolves."

"What?"

"You told your uncle that there are no wolves, but there are, plenty of them. They aren't quite as savage as Russian wolves, but you wouldn't want to run across a particularly hungry Mongolian wolf late at night. Nor a pack of them at any time of day, for that matter."

"You mind if I go and get my uncle out of the car?"

"Wait until the storm blows over. He'll be fine where he is. Wolves don't know how to open car doors. You're Major Bing, I take it."

"Let me guess, you are Mr. Ding."

The man's mouth did something that I took to be a smile. "Amusing, yes? That our names rhyme?" He indicated I should take the chair beside him near the stove. "We have business. Better to do it right now."

I waited until he sat, then did the same. "You have credentials of some sort? A secret handshake maybe? The chances of my running into the wrong contact out here is slim, but I don't want to chance it. Slim odds are not no odds."

"I have a tie with rutting deer on it, but it's in my suitcase. Would you like me to get it?"

"No, that's good enough for me. And your friend here?" I indicated the man who had grabbed my arm and pulled me inside. "He has a tie, too?"

"He wouldn't know how to use one. Not around his own neck, anyway."

The storm had nearly passed, and there was little sound except for a few late raindrops and the fire crackling in the stove. I decided it was time to take in my surroundings more closely. I would have liked a better view of the door, but my line of sight was blocked by a short, muscular man. He didn't appear to have a neck, nor any thought of moving aside. The room was even bigger than it had seemed on first impression, but with two of them and only one of me, I didn't think I could race around the center pole too many times before one of them nailed me. There were no windows to speak of, so jumping through one was not an option. The only thing left was sitting tight. Apart from my uncle's foreboding remarks—and he made those all the time—I didn't really have much reason to assume Ding would be a problem. I might have convinced myself completely if he hadn't had teeth like a piranha.

"You had trouble finding us?" Ding poked at the fire with a stick. "These maps aren't worth a damn. I think they're meant to confuse outsiders. Well, you made it, that's the main thing."

The rain seemed to have stopped, and I couldn't hear any more wind. "OK by you if I get my uncle now? He's looking forward to meeting you."

"Not quite yet." Ding looked at the muscular doorman and nodded slightly. "But my colleague can go out and keep the old man occupied until we're ready for him to join us."

"I'm not sure that's a good idea. My uncle doesn't do well with strangers."

Ding's mouth approximated the sound of a laugh. "They'll get on with no trouble, you don't need to worry."

When we were alone, Ding reached into his pocket and pulled out a brown envelope, no tape. "These are your orders. If you want to go over them here, that's fine with me. Or if you want to wait until later, that's fine, too. There are some time constraints, however. This job has to be done, completely finished, in two days."

"Then what happens?"

"Then we'll see."

Since I didn't know what had to be done in forty-eight hours, it didn't strike me as an insurmountable problem. Sometimes, jobs with short fuses turned out easier to handle. Lots of pressure to move, but little time to think and less time for long lines of authority to get wrapped around the ankles. At least it meant my uncle was wrong. Ding wasn't going to bury us right away.

From outside I heard the car door slam. A moment later, my

uncle stepped into the ger. He was laughing. "Off to a good start, eh, nephew?"

Ding stood up carefully. "Where is my colleague?" He reached under his jacket and came out with a pistol. For some reason I was relieved to see it was a Chinese model. I was even more relieved when Ding didn't point it at me.

"He's probably fixing his digestion around the corner," my uncle said, ignoring the weapon in Ding's hand. "He said something about mutton."

Ding reholstered the pistol and sat down. "Pull up a stool, Inspector."

My uncle sat.

"You don't remember me?" Ding put the stick in the fire again and stirred the embers. "It wasn't that long ago. Let me think." His brows went into thinking mode. "All right, a few years. Ten? Let's say ten."

My uncle looked carefully at the other man's face. He took in the jaw without obvious concern. "Never saw you before in my life."

"Ah, you see? That's because I don't think we ever actually met. It was more like a long distance affair."

My uncle closed his eyes. "If you say so."

"Ding, I think we're tired. And we could use some food."

My uncle mouthed the word, "Noodles."

"I have what I need for the job. How about you show us where we'll be staying. If I have any questions, we can talk in the morning." I heard a note of irritation creep into my voice.

Ding looked over at me as if he no longer knew who I was. "Staying? Here?" He looked at his watch. "That's not what . . . well, you were late arriving, and the storm has probably made these damn ruts they call roads too muddy. You'll get lost for sure trying to find the main highway back to the city. Give me a minute, I'll have to go outside to make a phone call. Make yourselves comfortable. I'll send the little bear"—he stopped himself—"my colleague in to keep you company."

"Be careful," my uncle said as Ding opened the door.

Ding turned. "What?"

"Wolves," my uncle said. "Mongolian wolves."

6

"You know him? If you knew Ding, why didn't you tell me?"

"One, what difference would it have made, and two, he says he knows me, that doesn't mean I know him. He's playing some sort of game. Let him."

"What did you do to the little bear?"

"Me? Nothing. He said he felt a little queasy from dinner. We exchanged a few words, then he started turning green and disappeared around the corner."

"Well, be careful what you eat at breakfast. We can't be stopping every few miles. And no, I don't know if they'll have noodles."

"Surely they have noodles. Once upon a time they looted any city they could find for two thousand kilometers in every direction. They must have brought back the local fare. How much mutton can one person eat?"

"I'm going out to get our suitcases. Do something with this stove or the fire will go out and we'll be cold tonight. Which bed do you want?"

"Does it make a difference?" He tested one, then walked the long way around the tent to test the others. "No difference. None of them will do my back any good. I'll take the one on the right. That way, when I lie on my right side, I'll be facing the stove."

There wasn't any sense asking how that mattered. I retrieved the suitcases and had just locked the car when Ding materialized out of the dark.

"It wasn't easy getting permission for you and your uncle to stay here tonight. Beijing wants the plan under way by tomorrow morning at the latest, and for that to happen you've got to be in Ulan Bator, not out here with the sheep. That means you'll have to leave before dawn."

"What about the quarry?"

"He's here. We know he's here."

"And the seal?"

Ding paused. "It's here."

"You just don't know where."

Ding snarled. "We know where, we know who, and we know how."

"You forgot the why. Why do you need me?"

"I don't. Believe me, I don't need you for anything, but someone back home thinks you have the magic touch. You have a golden résumé in Beijing, it seems. Too bad we're not in Beijing."

"Yeah, too bad." I looked around. "So why did we have to meet all the way out here a hundred kilometers from electricity and running water? There isn't any place in Ulan Bator, a nice restaurant maybe, where you could have handed me the envelope?"

"Making sure, that's all. No eyes or ears that we don't know about out here. By the way, getting lost like that wasn't smart. Don't do it again. People might not understand."

"Next time, be somewhere easier to find."

"Next time? I don't think so."

He stuck close beside me as I walked back to the ger. As I opened the door, he poked his head in and looked at my uncle. "Pleasant dreams, Inspector."

My uncle didn't say anything, but after I came in and shut the door, he got up and stood closer to the stove. "I was right. That man is a menace."

"We'll be done with him in a few hours. We leave tomorrow early. Get some sleep."

"After breakfast?"

"Before."

"Again we have to drive in the dark over the trackless wilderness? What makes you think you can find the highway?"

"Stop worrying. I have a map, don't I?"

My uncle laughed with the gusto of a condemned man, went back to the bed, and pulled the covers over his head.

Chapter Two

The return to Ulan Bator was less difficult than I'd feared. My uncle dozed in the backseat most of the way. Occasionally he sat up and looked out the window.

"Are we there yet?"

"We are. In fact, we passed it an hour ago. I'm hoping to get to the Gobi Desert before lunch. The intense heat and lack of moisture will do you good."

"Yes, well, wake me when we arrive. Better yet, push me out the door and let the wolves finish the job."

"We'll be in the city in about half an hour, assuming we don't run into a sheep."

"How do you know?"

"Because we just passed an enormous statue of Chinggis Khan on horseback."

"Really, why didn't you wake me?" He looked out the back window. "I would have liked to see it."

"Some other time. Ding said Beijing wants us in position by ten at the latest. Everything needs to be done in forty-eight hours."

"What's the crashing hurry?"

"He didn't say. Anyway, it will leave us plenty of time for sightseeing later. Better this way than something that has to be dragged out."

"I don't think I trust Ding."

"There I'll agree with you."

Once in the city, we crawled in traffic for half an hour until we got to the tallest building we could find, not difficult because it was taller by far than anything else for two hundred kilometers in every direction. Next to the building was an open square that fronted an elaborately decorated structure.

"The map says this is the Parliament Building. We can hope it has at least that right." With the crush of morning traffic, there was no way to move into the next lane. We sat going nowhere, staring at the building, for several minutes.

"You're going to have to park this thing," my uncle said finally, "and I don't know how. Maybe we should abandon it right where we are. Traffic isn't moving anyway. It's not as if anyone would notice for a while." He watched two men trot by briskly on small horses. "Proud fellows," he said.

2

In Parliament Square, we stood doing nothing but looking around for a few minutes.

"I've been thinking," I said, letting my eyes roam over the scene in case Beijing was working someone into position on the edge of the square to signal us the next move. Ding hadn't been expansive on this point. All he'd told me was that everything was under control and in place. As far as I could tell, there were only locals strolling around. "You need to send something to Miss Du. Nothing elaborate, just enough to keep her from calling her cousin with the bulldozer."

"Torpedo off the port bow," my uncle said.

From the far edge of the square, the funny little man with a three-day growth of beard and battered shoes appeared, seemingly out of thin air. Again his erratic motor pushed him from side to side but aimed well enough so that in thirty seconds he arrived in front of us. Again he presented postcards for sale. I was in no mood to haggle. I told him to go away. He grinned wildly and reminded us that his house had burned down. He needed money, he said, or his children would starve.

"We all have a sad story sooner or later, friend. Maybe tomorrow." I have a soft spot for starving children, but this was not the time or place to talk about it. All that mattered to me was that he was blocking my line of sight.

"You still owe me for the map," the little man said, "but never mind. Buy these. How about not tomorrow? How about right now?" He pushed a card at me. "Look, here's something nice. See? Horses crossing a river under the open sky. Brings tears to your eyes, am I right? You can have it for next to nothing. Even for nothing. A loan. If you don't write home with it by tomorrow, you can trade it in for something different."

"Not interested in sky," my uncle said. "You have anything else?"

The man quivered with pleasure. "Sure, plenty more." He produced a new card. "The best you'll find. Very rare."

My uncle stared at it. "This doesn't look like anything around here. Much too much green. Where do you hide all those trees?"

"You kidding? We have plenty of trees. Tons of them, birch trees out the arse if you know where to look." He gave my uncle a lopsided grin.

I snatched the postcard from his hand. "We're busy right now, do you mind?" I turned the card over. Written on the back was a small number 5. Hard to believe that we were hiring people with such crummy shoes, but you never really knew what Headquarters was thinking these days. "We'll keep this one. Good luck with your house," I said, "but we don't need any more of these. Not enough stamps." I pocketed the card.

"It's my birthday today." The man suddenly didn't look so down at the heels. "You can give me a present. Cash is always nice."

My uncle dug into his pocket. "What's this worth?" He held up some local currency that had the number 1,000 on it. "Here, go get yourself a bath. Buy some ice cream for the kids."

The man scuttled away across the square and disappeared so quickly it was as if he had never existed. I looked around. Across the street I spotted a bar under an English-language sign that read IRELAND'S FIFTH. It didn't seem likely to me that it would be open at this hour, but as we approached, I made out a hand-lettered sign hanging on the door that promised BREAKFAST ALL THE DAMNED DAY.

My uncle chuckled to himself as we went up the steps to the entrance.

"Let's go in," I said. "Something funny?"

"No, just the Irish."

The front door was unlocked, but our way inside was blocked by a middle-aged man, a European with thinning red hair and big hands. He looked somberly at both of us until I flashed the postcard. Without a word he stood aside and motioned for us to come in. There were no lights inside the bar, and barely enough daylight from three windows along the back wall to attempt walking without banging into something. I could make out a solitary figure at the bar, but I couldn't distinguish any features through the gloom. One of the tables was occupied.

"Who are those people over there?" I didn't know what the plan was, or even if there was a plan. All I could figure was that we were supposed to meet someone here. It might be I was wrong and this was the wrong place. I was just moving on instinct, that and a postcard with the number 5 on it. It couldn't be coincidence that the greasy little man had showed up for a second time out of nowhere.

"They're Kazakhs." The somber European who had met us at the door had disappeared into the darkness, his place taken by a very tall youth wearing a long white apron that brushed the top of his shoes. He handed me a menu. "They're not very bright on the whole, or so I'm warned."

"Is that a fact?" My uncle edged forward. "Would that be your opinion, as well?"

"If you know a smart Kazakh, I'd like his business card."

"It was a woman, a bank manager as a matter of fact, and I don't think she'd give you the time of day. Do you mind if I go over and say hello?"

"Doesn't bother me what you do. They've been waiting for someone, though they won't say who."

My uncle turned to me. "Come along if you want, but don't say anything until I give you a sign. Try to commit the conversation to memory, and be ready to write it down as soon you can find a piece of paper in this cave. Maybe there's something you can use at the bar, a napkin or a paper towel."

"Commit what to memory? What makes you think they know anything we want?"

"What makes you think they don't?" Before I could reply, he walked over to the table and spoke briefly to a man whose eyes shone through the darkness like those of an angry eagle. The man stood to shake hands and motioned to the others to make room for my uncle. It seemed awkward to go over at this point, so I stayed where I was and watched from across the gloom. At first, there wasn't much that you would have called communication going on. The five of them—two men and three women—sat very still. It turned out both of the men had fierce eyes, intense and unblinking. They listened to my uncle, barely nodded when he paused for a response on their part, and spoke no more than a couple of words each when he tapped his finger a few times on the table to indicate that it was their turn. After the second man had squeezed out his few words, he stared at my uncle, as if taking his measure, then stood and walked out of the place. The remaining four stayed quiet, almost motionless, until one of the women leaned across the table and began speaking rapidly in a low voice to my uncle. When she finished, she shook her head sadly. After a moment, the two other women took the last man by the arm and, with one of them walking on either side, led him away. When they had gone, my uncle started to get up as well, but something seemed to occur to him and he sat down again. At that point, he motioned for me to join him.

"This is my nephew," he said to the woman who had stayed behind. "He is a specialist in finding missing people, aren't you, nephew?"

The woman gazed at me. My uncle looked at the ceiling and smiled. "He is quite familiar with the events surrounding the disappearance of your mother. Whether he will be able to help, we'll have to see. First, he'll need to know something of what you saw the other day."

"Uncle, can I have a word with you?" I am a big fan of teamwork, as long as both parties know what they are doing. Back at the Ministry, teamwork was encouraged as the magical key to success; the praises of teamwork were sung endlessly at meetings; we were constantly reminded by brightly colored posters sent to each bureau monthly not to forget teamwork in everything we did. Teamwork takes communication, however. In this case, I had no clue what my uncle was up to.

"A word, of course, nephew. First let me introduce you to Kim Joo-si." He turned to the woman and said in Korean, "I leave it to you, Miss Kim, to explain things as you wish to my nephew. I have a phone call to make but will return as soon as I can."

Apparently, my team was signaling that I was to sit and listen to this woman. Apparently, she was looking for her mother, whether actually or metaphorically I couldn't yet tell. In any case, I wasn't interested in becoming a traveling missing persons bureau. I didn't know her; I didn't know her mother. Besides, if she was Kazakh, what was she doing with a Korean name? Was she the reason we had been directed to this place, or were we about to fall into a big hole of misdirection? Ding hadn't said anything about looking for someone's mother, or mentioned a code with the word "mother" in it. I looked at the woman more closely. There was nothing but an achingly sad expression, two melancholy eyes set in an oblong face that seemed etched into permanent despair. What she knew or didn't know, how she fit or didn't fit with what we were supposed to be doing in Ulan Bator, I couldn't glean. For some reason my uncle didn't want to take part in discovering her exact utility to us, or maybe he wanted me tied down while he went off to do something else. In any case, it wasn't good use of my time given that I had less than forty-eight hours to go. Equally relevant, just looking at her was about to get depressing. I did the only thing I could think of; I stood up to leave.

"Sit down."

Her lips might be sorrowfully composed, but that didn't stop them from speaking with considerable authority. I sat.

"You are interested in a certain seal and a certain man?" The woman had no hesitation about getting right to the point.

"Go on," I said.

"I know where you can find both." She was using Korean now, speaking in a loud voice, a little too loud considering I was right across the table.

"Lots of people seem to know what I need, yet I am left in the dark," I said quietly. "Excuse me for asking, but why should I believe you and not someone else?"

"You believe whatever you like. Most people do. I'm telling you as payment for your help in finding my mother. I have no money, otherwise."

I almost laughed out loud. Well, money or no, she had my attention. She'd given me a choice. I could take the bait about my predecessor, or I could follow up about the seal. I cared mostly about the former, but there was no sense letting her know that, so I focused on the latter. "What do you know about the seal?"

"It's worth a lot."

"A lot can mean anything, depending on who is doing the buying and who is doing the selling."

"You think I'm trying to sell it? Then you're a fool, a bigger one than I thought."

"I barely sit down and you already think I'm a fool? Not very nice. Or perhaps we've met?"

"Never. I dreamed of you last night, and in my dream you were a fool, but only a small one."

"You dream often of men you've never met?"

"Not often. Only when something is about to happen, something bad."

Automatically, I turned and swept the restaurant with my eyes. If something bad was about to happen, I preferred to see it coming. Now that I was more accustomed to the low light, I noticed a couple sitting at a table against the side wall. I could also get a better fix on the figure at the bar, a lanky man with a face like old leather. The tall waiter with the long white apron was nowhere to be seen.

"Nothing here to worry about," I said. "It looks quiet enough. Irish bars don't get rowdy until evening, right?"

The woman put one hand to her lips, whether contemplating my observation or hiding a smile I wasn't sure. "This one gets rowdy if more than two people are drinking," she said. "Don't worry, whatever it is I was warned about in the dream might not happen right this moment. But it will happen, it always does."

You should know, sister, I thought to myself, it was your dream. I tried to steer us back on track. "Maybe you can tell me more about the seal in the meantime." I quickly weighed my options. I could sit here sparring with her all day long, trying to figure out who she was. Or I could step on the gas. If she could go right to the point, so could I. "Can you get it for me?" I leaned forward a little to watch her reaction. Out of the corner of my eye, I saw the man at the bar move slightly. From then on, it seemed to me imperative to keep track of him.

"How come you don't ask about your friend?" In a flash, the woman's eyes became those of an eagle. If her fingers had been replaced by talons at that moment, I wouldn't have been surprised.

"Maybe I don't have any friends," I offered.

"That's not wise," she said. "Everyone should have friends. Of course, it's up to you. What about my mother?" The woman reached into her blouse and fished out a small sliver locket, which, when she opened it, revealed an old, slightly grainy black-and-white picture of a girl in traditional dress standing out on the empty grassland and holding a lamb. The picture had at one time been folded in fourths, and the upper right quadrant was missing.

"Very beautiful. Your mother when she was young? Here in Mongolia?"

"I thought you were supposed to know everything. That's what the old man said. No, this was taken back home, in the difficult times."

The man at the bar reached for his ear but missed. It was early, but he was already drunk. If he fell off the stool, he might knock himself out. That wouldn't be a loss as far as I was concerned.

"Sure," I said, "the picture was taken back home. Don't worry, I know plenty."

"Do you see the man at the bar?"

"The drunk? He seems unusually interested in us. A friend of yours?"

"No, not a friend. We work together sometimes. He has few talents, but he follows orders." She lowered her voice. "He's not watching me. He's watching that couple. They're South Koreans. They've been tailing me for days. By now, they're getting bored and stupid. As for the man at the bar, he's not as drunk as he looks."

A waitress came out of a back room and marched up to the table. She skipped the pleasantries. "You're going to have to order," she said. "If all you want to do is talk, there's a nice bench outside. This isn't a bus station, it's a restaurant."

I wasn't about to be chased away by a waitress, especially in front of the Kazakh lady. "That couple over there doesn't seem to be ordering anything. They're just sitting and pretending to be infatuated with each other."

"Tell me about it." She crossed her arms. "You want coffee?"

"No, I don't want coffee. What about juice? You have any in this place?"

"Juice? Orange, tomato, and apple."

"How about orange? Is it fresh?"

"Honey," she said, "it's fresh. I squeeze it all night long." She gave me a bland look. The man at the bar wheezed a laugh.

"I'll have the apple juice." I nodded at the woman across from me. "You want something?" I asked.

"Vodka." She ignored me and spoke to the waitress. "Polish. None of your Mongolian rot. Bring the bottle. Maybe two glasses. Mr. Apple will have some, too, won't you?"

When the waitress walked away, I grabbed several paper napkins off the next table. They were tiny, but I can write small. "All right with you if I take a few notes?"

She shrugged. "It would be better with a minitape-recorder. You ought to have one. It's more professional."

"Sure, I ought to be driving a shiny car and have shoes with new heels, but I don't, so do you mind?"

At that point, who should appear but my uncle? He was carrying a tray with a bottle of vodka and three tall water glasses. "The waitress asked me to bring these over. She's on a break, she said. If you ask me, she was in a hurry to leave. A little early for drinks, isn't it?"

"Not where I come from." The woman took the bottle, twisted the cap, and half filled each of our glasses. As she did, she sang in perfect English:

> *"It made him very sad to think*
> *That some, at junket or at jink,*
> *Must be content with toddy."*

I started to ask what the hell she meant by that, but my uncle quickly broke in.

"Cheers," he said.

"Cheers." She lifted her glass in a toast, drained it in one go, and poured herself another. She nodded at our glasses, untouched. "It's rude if you don't drink. In the rural villages, it's even an insult. That's how blood feuds start in my country."

My uncle rose to the occasion. "Never be rude in a strange land," he said to me. He turned to the woman and bowed slightly. "Here's to finding your mother."

"To your seal," she said and downed her drink. She looked hard at my glass. "Mr. Apple, I can't talk until you drink."

"Go ahead, nephew, don't disappoint Miss Kim." My uncle held out his glass to the woman. "Another? I have heard many times that Kazakh women are beautiful," he said.

"You've been with one?" She poured. "I thought your people were partial to Hoeryong girls. Very delicate, they say."

"Yes, quite delicate, though for some reason it's easier to get white apricots in season."

"Am I missing something?" I hadn't even smelled the vodka and the conversation was drifting away. We got reports from sources in Hoeryong all the time, but none ever mentioned apricots.

"It's a saying," my uncle explained, before downing his vodka in two swallows. He took a breath and seemed intent on clearing his vision for a moment. Then he continued. "The northern part of my country, especially the area around the city of Hoeryong, is noted for its beautiful girls and white apricots. The girls are all right, but at my age, I begin to prefer apricots."

I nearly spilled my drink.

3

From the window of our hotel room I spotted a statue of Lenin. His back was to me, and as far as I could tell, he was hailing a taxi. I decided to make a mental list of what we'd learned and hadn't learned up to now about what we were supposed to get accomplished in Mongolia. The list was lopsided. The list of things we hadn't learned was much longer. Meanwhile, the forty-eight-hour deadline was shrinking fast.

Staring at Lenin's backside gave me an idea. "That seal we're after is being used to stamp phony decrees." It wasn't meant as a conclusion based on any evidence, but with only forty hours left, we needed something to shoot at, even a wobbly hypothesis. I turned around to watch my uncle's reaction. "There are two possibilities as I see it—a counterfeit seal can be used to stamp real decrees, or it can stamp phony decrees. Either way, the result isn't legal. If we can figure out how it's going to be used, we might have a compass heading pointing us toward who has it."

"A shot in the dark, hardly worth the effort." My uncle wasn't looking at me. He was sitting in the only chair in the room, flipping through a booklet on shopping and nightlife in Ulan Bator.

Coming from him, that response was positively encouraging, so I ventured on. "Might be underworld, might be designed to undermine a government, might be—"

"Where did we leave off on the Blue Sparrow?"

"A severed right ear. It was an unsolvable case, you said. It also has nothing to do with our present problem, and I still don't know why you brought it up to begin with." I gave this some thought. Something clicked, which is what things do sometimes. No reason, they just click. "Wait a minute. Until the other day, I never had a single case that involved body parts, not human body parts, anyway. Some of them concerned bear gall bladders, but that's routine. Suddenly, you come at me with a story about a lonely ear, and then Miss Du shows up with a bag full of her dad."

"I never said Blue Sparrow was unsolvable. I said we didn't solve it, and we don't know if it's Miss Du's father yet."

"Can I remind you that we have to send her some sort of a report in the next few days or my house may be gone when we get back."

"No, she won't do that. She likes you."

"What are you talking about? She threatened to neuter me if I touched her."

"Pah. I think you are just skittish after your last"—he paused delicately—"experience. No need for that. Dust yourself off and get into the game again."

"The game, as you put it, can wait. I'm talking reality, cold cash. We haven't made any progress on Miss Du's case, and she gave us a lot of money, remember?"

"You're always complaining about money. Would you feel better if I gave it back to her?"

"My conscience doesn't need that much soothing. Let's just write down a few lines about what we've discovered and get them to her."

"We haven't discovered anything. Personally, I find it hard to believe that old Du would be rash enough to get himself dismembered."

"He's a forger."

"The best, and in my experience, forgers are not rash. They are meticulous to a fault. They can worry the hell out of the tail on a numeral. Every little thing is a problem a continent wide to them. It's annoying if you don't share their passion." He turned back the top of a page on bars and put the booklet on the low table that occupied whatever space in the small room the two beds and single chair didn't. "I suppose you can be dismembered for being annoying same as you can for being rash."

"Yes," I said, "it's better not to be annoying." I would have liked to look him in the eye to drill that point home, but his eyes had closed. "Uncle!"

His eyes remained as they were. "I'm thinking."

"Think about this. The seal, I'm telling you, is phony. I've got this feeling."

"So you say, and now you've said it twice. Repetition is not an antidote to uncertainty. You might as well get that through your head. As it happens, you could be right, but I have no way of knowing one way or the other. I take it neither do you."

"I know a good coincidence when I see one. A *phony* seal . . . and a forger? What if there's a link? What if Du is connected to this seal? What if he was hired to produce the counterfeit? It's a start."

"You mean, what if he faked his own death and then counterfeited his own fingers. The 'what if' approach to problem solving, is that where you're going with this? Yes, well, what if camels sprout wings? What if?" At this point his eyes opened and regarded me uncomfortably. "Phew, what a thought."

"All right, if you think I'm chasing my tail, come up with something better."

"You of all people don't need a tail. It would only make you easier to read than you already are, like a puppy that has chewed on the furniture. Don't flinch, that's not meant as criticism. I tell you such things for your own good."

"Maybe my own good is my business, uncle."

"Then have it your way. Your business is your business. Be my guest if you want to grow a tail. I'd simply suggest that we need an alternate hypothesis to the one you just floated. Keep yours if you want, but let's find another. With two you don't end up stuffing all the evidence into one bag, whether or not it fits. It's much too easy to fall into that trap. Bad investigations do that all the time. In the Blue Sparrow case—"

"Find me another bag. Let's forget the damned birds!"

My uncle rolled on effortlessly. "In the Blue Sparrow case we tried and tried to come up with another hypothesis bag. We knew we had to. Everything fit together in the investigation too neatly almost from the beginning. As you'll recall, it was a woman's ear that the vice minister of railways had found on his doorstep."

"Don't worry, I recall."

"The vice minister was a foul-talking man, a one-star general who thought the best way to get people to follow orders was to insult them in the loudest possible voice."

I sat down on my bed. "Will this take long?"

"It was a little like doing a jigsaw puzzle of a picture of yourself looking in a mirror. Obviously, we said to ourselves, this is a grudge crime. Someone took badly to being yelled at all the time."

"Sure, they cut off their own ear and put it on his doorstep. Very symbolic. Shouldn't have been difficult to find a woman with only one ear."

"That's exactly what we thought, until a week later. We made a list of everyone who might have a beef with the vice minister. The man had a career going back forty years. It was quite a list. I pointed out that most of the names were of men, most of whom didn't have shell ears or wear earrings. In fact, a good number of them were already dead of other causes. No matter, we had to check them all out. The byword of the Ministry in those days was 'thorough.'"

"Do you have another bag for us, or don't you?"

My uncle put his hands behind his head and leaned back. "Another bag? Consider this possibility—the seal isn't Chinese."

"I'm listening."

"It's Korean. Probably South Korean."

"No, that's crazy. It doesn't go anywhere. Why would Beijing worry about a phony Korean seal? The two of them, Seoul and Pyongyang, bark at each other all the time. Our standing orders from Headquarters are not to get between them on anything."

"We're creating hypotheses, not spinning answers. I'm not saying I'm sure. I'm saying it's possible."

"In that case, why not spin this—your people in Pyongyang forged it to use against the South."

"At least you're thinking. That could be right, it could be wrong, but it's a thought."

"Much as it pains me, I'll give you this, uncle, you know plenty, but you don't know Chinese like I do. I can't see any way Beijing would break a sweat if this is about South Korea."

"Pah! What you really mean is that you don't see why you were hustled off to this place. Maybe your presence is beside the point. Maybe it doesn't actually concern you."

That opened up a hell of a big bag all of a sudden, so big I walked into it without having to duck my head. "Meaning, perhaps, it concerns you?"

"Two thoughts in a row, very good. Leave that aside for now. Let's open a third bag and call it 'loose threads.' You are partial to threads, as I remember. What do you suppose all that talk you heard about corruption across the border actually meant? Do you imagine your headquarters really cares about corruption? Since when do Chinese care about corruption?"

He had something there. "I'd say they care about corruption when they're ordered to worry about it, or when they realize their last payoff had a long string attached."

"Let's pull on that. How worried were they when they gave you that order? To put it another way, what do you suppose worried the people who ordered you to worry about it? Let's add one final point to consider—we can be sure that whoever is behind the phony seal isn't after a big splash. No, this is not supposed to be high profile. More likely, it's supposed to be just enough to discredit whoever uses the stamp, which in this hypothesis would be the South Korean government." He picked up "What to Do in Ulan Bator."

"Why would someone want to discredit the South Koreans?"

"They're annoying?"

"For the moment, let's assume you're right. They certainly are all over this town, but we are still left with the central question: Who has the seal?"

"I don't know and you don't know, but it looks to me like someone certainly has a hunch, and they're playing it for all it's worth. Let's back up. If Beijing put this all in motion to get you here, who do *you* think they think has the seal?"

"People they consider my old friends, that's who."

"Again, that border! You're telling me Beijing thinks this is a North Korean operation? I thought you said it was South Korean."

"No, I said it was a South Korean seal. Whose operation it is remains to be seen."

Maybe all of this was pure speculation, but it didn't ring that way. This involved at least three capitals, maybe more. If this was such an important case, why hadn't they put a special team on it? I knew the answer before I even asked myself the question. They needed someone small, too small to attract attention. They also needed someone who thought like a North Korean, not just someone with a little Korean blood in his veins. They needed my uncle, and they couldn't get him here without me. My résumé, golden or otherwise, had nothing to do with it.

"This stinks," I said. "If I can book us a flight, we're going home tomorrow. Beijing can send someone else to handle things. If it were on the border in my jurisdiction, that would be a different story. This isn't my neighborhood. Not even close. Wrong latitude, wrong longitude."

"Not even if Madame Fang is part of it?"

"Be serious. She's too old for me. Besides, you said it yourself, she'd eat me alive."

My uncle had a gleam in his eye I didn't like.

"Don't tell me you think she's involved."

From behind me, I heard, "Do you want to close the door, or shall we let all the flies come in?"

Chapter Three

"Mei-lin, this is unexpected." My uncle walked over and took her hand. "Been in town long? Fascinating country, rather flat in parts. No doubt you're here for the wrestling matches— glistening, sweaty young bodies, muscles rippling, that sort of thing. Or maybe you've taken up throat singing. You were always good at playing two parts at once."

Madame Fang rewarded him with a disdainful smile. "Inspector, if I'd known you and your handsome nephew were here, surely I'd have come sooner. I've been here a week or so staying all alone in a lovely ger hotel at the edge of town. You should move your things and room with me." Madame Fang gave my uncle a look that would have sunk a thousand ships. She was dangerously annoyed and made no pretense of it. It didn't seem to throw my uncle off stride.

"No, we're comfortable here, aren't we, nephew?"

I nodded. "Perfectly comfortable."

"In that case," Madame Fang said, shifting moods abruptly, "why don't we all go out to dinner? There's an Italian restaurant downtown not far from here that's very good. It's Italian in its own way, of course, but the ambience is tremendous. They play music from the 1930s. It reminds me of restaurants in Shanghai when I was younger." She was suddenly sunny, cheery to a fault.

I like it when emotions arrive with plenty of warning. Madame

Fang preferred the neck-snapping variety. It didn't seem to faze my uncle, but it was getting to be too much for me. "Why don't you two go for dinner?" I suggested. "I have a few things to nail down. I'll probably be late; stay out as long as you want."

"It will be like old times, Inspector." Madame Fang laughed.

She was well over her annoyance and as dazzling as the Hope Diamond. I could see from his expression that my uncle would have meowed like a kitten for her if she'd suggested it.

"Do you still drink?" She patted my uncle's hand. "Or have you given that up, too?"

2

I headed for the square in front of the Parliament Building, not far from our hotel. At this time of the evening, the place was bustling, and the sidewalks all around were full of people. That was good. I moved into the flow of the crowd, blending in every way I could. I made myself walk like a man who would rather be on a horse than on a concrete sidewalk. I held my head like someone accustomed to being outdoors scanning the horizon; someone who ate large quantities of mutton; someone who knew how to survive long winters of minus thirty degrees. I swung my arms like a man who hated wolves because they killed my sheep. My sheep! I thought bad thoughts about Lenin and the Soviet secret police. Most of all, I convinced myself that I was not from China but from this place, had always been from here, back to the beginning of time. My ancestors, I felt deep in my heart, had ridden down fleeing soldiers of broken armies and laughed at the sport of doing it. There was also something about other men's wives, but I let that alone.

I knew instinctively what they would be looking for, the foreigner in the crowd, the slight swing of the arms or length of the gait that would stick out, the hesitation at the street corner, or the too eager step into the road against the traffic light. They'd zero in on anything that gave away the game, anything at all that stripped away the protective coloring. They were looking for me. I didn't know who might be behind, or in front, trying to mark me. I had to see them first. There was one thing working in my favor. It's difficult not to crane your neck when you're looking for someone out of doors. Inside, even in a big meeting hall, you can let your eyes roam, but outside in a crowd of people, if only a little bit, you have to crane your neck.

I spotted the first one off to the right, about fifteen meters away. There would be at least three more of them, each one covering one-fourth of an invisible circle. I spotted the second one. These weren't Mongolian security agents—wrong eyes. They weren't Chinese—wrong haircuts. They were North Koreans, always the same stupid shoes. I'd dealt with enough of them over the past few years to know how they took their time scouring the bushes for their prey. That was fine. They were exactly who I wanted to see because it told me what I needed to know. My uncle, not that it was a surprise, had been right.

A North Korean team like this wasn't here for the sights. They were here to snatch someone, not just anyone. They were here to find my predecessor and bring him back, either that or make sure he never left this place. They thought he was here, in Ulan Bator. That meant I had to find him first.

I eased my way across the street into the darkness of a narrow alley and watched. In another minute they closed the net and discovered it was empty. They exchanged a few sharp words, then headed back in the direction of their embassy, which I knew was about five minutes away. I gave them a head start and set off to follow at a safe distance.

Two big Mongolians blocked my way. "In a hurry?" One of them put his hand on my neck. And that, as we say, was that.

Chapter Four

You're on my territory, and you don't have permission to operate here."

I sat up. My head was clear. A quick inventory turned up no bumps or bruises. The only thing was my throat was a little dry. My eyes did a quick tour of the room. The lights were low, which was more soothing than ominous. There were no windows, but the place didn't feel cramped. It had an air of openness to it, as if the sky and open plains didn't pay attention to walls but seeped into everything. The man who had spoken was leaning against a desk, watching me.

"Where am I?"

"Not far from where you were a couple of hours ago."

"I'm a tourist." Anyone who started a conversation by telling me I was on his territory was not someone I wanted to sit and chat with. "You treat everyone like this?"

"No, just your type. You're a tourist? Pleased to meet you, I'm the king of Siam. Who did you think you were kidding out there on the square, walking around like you had terminal hemorrhoids?"

"I ride horses a lot."

A laugh rolled in from the hall, followed by a big man who had to duck as he came through the door. It was the man in the alley who had put me to sleep.

"Bazar here apparently isn't convinced. In case you're wondering, we didn't make you in the square. We picked you up at the airport. The rest was easy. We've been watching."

"What about those North Koreans crawling all over? You watching them, too?"

"This is a big place, but very empty, as you no doubt have figured out. We notice things."

"So what happens now?"

"That depends."

"How'd your boy do that, the hand on the neck thing? I'd like to teach it to my students."

"Oh, you teach?"

"Yeah, I teach riding."

Bazar laughed again.

"OK," said the man. "Fun's over. I need a statement from you." He turned to the big man. "Tell Tuya to come in. We're liable to be here awhile, so tell her to bring us something to eat."

With the big man out of the room, it felt like there was more air to breathe. "You think I could have a glass of water?"

"In a minute."

"We waiting for something?"

"No, I need you to listen."

"I can't drink and listen at the same time?"

"Not unless I say so."

"Speak, by all means."

He produced a tape machine, pressed the PLAY button, and stood back. What came out was short, less than a minute. "That's it? I was expecting something more. Moaning, or screaming, maybe pleas for mercy. What else is on the tape?"

"Nothing. A dog barking, that's all. You heard it all. It's a dog. I want to know what sort of dog. Big, small, English breed, Mexican?"

"What makes you think I know one from the other?"

He fussed with the tape player. "Listen closely this time." He closed his eyes and played the tape again.

I listened. "That's not a dog."

"It's not a canary, that's for sure."

"No, it's a seal, maybe a sea lion."

"You mean this was taped in a zoo?"

"Seals do live outside of zoos, you know."

"Not around here they don't. Like where?"

"Like everywhere there's ocean."

"In China? I need it to be in China."

"How about close, near the port of Rason. They have seals there. I know because . . . one of my students is from there."

"In North Korea, seals?"

Strange he should know that Rason was in North Korea. I wouldn't have bet a Mongolian police inspector would know something like that. If I hadn't been suspicious, I would have been impressed.

"How do you like that! That explains plenty." He stepped into the hall. "Tuya, I'm waiting. Do you mind?"

"Momento." A young woman brushed past him into the room carrying a tray, which had on it a pitcher, three glasses, a notebook, pens, and a small pile of what appeared to be flat white rocks. Not unusual, except she was carrying it behind her back, with both hands. She put down the tray, retied her ponytail as if she were standing behind herself, and then looked at me languidly. As soon as she did, I prayed for an early death because I knew I was going to fall for her, and it would end badly. She was slim and tall; she moved like a flower in the wind. The only thing wrong was the way she had her arms behind her back. It was unnerving.

"Tea?" She was holding a glass up for me, in the proper fashion. "It's Mongolian tea, I don't know if you'll like it." She could have poured mud in the glass, it didn't matter. If she was giving, whatever it was, I was taking.

"Yes, thank you."

"It's salty milk tea."

Didn't matter. Didn't matter.

"Here." She put a little in the glass and handed it to me. "Have a sip first. If you like it, I'll give you more."

More! I heard soft zither music in the word. "Delicious," I said. "Superb."

"You haven't tried it yet." Her eyes narrowed slightly in suspicion. "Maybe you should eat something with it." She took a couple of the stones and handed them to me. "They're cheese. Are you hungry?"

Just then the man walked back into the room. "Thank you, Tuya. Set up to take notes. As soon as our guest has had his tea, he'll begin telling us why he is here."

Tuya sat down. "Allegro," she said. "Anytime."

The man took some cheese stones for himself and chewed one slowly. "Tuya went away to Italy a few years ago. She was supposed to learn Italian and work in a restaurant, but it turned out not to be the case. They wanted her for something else. Some bigwigs thought she was the very thing they needed at their parties. She told them what to do with themselves and left. She went out the door and didn't look back. You'll notice she's tall."

"I did notice that."

"And that she carries herself very well."

"Unusually, you might say."

"That's her training. After she left the party animals she talked herself into a European circus for a season. When the circus went into winter quarters, she came back here and enrolled in the UB School of Contortionism. She was finishing up with honors when I heard about her. It was a perfect fit. She works flexible hours."

Contortionism, that explained the odd way she'd carried the tray in the room. Unbidden, certain possibilities flashed through my mind. I put them aside, though not too far aside.

The man frowned. "Tut! I can see what you're thinking, and you might as well forget it."

Tuya smiled to herself.

The man continued. "She's a gem. I can't even tell you how

many jams she's gotten us out of. It's amazing how many times you end up needing someone able to do so many things with their thighs."

Tuya smiled again, modestly.

"All by herself, she's stopped several suspects dead in their tracks. No need for weapons, no need to chase them down the street. Next thing they know, Tuya has them in handcuffs. One of them fainted when he saw where she'd put her head."

I replaced the glass of tea on the table nearby. "Well, this has been interesting. Wonderful snacks, but if we're done, I'll be going. My tour bus leaves in a few minutes."

"I wouldn't try to leave. Even if Bazar is napping outside the door, he is a light sleeper. Bazar, you awake?"

"Yeah, boss, wide awake."

"Good, stay that way." The man rubbed his hands together. "Let's begin. For the record, Tuya, please insert the standard opening about how the subject walked into the office on his own and asked to speak to someone in authority, etc., etc."

"Whoa," I said. "Who walked in where? Let's simplify the process. Why don't you write the whole thing and have me sign later? You can bring it—two pages, six pages, makes no difference—to my hotel room tomorrow morning. My room faces Lenin's posterior. That way will save everyone a lot of trouble. Tuya can probably write it by heart, with one hand behind her back. I mean, in a manner of speaking."

The man looked shocked. He had an unusually expressive face, though I couldn't be sure if it was expressing what he felt or what he wanted me to think he felt. Otherwise, there wasn't anything about him that stood out. Medium height, medium build; I wouldn't have looked twice at him except that he was standing directly in front of me. "This isn't a confession we're talking about. Tuya wouldn't even know where to start, other than the standard opening. That's why you're here, to tell us why you're here. It wouldn't do me any good to make something up, would it? Don't worry about the intro. That's just boilerplate. If I put down we beat the stuffing out of a suspect and dragged him by his hair into headquarters, it upsets the magistrates. They're trying on democracy for size, and no one has figured out yet that police work isn't democratic. It's coercive, though we're not supposed to use that word anymore."

"I'm in custody? Under some sort of arrest? Preventive detention? I'm a citizen of the People's Republic of China, and I'd advise you as a new-made friend to keep that in mind. You can look at the first page of my passport, if you don't believe me. Incidentally, we haven't introduced ourselves."

"Oh, don't worry. We've already looked at every page of your passport upside down and backward. As for advising, let me advise you that this is Mongolia. Friendly as I am, it saddens me to say you don't have any rights here, no rights, no jurisdiction, no status. In other words, I don't give a damn about your People's Republic, and I don't care who is supposed to show up in a couple of days."

I was about to ask what he meant, but at this point he had a full head of steam and wasn't going to stop for a simple question.

"Maybe the rabbits in the Foreign Ministry would twitch their noses and swoon in fright if you waved your august Chinese nationality at them, especially this week, but I don't care. Bazar doesn't either, do you, Bazar?"

"No, boss, I had Chinese for lunch."

Tuya put her arm behind her back and picked a couple of cheese stones off the tray. "Tell me when we start. You want all this stuff included, or do I wait some?"

"I think we're ready." The man turned a chair around and sat down, resting his chin on the back. It wasn't much of a chair, all plastic and metal. My uncle would have scoffed at it.

"Something the matter?" The man waved his hand in front of my face. "Are you with me?"

"Yes, I'm with you, but I still don't know who you are."

"Good. It's not important. You can call me Bat Man." He

nodded slightly at me. I nodded slightly back. "This really isn't difficult. All I want to hear is what you're doing in my country. Simple, yes? Simple Simon met a pie man." He grinned. "I watch movies; you want to hear my imitation of Clint Eastwood?" Then he frowned. "You rented a big car, drove out to the national park, went in circles a little, stayed overnight at one of those camps, then rushed back to Ulan Bator early the next morning. How come? You didn't like the scenery? Incidentally, you shouldn't use your horn out there in the countryside, it scares the livestock."

"I liked the scenery fine." There was no sense relating the conversations with my uncle in the car about the landscape. Maybe he already knew.

"When you got back, you made contact with a yak."

"I did?" This threw me off.

"The funny little man with the postcards. He's a yak, someone who isn't what he seems to be. Then you went to the Irish bar and met a known Kazakh agent."

"I did?" It was starting to sound complicated, hard to explain. "I never saw her before in my life. How would I know she was an agent?"

"In fact, the little Kazakh group was having its monthly meeting when you walked in. It was going to be an important meeting—unusual, extremely urgent, tip top. We were worried it was going to be a problem for us in view of the special security arrangements that are supposed to be in place. You and that uncle of yours interrupted the proceedings, and the birds flew away before we could find out what they had in mind. The presidential security people are hopping mad. If they had gotten to you before I did, things wouldn't be as pleasant as they are at this moment."

"A thousand pardons." What special security arrangements? Which brought us back to the question I hadn't asked: Who was showing up in a couple of days? Not counting the North Koreans, I hadn't seen signs of anything unusual. "It wasn't intentional, believe me. We didn't even know those Kazakhs would be there. We just stopped in for a drink.'

"Is that a fact? Then why did the yak send you?"

Excellent question, I had to admit. Another excellent question: How did this Mongolian cop know what was on that postcard? Unless they'd dragged the funny little man in and dunked his head in a water pail until he talked. Or maybe he was working for them, part-time.

"This yak fellow kept showing up, unbidden," I said. "It got to be a little annoying. If you know so much, you ought to know we had no connection to him."

The man smacked his forehead. "Yeah, I should know that, but I don't. Why don't I? Maybe you have an explanation. See, that's all I'm after, a simple explanation. You must have a dozen of them, prestamped and ready to drop in the mail. How about you try them out one at a time? I'll give them ratings, sort of like they do at the Olympics. It's a democratic approach; I'll even throw out the lowest score, the one from the East German judge. How's that? We'll look at the top three, maybe get them in rank order, and then put them to a vote at the national elections. When are the elections, Tuya, this coming December?"

"Year after that."

"OK, year after that." The man took a couple of cheese stones and handed one to me. "Meanwhile, you can stay in a hole in the ground and rest at our expense. We haven't fixed up the jails yet, but the old ones are pretty nice even in their original state. Well, for holes, they're nice all except in winter, which lasts pretty much from October through April. Don't worry, it's easy to count sheep in this country. Believe me, you'll have no trouble getting to sleep. How about it?"

He poured himself a glass of salty tea and drank it down noisily. "Or, we can do it different if that doesn't sound good. Like, maybe you tell me something I can believe from the start. See, I'm reasonable, I'm open to alternatives. I'm good cop, bad cop all rolled into one. We're shorthanded these days, no one has the budget to hire enough staff, but that's all right. It means I get to choose. Three days a week good cop, three days a week bad cop. And on the seventh day I rest. What am I tonight, Tuya? What does it say on the rota on the wall next to the desk?"

"Ummmm, good cop."

"How about that!" He radiated goodwill. "You, my friend, are in luck. Tomorrow might not have been nice." The man shouted out the door. "How about it, Bazar? What are you today?"

"I don't know, boss. I lose track."

The man turned back to me. "So, over to you. I'm listening, Tuya is listening, the hidden recorder that we got for half price from Russia on the Internet is listening. Talk to me."

I thought about it. I wasn't here working against the Mongolians. They hadn't caused me any trouble. As far as I knew, there wasn't a single Mongolian living in my district at home, though lately we'd noticed a few of them riding the train from Tumen into North Korea. Taking the long view, I didn't particularly care if they had occupied Beijing a few hundred years ago. Right now, they were minding their own business. I liked what little I'd seen of their operations. They seemed to have a pretty good handle on what happened within their borders. What I couldn't figure out was what had them so rattled.

"Maybe if we work together, we can help each other out," I said, feeling my way along. "We both seem to be running out of time, and we might actually be in the same sinking boat. There's no reason not to cooperate." Actually, that was not quite true. There was one reason of undeniable weight—I didn't have approval to cooperate with the Mongolian police. Beijing wouldn't like my getting into its liaison shorts, creating a working relationship with a foreign service on the spot without proper say-so. The explanation that there hadn't been time to fill in all the forms would cut no ice.

On the other hand, Beijing hadn't done much in the way of

briefing me about what I was getting into, much less how I was supposed to wriggle out if something went amiss, "amiss" being a fair description of the current situation. Something was amiss, otherwise I wouldn't be sitting here. As a matter of fact, if I lingered on the thought, it was hard not to come to the conclusion that someone in my own ministry had set me up.

I took a deep breath. Lack of sleep, spending too much time with my uncle, something was getting to me. No one was trying to set me up . . . not today, anyway. I exhaled slowly and tried to look sincere. "I'm looking for a friend." This was one of those times when I was going to have to roll the dice in the dark. "Maybe you know him."

"Not likely." The man gave me a puzzled look. "But what the hell, you can never tell. Try me."

If my uncle was right, and I had to admit it was starting to look like he often was, Beijing obviously wanted that missing state seal back in South Korean hands very soon. Everyone was in a hurry; no one would tell me why. Ding said Beijing wanted the operation over in forty-eight hours. The Mongolians felt pressed by a special security window that seemed poised to open any moment.

The woman in the bar—a Kazakh who apparently drank early and often—wanted to locate her mother, for reasons that didn't interest me. What mattered was that she also knew, or said she knew, where the state seal was, *both* the seal and my predecessor. What did someone from Kazakhstan care about either one? At first glance, I'd dismiss her as a crank, but then, why were the South Koreas following her around? Unless, of course, they thought she had the seal, or knew where it was.

That's when it hit between my eyes. The Mongolians had been monitoring the meeting of that Kazakh foursome in the Irish bar. Even if it was just a tape, by now they would have transcribed my conversation with the woman, and they'd know I was looking for a seal, even if they didn't know what sort or why. Yet none of that had come up so far in the little dance this man and I were doing.

He was holding back that card, except in a curious way he'd turned it over for me to see. He was the one who had let me know they were watching the Kazakhs. He was enjoying himself, stringing this out. In his own way, the little bastard was as double-jointed as Tuya.

"I don't know what my friend looks like anymore," I said. "Haven't seen him in a long time. We were boyhood chums, you might say, went through school together, and then lost touch a few years later. Maybe a phone call once in a while. He travels."

"Sure, friends across the years, that sort of thing. What makes you think he's here?"

"This I also don't know, actually." It helps to touch ground truth now and then in these sorts of sessions. "Someone told me they'd heard he was in Mongolia." Overdoing the truth isn't a good idea, but coming close twice couldn't hurt. "Naturally, as soon as I heard that, I decided to come and see."

"That happens a lot; missing Chinese turn up in Mongolia, and their friends pour over the border to restore old ties. People think we're a backwater, but we're not. We're very modern. In fact, we're thinking of starting a Web page, www.visitmongolia/findfriends. Only one problem. I think it should be dot org, but Bazar says it should be dot com. You still think it should be dot com, Bazar?"

"I'm thinking, boss."

"This is part of our new ethos. Kicking around ideas instead of people. Not as much gets done, but no one's nose gets out of joint. You may have noticed Bazar's nose is broken in two places; that happened under the old regime."

Tuya put down her pen. "I'm skipping that part about Bazar's nose."

"Tuya, believe me, if you don't want to stick Bazar's nose in this, we leave it out." The man stood up and pushed the chair to one side. "Why don't you admit it?" He parked his face close to mine.

"Sure," I said. "Admit what?"

"That you're here as a security advance for your premier."

This was news to me. It shouldn't have been. When someone at that level traveled, even if it was nowhere near our area, we were supposed to do a special check and report any rumors about threats. I never heard anything about the premier traveling, but it wouldn't enhance my stature to admit that. "Is it a crime, to advance for a VIP?"

He smiled, probably the way a Mongolian wolf smiles at a lamb. "We're supposed to have liaison agreements. Here we are, busy trying to prepare things to guarantee an uneventful visit for your man, and you are for some reason out on the street exciting the North Koreans. It's like you put a stick in a beehive and stir it around. Already you have more security people in town than we have on our entire force. A lot of them are posing as journalists, but they don't seem to know which end of the pencil to hold. I have a whole stack of reports about someone's lady agent walking around in a lace dress that no one knows how to describe without getting into trouble."

Tuya blushed.

"We're trying to find out whose she is. The North Koreans ran the other way when they saw her; that's how we first knew they were around."

"Yup." I gave my best imitation of laughter. "Like bees, buzzing." What was he talking about?

"You have some game with them?"

"Me? Not me, someone else maybe. I just wanted to make sure they were in the open. I don't wear lace, so I have to take another approach."

"Well, don't. We put them on little leashes once we mark them, and I don't want them jumping around. You take care of the North Koreans on your soil, we'll do it on ours, all right with you?"

"Sure, that's the way we like it."

"Good, then get the hell out of here. You are lying through your teeth, and if it weren't antidemocratic, I'd knock them out myself. I could hold you as a potential threat to the Chinese premier and his party, but then if it turned out you were actually here to protect him like you say, I would hear about it until—" He stopped. "Uh, what seal?"

"I never know what you're going to say next."

"Never is a long time. What seal are you looking for?"

"You won't believe this."

"Don't tell me, you don't know."

I shrugged. "I think the North Koreans know, and that's why they're buzzing around. They know what it is, but they don't know where. They want to make sure I don't find out before they do."

"A lot of trouble for a lousy chop, or am I wrong?"

"It's complicated."

"I'll bet."

"It's forged."

"Tsk, tsk. We can't have that. Someone using it to sign your checks?"

"Not mine. Seoul's."

"Ahhh." He sat down. "So, what is this to you?"

"That's what I don't know."

"But you're here looking for it. Not by yourself, either. You have your uncle in tow."

"He's harmless."

"Inspector O? Harmless." He laughed. Bazar's laugh came bouncing in from the hall. Tuya looked up to give me a ravishing smile. With everyone so jolly, I figured I should join in. The man stopped laughing long enough to say, "He's harmless, and the next camel you see will be on roller skates." This brought howls of laughter from the hallway.

They were having such a good time that I hated to break things up. "The fact is, he didn't want to come here," I said.

"In that case, why is there a meeting of the clan?" The man

indicated to Tuya that she should stop tickling me with her smile and start taking notes again.

"What clan?"

"There you go. Dumb as sheep dip. You really don't know, do you? The beauty queen Fang and her wingman. They showed up a week ago. He's vanished, gave us the slip, which has caused a lot of nasty messages to come down on my head from on high."

"I feel your pain."

"Thank you. Now here we are, with your caravan due to arrive bearing gifts. Don't say it, don't tell me this is all news to you."

"I'm not saying anything." Madame Fang had come with someone in tow? And now she was out having dinner with my uncle, all under the watchful eye of Mongolian security? "I have a suggestion. It's the only thing that is going to work."

"You're going to slit your throat."

"No. Better than that. You're going to help me, and I'm going to help you."

The man turned to Tuya and indicated that notes were unnecessary at this point. She put down her pen and hoisted one leg behind her neck. "I've got to loosen up a little," she explained. "My joints get stiff sitting in this chair all day long."

If she hadn't been gorgeous, the effect would have been less charming. As it was, I figured I could come home to that four nights out of five.

"Soothing words I don't need," the man said, ignoring Tuya's posture. "Other than soothing words, what have you got in mind? It can't be anything long-term. I have maybe thirty-six hours to keep this pot from boiling over."

"If you're not going to tell me what's on your stove or why, there's a limit to what I can do for you sitting here." Ding's operation was keyed to the premier's visit. That at least was now clear.

"You expect me to let you walk out the door, is that it?"

"If Tuya is assigned to tail me, you won't hear any objection."

Tuya's other leg joined the first behind her neck. "OK," said the man, "but it looks like she may have to walk on her hands. Tuya, you want the job?"

"Some other time," she said. "Bazar needs the fresh air more than I do."

"All right," the man said to me. "Let's say you walk out the door, Bazar follows as inconspicuously as possible ten meters behind. How does this help me?"

Tuya lowered herself off the chair on her hands and rolled out of the room. I must have blanched, because the man gave me a reassuring pat on the shoulder.

"Tremendous asset for the force, once we figured out how to deploy it," he said. "You should look into the option."

I took a deep breath. It rattled me, somehow, seeing Tuya do that. "Over drinks sometime, you can explain it all to me."

"Well, there is a certain shock value involved." He looked into the hall, watching Tuya roll away before returning to the subject at hand. "You still haven't answered my question—how does your walking out of here help me?"

"I know some things you don't."

"That's been my point all along."

"I can't tell you anything right now, but what I know can turn down the heat on that pot you're worried about."

"So it won't cause any trouble to the visit by your prime minister?"

I may have grinned slightly.

He frowned. "And how can I help you?"

My uncle might have figured all of this out without ever leaving his workshop. I had to run into a bull of a Mongolian policeman and get fed saltwater by a beautiful woman who wasn't particular about where she put her arms. But I'd learned over the years that it didn't matter in my line of work; whatever got you where you needed to be was all right. I had almost all of the pieces. They weren't what you'd call little. They were big, bigger than the sort of thing that normally showed up on my desk. I knew how to deal with people. Countries and continents I left for someone else, or I had until now. The Chinese premier was showing up in a day or so, but for some reason he needed to know that two pesky details—a phony seal and a renegade intelligence officer—had been taken care of. That's what no one in China had bothered to tell me. I still didn't know why, but why could wait. At least I was sure I knew what, some of what, maybe most of what. That's what this Mongolian cop had laid out on the table for me. I decided he wouldn't appreciate a hug, so I just smiled.

"How can you help me? You already did."

Chapter Five

You tried to blow him up?"

"Yeah, tried is the operative word."

"A problem?"

"The bastard doesn't care fuck about safety."

I indicated puzzlement, which he only sensed since he couldn't see my face. I was standing behind him, and it was very dark. We were in some sort of combination toolshed and classroom on the outskirts of town.

After I left the police station, around two in the morning, I made a couple of moves to lose Bazar as quickly as I could. I felt bad about doing that, but I had picked up someone else on my tail, and this second tail was doing a better job. It's hard to get anything done with two different services right behind you. One of them had to get lost, and I nominated Bazar. Once I'd shaken him, I kept moving in widening circles. I couldn't spot whoever it was that stuck with me; each time I put myself in position to get a look behind, he disappeared. I knew he was there, though. I had the feeling it was a singleton, not a tag team.

After nearly an hour of hide-and-seek, we were in a grassy area that seemed deserted. The closest ger was half a kilometer away. A couple of cows walked up to me. They stopped a few meters away and gave me their undivided attention. If I'd been trying to hide, having two cows staring at me would have been a dead giveaway, but luckily I wanted to make sure whoever was trailing behind got a good fix on my location in the darkness. There were no more streetlights and barely any moon. A moment later I spotted what looked like a partially collapsed shed beside a large pile of stones. I moved in the opposite direction for about twenty meters. Three or four logs lying against each other appeared out of the darkness. I pretended to stumble on them, cursed loudly, then got as low as I could and doubled back into the broken doorway of the shed. The cows lost interest. The shed had a broken blackboard and five or six chairs tumbled about on the remains of a concrete floor. There was a row of hooks on one wall with various tools, a bit and harness, and five or six leather straps hanging from them.

Five minutes passed before I heard someone moving across the grass. The sound stopped, the cows grunted, and then a human head poked into the shed. I brought one of the chairs down on it. The chair broke, but not before it did its job.

Luckily, the owner of the head was stunned but not unconscious. It was one of the North Koreans I had spotted in the square earlier that night. After tying him to the what looked like the sturdiest of the remaining chairs with the leather straps, I brought him to with a couple of hard slaps on the face. As he looked up, I stepped behind him. I asked him a few easy questions to get things rolling. That's when he said the bastard didn't care about safety, which I found puzzling.

"What, you don't believe me?" He started straining against the straps, but they were tight.

"How doesn't he care about safety? You're saying he's reckless?"

"Yeah, that's it. Reckless. The bomb was rigged to the seat belt. When the metal fitting clicked into the buckle, it was set to go boom. It was foolproof, a prizewinning concept; not a single failure yet. We've never tried doing anything with the air bags, too many complications."

"But this time? No boom? Faulty engineering with the seat belt design?"

"Nothing wrong with the engineering, nothing wrong with the components. It was human failure. The son of a bitch doesn't drive with his seat belt buckled."

"Why not just kidnap him? That can't be so difficult."

"Says you. We tried. First, we tried to invite him back, you know, the rat-takes-the-cheese sort of thing. No luck. Then we tried to screw with his GPS, sort of misdirect him into our hands."

"Very imaginative."

"Yeah, but nothing doing. He didn't turn it on. So next we thought about snatching him. Our planning people looked at it. Everything in a grab-and-run scenario is premised on sea exfiltration. Everything—transport, logistics, timing."

"So?"

"So, you may have noticed, there is no sea near this shit-can country. No one could come up with a workaround fast enough. Finally, a few days ago, the order came to send him to the moon."

"That's code?"

"A figure of speech. My wife says I overuse it. Just means use a pistol, nothing fancy. It's sort of embarrassing, lowest-common-denominator type of work."

"For fun, try to guess what I'm about to ask."

"That's easy. What's the next move?"

"Very good. What's the next move?"

"We had the airport covered, and he showed up in pictures carrying the baggage of the lady with the hips. What she wanted with him I don't know, but they checked into that hotel with the swank gers on the edge of town. They had a car, so we figured it would be easy. Like I told you, nothing worked. Finally, we got the order to lay off, just watch him, which we did, until we lost track of him about a week ago. So the next move is to figure out where he is before anyone else does, and then we finish the job."

"You said there was a woman with him. What if she was in the car when it blew up?"

He shrugged his shoulders as well as he could. "Tough on the hips, I guess."

"The Chinese want him big-time, you realize that?"

"Tell me about it. Luckily, they don't have any better idea where he is than we do. They're tripping over themselves." He paused. "No offense. It's just my observation, honor among thieves and so forth. I'm guessing you're Chinese; you speak Korean like a Chinese, no offense." He paused again. He was talking fast, trying to keep me occupied. That was good. It meant he had zeroed in on the idea that his situation wasn't ideal. "I think your people have sent at least two special teams out here to find him, plus an army of beaters. One of the disadvantages of having so many people, I suppose."

Again I emanated puzzlement.

"More people, more idiots. It's simple math. No offense."

"You're sure they haven't located him?"

"I'm not worried; we have that angle covered. Between you and me, we have a good fix on Chinese operations. If you're going to ask how I know, don't bother. It's not my area, and I make sure to stay away from it. Intelligence, counterintelligence, you can twist your privates into a pretzel trying to figure it all out. I'm simply an operations type. What really worries me are the locals. No way to be sure of them. They hardly have any people."

"Fewer idiots."

"Yeah, you might say. And they're good. Even that big guy who was tailing you knows his stuff. I happen to have a few tricks more than he does, that's all. As soon as we spotted you at the airport, we thought we had an inside track. It was a cinch you were going to lead us to our man, but that didn't pan out. We picked you up again when you got back to town, but then we lost you in the square last night. At the embassy we got chewed out but good when we reported in. Luckily, I couldn't sleep and was taking a stroll when I saw you leave the police station. They work you over?"

"They're gentlemen."

"That's good." He moved his shoulders as much as he could against the straps. "I'm beginning to think we're right, that you don't know where the man is either."

"You think so, huh?" He had fully confirmed one key fact that up to now I'd only surmised, that my predecessor was somewhere in Mongolia. The North Koreans might be wrong about a lot of things, but not about this. He was the "wingman" that the Mongolians had spotted and then lost. "Maybe I didn't know before. Let's say you gave me an idea. Let's say I owe you. What would be fair payment?"

"How about you start by untying me."

"Can't do that. Not yet, anyway. You didn't let anyone know you were following me?"

He hesitated a fraction too long. "Yeah, that's what we always do. Check in to make sure we have backup."

"You used smoke signals, perhaps? You said you were just out for a stroll by yourself when you spotted me. I think you just took out after me and that big Mongolian without letting anyone know. Tsk, very bad operational practice. You don't even have a phone on you. I checked."

"Maybe I lost it."

I smacked him on the back of the head. "Don't start with me. How many are on your team?"

He looked down at the floor.

"Three?" I moved around in front so he could see me.

"Come on." He sounded impatient. "You know I won't give up that sort of details."

"I think you will." I pushed the chair over on its side and stepped on his hand. "I'll grind the little bones in your fingers into powder. There won't be enough to glue back together, much less heal. You might as well audition as a sea lion in a circus."

"Hey!" He twisted his head around as far as he could so he was looking up at me. "What's your problem? It's my job. Nothing to do with you."

"That's what you say." I put some weight on the foot covering his hand. "I'm willing to believe you, but that doesn't save your hand." I moved my foot a little.

The night was cool, but he was sweating. His eyes went from my face to my foot. "You can't let me get up from here. You know you're going to have to kill me. Then they'll send someone to even things up. Maybe not right away, but sooner or later. Why start a vicious cycle like that? Let's think about it. Hey!"

I stepped hard on his hand. "I'm not interested in killing you. I just want us to be friends, maybe something on Facebook. Could be a while, though, before you can type. At this point, if they put your hand in a cast for five or six months, you might get use of a couple of fingers again. Might. It all depends on who sets the bones. The bones in your hand are real small. Did I mention that? They're tiny. It takes a skilled surgeon a week of operations to sort them out. You know any skilled surgeons in one of your top-notch hospitals?"

"I know three of them. Four counting me."

I eased off his hand a little. "That's better. Next question."

"No more questions."

I lifted my foot completely off his hand for a second. His face relaxed. Then I stepped down hard. He screamed.

"You don't tell me what to do," I said. "You tell me what I want to know. Are we clear?"

"Yeah, yeah." It was whispered.

"What's he doing here?" I already knew. I needed to know if the North Koreans knew.

"We heard he wants to go home. No one told us that exactly, but we heard." He had his eyes focused on my foot. His eyes were practically popping out of his head, willing my foot not to move. "I can't be sure. All I can do is tell you what we heard."

"That's good. You heard he wants to go home. And where is that? Where is home?"

"China."

I moved my foot a little; he screamed again.

"I already knew that," I said matter-of-factly. "You care to be a little more specific? Maybe save your thumb?"

"They didn't tell us! What the hell would they tell us for? They don't give us bio sheets, nothing like that. We're like dogs with a sock. Smell this. Find who it belongs to."

"Maybe you could find him easier if you knew something about him, did that occur to anyone? Like where specifically he's headed on his way home? Makes sense, don't you think? People usually go the shortest distance between two points."

"Sure, it makes sense, but so what? We're not supposed to know too much about him. It's no different from tracking an animal. Who knows what a deer thinks? Who cares? Anyway, we're not supposed to get him in China. We can't operate there, not normally. We're supposed to find him here."

"And when you find him, then what?"

"I told you what my orders were."

"Send him to the moon."

"Yeah, that's it."

"What if he's not armed?"

He made sure my foot was nowhere near his hand and then grinned at me. "It's easier if they're not armed."

I set him upright on the chair again, then pulled the harness down from the wall, crammed the bit in his mouth, and tied the whole thing tight on the back of the chair.

"Give my regards to the cows," I said and scrambled back out of the shed into the night. With barely any moon, there were no shadows, which may be why I nearly bumped into a hulking figure standing a few meters away near one of the piles of stones. Bazar put his finger to his lips and indicated with a frown and a nod of his head that I should keep walking. That seemed like a good idea, and without any words between us, we parted company.

Chapter Six

I found something out," I said to my uncle as soon as he closed the door to our hotel room.

"Long time no see." He sounded unconcerned, but I noticed he watched closely as I moved into the room. "Everything all right?"

"Fine," I said. "Everything's fine. How was your dinner?"

"Dinner? You mean last night? It was good, if you enjoy that sort of thing. The restaurant was overcrowded. Too many South Koreans."

"You really don't like your countrymen, do you?"

"No, in the aggregate they're fine. It's one by one that they can get on your nerves."

"Guess who is about to visit here?"

"The Chinese prime minister. I thought you were supposed to know these things."

"How did you find out?"

"The waiter at the restaurant mentioned it. He and Mei-lin had quite a conversation about the details."

"Madame Fang knew, too?"

"Of course she knew."

"OK, next question, who is the prime minister bringing with him?"

"A long convoy of happy capitalists who think this place is a fat pig ready to be carved up."

"Really?" I hadn't focused on this possibility. "You think this is all about money?" Our earlier conversation about whose phony seal was rolling around, and why, jumped up and bit me. "Don't tell me you think Beijing wants to discredit the South in order to steal a couple of lousy business deals."

"Steal? Did I say steal? I did not. I'm sure your capital just wants to get the South dropped from consideration for a few strategically important ventures. The South Korean prime minister was here last month. He initialed a stack of memoranda with the Mongolians on investment. These were only MOUs. The details remain to be worked out and the final agreements signed."

"And you know that because . . . ?"

"Because there was a picture of him and his business pals with sloppy grins on their faces in the hall to the men's room in the restaurant. That was where they held the final banquet."

I must have frowned.

"No, not the toilet, the banquet room. A South Korean reporter was sitting at the next table, and she told me they were all drunk out of their minds. At the banquet, which she attended apparently, she was wearing a lace dress that should not be allowed in public according to the waiter. He told me in confidence that he had reason to doubt that she was a reporter at all."

"Hooker?"

"Lower than that in his estimate. Intelligence. Halfway through dinner, she invited herself over and sat down. She kept rubbing her ankle against my leg under the table. I guess maybe I still have it, huh?" He smiled faintly. "I think she was trying to get up Mei-lin's nose. If so, she succeeded. They seemed to know each other."

I was skeptical. "The South Koreans are moving to close some deals with the Mongolians. Hooray. So what? That's what the South Koreans do. They roam around Asia and close deals. We have scores of them in Yanji."

My uncle lay down on his bed and closed his eyes. "Maybe it's that simple, but I don't think Beijing is comfortable with the thought of so many South Koreans in Mongolia. They want to knock those deals loose and then move in to pick up the pieces."

"Pieces of what?" I tried to remember if I'd ever read anything about Mongolian resources. "Gold mines?" Something about gold and Mongolia rattled in my memory.

"Better than gold—coal, a lot of it, not to mention uranium and rare earth mines. To top it off, a deal on construction of a rail line to carry away all the goodies."

"Since when do you know anything about rare earth mining? Or did the lady with the lace dress have some insights?"

"She was dressed demurely enough for our conversation, fortunately. Otherwise Mei-lin would have yanked my arm out of its socket dragging me away." He sat up suddenly. "From the way things are moving, I'm pretty sure Beijing has lost control of this operation, whatever it is. After all these years, there's one thing I know in my bones—your people don't like what they don't control."

"And your people do?"

"We don't control anything, which means it's never a problem. Chinese, on the other hand, are historically conditioned to think they control plenty, or ought to. Beijing's anxiety won't drop to normal levels of paranoia until your bosses think they've got firm hold of the reins again."

"Yes, pretty important not letting someone else hold the reins."

My uncle went to the window and pulled the curtains shut. As he did, I could see that Lenin hadn't budged.

"What's more, your friends in Beijing are no doubt fretting that unless they regain control, the whole thing will blow back on them," my uncle said. "Believe me, all of us living on the periphery know that nothing in the world is as dangerous as a fretful Han

Chinese official. In MPS Headquarters, right outside the minister's offices, we had two five-drawer safes full of files. All ten drawers were marked *How to keep the Chinese off your neck.* Over each safe was a big sign, in blood red. 'ATTENTION! NOT TO BE MOVED TO STORAGE. NOT SUBJECT TO PERIODIC EVALUATION FOR DESTRUCTION. THIS MEANS YOU!' "

He picked up the brochure on Ulan Bator nightlife and flipped through it once again. "I wouldn't be surprised if someone is digging through those files right now, trying to answer a crash request for a review of current Chinese operations that might go bad and leave everyone on the border in pain for months. Pyongyang must know something is up."

I didn't say anything about the North Korean team I'd spotted, or the conversation I'd had with the man in the shed. All I said was, "How?"

"The roe deer always knows when the tiger has a thorn in its paw."

Roe deer? I'd never heard my uncle describe his former colleagues in such unflattering terms. "So what does all this toing and froing of officials have to do with the counterfeit state seal?"

"That's your job to figure out, not mine. Not withstanding Beijing's stubborn belief in my nonexistent continuing access to North Korea, I'm only along to provide commentary on the treeless plains." He paused, meaningfully. It was the sort of pause that always means trouble. "How about we take a trip out to the east? There are supposed to be mountains there that disrupt the sky a little. We can drive; I'm not going in one of those little airplanes we saw at the airport when we landed."

I was right—trouble. He didn't care about the mountains, and for all his complaining about the sky, he didn't care enough about that to take another long drive. It was a simple equation. If he wanted to go east, I didn't, at least, not before I knew what he knew. He wasn't going to just tell me; that would be too simple. It wasn't in his genes. Well, I had genes, too.

"Not so fast," I said. "We agreed that the whole reason for this trip was to bring you here to deal with your old colleagues. We already did our driving when we went to see Ding. That's enough."

"Oh, really? The reason we're here is for me to deal with the North Koreans? Was that supposed to be in one of my hypothesis bags? I thought it was in yours. I don't work for Beijing, though no one seems to be able grasp that idea. I actually have other things to do."

"For instance."

"For instance, consult the medical profession."

This was news to me. He'd never gone to a doctor in the time he'd lived with me. Never even complained, except maybe about his back, which he thought was a body part that had no purpose except to cause problems.

"Are you sick?" I dropped my suspicion momentarily but picked it up again a second later. He looked in good shape, and if he was sick, my uncle would not go to a doctor in Mongolia. No, he knew something.

"I'm not sick. I have to go see a doctor at a clinic, that's all, and you need to drive me. It's four hours away, more or less."

"Four hours?"

"Three hundred easy kilometers, more or less."

"There isn't a clinic closer than that? And you don't know for sure how far it is? More or less could be anywhere in this country." All of a sudden, something rang a bell. It wasn't mountains, it wasn't sky, and it wasn't a clinic four hours away. My uncle must have heard something from Madame Fang. Whether a slip of the tongue, which I doubted, or a deliberate message beamed from her necklace, I didn't know. Of course, I'd stumbled across part of the same information, though under less comfortable circumstances. The Mongolian police detective had suggested that Madame Fang arrived in country with someone—a gathering of the clan, he'd called it. After some persuasion, the odious man in the cowshed confirmed Madame Fang had arrived with the quarry his gang was after, but they'd lost him. They'd lost him because they hadn't thought to drive four hours cross-country to a clinic in the middle of nowhere.

Or maybe not. Maybe Madame Fang was playing with us again. Maybe she wanted us out of town exactly because that's where her wingman was, or was about to be. Maybe she was using us as rabbits leading a pack of dogs off to where they wouldn't find anything but a lot of sky. If you came right down to it, what was she doing with a wayward MSS special bureau director, once defected, here in Mongolia, anyway? For that matter, what business did she have in North Korea to start with?

No, I wasn't going to jump in a car after too little sleep and drive on a monotonous road just because my uncle was hypnotized by Madame Fang's pearls. Not without a fight. "I don't think we should go off for drives anywhere. We'll be wasting time. Besides which, you've done nothing but complain about the car. Is there anything you haven't objected to since we arrived?"

"If we leave at five in the morning, we can be there by ten or eleven at the latest, assuming we drive straight through. I'm leaving us some margin for error." My uncle put the brochure back on the little table and lay down on his bed again. "That Irish bar we visited isn't listed as one of the places for people to go. Curious." He shut his eyes. "Turn off the light. Maybe we can get a few hours of sleep. I don't want you nodding off at the wheel. Where is our car, by the way?"

I was too tired to fight; there was only strength to retreat to a last defensive line. "Why decide right now whether to go to this fairy clinic? Let's think about it in the morning. I'm tired, it was a long day." This was not met with any sympathy. "Did you write a note to Miss Du yet? Let's do that over breakfast. Maybe by then you'll feel better and we can skip the long drive." He wouldn't take that, but I didn't care. I was just keeping the conversation going while I worked my way to asking him what he knew about Madame Fang's wingman.

"You left the car in the middle of the street, oddly enough." He yawned and pulled the covers over his head. Before I could reply, he was snoring softly.

"Good thing it's red," I said to no one in particular. "We won't have any trouble spotting it."

2

An hour later, my uncle was up and dressed. The sun hadn't come anywhere near the horizon. He sang loudly in the shower, some song about an affectionate bosom. When I buried my head in the pillow, he bumped into the bed a couple of times walking back and forth.

"You must have had quite a time last night," he said when I was finally awake. "You were talking in your sleep."

"What did I say?"

"Mostly incoherent, but very emphatic. Do you have a guilty conscience? Don't bother; it isn't worth a bad night's sleep, whatever it is. Let's go get the car."

"I'm exhausted and hungry. I think we should talk about it over breakfast."

"You stay here and sleep if you want, it doesn't matter to me. I'll drive myself."

"You aren't authorized to drive the car, and you can't go five hours out of town without me."

He smiled. "Want to bet?"

I showered and dressed in a hurry.

"Been with cows?" My uncle pointed at my shoes as we stepped outside into the first signs of sunrise. The light was pale gold; each building it touched took on the hue of the earth so that, for an instant, the city seemed a dream of the past. The new glass buildings stopped preening, the streets were quiet, and from somewhere nearby a horse whinnied.

"Cows?" I looked down at my shoes. "Can't avoid them," I said "They wander around everywhere. Let's find the damned transportation."

My uncle was partially right about the car—it had been moved to the side. To the side and a kilometer away on a field next to a solitary ger. For a moment I worried it might be the same field I'd been in the night before, but there wasn't any shed in sight. I decided fields all looked pretty much the same at this time of the morning.

We only found the car because a traffic cop walking along the road remembered seeing it being pushed by a couple of men he recognized from an argument the two of them had been having in the middle of the street a week ago.

"They gave me a lot of gas about their rights. I told them to get out of the street or I'd make them collect all the pony crap from here to Chinggis Khan's tomb."

"I thought no one knew where the tomb was," my uncle said.

"Yeah, well, that's sort of the point." The cop looked peevishly at my uncle. "Lucky for you I didn't ticket your car. Next time I will."

When we finally spotted the car, my uncle was in favor of knocking on the door of the ger and finding out who the hell these people were. I was for getting in and clearing out. The problem was settled when a wiry man with a mustache emerged from the ger.

"Welcome," he said. "Admiring the vehicle? Quite something, isn't it? Red like the blood of the sun, burly as an ox, runs like a camel in heat. I hate to sell it, but my cousin's house burned down and I want to help him out." He hitched up his trousers and then reached in his back pocket for a small blue book. "Make me an offer, in dollars."

He waved the book at us.

"We can't pay," my uncle said.

"No funds?"

"Plenty of funds. But it's ours, we own it, and where I come from, you don't buy back from crooks what you already own."

The man smiled. "If it's yours, why is it sitting in my field?"

"You said it was in heat?" My uncle smiled back. "Maybe it was attracted to something in your person."

"Good way to die, talking like that," the man replied evenly. He returned the little blue book to his pocket. He didn't seem to be armed, but there was no sense standing around to find out.

I showed the man the keys. "We're going to get in the car and drive away. I'm betting you don't want any trouble. Find yourself another car to sell illegally."

"You have the keys, good for you. Bet you wish you had the spark plugs, too. What will you give me for them?"

"This car doesn't need spark plugs. It's diesel."

"You don't say." He frowned. "In that case, take it off my property. Diesel attracts a lot of the wrong sort of people." He stared at my uncle, nodded at me, and disappeared back into the ger.

Once we had maneuvered through the early morning traffic and were out of the city again, I turned to my uncle, "You know where we're going?"

"This road is fine. Don't turn off onto one of those dirt paths. We'll be in Ondorkhaan before dinner. Maybe before lunch."

"Where we will be doing what?"

"The name of the town means nothing to you?"

"Should it?"

"Hell of an education system you have in China."

"Yours is superior, I take it."

"It leaves inquiring minds. That's a plus, I'd say."

"My mind is inquiring, which is how we got into this conversation. I enquired what we'd be doing in the town of Ondorkhaan."

"It's near where Lin Piao's plane supposedly crashed."

I nearly drove us off the road. "You're investigating Lin Piao's plane crash? That was 1971!"

"Don't be ridiculous. I'm just remarking on the irony. A town in the middle of nowhere, site of one of the most fateful assassinations in recent history, and that is where we are headed to stop an assassination of possibly similar import, if lesser profile."

"First of all, Lin Piao wasn't assassinated, his plane went down. Sometimes planes do that. The KGB investigated and said there was no evidence of foul play."

"Good for the KGB. You believe those lying thugs?"

"It was a long time ago, uncle. Lin Piao had to leave in a hurry, before Mao got to him. Maybe the plane hadn't been serviced right; maybe the fuel hadn't been topped off."

"Just dropped out of the sky, did it?"

"That's not why we're on this road. We're not going to see a doctor; we're not going to visit a clinic. This has to do with Madame Fang and whoever came to Mongolia with her."

"No, you're wrong. We are going to see a doctor."

"About an assassination?"

"I have a theory, nephew, and I'll need your help once we get there. We'll have plenty of time to go over the details while we sit in the doctor's waiting room."

"I ought to turn this car around and go back to Ulan Bator."

"But you won't."

3

The drive was along a two-lane highway through mostly flat countryside. In the distance were windswept hills that never seemed to change; if it hadn't been for the bumps and ruts, we might have thought we were standing still. It was not the sort of drive you want to take on one hour's sleep. The land was dry, and the sky—

need I mention—was enormously blue. I waited for my uncle's inevitable comments.

"I've seen enough sky for a lifetime," he said at last. "It's unnatural. It may even be dangerous. With this much sky overhead, who can say it won't just fall down and flatten us at any moment. Maybe that's why this damned place is so flat, maybe it's happened once before. Don't stop moving, that's probably the only thing that keeps us safe."

"Listen, this was your idea, driving all the way out here. You're worried the sky is going to fall on us? I can make a U-turn right here; you won't hear any complaints from me. I should have done it an hour ago."

My uncle was not about to be shaken off his focus. "Did you hear that girl singing the other night outside our hotel window? Talk about melancholic! This is where it comes from, all this emptiness." He waved his hand out the open window. "These people must be lonely from the moment they're born."

"They don't strike me as melancholic at all. They're actually very good-looking and optimistic, I'd say. The girls especially. They have an independent stride, like a high-strung pony, nothing mincing about it."

"Pah! Next you'll insist this isn't empty countryside. I'll tell you what it is. It's a wormhole to the Universal Vacancy. It's not even in the middle of nowhere. To be in the middle of nowhere, nowhere has to be a place. This is not a place. It's nothing." He put his head out the window and looked at the sky for a few minutes as the wind blew against his face. "If I knew a melancholy song, I'd sing it right now," he said and pulled his head back inside. He tilted the seat back slightly. "Wake me when we're there, if there is a there there."

4

"May I help you?" The nurse had on a pale green uniform. Her hair was short, dyed light brown. When she stood up from behind her desk, she was square, broad shouldered, maybe eighty kilos, though nothing fat about her. She was more like one of the huge boulders that lay scattered at the base of the hills we'd passed kilometer after kilometer during the long drive.

"Is the doctor in?" My uncle spoke to her in Russian. It surprised me when she answered in the same language.

"He's out. He'll be back by three o'clock. That's when he sees patients. Would you like to wait?"

"Sure, we'll wait." My uncle took out his wallet. "How much is it to wait per hour?"

The nurse avoided his eyes. "It depends."

"I need to walk around while I wait. That way my back doesn't get bad. It's why I'm here, my back. So if I wait and walk, that's good therapy." He pointed to the doorway behind her desk. "Walk into one room, walk into another room. Gives me a chance to stretch. Always a good idea to keep moving." He pulled out fifty dollars and put it on the edge of her desk. "Good for a couple of hours?"

"Make sure you've walked back to this room by ten minutes to three." She sat down and started going through a pile of charts on her desk. "Fifty gets you very little hereabouts." The fifty-dollar bill seemed to walk by itself to her right hand. "Seeing as you are a stranger, you get a break, but only once. Don't forget, ten minutes to three, make sure you're sitting here." She looked at me. "You got a bad back, too? Or another type of complaint?"

"Me? I'm fine. I'm just the old man's driver."

"Then go wait in the car. This room is for people who need to see the doctor."

"I could stand to have my blood pressure checked. It goes up when I'm around bossy people."

She smiled. It rearranged her features but not in the most flattering way. "How come a nice Chinese boy like yourself is all the way out here in this lonely place?"

"I told you, I'm a driver."

"No, you're not a driver."

"Is that so?"

"Your left arm isn't sunburned. All the drivers stick their left arm out the window on long trips. You're a cop of some sort. He is, too. I can always tell."

"Maybe I'm a Japanese driver. Right-side drive."

She glanced at my right arm. "No sale."

"In that case, maybe you can tell me why I'm here. The old man says that there was a plane crash nearby."

"News to me. We had two motorcycles collide on the main highway near here a few days ago. It was a big mess. Last year in January a truck ran off the road during an ice storm. No one could get to it for weeks. You talking something recent?"

"Forty, forty-five years ago."

"Forty-five years, and you're only now getting to it? You must drive extra slow."

"How come a smart woman like you is stuck in a lonely place like this?"

"The doctor needs a nurse to run his clinic. There isn't much else around for the people when they get sick. Or lonely. It's usually slow this time of year, but it gets busy in late summer."

I began to wonder what my uncle was doing in the back room. "What sort of people do you get in here?"

"Normal people. Herders with sprains, children with fevers, a few TB cases."

"Gunshots?"

"Not since I've been here. People aren't all that angry, and they know how to handle weapons. The men go out hunting wolves in the mountains once in a while. The worst that happens is one of them slips on the ice and breaks his wrist."

"Nurse!" It was my uncle from somewhere inside the treatment area. I took off in that direction, but the nurse was quicker and blocked my way.

"Sorry, we have rules."

I slipped around her. "So do I."

My uncle's voice came out of one of the rooms again. *"Nurse!"*

I followed the sound down the hall. The first room I passed had two women in it. One of them, sitting up and covering herself with a blanket, looked at me fearfully. The other seemed too sick to care. She raised her head slightly, then fell back. My uncle was in the next room, standing beside a bed on which a man lay, writhing. It was dark—no lights, and a heavy curtain covered the window.

"I think he's been poisoned." My uncle whirled around. "Get the nurse in here. Where the hell is she?"

The man seemed to leap up from the bed. He flailed his arms and bent backward so far I thought he would snap his spine. Then he fell heavily onto the bed again and was still.

"Damn," my uncle said.

"What happened?" The nurse burst into the room. She looked at the man on the bed. "What have you done? Get out!" She put her fingers on the man's neck to check for a pulse.

"Don't bother," my uncle said. He turned to me. "Your fish won't make it home."

The nurse whirled around. "What fish? This patient was perfectly fine. Not a thing wrong with him. Now look. What did you do?"

"Me?" My uncle was calm. "He wanted some water, so I gave him a glass from that pitcher." He pointed. "Who else has been in here?"

"Get into the waiting room and don't leave," said the nurse. "I'm calling the doctor."

"Maybe you'd better call the police," my uncle said.

"I'll handle things." The nurse picked up the water pitcher and dumped the water down the small sink beside the door. "Do as I say."

My uncle motioned for me to come with him. He sat down in the waiting room. I remained standing. "Let's not wait around," I said.

"And do what? Make a run for it? Bad idea. She's not going to call the police."

"How do you know that?"

"Blue Sparrow. Besides, she poured the contents of the pitcher down the sink. The police won't like that. She's calling the doctor right now. Didn't I tell you? The vice minister called his political officer."

"You mentioned a fish."

"Yes, he was waiting here for us. He said he knew where the seal was, and that he'd be more specific once he was sure you'd protect him."

"What was he doing here?"

"Pretty out-of-the-way place. He must have figured it was safe hiding right under their noses."

"Under whose noses?"

"The North Koreans, who else? This is a North Korean clinic. The doctor is North Korean, part of a health agreement Pyongyang has with Ulan Bator. These clinics practice traditional medicine. People like it better than the modern stuff, mostly because they think it works."

"I guess it wasn't as safe as he thought."

"We all make mistakes, though they're usually not as fatal as his was. You think he misjudged all on his own?"

For once I was not just with my uncle, I was way ahead of him. "Someone lured him here. Rat takes the cheese. You think the doctor knew?"

"If he didn't, the nurse seemed to."

"She let you back there. We walked right into it."

"Maybe. Or maybe she meant for me to keep him safe until the doctor showed up, and we figured out some way to get him out of here."

"Didn't he say anything else about the seal?"

My uncle did something I'd never heard him do. He groaned slightly. "It was like a script from a bad movie. He said he knew where the seal was. He started to say something else, then his throat went dry and he pointed at the pitcher of water."

"Why'd she pour out that pitcher right away?"

"You tell me."

"Let's go back and check his things. He must have brought some files with him to make himself more valuable."

"Don't bother. They won't be in the room. He was too nervous. I think he had the feeling he was right on the edge of disaster."

"So which was it, did he think it was safe here, or did he think it wasn't safe?"

My uncle gave that some thought. "Maybe he figured it was safe until he saw something that changed his mind."

It wasn't a bad thought, so I followed it. "What if he saw someone he knew, someone he didn't want to see?"

"Could be. Or maybe something that didn't fit. He got agitated when I walked in, but he relaxed a little when he saw it was me."

"How'd you know he'd be here?"

My uncle shook his head. "Not important."

"Not to you, maybe, but it is to me. It was Madame Fang, wasn't it? She brought him here."

"At the moment, we don't need to worry how he got here. We need to find what he carried with him. If he had files when he showed up on my side of the river, he'll have taken files with him when he swam back. We'll ask the doctor when he arrives."

"The doctor? You said he was North Korean!"

"What is that supposed to mean? You think his heart doesn't beat exactly like yours?"

"I wasn't implying anything. I'm half Korean, you seem to forget."

"No, I don't forget. Sometimes I just don't know where it's hidden. Do you?"

Insanity! No matter where we were, no matter what was going on, the slightest spark could ignite this blaze. "Why are you always irrational on this point? I am who I am. Nothing is hidden."

His lips tightened into a straight line, turned down at each corner. "I won't raise it again."

"Yes you will. You'll keep at it forever and then some. I can't help it if I have a drop of Chinese blood in me. In fact, I'm proud of it."

My uncle looked away. He seemed drained. It was my fault; there was no need to have said that. We sat in the worst sort of silence for a few minutes. It was too much for me, so I broke it. "What now?"

"Nothing to do but wait." My uncle took a piece of wood from his pocket, a small piece of pine, and smoothed it between his fingers. "The doctor is due back in an hour, if the nurse is right."

5

"Good afternoon." A man came in the front door and looked at us with surprise. "Have you checked in with the nurse? I didn't know anyone was waiting. Let me wash up and I'll be right with you. I don't want to shake hands, there's a flu going around." He walked over to my uncle. "I'm Dr. Lim." He was the calmest person I'd ever seen in my life. Just looking at him lowered my blood pressure.

"Whenever you're ready, Doctor." My uncle pointed at the door to the patient rooms. "I think your nurse is in the back. She might have something to discuss with you first. Didn't she call you?"

The doctor's eyebrows went up slightly. "Well, then, why don't I go back and see what she has to say. If you don't mind waiting a bit longer." He smiled at me. "Are you two gentlemen together?"

My uncle nodded. "Yes, this is my friend and colleague. He was kind enough to drive me here. I would have driven myself, but he insisted."

"A good thing, too." The doctor looked closely at my uncle. "I don't think you should be driving. I think your pressure is a little high, and you're prone to fatigue. Nothing to worry about, though you have to watch your diet."

The doctor disappeared through the door.

"She didn't call the doctor." I stood up. "She must have called the cops. Let's get out of here."

"Don't worry, she called him. He already knows what's what."

"He's certainly calm about it, and a liar to boot. What weird courtly ritual were you two acting out?"

"You never saw people being polite to each other before?"

"Yeah, but usually not at a murder scene."

We waited a few minutes, heard voices from the back, and then the doctor came through the door, wearing a white coat. If anything, he looked even calmer than before. He pulled a chair over in front of us and sat down.

"The nurse is pretty sure it wasn't poison," he said. "Based on the symptoms, I'm not ready to say one way or the other. There might have been something in that pitcher besides water, but I doubt it. She admitted to me she shouldn't have dumped the contents down the sink, but there will be a residue and I've locked the pitcher away for safekeeping. It's possible he died from some sort of seizure. There will have to be an autopsy to be certain, and I don't have the right facilities for that. Even if I did, the agreement of my service doesn't call for me to do that sort of thing. It's up to Ulan Bator to make the decision on what to do next. It would help to know if he had a history of seizures. Do either of you know?"

We both shook our heads.

"Well then, let's go on the assumption that something sudden brought it on. Did you say anything to him to get him riled?" The doctor looked at my uncle. "Was he agitated about something?"

My uncle shrugged. "I'd say he was nervous. You knew who he was, of course."

"You mean did I know who his records say he was, or who he was?" The doctor reached back and took a file off the top of the pile. "He gave us the name Naranbaatar. Had a few pieces of identification with him. Said he had a history of knee problems, that this complaint kept him off horses and indoors most of the time, which explained why his complexion was so smooth. All baloney, but I'm not here to question people. He might have told me he had a jet engine up his ass and could fly to the Altai Mountains, wouldn't matter to me. I knew right away he didn't need treatment, that he needed a place to hide, so I hid him."

"You do that often?" It was the natural question I would have asked if this had been my case, in my district, in my country. But this wasn't my territory, even though what had happened in the clinic was distinctly my concern. I backtracked as best I could. "What I mean is, how long had he been here?"

The doctor had been about to parry the first question, but he switched quickly to respond to the second. "About a week. A couple of days ago, there was a motorcycle accident. Two motorcycles coming too fast down the highway. One hit an oil slick and crashed into the second. The motorcycles must have flown twenty meters through the air all tangled up before they came down on each other. One of the riders was caught in the wreckage. The gas tanks caught fire; there wasn't much left of him. The other rider was thrown clear and badly injured but still alive when they brought him in here. He died an hour afterward, nothing I could do. When Naranbaatar saw his face, I thought he might have a heart attack."

"He recognized who it was?" I couldn't help sliding back into interrogation mode. "And you, Doctor, did you also recognize who it was?"

The doctor was unflappable. "No, but I recognized something on the remains of the jacket of the other one when they brought the body in. There was an unusual design sewn into the cuffs. One of the security officers from the North Korean embassy had a jacket like that. He wore it when he came by once in a while to check on us."

"He showed up on a regular basis? How often?"

"Roughly? Three or four times a year. From November through March they don't bother because it's too cold. Without looking at my records, I'd guess late April, June, September, and October were usual."

"But this year the first visit was in May?"

"This year it was still snowing for most of April. What a winter! People said it was the worst in memory. There were dead animals all over the place, frozen stiff. Once the thaw set in, it was a health hazard. Have you ever tried to get rid of several hundred thousand putrefying sheep?"

My uncle wrinkled his nose, but it wasn't at the thought of decaying sheep. He could tell the doctor was avoiding the question. "So this year, May was the first visit? Is that the only thing that caught your attention, that and the sleeve cuffs?"

"The normal security visitor had already stopped by a week before the crash. This second visit was unusual. It was even more unusual because they don't often travel in pairs this far out in the countryside. I think Naranbaatar recognized the one who was brought in alive. That was strange because, as I said, this wasn't someone I knew."

"You know all the security people?"

"All the regulars who are assigned to the embassy, yes."

"Your patient, Mr. Naranbaatar, didn't say anything once he got over his initial shock?"

"No, he just stopped talking to us and took to his bed."

"The nurse said there was nothing wrong with him when he checked in."

"That's right, there wasn't."

I lowered the boom. "You knew who he really was, didn't you, Doctor?"

The doctor looked at me and then turned casually to my uncle. "I'm ready to examine you now. The nurse said you have back problems. Shall we take a look?"

"Why not?" My uncle stood up stiffly. "I'll follow you, Doctor."

A thought occurred to me. "Have they come out yet to investigate the accident?"

For the first time, the doctor showed a hint of annoyance. "The Mongolian police? Of course."

"No, I mean the embassy. I'd be suspicious if I were them."

"Are you? My nurse told me she thought you were both police of some sort."

"Your nurse is very perceptive, Doctor." My uncle walked slowly to the hallway door. "Yet she doesn't have X-ray vision."

The doctor smiled. "In that case, take off your outer garments and put on the gown hanging on the back of the door, Inspector. I'll be in shortly."

As my uncle disappeared through the doorway, the doctor unlocked a glass cabinet in the corner of the room. I strolled over to check what he was retrieving.

"You still haven't answered my question, Doctor. Did the embassy come out to investigate yet?"

"How could they? These weren't members of the embassy staff; they may not have even had proper entry papers."

"But you said the first rider was the embassy security officer."

The doctor looked at me coolly. I knew what he was thinking. He was thinking that I was playing a game with him. He hadn't said any such thing.

"Really," he said, "if I had the time, I might enjoy this interrogation. I said I thought I recognized the jacket, that's all."

"There wasn't any identification on the body?"

"Paper? If there was, it was incinerated."

"Tattoos?"

"This isn't a morgue, it's a clinic. The local police bundled up the remains and sent them back to Ulan Bator. You can check with them if you like."

"But you're a curious, observant man. You have a theory about all this, don't you?"

"No, I avoid the world of the hypothesis unless it has to do with the ailments of my patients. That's why I became a doctor."

"You have a dead patient in the back room. Two days ago, he

was half frightened to death by something he saw, and a few hours ago, something he didn't see took care of the second half. It wasn't a seizure, and you know it or you wouldn't have stayed out here talking to me. I'm going to ask you one more question. You don't have to answer; I don't have any authority, and you don't have any obligation. Who were those two motorcyclists?"

He almost decided not to answer, I could tell from he way his breathing changed, but then he sat back in his chair. "I only know what I hear. They were part of a team sent to keep an eye on the transit camp of North Korean refugees. It's not far from here. Pyongyang tried to complain about the camp when it was first set up, but the Mongolians told them it was on their territory and their own sovereign business. The North backed off, but still does its best, very low-key, to keep tabs on what is going on, who is there, who leaves, and who stays. It's all relatively smooth. Nothing like on your border."

"My border?"

The doctor took a small bottle from a shelf, then locked the cabinet. "You're not Mongolian. You aren't Korean, not all Korean, anyway. I don't need X-ray vision to tell me that."

6

"That does it." The doctor washed his hands in the sink. "You can put your shirt and trousers back on, Inspector. When you're dressed, take a seat over there and we'll talk about what you need to do for your back." He pointed to a desk in the corner. "Your colleague is welcome to join us."

My uncle sat up from the examination table. "That nurse of yours is very efficient. I assume she called someone in the police agency in Ulan Bator."

"I think your back might be a problem because you are prone

to sticking your nose into other people's business," the doctor said evenly.

"Better there than up someone's backside." My uncle retrieved his trousers and his shirt. "Let's not get at each other's throats, Doctor."

"She didn't talk to the police," I broke in before they could begin their courtly dance again. "She talked to some fellow from the Special Service. His name is Bat something."

"Batbayaar." The doctor didn't look up from the form he was signing. "The man's name is Batbayaar. You're going to ask how I know him, so I'll tell you and spare everyone the trouble of a game of hide-and-seek. The Chinese prime minister is about to visit Ulan Bator, as you no doubt know. Every time an important foreign visit is planned, the Special Service sends a notice to police in the outlying areas to be alert for unusual events, shady figures lurking on street corners, that sort of thing. Our local police pass these alerts on to us. The motorcycle accident must have caught Batbayaar's attention. I say that because he sent an urgent follow-up request for us to be on the watch for strangers seeking medical attention or people posing as family members or acquaintances inquiring after accident victims. I couldn't tell you what piqued his interest, though I assume he keeps tabs on the undeclared North Korean teams." The doctor put down his pen and looked casually at me. "As he does any undeclared Chinese operations."

"How do you know your nurse didn't tell Batbayaar about the suddenly departed Naranbaatar when he first showed up?" My uncle slipped a little steel into his voice. "For that matter, how do you know she didn't tell the North Koreans?"

"Because I didn't." The nurse stepped into the room. She gave my uncle a nasty look. "I wouldn't do such a thing. The doctor insists on confidentiality for the patients. If there were some reason to breach that, it would be up to the doctor to decide. It's not a decision I would take on my own."

"Of course not," said my uncle. "Certainly not for fifty dollars."

This caused some bad feelings, but there wasn't much the nurse could do other than to glower and stalk out of the room.

"Doctor, you took something from the cabinet before we walked in here. Would you mind showing it to me?" I planted myself next to the desk.

"You're a little out of area to be throwing your weight around like this, I'd think. You realize, of course, I don't have to show you anything. I've told you more than enough already, and then only because I have respect for the Inspector here." He turned to my uncle. "These are some pills I want you to take." He held up the small bottle he had removed from the locked cabinet. "Once a day at bedtime. Take them until they're all gone. I'm sure they'll do you some good."

"What are they, if I may ask?"

"Just a traditional herbal mixture."

"Very good of you, Doctor." My uncle stood up, took the pills, and looked the doctor in the eye. "I must say, I admire your work out here. Perhaps we'll see each other again."

"Perhaps." The doctor walked us to the front door. "Drive carefully on your way back. Don't hesitate to call me if you need anything else. Good-bye."

When we were in the car and on the main road again, I told my uncle to look at the bottle the doctor had given him. "It's not just a regular old herbal concoction," I said. "He had it under lock and key."

"Is that so? I wonder if it belonged to poor Mr. Naranbaatar."

"You were awfully chummy with the doctor. Old friend of yours?"

"Never saw the man in my life. Something wrong with countrymen being polite?"

Neither of us spoke for the next several monotonous miles. "You're sure Naranbaatar was who you think he was?"

"Give me some credit now and then. I'm sure. A little older and thinner, but he had an unusual way of squinting his eyes whenever he got excited. He still had it."

"I have a bad feeling about this. For one thing, how do I explain to Beijing that he died in my presence?"

"He didn't die in your presence, he died in my presence."

"Even worse."

"You won't get a medal, I suppose. At least you kept him from falling back into the hands of the North Koreans. That's something."

"Someone is going to say I killed him."

"You? Why would you do something like that? You don't have any motive." My uncle adjusted his seat belt. "Do you?"

I hit the next rut in the road with considerable precision.

"No, I thought not. On the other hand, your friends might say I had a reason to do away with him. If they think I still work for Pyongyang, they could reason that I was sent here to make sure he never made it home."

"Except Pyongyang didn't send you here, Beijing did."

"We both know they'll never admit that."

"What about the seal? He must have had it someplace he thought was safe. What about that Kazakh woman in the bar? How would she know where he put it?"

"Best way to find out is to ask. We'll go back to that Irish bar. She seems to know how to drink."

"You really think he died of natural causes?" I thought about it. "I don't know if I trust that doctor. I certainly don't trust that nurse." I thought about it some more. "So much for not using seat belts," I mused.

My uncle gave me a quizzical look. "All this open sky is making you cryptic. You want me to drive?"

"No, I don't."

"If we go by that statue of Chinggis Khan again, let's stop. It says in the booklet in the hotel that you can climb up inside it and look into the 'vastness of history.' Who writes things like that?"

"I have a hypothesis for you about that motorcycle team."

"Did you hear what I said about the statue?"

"Yes, I heard, but I still have a hypothesis. While you were in the examination room, the doctor and I had a brief conversation."

"You didn't rough him up, I hope."

"No, not even figuratively. I was very polite."

"He dodged."

"Some. Finally he told me that the two riders who died were part of a team to watch a refugee transit camp."

"He said that? I thought doctors never lied. They were obviously sent out to run down rumors that the redefector was hiding out in the countryside around here. One of them must have been someone who knew what Naranbaatar looked like, someone who could recognize him. That's what caused Naranbaatar to go into shock; he knew Pyongyang had located him, and he figured he was trapped. When we showed up, he had a momentary surge of hope."

"Surges of hope don't kill people," I said, and that ended the conversation for the next fifty kilometers, when a lone motorcycle roared past us going toward Ondorkhaan at a high rate of speed.

"In a great hurry," my uncle observed, "to get nowhere special."

Halfway to Ulan Bator we passed a truck pulling a heavy bulldozer on a trailer.

"There's some paper and a pen in my bag on the floor in the back. Get it out and write the note to Miss Du. It will give you something to do for the next three hours."

"I can't." My uncle shook his head. "Writing makes me carsick. Don't worry, we'll do it tonight."

Chapter Seven

The room was not unoccupied when we got back to our hotel. It hadn't been cleaned either, but the main problem was Batbayaar, lying on my uncle's bed. His head was propped up with several pillows, and he was breezily going through the brochure on local nightlife.

"I never realized how exciting it was around here," he said. "Plenty to do." He looked over at us. "Your trip was good? I wish you wouldn't launch out of town without informing me. It burns a hell of a lot of gasoline."

"We haven't met." My uncle put out his hand. "You must be Batbayaar. I figured you'd come by at some point. Might be a good idea if we went out for a drink and a chat. Plenty of good places to go. A nice Irish bar around the corner not far from here, maybe you know it."

Batbayaar stood up and shook hands. "A pleasure, Inspector. We have things to discuss." He turned to me. "You must have business to attend to, threads to tidy up, that sort of thing. Try not to lose Bazar this time. You never lived on a farm, did you?"

"No, why?"

"You don't know the right way to put on a harness. That's got some people mad at you, and I don't want the disagreement to go any further, not around here anyway. If you have scores to settle, take them across the border." He smiled, though it was that grim sort of smile, like a mounted archer reaching for his best barbed arrowhead. "Don't test me on this, and don't bother waving your passport in front of me. I'm not impressed."

"I can't wave it at you. You never gave it back."

"Oh?" Batbayaar reached into his breast pocket and came out with my passport. He threw it on the bed. "Must have slipped my mind. You have twenty-four hours to leave. That's already been entered in the system. I'd suggest you not think about an overland route. You definitely don't want to go through Ondorkhaan again. Such a long ride with so many empty stretches."

"The airport?"

"Exactly what I had in mind."

"What if I said I had a few things I needed to do and it would take me a couple of extra days to do them."

Batbayaar gave me a doleful look. "Tell it to the wind."

"For the record, are you forcibly deporting me? Declaring me persona non grata? Only hours before my prime minister arrives? How do you think that will look?"

"I don't throw people out of the country, if that's what you mean. I'm inviting you to catch a plane. Actually, I don't give a camel's ass how it looks. Image is not at the top of my list of concerns at the moment."

"We'll see about that. All right, twenty-four hours." I looked at my watch. "I've got plenty to wrap up before that, and I'm not going to duckwalk just so Bazar can keep up. If he wants to follow me, then he'll have to pick up the pace. Oh, and say good-bye to Tuya, will you?"

"If I see her before you leave, I will. She's on assignment. Hell of an asset."

My uncle was waiting impatiently at the door. "Pity," he said. "Such a lovely country. I was just getting used to it. I even thought of going for a few throat-singing lessons. Maybe on the next trip."

As they walked down the hall together, I heard my uncle say, "You shouldn't be too hard on him; he's only part Chinese."

2

Getting two tickets on the next day's afternoon flight wasn't easy, but Batbayaar must have had a lot of pull because after the reservation clerk put us on hold for a long while, she came back with the news that a couple from Australia had canceled and we could have their seats. At the airport, my uncle waltzed through the immigration check; I was held at the desk for nearly forty minutes while they examined my passport, made several phone calls, and stood around uncomfortably waiting for instructions.

"I've got to board the plane," I said at last, pointing down the passageway to the departure gates. "The whole idea is for you to kick me out, not hold me here. You're not sticking to the script."

"Try not to interrupt," said one of the immigration officials. "We can't stamp your passport until the final checks come through, and nothing is moving. Relax, we'll get you out of here one way or another."

"I work with your Special Service. Does the name Batbayaar mean anything to you?" It obviously didn't. "What about Tuya?" One man smiled to himself. He was my target. "You know her?"

"She came through my line once. No one ever handed me a passport like that before, I'll tell you that. You a friend of hers?"

"You might say."

"OK." He stamped the passport. "Don't show your nose around here again. That's friendly advice."

My uncle was in the passenger waiting area, thumbing through a small book. He held it up for me to see. "Instructions on how to build a ger," he said. "Very interesting. Maybe I'll try when I get home."

"You going home?"

"Sooner or later. I might have to wait a few centuries for your little confrontation with the North Koreans to blow over."

"Batbayaar told you."

"He held back a lot of detail, but he said that after Bazar told him about the man with the bad hand he got so mad that he thought of wrapping you in a blanket and letting horses loose to trample it. Fortunately for you, some woman named Tuya changed his mind."

"He was angry."

"Furious."

"I thought he didn't like North Korean squads roaming around his kingdom annoying people."

"He's not fond of them, no. Organized intrusions on his territory rub him the wrong way, but he doesn't have anything against North Koreans as individuals. He prefers them to Chinese, as a matter of fact."

"I'm not reacting, if you'll notice."

"North Koreans and Mongolians are a lot alike, though since they're deemed to be underfoot, the illustrious dragon throne in Beijing doesn't notice such things. A shared danger of being squashed by the Middle Kingdom tends to bring out shared traits. We had an interesting chat about that, that and a few other things."

"Should I ask about what? Or do I just dismiss it as the mice squeaking among themselves?"

"He had a few observations about that Kazakh woman in the Irish bar."

"Like maybe she is a congenital liar and a drunk."

"No, actually she is a PhD in mining engineering, a devotee of the English operettas of Gilbert and Sullivan, and a successful collector of weak-willed men."

"Then it's lucky we got out of there when we did. I'm going to the little bookstore to pick something up, a memento from the trip. That book on how to build a ger looks useful, since my house probably won't be there anymore. I wonder if Miss Du's cousin took your tools or if he just smashed them along with everything else."

"You worry too much. Go buy a postcard or something."

I was in the bookstore, browsing through the picture books, when someone tapped me on the shoulder. I tensed.

"*Calmati*, Inspector. It's only me."

"I don't know Italian," I said, "but I hope that means we're going to run away together to a cabin in the Swiss Alps." I caught myself. "No, not the Swiss Alps. The Italian Alps. Can you cook? Never mind. Food is irrelevant." I turned around.

"Very nice to see you," Tuya said. "I hurried over here to say good-bye. My boss was angry when he found out about what happened in that shed. You OK?" She was standing naturally, all limbs properly arrayed.

"Fine," I said. "Too bad I have to leave in a hurry like this. I was hoping we'd have a chance for a cup of salty tea or something." I wondered if I could fold her up and put her in my carry-on bag.

"I can't stay; I have to get back to the office. Nice thought about the cabin, though. Maybe I'll call you sometime. Or you can call me."

"I don't have your number."

She put something in my hand. "Now you do." She pulled a book from the shelf. "This one is nice. It will help you remember."

"You going to roll out of here?"

She smiled. "I think I'll walk. Good-bye, Major. Take care of yourself."

When I got back to where my uncle was sitting, he was sketching on a small piece of paper. "It's a collapsible bookshelf for a ger. See how broadening travel is?"

"We're boarding," I said. "You want the window seat?"

3

My uncle was tense and distracted until we took off. "These things . . ." He indicated the airplane. "Very ungainly looking until they leave the ground. I hope they've done the math right on flight."

"Put your seat back and relax. There's nothing we can do about it now." I figured I'd make conversation for a few minutes until the sound of the engines calmed him down. "What was the story about that Kazakh woman's missing mother?"

"A tale she tells strangers on whom she has set her sights, according to Batbayaar. She got that locket she pulls from her blouse from an itinerant vendor near a place called Tsambagarav Mountain where her people live. Maybe it's in that book you bought at the airport. They train eagles, which goes a way toward explaining the looks those men gave us."

"We're supposed to think she didn't know anything about the seal?"

"That's what I wondered. Batbayaar's view was that she probably did know something. She and the doctor's nurse are related in some obscure and distant way. They both work, off and on, for the South Koreans, who, as I told you, are nosing around for investment opportunities."

"What? Batbayaar told me she was part of a Kazakh intelligence team."

"That, too. And, for a while, they were apparently both working for someone Batbayaar could identify only as 'K.'" My uncle closed the window shade. "You wouldn't know who that was, I don't suppose."

"Are we still in Mongolian airspace?"

"Funny, that's the same question Lin Piao asked."

"Never mind Lin Piao. What about that bottle of pills the doctor gave you? Have you opened them yet?"

"They're in my suitcase."

"They're where? Your suitcase went into checked baggage. We'll probably never see it or that bottle of pills again. I told you, there was something funny about them."

"Maybe one or two." He looked around. "Where are the exits on this plane? Is there one up front? I don't like the thought of having to crawl backward in an emergency."

"We're not going to fall out of the sky, don't worry." I thought it over. "So, Mr. Naranbaatar didn't die of natural causes after all."

"Of course not."

"The nurse?"

"You can speculate; I'm not going to bother at this altitude. What's clear is that your predecessor didn't have much luck under the cloak of Naranbaatar, that he had a lot of people hoping he would drop dead, and that there was no way he was going to get home."

"You don't care who killed him?"

"There were a hundred arrows in the air at the same time, all aimed at him. It really doesn't make much difference which one actually hit a vital spot."

"Maybe not, but maybe if we knew it would tell us where the seal is. We still have to worry about the seal, you know. You said Batbayaar told you the nurse and the Kazakh woman are related. The Kazakh woman said she knew something about the seal. I'd say she knew because the nurse told her."

"Reasonable, but the South Koreans could have mentioned it to them. Seoul seems to have had some inkling about the seal. There is probably a need to put it under a microscope to see if it is really counterfeit and, if so, who dropped it into their carry-bag on the way to Ulan Bator last month."

"The list can't be infinitely long. Who had motive? Who had expertise to forge a government seal? Who had access to the prime minister's official baggage?"

"I know a fish who had the answer to all of those questions."

"But he's dead."

"As a doorknob." My uncle raised his window shade again and looked out at the featureless landscape below. "Next time we're here I want to go to that statue we passed, and then to the mountains out west." He pulled a postcard from his pocket and waved it at me. "A lot of interesting trees there."

PART III

Chapter One

My first day back at work, no one would look me in the eye. Li Bo-ting seemed especially out of sorts. He didn't come to my office to say hello. There wasn't even the standard short memo from him on the desk welcoming me back. When I called him to ask for the past several days of daily logs in order to catch up on what had happened in my absence, Li paused and then said they weren't available.

"Not available? Where are they, getting their nails done? I'd like to see the logs, Bo-ting, now. If they're not up-to-date, don't worry. Just bring them over. And tell Mrs. Zhou to bring in some tea." Mrs. Zhou responded more favorably to Li Bo-ting than she did to me.

There was another pause, this one definitely more uncomfortable than the first.

"Li? You there?"

"I wouldn't mind getting something to eat. Why don't we meet in five minutes out front?"

As a rule, there's no sense barking at people, least of all my deputy. "Fine, I'll look at the logs when I get back. Where is the new man, Jang, by the way? He wasn't at the duty desk when I came in. He's supposed to be here by 7:00 A.M., or is he doing his nails, too?"

"See you in five minutes."

Li was always efficient, and sometimes brisk, but he was rarely this abrupt. Whatever was bothering him wasn't trivial. I thought longingly of Tuya's ability to get out of tight spots. The phone rang, and for an instant I hoped by some miracle it might be Tuya.

"Go ahead," I said.

"You made it back, I see." The sultry voice of Madame Fang reached out and caressed my right ear.

"I did, and I'm glad to be home." I would have been less surprised if it *had* been Tuya. "Can I be of service?"

"What did you have in mind?"

I looked up at the clock behind my desk, with the junction box and all its special connections. This was a conversation I didn't need recorded. "I'm about to leave for an appointment. If there's something you need to discuss, maybe we can meet later today. You want to come in here?" I knew she wouldn't.

Throaty laughter over a phone is never appealing, but hers managed to break the mold.

"In that case," I said, "let's meet somewhere else."

"Two o'clock," she purred. "Should I bet that you won't be on time?"

"Don't bother." I hung up.

It would have been smarter to tell her to get lost. Meeting Fang Mei-lin at Gao's place, which was the only thing she could have meant by asking about making a "bet," was a very bad idea no matter which way I looked at it. What was she doing calling me, anyway? Her links were with my uncle. If she wanted to see him, why didn't she go over and knock on his door? She'd been there before.

Li Bo-ting threw away a cigarette as I came out the door. He rarely smoked, so if I hadn't already known he was nervous, the cigarette would have told me.

"Not good for you, Bo-ting."

"Better than a bullet in the back of the head," he said, but he didn't laugh. "Come on, just walk for a bit."

I figured he wanted a chance to think, so I fell in step beside him without another word. After fifteen minutes of turning into alleys, doubling back, and ducking into rear entrances and coming out the side doors of old buildings, I thought it was fair to say something.

"Are we there yet?"

"You'll see. Getting tired?"

"I'm right beside you, aren't I?" Only I wasn't. He had vanished. I stopped to look around. There was a low whistle, and as I turned to locate the source, I saw Li's head barely above ground level.

"Stay with me," he hissed. He had gone down a stairway into what looked to be the basement entrance of an abandoned warehouse. The door was old, but judging from the way it glinted in the sun, the lock had been replaced not long ago. Li found a key in his pocket and motioned me to go ahead of him.

2

When I came to, it occurred to me that the Mongolian way of putting someone down had its advantages. My head was throbbing so hard that my jaw ached, but after I opened my eyes I saw I was much better off than Li. He was lying next to me, with a bullet hole in the back of his head.

"Too bad about your deputy."

The voice rang a bell, but a bell wasn't what I wanted to hear at the moment. I closed my eyes again and thought about all of my creditors that would never get paid. "Never smart, murdering an MSS officer," I said quietly in order not to give my headache more noise to feed on.

"If killing one is bad, imagine what sort of trouble two will cause."

That brought forth a low chuckle to my left. To my right, a throat was cleared. If I had to guess, I'd guess there were three of them, but I didn't really care. It wouldn't take three of them to pull the trigger if that's what they wanted to do next.

"Untie the bastard." The bell had turned into a gong parading back and forth across the room, reverberating in my skull.

"What?"

"I said, untie the bastard. How come I have to repeat things for you all the time? Are you deaf? Maybe we should cut off an ear and show it to the doc."

"I heard you fine. You said untie him. I just don't think it's such a good idea, that's all. But you're the boss."

"You bet your tattooed ass I'm the boss. And I'm not kidding about your ear."

Out of the haze that was clearing from my vision, I recognized the man standing over me as a member of the noodle shop quartet. "Hey, Wong," I said feebly. "Long time no see."

"Fuck your mother," he said. He pulled a knife from his belt and cut the terrycloth ties around my wrists. "Get up."

"You mind if my head stops spinning first?"

He kicked my leg. "Yeah, I mind. Get up."

"Easy." The voice across the room stopped driving marlinspikes into my brain. "We'll deal with him later. Let's move out. I don't like it here. Too confining. Reminds me of prison. Go on, help him up."

Wong grabbed my collar and yanked me to a standing position. "Don't even move sideways without my say-so."

The sudden move set back my vision, but I could make out what was at my feet. I looked down at Li. "What about him?"

"It never fails—he's a talker, I should have known. Put a sock in his mouth."

3

I was in the backseat of a car, trying to make the dizziness go away and not to vomit. There was ringing in my right ear, but the voice beside me was crystal clear.

"I'm on retainer, you might say. I do some work; I withdraw some funds. It's all on the up-and-up."

"Sort of like a lawyer," I said, trying to be conversational.

"Yeah, you might say just like a lawyer."

"Not a lot of lawyers threaten noodle shop owners with bodily harm." What the hell, I wasn't in polite company. No reason to be polite.

"Oh, you'd be surprised. They don't eat noodles with their golden chopsticks, but they know that lots of other people do. There's money in noodles if you know what you're doing." My memory clicked in, and so did the voice.

"You are the noodle racket king, I take it?"

"Take it any way you like."

The driver laughed.

The dizziness cleared. I found myself wedged between Wong and the noodle king. When we emerged from the garage into the light, I could see that the area around Wong's eyes was scarred from the boiling water the cook had thrown in his face. Up front, I saw two hands on the steering wheel. They must have ditched the man the cook had cleavered.

"You'll notice you're not handcuffed." The noodle king had a way of sounding like he was granting big favors.

"I noticed."

"Not gagged, either."

I nodded, but kept my mouth shut.

"We want to drive out of town without anyone noticing; here we are, four businessmen on an outing. It would look odd with three of us in back, it might attract attention of a traffic cop, so Wong here is going to move up in front. First, he has a present for you."

Before I could react, Wong jabbed a needle in my thigh. I watched him press the plunger, and then I wasn't here, there, or anywhere. My vision was still good, and my hearing was fine, but I couldn't make my muscles pay attention. It wasn't paralysis. It was as if all will to move or speak had disappeared. My body felt like air.

Wong put his face in front of mine and looked into my eyes. "OK, it's good for two hours." He opened the door, climbed out of the car, then reached in to drag me over to where he had been sitting. "Comfortable?" He put my hands in my lap. I could only look straight ahead. When my head sagged, the noodle king propped it up again.

"What about the neck? They didn't fix the neck thing yet, did they?"

Wong slammed the door, slid into the front seat, and we drove out of a fenced lot filled with shipping containers onto the street. The driver took a couple of quick turns; from the look of things I had the feeling he was heading for Aidan Road.

"We call it our velvet rope," the noodle king said helpfully, like he was a docent and I was a paying visitor at his Museum of Triad Technology. "That medication doesn't leave any marks. It's better than terrycloth even, nothing to suggest a corpse has been bound and gagged. We tried tape, but tape is the worst; there's always some sort of residue. No one wants residue."

A little residue never hurt, I thought.

The driver looked at me in his rearview mirror. It was Miss Du's chauffeur. He smirked. I would have smirked back if my mouth had been attached.

The noodle king kept up his end of the monologue. "Of course, getting the dosage right is tricky. You should have seen the first one. He drooled the whole way, no control over his functions at all. The chemist was mortified when we told him. You OK?" He poked me in the neck. Suddenly he screamed, "Pull over!"

The driver swerved and braked hard; Wong twisted around with concern on his face. "What?"

"You didn't fasten his seat belt. Look at him!"

I'd been thrown against the rear window and then forward onto the back of the driver's headrest before sliding off the seat.

Since I couldn't move, I figured I might spend my last moments staring at the floor mat.

With some difficulty, the noodle king lifted me back into a sitting position. "Where the hell is the buckle to his seat belt?" He fumbled around before finding it tucked behind the seat cushion. "Doesn't anybody use these things?"

Wong paled slightly. "You sure you want to buckle that?"

"Don't be an idiot. They wouldn't touch this car. They need us more than we need them." There was a loud click. After a brief eternity, Wong exhaled.

"Let's move." The driver sounded impatient. "I have to be back in Yanji by four o'clock."

"Fancy that," said Wong. "Can't keep the lady waiting."

"Shut up, the both of you. Wong, it's not working; when does he get sleepy? He's still awake." The noodle king waved his hand in front of my eyes.

"Relax, it takes twenty minutes, more or less. By the time we're on the highway, he'll be out."

Wong hadn't impressed me as the scientific type, but for some reason he seemed to hold the group's medical expertise.

The driver turned on Juzi Street, which goes out of the city to the highway. Miraculously, my sense of direction was still working. If we went left when we reached the highway, we'd be heading toward Changchun. A right turn would point us toward the town of Tumen, on the river. Now would be a perfect time to jump out of the car, but I knew it was an idle thought. I had no will to move a muscle. Worse, I could feel myself getting drowsy. Wong seemed to know his stuff. Just before I fell sideways against the door and into a deep sleep, I felt a right turn. Tumen! One thought shone like a neon sign against the darkness swallowing my consciousness: This is my chance to give Handout his walking papers.

4

A train whistle followed by the rumble of a locomotive pulled me back from wherever I had been. I was handcuffed to a metal bar bolted to the bare brick wall of a warehouse. On first glance, I was alone, but there were enough stacks of shipping crates piled five or six high that I couldn't be sure if someone was hidden from view. The handcuffs were tight. They had already left marks on my wrists. A hopeful sign. The noodle king had said they were fussy about leaving marks on a corpse, so maybe I wasn't corpse material.

From the far end of the room I heard voices. Two men appeared, the noodle king and someone I recognized from the WANTED photographs we kept on the wall near the duty desk in the office.

"Well, look who we have here!" the second man said. "A very big fish in our lovely net." He moved closer and stared at my wrists. "Get those cuffs off him, they're leaving marks."

"Too late," I said. "I have delicate skin, easily marred."

"Tough. In that case, we'll have to boil it in a vat of noodles until it slides off the bones." The noodle king unlocked the handcuffs. "Wong knows better than to do something like this. I'll talk to him, Doc."

"Yes, talk to him." The second man had a scar that went from his right eye down his cheek and disappeared under his jaw. His right ear was mangled, though you could barely see it because he wore his hair long, over to the right. "When you're done talking, get rid of him."

"Of Wong?"

"I heard what I said, and I only got one ear. What's your problem? I'll say it once more, and this time pay attention. Cut off his head or something." He turned to me. "Any objections from the MSS contingent here?"

This second man went by a long list of aliases. The last time I'd looked at the file, he had taken to using "Mike," or on occasion "Dr. Mike." Apparently, he'd picked these up during his years in America running a prostitution ring supplemented by illegal snake-fish sales to fancy restaurants in New York City. MSS Headquarters had sent messages wrapped in large-denomination dollar bills encouraging him to stay in the States, but he got greedy and ended up being deported around ten years ago. His original territory had been in the south of China, but too many new gangs had established themselves there during his absence, so when he returned, he decided to move his operations to the northeast. He put out the word that he wanted "elbow room." It didn't take him long to regret that decision. People in the northeast weren't devious enough for his taste. He was used to southerners, who smoothly said one thing and did another.

At the moment, he was standing half a meter away from me, blinking slowly as he examined my face. No one in MSS had been this close to Mike in years. Several operations had been launched to capture him, but he was good at disappearing at the last minute. Before Madame Fang had appeared on my doorstep, I'd been reading reports that he was moving in and around Tumen, scouting new opportunities. I'd been doubtful, but the source, whoever it was, obviously deserved a bonus. If I ever got out of here, I'd pay it from my own pocket.

"Mike," I said conversationally, "I've been meaning to send you a note about the rules in my sector. There's nothing too onerous. We can go over them at some point, whenever it's convenient. I take it now isn't good."

"Yeah." Mike smiled, which turned his scar into a coiled snake. "I've been waiting to hear from you. Meantime, I'm picking up rumors about a hard strike you been organizing against me and my associates."

"Really? Who told you that?"

"Your boy Bo-ting, for one." He turned to the noodle king. "He didn't know?"

The noodle king shrugged uneasily. "It didn't seem like a good idea to tell him. I thought about it, but there were complications."

"Complications." Mike frowned and ran a finger along the length of his scar. "You were supposed to make sure he was on board. Now I see him in handcuffs."

"Yeah." I held up my wrists to underline the point. "They left marks."

"Shut up." Mike suddenly raised his voice. He pulled a nasty-looking pistol from his belt. The file had said he had serious problems with anger management, something that wasn't working in my favor at that moment. I could see the muzzle of the pistol was a few millimeters from my nose.

"It's OK," I said. "I'm not the one that double-crossed you."

"Double-cross?" Mike swung the pistol away from me until it rested under the chin of the noodle king. "Meaning what?"

"Nothing, he's blowing smoke. I wouldn't double-cross you; you think I'm crazy? Wong might do something like that, but not me. Not me."

Another train whistle sounded, this time with considerable insistence. Wong came running in, as if on cue. ""Come on, we've got to get him boxed up and on the train." He pulled up short when he saw our friendly tableau. "Hi, Mike. Didn't know you'd be here."

Real fast, Wong's cheek started to twitch.

"Why wouldn't I be here? This is my territory, isn't it? You work for me, don't you? How come you're putting him in a box? I thought he was on the payroll."

"Complications." Wong looked at the ground.

"You were planning on boxing him up? Killing an MSS chief, I'd say that's complications. Killing an MSS chief is bad, but doing it without my say-so? Real bad." He hit Wong across the face with the pistol. "Who's paying you?"

Wong put his hand to his nose, which was bleeding, and took a step back. "Calm down, would you? No one is paying me. No one but you, I mean. We had to move fast, that's all. This hard strike thing was about to get serious, and our friends across the river—"

"I don't have any friends across the fucking river!" Mike was shouting. "Do you?" All at once, his voice dropped to a hoarse whisper. "That's interesting, Wong, if you have friends across the river. Me? I'm sick and tired of dealing with those Koreans." He took out a handkerchief and handed it to Wong before continuing. "They're trouble all the time, always gaming which way to move. Did they pay you to bundle this guy up and send him over to them? Or did they ask for his uncle, and you got the wrong goods?" He took a step back. "You got trouble with your cheek? It's dancing across your face."

The noodle king had moved to put a big packing crate between him and the pistol. "Take a pill or something, would you, Mike? Think calm thoughts. We'll go and get a good dinner afterward. Maybe a sauna and a rubdown."

"A good dinner? In this town? You kidding me? The skin on the dumplings around here is thick enough to choke a pig." He jerked the pistol back in my direction. "I'm saying he doesn't go across the river. Anyone object?"

The noodle king looked at Wong. Wong looked at me and then folded over as if he had been shot, which the near-simultaneous sound of a gunshot strongly suggested was the case. Mike disappeared without saying good-bye. The noodle king stood still, sort of like a statue about to wet its pants.

"I say we all take a little train ride to Rason." Uncle O stood up from behind a crate, holding a small pistol with a mother-of-pearl handle.

"Uncle, what a pleasant surprise. How did you come by such a cute gun?"

"Mei-lin gave it to me as a present last night. It was our twenty-fifth anniversary."

"You're married?" I nearly choked on the image.

As he turned Wong over with his foot, my uncle laughed in a

charming manner, completely unlike anything I'd ever seen from him. "No, twenty-five years since our first encounter. This man, incidentally, is completely dead. I thought I was aiming at his shoulder." He pointed to the noodle king, who was still frozen in place. "What about that one? Let's cuff him, to hell with the marks."

Chapter Two

We were in a very large wooden shipping container, a cube maybe two and a half meters on a side, resting on a flatcar coupled to a freight train bound for Rason, or so my uncle said after checking with the freight office minutes before the train pulled out of the station. After crossing over the Tumen River bridge into North Korea, the tracks paralleled the river most of the way. Since there were four of us in the container—my uncle, myself, the noodle king, and Wong's body—it was not the most pleasant train ride I'd taken, but my uncle, surprisingly, seemed not to mind. The noodle king, however, seemed uncomfortable, though whether because he was sitting close to Wong's body or because he was bound and gagged was hard to tell.

"Too bad we don't have a better view," my uncle said, looking through a small crack in the boards of the container. He moved away and sat near a cloth bag he'd brought with him. "I'm sorry about Lieutenant Li."

"How do you know about Li?"

"You were supposed to meet Mei-lin at Gao's. You didn't show up, so she phoned me. I called your office, and the Shanghai spider said you'd both gone out and hadn't returned."

"We went for a walk."

"Sure, I do it all the time, walking in geometric patterns, doubling back, disappearing into buildings and coming out another entrance. It's probably the healthiest way to walk, except in Li's case, it didn't turn out that way. I chatted with the people Li was trying to shake. They told me where they'd lost him, and from there it wasn't hard to find the place. You'd just left, but Li was still there, dead."

"Yeah, well, as of this moment that Mike character has become target number one for the hard strike. I'm not letting him out of my sights next time."

"Mike had nothing to do with what happened to Li. He'll probably lose his temper again when he finds out. That was Wong and the big noodle over there." The noodle king was trying to say something, so I ripped the tape off his mouth.

"*Yow!*" was the first thing that came out. "Easy! That tape, take off that tape easy, would you?"

"It's special," I said. "It leaves marks, sorry. We'll see about putting your lips back on when we get to where we're going."

"Listen, I didn't have anything to do with Li, understand? That was totally Wong. Maybe I push people around, but I don't go in for killing them. Wong acts—" He stopped and looked at the body. "Wong acted on impulse. It was always a bad trait."

"What did Mike mean about your not telling me? What's the secret?"

"I don't know. Mike is funny sometimes."

"You want to talk about funny? My uncle aimed at Wong's shoulder and blew his brains out by mistake. Don't press me. These train tracks are in terrible shape; his aim is liable to be even worse here. Take another stab at answering my question, why don't you?"

"Sure, have it your way. Mike wanted us to bring you on board, that's all there was to it. He had your deputy Li Bo-ting on the payroll part-time, but that wasn't enough. Deputies don't count, according to Mike. He already has the MSS chiefs in Changchun and Shenyang. He wanted a full house."

"What about Harbin?" My uncle had to shout the question over the clatter of the wheels as we picked up a little speed.

"Harbin? You kidding? The chief there is a crook. We couldn't convince him to come in with us, so we were going to have the Russian mob tap-dance on his head. Not that they do such a good job these days."

I gave it a moment's thought before I grabbed the noodle king's neck. "Where's Mike, and don't tell me you don't know where he hangs out or I'll dangle you under the wheels of this train until you look like a plate of leftover tripe."

"Here there couple of places he moves around let me think will you?" This was said in one unpunctuated nervous burst. At least I was getting through to him.

"Good, think about it." I fastened the tape back over his mouth. "Just sit there and think. The next time I take this stuff off, you'd better have the right answer or I won't think twice about turning you into tripe. We're not on Chinese territory at the moment, we're in North Korea. That means there aren't any special rules weighing me down."

My uncle motioned me over. "You wouldn't really dangle him under the wheels, would you?"

"Sure I would. Wouldn't you?"

Again my uncle looked out of one of the cracks. "I hate to say this, but I will anyway. It looks exactly like Mongolia."

2

An hour later, the train squealed to a stop.

"We're at a junction." My uncle crawled to the back end of the crate and peered outside. "I had to memorize the rail lines in this part of the country one time when we were chasing a smuggling ring. The tracks split here. One branch leads over to Khasan on the Russian side; the other route goes south and ends up in Rason. The stationmaster here might decide to take off a few freight cars to send to Russia. He's not supposed to, but the Russians pay him extra for Chinese railcars. Let's hope he reads the freight manifest right and keeps us hooked up on the Rason route. While they're decoupling and rearranging, the train guards will use the chance to stretch their legs and do a quick inspection. They'll probably bang on a couple of crates and make some noise for the hell of it. Make sure Mr. Noodle over there stays quiet."

We heard someone clamber up onto the flatcar our crate occupied. My uncle looked at his watch and started ticking off the seconds with his fingers. When he was at fifteen, we heard a female voice say, "Not tonight, sweetheart."

My uncle smiled to himself. "That's MPS talk for 'nothing here,'" he whispered. "The number code on the back of the crate is for special Chinese cargo bound for Rason. They have orders to expedite anything with that code. Normally, they think 'expedite' means whenever they feel like it, but there's no fooling around with this code. If anything marked with it is held up for more than two hours at any station, heads roll. This is the last rail junction before Rason. Once we leave here, the rest of the way should be easy."

"Good," I said. "Now maybe you'll tell me, what's in Rason that we need to see?"

"I thought you knew. Batbayaar said he played you a tape, and you told him it was from around Rason. What would a Chinese MSS officer know about a North Korean port, he thought to himself. Same question occurred to me. What would you know about Rason? It's not in your sector, is it?"

"Funny, I had a question, too, when I listened to the tape. What did the Mongolian Special Service care about a recording of a seal barking? I just took a guess that it was from around Rason, but if it was, why did the Mongolians care?"

"Did you have an answer?"

"I didn't right away, but then you said something that nudged the piece into place. You told me the Chinese wanted access to coal and rare earth mines, and they also wanted control of the railway in Mongolia to transport all of that stuff out of the country. What you didn't mention was where it would all be going—to the ice-free port of destiny, the Sea of Japan's shining star."

My uncle shook his head. "They don't teach geography in China? East Sea, East Sea, not Sea of Japan. They don't own it; they don't name it."

"We hear that Pyongyang is pushing for Mongolian participation in Rason to dilute the Chinese presence there. The Mongolians aren't sure of their footing—they get dainty when it comes to standing up to the Chinese—so they've been trying to develop agents around the port to get a better idea of what's going on and where it's safe to step. You know, the usual—dock workers, taxi drivers, prostitutes. Maybe the tape was a recording of a report phoned in from one of their new agents, and they were trying to figure out from the background noise exactly where it originated, whether their source was really in place or was calling in from the corner drugstore in Ulan Bator."

The train started to move.

My uncle looked skeptical. "How, sitting in Yanji, would you know anything about these things?"

"It's my job, that's how, and that's all I'm going to say." I looked over at the noodle king, who had his eyes closed but was listening intently. I should have blindfolded him and put his head in a bag. "What happens to him?" I asked.

"He goes on a coal freighter to Shanghai. If he survives the trip, he'll be a lifelong advocate of clean energy. He'll also be so seasick he won't be able to stand for weeks. Since he's wanted for the murder of the deputy chief of the Yanji MSS special office, it won't even cross his mind to complain about how you broke both of his legs before pushing him down the coal chute."

"I'll break more than his legs."

"He's from Fujian, isn't he?" My uncle slid over to where the noodle king was turning various shades of pale. "Listen, you, I'm going to take the tape off your mouth, and then we're going to have a conversation. Does that meet with your approval, or do we start taking you apart?"

The noodle king opened his eyes and indicated he wanted to talk. My uncle ripped the tape off.

"*Hey!*"

"Yeah, it hurts. Lay off kissing for a few months. You were in Yanji gathering up noodle shops not long ago, am I right?"

"So?"

"Did Mike ever come to town to check how you were doing?"

"Maybe."

"Where did you meet?"

"I can't remember."

My uncle knocked him on the side of the head, pretty hard.

"Did that jar anything loose?"

"It's no good, uncle," I said. "He doesn't care about his head. He cares about his hands. Go ahead and give him a little of what I did to that guy in Mongolia."

The noodle king shot me a look you wouldn't have thought a man in his circumstances would have had in him. "Come on, what is this rough stuff? What did I do to you?"

Word had spread fast from the cowshed. "You killed Li," I said. "That's for starters."

"It was Wong, didn't I already say that?"

"Wong worked for you."

"Wrong. Wrong, wrong, wrong. Wong was a subcontractor. Mike didn't want permanent staff. He wanted to be able to take people in and get rid of them whenever he felt like it. No strings, no blood oaths, no pinkies cut off. Simple business. He said it was cost-effective."

"I'm asking you one more time. Where did you and Mike have your meetings?"

The wheels clicked and clacked. A rock landed against the crate. The train heaved to a stop, and we heard the train guards climb down several cars away to shout threats at someone. Then we started moving again.

"What a shame. Time's up. Show me your left hand. I'll tell you your fortune."

"Gao's. We met at Old Gao's. Always the third room."

"That's the one in the back, the smallest one," I said.

"You and Mike did some gambling?" My uncle ignored the observation. "I don't think Mike likes to gamble."

"Not unless it's a sure thing."

"Then it's not gambling, is it?"

"I guess not."

"So, Gao let a couple of thugs take over one of his rooms, eating into his profit-making space. Is that right?"

"No," I cut in again. "No, that's not right. Gao worked for Mike."

"You knew that?" my uncle asked, a coating of ice in his tone of voice. "You knew that all along?"

"We knew Gao wasn't an independent. No way someone taking in that much money could stay independent. We weren't sure who he worked with. I wanted to put a twenty-four-hour watch on the place, but the idea panicked a lot of people in Beijing. What if we ended up with a long list of officials frequenting Gao's? Arresting a mayor or a city party secretary is all right, but a provincial governor? A vice premier? Not something you want to try."

"I thought you spent a lot of time there."

"Nah, not as much as you think. I knew most of the regulars who showed up, but Gao would have kept me out of the way when someone really big was there. I figured putting the place under surveillance might be useful; it would have given me a good excuse for being there once in a while."

"Maybe you could even have put your losses on an expense account."

The thought had crossed my mind more than once.

"I forgot, you are the only pure soul in the kingdom. You'd think about something like that, but you wouldn't do it. We would starve first." My uncle shook his head. "Why didn't you do the surveillance on your own and keep a list in your desk of whoever showed up? Lists of names come in handy sometimes."

"I know, that's what I tried."

"Don't tell me, you assigned Lieutenant Li to the job, and he came back with nothing."

"Almost nothing."

"You let him get away with that?"

"He told me his sources were warning us off."

"How do you know his sources didn't work for Mike?"

"Twenty-four hours ago I would have laughed that off. Now? I'd say it's possible. Maybe even likely."

"If you had a dirty mind, you might even suppose that's why the Third Bureau had taken up residence in your office. Checking to see how far Mike's influence went, assuming the Third Bureau is nothing but virgins who never took Mike's money."

I considered this. It made good sense. In fact, it jarred all my suppositions loose and rearranged what was possible. "Remember you recommended a different bag for each hypothesis? It's time for another one."

Our shipping crate swayed slightly as the train slowed and then stopped.

"Rason," my uncle said. "We're on the edge of Pier Three. The Chinese run it like they own the place. Maybe some of your creepy friends are involved." He gestured at the noodle king. "In less than an hour, one of the stevedores will check the shipping numbers on this crate, hoist it into the hold of a freighter, and off you go."

"So you were only kidding about the coal chute." The noodle king looked relieved. "I knew you were only kidding."

"Not coal," my uncle said. "Scrap, garbage, string, old toothpicks—that sort of thing, but they sneak those ships around

like they're hauling contraband. The U.S. Navy may mistake it for
a shipment of plutonium and blast it out of the water. We'll try to
find something buoyant to leave with you. Try to remember not to
breathe as long as you're underwater," my uncle added helpfully.
He turned to me. "This way." He counted over three boards from
the corner and pushed the fourth open. "When I say go, you go—
jump down and run like hell to the nearest cover. I'll find you."

"What about him? Won't he yell?"

"He might, at which point the guards will fill this crate with
lead. You know any Korean?" my uncle inquired of the noodle king.

The noodle king shook his head.

"Nothing at all? How do you talk to your contacts over here?"

"We use Chinese. They come over to our side. Shit, don't leave
me here; I'll get you a lot of money if you take me with you."

My uncle looked at his watch. "It's five o'clock. The local guards
are napping, the train guards have gone off duty, and the stevedores are on dinner break. Everything starts to move again at five
thirty. You have five minutes to tell me what you know. I'm not
giving you the whole half hour because I don't like you."

"Ask, ask, don't sit there, ask!"

"What does Mike have to do with the counterfeit state seal?"

The noodle king dropped below pale to pure white, white
enough for the Peking opera. "I don't know what you're talking
about," he said. "I don't know about any seal."

"Good." My uncle sounded pleased. "That's what I hoped you'd
say. Now I don't feel guilty about leaving you for the dogs."

"What dogs? I don't like dogs."

"What, you think Koreans only *eat* dogs? This ship sails with
high-value cargo buried under the garbage. That means there are
special State Security Department guards, Black Guards we call
them. They walk around with dogs that haven't been fed in days.
When the guards see something they don't like, they let the dogs go
after it."

This was all news to me. In all my years of reading agent reports from this side of the river, I never saw a mention of Black Guards or killer dogs.

"OK, OK, but if Mike finds out, he'll murder me."

My uncle laughed.

"He'll slice me up. I saw him do that once to someone, and then throw the pieces into a pot of noodles."

I thought of the dried ends. Apparently, my uncle did as well. He shifted uneasily. "Never mind that," he said. "The seal, what did Mike have to do with it? Was he going to use it, or was he just a conduit?"

"That isn't my department," said the noodle king, "but I'm the type of person who keeps his ears open. I overheard Mike on the phone a couple of times. He was talking to someone in Fujian about a character named Hu, or maybe Du."

"So what?" My uncle narrowed his eyes. "Are you screwing with me? Because I'm not in the mood"—he looked at his watch—"and we're almost out of time. What do I care about some character named Hu?"

"I don't know."

My uncle stood up. "Here, doggie, doggie."

"*Wait!* I don't know exactly. I seem to remember. It was Du, and I heard Mike say that if Du didn't finish the job before the sun set, he'd lose a finger for each hour of overtime. I didn't think anything of it. We used to cut off our fingers all the time as a sign of loyalty. Not me, I didn't, but a lot of the guys did." He looked over at Wong.

My uncle turned to me. "Unbelievable. This guy's about to lose his liver to a German shepherd and he's still playing games with me."

I figured this was meant as my opening. If my uncle was playing bad cop, that left me the job of pretending to be kind to this loathsome son of a bitch.

"Maybe he's not fooling around," I said. "Maybe that's all he knows. Mike ran things real tight. That's why we infiltrated Li into his group." At that moment I wished we had infiltrated Li into the group. Then we could have given him a medal at his funeral.

From the outside, we heard boots crunching on gravel. The noodle king stifled a sob. My uncle hissed at him, "Shut up."

Someone clambered up onto the freight car and walked around to the back where my uncle had said the numbers were. A moment later, we heard a man's voice shouting in Korean, then a stream of liquid against the side of the crate. Laughter. More shouting. The boots jumped down and crunched away.

My uncle closed his eyes. The air turned acrid.

For the benefit of the noodle king, I gave a rough translation. "The guard read the number on the crate, proclaimed that he was going to water the flower of Chinese-Korean friendship, and did so."

"Typical," said the noodle king. "We send aid, they give us back shit."

At that my uncle reached under his jacket and came out with a 9 mm pistol, no mother-of-pearl handle. "If I had on boots, I'd make you lick them." He stood up. "I ought to put a bullet between your eyes, but what good would that do?" He tucked the pistol back in his belt. "Instead, I'm going to tape your mouth, put a flour sack over your head, and wish you good luck. The MSS representative here will observe and attest that everything is done according to international human rights standards."

"Wait, wait, wait." The noodle king had slid back as far as he could against the wall. "I told you, there's a lot of money if you let me out of here."

My uncle turned to me. "You interested?"

I shook my head.

For an old man, my uncle moved like lightning.

3

Once we were clear of the train and onto the dock, my uncle slowed to a leisurely pace. "If anyone stops us, let me do the talking," he said.

"What about the Black Guards and the dogs?"

This drew a short laugh. "No such thing."

"What happens when they find the noodle king?"

"Depends on who gets to him first. If the stevedores find him, they'll haul him into a room with the Chinese gang leader, an ill-tempered sort named Tun Fan-xi who controls the docks. Our friend there will come out not long afterward neatly packed in several suitcases, one of which will be sent to Mike. If my old MPS colleagues find him first, they'll argue about what to do and then turn him over to Mr. Tun. Different road, same destination."

"More body parts. This is incredible."

My uncle shrugged. "It's the trend."

"You know, he heard us talking."

"Good for him. He won't live to tell anyone. Incidentally, if I ever mention the urge for noodles, shoot me."

"Speaking of guns, what are you doing packing so much fire-power? All of a sudden you're Hopalong Cassidy? What happened to that cute pistol you used to shoot Wong with? And where did you get that 9 mm?"

"The little one is on the floor of the warehouse. Don't worry, they'll figure a jilted girlfriend finished off Wong. It doesn't have any prints on it. As for the other one, I know a few people in Harbin who deal in this and that."

We came upon a guard post at the entry to the pier. The guard barked an order. My uncle barked back and flashed a pass. "Keep walking," he said to me in Chinese. "Look important. Wait a second or two, then sneer, just a little, like everything within sight is beneath you, distasteful, pitiable."

I sneered.

"Enough," said my uncle. "More than enough. Chinese around here sneer when they think they're almost out of sight of the locals." We walked for a few more minutes, turned down a street, up a small hill, and ended up on a weathered bench facing the port. "You said you had another hypothesis. Let's hear it."

I was about to explain when two cars—one black, one brown— barreled past going in the direction of the wharf. We could hear a commotion, then the black car tore by going in the other direction. The brown car followed a few minutes later, two uniformed police in the front seat looking out their windows, searching the area. The car slowed to a crawl as it pulled abreast of us. The driver's eyes drilled into me. I stared back, unsure whether or not to sneer. The car drove on. My uncle was sitting back the whole time, relaxed.

"Idiots," he said. "They were waiting for us to break and run. That would have made their life easy. You should have given him a good sneer."

"Do we want to stay here talking?"

"Sure. If we move now, they'll want to know where we've gone. When they drive by again and we haven't moved, they'll figure one of us is paying off the other. The noodle king didn't give them a description; otherwise we wouldn't still be here. What's your new hypothesis?"

"It's complicated," I said.

"Straight lines are way overvalued," he said.

"So far we've been dealing with a lot of different threads. Some of them have crossed, some of them haven't. I think it might be good to start at the beginning, at the point of origin."

My uncle took a piece of wood from his pocket. "It's elm," he said. "Good for the concentration. Want a piece? Go ahead, pull a thread."

"My predecessor—his true name, as you probably know already, was Lu Xin, but we found out subsequently that the North

Korean Operations Department called him 'Y'—had a central role in creating this mess. Lu wanted to come home, but he didn't know how to do it. For sure, his employers in Pyongyang wouldn't let him go with all that he'd learned about their operations. We already know what happened when he finally did leave. They kept him on a leash as best they could. He bided his time and pretended to be content."

"No, he didn't just bide his time. He got word to Fang Mei-lin at least a year ago."

"Ah," I said. This filled in a gap in my hypothesis, sort of like an avalanche can fill in a small valley.

"They used to be lovers, but she got tired of him. I won't give you all of her complaints."

"Ah." Another valley of doubt disappeared. "That helps with a few loose ends. She told you this, that he got word to her?"

"Knowing him a little, and knowing her a lot, I'm willing to bet he used her to deliver the news to MSS Headquarters that he was ready to come home." My uncle smiled. "I only bet on sure things."

"Then it isn't gambling, is it? Not to rake over old coals, but whom did she leave the note with? The one you claimed you didn't have and never saw."

"As a matter of fact, I never did see it, but there are two excellent possibilities. She might have given it to your Lieutenant Li, who apparently lived a life of intrigue beneath his dull, loyal exterior. Or she gave it to that old crook Gao. That would explain why she went there, I suppose. But Gao worked for Mike, you might object. Sure, Gao worked for Mike, and he worked for Pyongyang, and he no doubt worked for your Third Bureau, but most of all, he worked for himself. He would have calculated where Mei-lin's note would give him the most advantage, and if putting it in two places at the same time looked like a good way to double his profit, he would have done that."

"Shall I continue with my hypothesis?"

"I wish you would."

"Lu Xin, we might suppose, judged the time was ripe to try to move when he learned that Beijing had put in play an elaborate operation to discredit the South Koreans and clear the way for China to take control of most, if not all, of Mongolia's resources—rare earth deposits, coal, uranium, and timber."

My uncle's eyebrows went up.

"Just wanted to make sure you were listening. Except for the trees, this is pretty much your theory, but it fits, and I'll buy the whole thing from you."

"Consider it a gift."

"The key was a phony ROK government seal—made by the now-deceased Du, an expert Chinese forger working for a Fujian gang, which for some reason assumed this was a North Korean operation, exactly as Beijing hoped. At this point, we don't know who Beijing employed to put a North Korean gloss on the operation, but it wouldn't have been that hard to do. Like that Kazakh woman said to me, people believe what they want to believe. When Lu Xin got wind of the operation—and that's why this is still a hypothesis, because I don't know how he would have done so—he decided the storm it would produce, especially if the seal were to disappear for a short time, could supply cover for his own plans. With a few minor alterations, using a storm in the east to move in the west is standard MSS procedure. It probably goes back a few thousand years to some smart scholar in the Three Kingdoms, but who cares? The question was, how to create the storm?"

"Maybe when he learned that the gang had 'lost' the seal before handing it back to MSS, he made up a story and somehow passed the word to MSS that the seal had been moved to Mongolia, where the North Koreans intended to use it to embarrass Beijing."

"You're telling me you think he never had the seal?" If I'd been wearing a hat I would have taken it off to my uncle. "How'd you come to that conclusion, if you don't mind my asking?"

"It fits nicely in the hypothetical bag, that's all. Also fits with what you call standard operating procedure."

"Three Kingdoms, almost certainly."

"I'd guess there might be a hole or two in your overall theory, but nothing ever fits perfectly in these episodes. Leave that aside for now. How do you suppose he passed word to MSS about the Mongolian angle?"

I had already thought about that. "Madame Fang."

"No, no, not likely." My uncle waved the thought away impatiently. "He might have used her to pass on to Beijing his plea to come home, but he wouldn't give her anything that sounded too operational. For this to work, it would have to get to MSS through a believable reporting channel, an existing agent with a record. It couldn't be traceable to him; otherwise they'd wonder why he was giving this sort of information to them at the same time he said he wanted to come home."

I groaned. Mrs. Zhou's missing pages. I knew where they were. "Handout. He must have been working Handout for all of these years, saving him for the right moment. Lu Xin is the one who originally recruited Handout. When he got to Pyongyang, he must have figured out a way of keeping in touch with Handout. He took all of the relevant information in the case file with him, except for the fact that he was the one who recruited Handout."

"I thought you told me that Fu Bin controlled Handout."

"I never told you anything of the sort. Where did you hear that?"

"Who can remember where one hears things these days? So much information piling up."

"How much do you know that you aren't telling me?"

"Probably as much as you know that you are holding back. Want to put some cards on the table?"

"I thought you said gambling rots the mind."

"It does. Nevertheless, if we are going to get something believable back to Miss Du before she bulldozes your house and we're left with nowhere to live, we need to understand one or two more minor points."

"Like how her father ended up working for Dr. Mike?"

"Among other things."

The thought of my house in rubble overcame my training in security. Besides, we were sitting on a bench in North Korea. "At some point, Handout also became a Third Bureau bird. That may explain why Fu Bin disappeared so quickly once Handout passed him the message about the counterfeit seal. If there was ever a review of this seal fiasco, Third Bureau didn't want to be anywhere around. That's probably also why Li Bo-ting didn't want me to get rid of Handout right away; someone in MSS wanted to keep him in play a while longer."

My uncle didn't reply, other than to pocket the piece of elm that he'd been smoothing. Finally, he sighed. "I'll admit, I badly underestimated Y. He gave MSS just enough information to get them worried, but not enough for them to know exactly where to move next. He always seemed an odious type to me." That little bomb exploded on target. My uncle gave me a moment to recover. "You knew, of course, that he'd been working for Pyongyang for a long time before coming over."

"Ah, actually, no. I didn't know that." Things were starting to unravel faster than I could gather the threads up again.

This gave my uncle a shot of energy. He seemed reinvigorated at the idea of piling on surprises. "In 2007, someone tipped off your man Lu that a special investigating team sent by Beijing had discovered that he had helped Pyongyang to identify and kidnap a team of four South Korean military intelligence agents on the border. That episode went back to 2005 or 2006, when this particular agent team was setting in place a plan to entice North Korean generals to defect. Beijing obviously didn't care what happened either to North Korean generals or ROK agents, not in the abstract, anyway, but it didn't like the idea of Seoul using Chinese territory as a playground. It liked even less the chief of Yanji Bureau helping out North Korean counterintelligence."

"And?"

"And after a rough couple of weeks of interrogation, the North executed three of the four South Koreans, along with several high-ranking army officers who had been in touch with them."

"Number four?"

"The fourth signed a confession and was moved to a safe house where he was kept in isolation for a year or so. Eventually he became an instructor for the army's Reconnaissance Bureau. He was very effective, from what I heard, until he developed a drinking problem."

I'd heard almost more than I could absorb. I stopped talking and watched the ship being loaded at the pier. The cranes lifted the shipping containers from the train, swung them over the open hold in the ship, and lowered them.

"You know a lot that you've been holding back. We need to put all the pieces together. Not a few, not some, but *all* of them."

"In that case, I don't know any of this, and I'm not telling it to you."

"Fortunately, I never listen to a word you say."

"You should have already figured out that when Lu or Y—"

"Or K."

"Or whatever we decide to call him realized that he was about to be arrested, he disappeared with two briefcases of files filled with the coded names of agents and operations against the North. These were from files from your office, need I remind you. Didn't anyone do an inventory?"

"I wasn't there for the year after he left. I didn't do the damage evaluation. My own headquarters didn't even tell me any details about the defection until recently." I hadn't known anything, but Lieutenant Li did, and so, I'd wager with no fear of losing, did Mrs. Zhou.

"When he bumped into me in Pyongyang and announced he was defecting, we actually already knew each other slightly. In those days, I went through Yanji once in a while on liaison trips. Lu always turned up at whatever restaurant I wandered into and struck up a conversation. He was a desultory conversationalist, had a limited number of topics and didn't make those very interesting. I waited, but he never made a recruitment pitch. Didn't even buy me a drink. Anyway, as I told you, I tried to get him to go home when he showed up in Pyongyang, but he wouldn't budge. Of course, at the time I didn't realize he had such a persuasive reason for staying."

"According to you, your paths never crossed again until you saw him in the doctor's office."

"Our paths didn't exactly cross, no."

"But you heard things."

"It's hard not to hear things in Pyongyang. With this sort of incident, no one is authorized to tell anyone anything, which means everything is a rumor, even if it's accurate."

"And you heard what?"

"I'll summarize what I remember, as long as it's understood that I don't remember as well as I used to." He stared far off into the distance. "Funny, I could still tell you details about Mei-lin when we first met, how she lit a fire in me that to this day hasn't died down." He stopped. "Well, you want to know something else. This is everything I can summon out of the library that used to be my memory. I don't need it taking up space anymore."

"Go ahead."

"After a thorough debriefing that lasted six months, Pyongyang faced the problem of what to do with Lú. His knowledge of MSS operations was extremely useful at first, but without constant refreshment, they knew it would become dated. A decision was made to park him at a desk and use him to concoct ways to engage the MSS from a distance, sniff out Chinese operations in the North, and string them along. By watching how MSS handled his bait, Pyongyang figured it could determine how much and in what way Chinese operations had been modified, new techniques employed, and technology integrated."

"Which brings us to Handout."

"On that I can't help you, because I don't know anything about operations or agents."

I didn't laugh in his face, much as I wanted to. He knew plenty about operations, though for once he might be telling the truth—he might not know about Handout.

"Very well, then I'll tell you what must have happened. Interrupt me if you find yourself in possession of a stray fact that bears on the discussion." I thought back to what I'd read in Handout's file, those sections that had remained in the file in the office. "While still in China, Lu had recruited an agent, Handout, to work against the North Koreans. Handout had volunteered, but there's no record of the reason. Lu either kept it to himself or expunged it from the files before he skipped out. When he defected, he withheld knowledge of Handout from your interrogators. It wouldn't have been too hard to do; Handout wasn't a very useful agent and even in a six-month debriefing would have been at the bottom of the list of things your boys would have asked about. And he wouldn't have answered anything about which he wasn't specifically asked."

"Three Kingdoms again?"

I shrugged. "More like common sense. I'm sure your side does the same. You certainly do."

Silence.

I continued with my review. "Once he was settled into his desk job, he could carefully explore the North Korean files to look for signs of Handout, little footprints that had been part of their previous operations. He couldn't be sure who on the Chinese side would pick up handling Handout once he left; for a while he could be sure that no one would trust Handout, who would certainly be put on a shelf by MSS until he could be vetted all over again. I say all over again, but I'm not sure how thoroughly it was done the first time through."

"He certainly would never have checked out if he'd been one of ours. The agent of a defector coming out clean in the wash? Ha!"

"I thought you didn't know anything about operations."

"Common sense."

"Lu would also have been alert to the possibility of Handout stumbling into Pyongyang's counterintelligence nets. If he ever did get tangled, Lu must have steered suspicion away, making sure his boy never came to the full attention of the North Koreans. At the same time, he filled Handout's reports with as much straw as he could get away with so that Handout was never too valuable to the Chinese. That way, in case the North had another line into MSS, one that Lu didn't know about, Handout wouldn't be high on the list of Pyongyang's candidates for elimination." I hadn't considered the last thought until I said it, but it sounded all right on first hearing. I wasn't sure my uncle would agree. "Plausible?"

"Elementary. To this point, everything you've got in your bag is very simple. Tell me when it is about to become complicated."

"Thank you, I will hold up one finger." I smiled sweetly and demonstrated. "By this time, Lu had become, even in his own mind, Y. The plan became more complicated the more he thought about it, befitting a man who had nothing much to do all day long but plot. When the time came, he decided he had to reinvent himself as K, and as such use Handout to establish contact with the Tumen office of the MSS. Why? He already knew from North Korean reporting that his successor was Inspector O's nephew, and so he calculated that would be the ideal place to set things in motion. It was convoluted, with a lot of dark corners and loose ends. Exactly for that reason he figured that he could get away with it long enough to skip out of North Korea and back to his native land. He knew it wouldn't take anyone very long to figure out K was Y, but he didn't need it to last forever. Having a ghost image in the picture would keep information in separate files for a few months. That would create a gap big enough for him to slip through."

"What if someone had cross-filed the information? It would have become obvious almost immediately that they were the same person."

I smiled. "Cross-filed? Does anyone bother to do that anymore? Everyone is drowning in information these days. Who can afford to take the time to cross-file? Does Mrs. Zhou cross-file everything? We'd run out of file space in a week."

"Very risky, very convoluted," my uncle said. "I would never have done it that way."

"Ah, but you see, uncle, you're Korean, while Lu is Chinese."

"And never Mark Twain shall meet."

"What?"

"I said, I can't get over how similar in some ways this is to the Blue Sparrow case."

"Not now, not here. Sitting in enemy territory is not the best place for storytelling."

"Enemy territory?" My uncle looked taken aback, something I rarely saw from him. "Enemy territory? This is Korea; this is your homeland. Your father's grave is here, as is his father's and his father's before him. How can it be enemy territory?"

"I didn't mean that. You know what I meant."

"All I know is what I see and what you say. It baffles me sometimes, I have to admit."

"Go ahead, this is a pleasant spot, no one around." I needed to make amends, quickly. "What about the Blue Sparrow?"

"You sure you want to listen?"

I closed my eyes. "You have my complete attention."

"To review: The case got more convoluted the more we sank into it. We tried and tried to come up with another bag for our working hypothesis. We knew we had to. Several of us worried that things fit together in the investigation too neatly almost from the beginning. As you'll recall, it was a woman's ear that the vice minister of railways found on his doorstep."

"Right ear." I opened my eyes. "With a pearl earring."

My uncle looked at me suspiciously. "The vice minister was a loud-talking man so we suspected, but weren't sure, there might a connection between the ear and his brusque style."

"You made that point already. Maybe it wasn't the ear, maybe it was the pearl."

Another look. "That's unlikely. Did I also tell you that he was built like an East German boxcar gone to seed? We learned that it annoyed some people simply to be in the same room with him."

"It annoyed someone so much that she cut off her own ear and put it on his doorstep? As I said before, it shouldn't have been hard to find a woman with only one ear. And in my experience, women don't cut off their own ears."

"Did I mention we made lists of everyone who might have had a grudge against the vice minister?"

"You did. Come on, uncle, this isn't a real case, is it? You've been making it up as you went along."

"Of course it was a real case. It's one reason why I never made chief inspector."

He had never talked much about his career, so this jarred me. "All right, you went down the list of everyone who might have a grudge. It was a long list. Then what?"

"In those days, we were trained to be methodical, and that meant a lot of shoe leather. We didn't have computers. Headquarters assigned eight people to the case, and each was given one province. Inherently, the workload was uneven, though there was some effort to smooth out the inequalities as things proceeded. If we found that the general had been in a particular province for any length of time, we devoted a second person. I remember the inspector who got Yanggang Province ended up with not much to do. The general had been there only once, to go hiking. By contrast, after he became vice minister, he often went to Wonsan to eat seafood and sit on the beach. He put down in his travel orders that he was going to give guidance and investigate conditions at the railcar repair facility there, but no one believed it. The point is, he met a lot of people in Wonsan and that meant a lot of grudges, so naturally Wonsan, even though it was just a city, got its own investigator. I had a pretty good idea that Wonsan would end up having nothing to do with the case, and on this, at least, I was right. It wasted a lot of manpower that could have been used elsewhere, but that's a hard argument to make when people think that being methodical is a substitute for using their imagination and experience."

"Did anyone look for other body parts?"

"Like fingers?"

"Like anything. I would have thought one team would proceed on the basis of hypothesis A, a nasty grudge, and another team would look at hypothesis B, murder. I'd even have assumed, for the sake of argument, that the vice minister committed the murder himself and put the ear there to shuttle the investigation off on the wrong track. Maybe he had railroad images in his head."

My uncle smiled. "You are your father's son, and yet you are my nephew."

I wasn't sure what that meant. It might have been praise, and considering the circumstances, for once I gave myself the benefit of the doubt.

The brown car with the policemen in front cruised by again. About thirty meters past us, they pulled over and turned off the engine.

My uncle took this in without much interest. "Where's the seal, do you think?"

"Don't play games. You already know, don't you?"

"No, I don't know. Although I have a hunch." He stood up slowly and began strolling in the opposite direction from the car. "Let's go home."

Chapter Three

The return trip was easier than I would have guessed, and was more comfortable than the shipping crate. Back in Yanji the next evening my uncle went straight to his workshop to commune with his woodworking tools. I never saw a man so happy to be reunited with a Turkish saw. The first thing I did was to call the office. Waiting for the connection, I started having second thoughts. It had been almost two days since I'd disappeared. My unexplained absence and the discovery of Lieutenant Li's corpse must have set off alarm bells from one end of the Ministry to the other. They would have instantly concluded that, like my predecessor, I had defected to North Korea, and that my uncle's presence for the past two years had all along been meant to facilitate the operation. As far as the Ministry was concerned, it would all fit neatly with what had already been suspected in some quarters. A terse message from the Mongolians would have told them that K had been murdered, poisoned. The boulder-sized nurse would have implicated both my uncle and me in K's demise. The nurse's story was unlikely to stand up under serious investigation, but the Mongolians would be doing the investigating, and MSS—having only one hypothesis bag—wouldn't be looking for alternative explanations.

No, calling wasn't going to do me any good. It would simply raise the level of tension. Before the second ring, I hung up the phone. Yanji was probably already crawling with special MSS teams gathering information, questioning people, rooting around for evidence to confirm what they'd decided already—that I was a traitor and had doubtless benefited from a hidden support structure long in place.

It would be best if they didn't suspect I had returned, at least not before I had a chance to get in touch with someone in the Ministry who would listen to my explanation. If the teams had been watching the house, of course, they'd already know where I was, but the chances of that were slim. They thought I'd defected, and defectors didn't return home to make sure the windows were closed or the lights had been turned off.

The lights! I hurried back to my uncle's workshop.

"Turn off the lights. Were your shades closed when we left?"

My uncle was working on an old set of sketches. "Why, are we under air attack?" He didn't look up.

"No, but I don't want anyone to know we're home."

"So if the shades had been closed while we were away, it would be no problem if we left on this light because no one could see."

"Uncle, if they think we're here, they'll bust in with guns blazing. You'll never get those plans finished."

"Why didn't you say so? Turn off the light, by all means. I can sit in the courtyard and sketch. No one can see me in there. I promise not to sing."

"And don't answer the door. Even if it's Madame Fang."

"*Especially* if it's Madame Fang. Where are you going? If you see Gao, make him cough up the money he owes us."

"I'm not going to see Gao. I'm not going to see anyone until I get back to the office and put things straight."

"Tell me how it turns out."

"I'm taking two empty bags for hypothesis, do you think that will be enough?"

"Better take three."

"Uncle, you realize they probably think I defected and that you helped me."

"What a thought! And yes, it already crossed my mind."

"I also don't know who is on our side in all of this."

"Don't worry, the advantage is with the defenders if they are on the high ground."

"Are we?"

"We'd better be."

2

At some point, a team was going to be sent over to the house to do a thorough, regulation-style search: bookshelves ripped from the walls, floors pulled up, water pipes cut open, the entire ceiling taken down. There were a number of reasons to avoid things getting to that point, not least that they never cleaned up or repaired the damage if they didn't find anything. Nothing of mine would cause problems—my wife had taken all of my money, which meant, fortunately, there wasn't any unexplained cash lying around. My main worry was that I couldn't be sure what my uncle might have in his workshop beside tools or in those notebooks other than plans for bookshelves.

I needed to get to the office pronto, as Tuya would say. I couldn't roll there like her and didn't want to chance using my bike. My best alternative was a car, which, of course, I no longer had. There were usually taxis waiting in front of the New Sunspot, a curry restaurant about ten minutes away. I avoided curry, so none of the staff was liable to recognize me. However, most of the taxi drivers had done jobs for MSS at one time or another, meaning the odds were at least a few of them would know my face. I had to hope I could spot a new driver and slip into his cab unnoticed by the others.

Luckily, it was near dinnertime; most of the drivers were either in the restaurant or napping in their cabs. One of them was reading a newspaper. I jumped in the back.

"Extra money if you get me to the pharmacy before it closes."

He looked in the mirror as he started the engine. "Depends," he said.

I retrieved the two hundred yuan that I keep in my wallet for an emergency. "Here," I said. "This is yours if you don't get stopped for speeding or going through a red light, and you'd better do both."

We pulled away from the curb, tires squealing. Everyone in the restaurant must have run to the window to see what was going on, but I was already hunched down in the seat.

"That's good," I said. "I'll put in another fifty if you don't get into an accident."

The driver grinned into the mirror. "You're a regular cash machine. What's your hurry? And which pharmacy are you so hot to get to?"

"There's a place not far off Renmin Road, on Juzi Street. Know it?"

"Sure, I drive a cab, don't I? There's a pill joint closer if it's such an emergency."

"No, the place I'm going has bear parts in the back. I need some for tonight, if you know what I mean. Let's move it, we're practically standing still."

The driver accelerated. "Oh, that's the happy game. I hear starfish do the trick. You ever tried them?" The cab cut between two buses and lurched around a corner. "Me, I stay away from that stuff." He grinned again, this time to himself. "Don't need it."

"Good for you. Take the next left and cut through the alley."

"You want to drive?"

"No, I just want to get my bear parts, and you want your two hundred yuan."

"You said two fifty."

"Sure, but you still might crash this thing. Next right. About fifty meters, then pull over." I threw the money into the front seat before we stopped rolling and jumped out. "Have a good night." I slammed the door and took off down the street.

The driver stuck his head out the window. "Make way, man in a hurry!"

I ducked into the pharmacy, waited until I saw the cab pass by, and then went back out to the street. The office was a block away. Since no one would be expecting that I'd show up, I wasn't worried about running into extra security around our building. It was going to spoil the element of surprise if I went in the front door, though. Whoever was at the front desk could identify me as I stood in front of the camera. Going through the Bank of China might work, assuming I could get in. It was past business hours, but there was a night janitor. I rang the night bell and waited. Nothing. I tried three long rings.

The janitor appeared, lifted the grate, and unlocked the door. "Yeah?"

"Buzzer on our door is out. I need to go through."

"Funny, you're the only one tonight with that problem." She stood aside and let me pass. "I heard you had taken a trip."

"Oh?"

"None of my business." She locked the door and pulled down the grate. "You want me to turn on the lights so you can find your way to the back?"

"Thanks. Let's just keep things as they are."

She nodded. "Did I see you?"

"No."

"That's what I figured. Sometimes people ring the bell and then run off. I've got offices to clean. Don't trip on the threshold on your way out." She picked up a pail and a mop and padded away.

No one was around when I slipped into the MSS building from the old front entrance. The door opened to a dark hallway that wasn't much used, went past the Level 1 steel door to the file vault, and led to my office. I stepped in, turned on the light, and shut the door. Even before I sat down, the phone rang.

3

I let it ring. After the fourth one, it stopped for about ten seconds, and then piped up again. My plan had been, after collecting my thoughts, to call Beijing and tell them I was back. Obviously, this wasn't going to work. Someone hanging around the office would hear the phone and come in to answer it if it kept ringing. I took a chance and lifted the receiver.

"I thought your uncle was going to send me a report, or is he still duck hunting?" When she was angry, and, worse, made a point of sounding angry, there was a thick layer of Yunnan in the woman's voice that wasn't appealing.

"Ah, Miss Du, what a surprise." I spoke softly. "I'm in a meeting. Let me call you back later."

"Don't whisper at me, buster. My cousin's bulldozer will be there at dawn if there's no report from you by midnight tonight. I'm through with this runaround. Clear?"

"Perfectly. Don't worry, we're making great progress. It's all about—"

She hung up, saving me the trouble of having to invent what I meant by progress.

I looked at the clock behind my desk. It was still slow. The junction box with all the wires needed a special tool to open it, so I pulled the whole thing, clock and all, down from the wall and put it in the bottom drawer of my desk. I dialed the special emergency number to MSS Headquarters.

Just as a voice on the other end of the line answered with perfect duty officer protocol, "Go ahead," there was a soft knock on my door.

I hung up. "It's open." I placed both hands on the desk. That way there wouldn't be any questions about my intentions if this wasn't a friendly visit.

In walked the older man with the brush haircut. "Figured you'd be back," he said. "Mind if I sit?"

I motioned with my head toward a chair. Too soon to move my hands. "Is the Penguin joining us? Or Miss Bao? I'll have the table moved in for her."

"Don't bother, I'm by myself. It's just us, for now. My name's Wu. We skipped the introductions last time we met. That was around two in the morning, and you were in a bad mood. I guess this is better." He took out a pack of cigarettes. "You smoke?"

"Not lately."

He put the cigarettes away. "We friends yet?"

"Why, you going to shoot me?"

He laughed. "No. You might want to do that yourself later, but not before we have a conversation."

"I didn't defect, if that's what you want to know."

"I can see that. Let's not jump ahead, all right?"

"You mind if I make a phone call before we get started?"

"Sure, be my guest." He looked at the bolt holes and wires on the wall where the clock had been. "We have all night."

"So there is no misunderstanding, I'm going to pick up the phone and dial home." My uncle answered on the third ring.

"Uncle, Miss Du called me a few minutes ago. If you don't get something down on paper for her about the investigation, her cousin is going to be at the house with his bulldozer at sunrise. She means business. I think she hates men."

"Can I turn on a light yet? It's damned dark in here."

"Go ahead. I'm at the office. It doesn't matter anymore who knows we're home."

"You doing all right?"

"Fine."

"Don't forget what I said about the high ground."

"Write a page, even a half page for Miss Du, would you? You have her phone number; it's on my desk in the library. Call and tell her that a report will be waiting when she arrives tomorrow morning. I'll be back late." I looked at the old man, who nodded slightly. "See you when I see you." I hung up.

"Miss Du? Tough as they come. You have business with her?"

"Nothing productive. You want to hear the story?"

"Depends on where it fits. Let's start at ground zero. I warned you about Ping Man-ho, remember? You do any research?"

"I've been busy, you might say." Also, the person who said he'd keep his ears open about Ping now had a bullet in his head.

"I also warned you about your uncle, didn't I? What happened in Mongolia?"

"Plenty, most of it confusing. Whose idea was it to send me there in the first place?"

The old man pointed a finger skyward. "Up top."

"How does Fang Mei-lin fit in this?"

"Excuse me, this is my interrogation. If you want to ask questions, get your own."

"Sure, why not? If people aren't giving me fuzzed-up orders, they're grilling me. I've about had it. On top of which, my deputy was killed by a gang that has its sights on moving into my sector."

"Who killed Wong?"

"Huh?"

"Wong was working for us. He was getting us close to Mike. Who killed him?"

Click. Li, my trusted deputy, was working for Mike, so Wong was ordered by MSS to kill Li. One loose end tied up, but I didn't especially like it. "What makes you think Wong is dead?"

"Something we found in a warehouse in Tumen we've been checking now and then."

"Tumen is my territory. Did you bother to let me know, or was that too much trouble? What if we were both watching the same warehouse?"

"Were we?"

"I don't know. Were we? What did you find that made you so sure Wong was dead?"

"Blood, his blood, on the floor. We keep samples from all our officers, just in case. Sounds grim, but there you go. It came in handy on this one, and this isn't the first time."

"People bleed sometimes."

"Especially if they're shot. It was a small-caliber weapon, something like a woman carries. Nice and dainty."

"Yeah, well, maybe it was a woman with one ear."

"No games on this one. Beijing is not pleased with the turn of events. Incidentally . . ." Wu yawned. "The body showed up at a North Korean port a day ago. Kind of strange for a corpse to buy a railway ticket. You know who killed him or don't you?"

"I don't."

Wu's eyes narrowed, and he stared at me for a long minute. Then he pulled a gun out of his pocket and put it on a small table beside the chair. "This is the gun. It had been fired once. No prints, which always impresses me. It was made in the U.S. You recognize it?"

"Nope. I don't hang out much around people who favor pearl handles."

"You have your weapon nearby?" He didn't tense up, which told me he already knew the answer.

"It's in the desk drawer, unless someone has been in here already and took it. You want me to look? Maybe you should frisk me, too, just in case."

"Don't bother." He reached in another pocket and came out with what looked like my pistol. "Here it is. I was in this afternoon poking around."

"Find anything else of interest?"

"The sign-out sheet for an agent's file."

"We had that conversation already. I was looking at Handout's file because I was going to take over control from Fu Bin. You know who Fu Bin is?"

"Never heard of him."

"You don't deal with the Third Bureau?"

He made a face. "I wash my hands afterward if I do."

"Fu Bin was from the Third Bureau, doing what here for four years I have no idea. Or at least, I didn't at the time. After getting knocked out once or twice, a few things became clearer."

"That's good. Clarity has advantages on occasion. Sometimes things are better left vague."

"So where do I fit? In the clarity bin?"

"You were supposed to bring Lu Xin home."

"Too bad no one bothered to tell me."

"Yeah, well, no one told me either, and I was supposed to be in charge of cleaning up after this operation."

"Which operation is that?"

"Leave that in the vague bin. I don't think you killed Lu. Did you?"

"For the record or just among friends?"

"Up to you."

"I didn't kill him. I'm not sure who did. My uncle said there were a hundred arrows in the air from people trying to get him, meaning it didn't really matter which one hit home."

"Your uncle said that? Very pithy. Maybe I'll use it."

"For all I knew, I was sent to Mongolia to recover someone's state seal. I wasn't told whose, and I wasn't told why."

"So, did you recover it?"

"Has the premier been to Ulan Bator yet?"

"And back."

"No problems?"

"If you didn't get the seal, just say so."

"OK, I didn't get the seal. You know a character named Ding?" He nodded.

"Give him a raise. Maybe he can get his teeth fixed. Otherwise, he gets a failing grade. He wasn't that helpful."

"He wasn't supposed to be." There was an odd pause after that. "He gave you an envelope, that's what he does."

"What about the yak?"

"We don't have any animals on the payroll."

"The funny, dirty little man. The Mongolians called him a yak—something that is different than what it appears to be. He earns his money passing messages, too?"

"Oh, him. Yeah, sometimes. He's also good with a knife when he needs to be."

"I think I may owe him for a map."

"You can pay next time you're there."

I left that alone. "Anyone we missed?"

"Did Lu Xin know where the seal was?"

"Maybe. He indicated to my uncle he did. I don't know if the North Korean doctor at the clinic where Lu was hiding also knew. The doctor's a smart man. You should look into having a talk with him."

"It was that damned Kazakh woman, wasn't it?"

"I couldn't say. According to the Mongolians, she collects weak-willed men. I need to keep my distance."

"How long did the Mongolians hold you?"

"Don't tell me that Bazar works for you."

He shook his head.

"Please, don't let it be Tuya."

"Who?"

"No one, just a tea lady." If Tuya worked for MSS, I would never forgive myself.

"How about answering a question for a change? How long did the Mongolians hold you?"

"Not long. They put me out for a while. One light touch and I was gone. It's a pretty good move, doesn't leave any aftereffects. Maybe we can ask them to teach it to us."

"Sure, why not? What did they want to know?"

"About sea lions."

The man took off his tie and draped it over the back of the chair. "Sea lions, huh?"

I could see he was disappointed. "Something wrong?"

"It's Rason, and it's causing me more headaches than anything. I'm supposed to be at the end of my career, ready to retire, but what do I get? Rason."

"You're the third person who said 'Rason' when I mentioned sea lions. What am I missing?"

"Nothing. There's no direct link with sea lions. But in this case, if you know a little, you know a lot. It's all about context. Rason shows up in your reporting, doesn't it?"

"Now and then."

"That means you know the place has a lot of people salivating. The triads are already there."

"So I've heard."

"The Mongolians are doing some light-footed reconnaissance."

"Yeah, but what's the fascination? It's a port, not very big."

"Oh, you been there?"

"A flying visit, you might say."

"Meaning, you were in North Korea after all."

"Sort of like Lenin going back to Russia in a sealed railway car. Only in my case, it was a shipping crate."

"Enough." He stood up. "I can't write this down because no one will believe it."

"You're not leaving, are you? This is getting to be an illuminating session, lots of clarity. How about we leave something vague, a loose thread here or there? Think anyone would mind?"

"They don't like loose threads in Beijing anymore. They used to; I don't know what happened. Damned shame. Though I can tell you, they want to know what happened to that state seal. They don't want that left flapping in the breeze."

"I have a theory, if you want to hear it."

He sat down again. "This is going to be good. I'll bet you and your uncle kicked it around already."

"Can you pocket those pistols or something? They make me nervous."

He put the pearl handle in his pocket. "This other one is yours. Want it back?"

Not in a thousand years was I going to be caught holding a pistol alone in the same room with a grizzled special section squad leader. "No thanks. You keep it. I'll get another one later if that's how things break."

He shrugged. "Have it your way." He put my pistol in his other pocket. "You were saying?"

"It's only a theory. It ties together, though, especially if you figure in Miss Du."

Chapter Four

The next afternoon, all four of them were in the library, seated uncomfortably around my uncle's desk. We only had three chairs, not counting the one where my uncle was sitting. That left Gao on the stool with the poplar seat. He still owed us money, and his left ankle was still in a cast.

I was standing behind Miss Du in case she jumped up and moved menacingly toward my uncle, as she had in our first meeting. She had on a peek a boo lace dress—made especially for her in Yunnan, she told me at the front door. My uncle seemed very uncomfortable at first when she came in and sat down. Each time he looked at her, he glanced at Madame Fang first.

Wu had joined us. I wasn't sure it was a good idea, but my uncle told me not to worry. Wu stayed in the background, leaning against the bookcase closest to the door. The last to arrive was Ping Man-ho, wearing his trademark Hong Kong suit. In honor of the occasion, he sported a dove gray shirt with a pale green tie. Gao muttered under his breath when Ping appeared, but Ping paid no attention and seated himself comfortably next to Miss Du. She studiously refused to acknowledge his presence, which made me think they had crossed paths once upon a time.

As soon as Ping was seated, my uncle cleared his throat. "I'm grateful to you all for coming with no more than the normal complaints," he said.

"No speeches, just tell us what this is about, OK, and let us go home." Gao looked over at Madame Fang. "Some of us have to work for our food, you know."

"Ha!" Madame Fang hurled this at my uncle. "I wish you'd told me who was going to be here. I might have made other plans."

My uncle put up his hand. "Enough. I didn't invite you here because I expect you to become friends, though I think you are all acquainted in one way or another."

Four sets of eyes instantly turned to examining the floor; three pairs of lips compressed into thin frowns. The exception was Ping Man-ho, on whose handsome face there lightly danced the briefest of self-satisfied smiles. I didn't know why my uncle had insisted I make sure he was in attendance, though Wu's interest in Ping and Li Bo-ting's odd reaction when I'd mentioned his name at the dumpling restaurant told me it wasn't just because of his taste in suits. Whatever the reason, I found myself watching him closely.

"I, for one, would like to know what this is about. You owe me a report. You promised a report. Instead, I have been brought against my will to a meeting with people I wouldn't otherwise ask for the time of day." Miss Du did not single out any of the others. It was a sort of blanket petulance.

"How nice of Your Highness to put up with us." Gao appeared to take in Miss Du's outfit for the first time. "You have enough money; next time, OK, why don't you buy the whole dress?"

My uncle rapped his knuckles on the desk. "This isn't a primary school play yard. We have a number of things to discuss. At the conclusion, I expect we will have the answers to several important questions."

"What questions? I don't have any questions, OK?" Gao said. "And since I don't, I'll take my leave, OK? Some people in here, OK, owe me money, and I can't afford to sit doing nothing." With some effort, he pulled himself up and looked around for his crutches, which I'd put in the hall so he couldn't bolt out of the room.

"Sit down. You will speak only when I tell you to, and you aren't going anywhere until I say you can." My uncle sounded completely in charge. Madame Fang shivered slightly with what I took to be excitement at this display of authority. She had on a necklace with two strands of pearls, and she fingered one of them provocatively before dropping it onto her blouse, which was some sort of satin, designed to make clear what she wanted to make clear.

Miss Du craned her neck around and looked at Wu. "Who is that man and what is he doing here? Is he one of the private investigators you've hired to pad the expense account? Has he got any credentials, or shouldn't I ask?"

Wu didn't bother to respond. He simply looked at Miss Du as if he'd dealt with her type plenty before. My uncle rapped his knuckles on the desk again. "Mr. Wu is competent, knowledgeable, and experienced. He has a special interest in these proceedings, but he isn't a direct participant. So you might as well pretend he isn't there and face me. I'm the one who is going to ask the questions, and I'm going to listen very carefully to your answers."

My uncle took a small box out of one of his desk drawers and put it on a shelf behind his chair. "You may think you don't have to answer the questions I am going to ask, but you would be wrong. Major Bing"—he indicated he was referring to me—"is fully empowered to enforce the rules of interrogation."

I put on an impassive face. There are no "rules" of interrogation, and I had no power to enforce anything that took place here. I couldn't step on anyone's hand or slap anyone around. My job was to keep the four of them seated and sufficiently intimidated so they would jump through whatever hoops my uncle produced. What those hoops were I didn't know for sure, since he hadn't told me what to expect. If something happened, I could take care of the two women and Gao with no trouble, but Ping looked in pretty good shape and I didn't want to have to tangle with him if I could avoid it. I'd been knocked around plenty for one month already.

"The first order of business"—my uncle peered grimly at each of the four in turn—"is to inform you that Naranbaatar is dead, murdered most foully."

This news was met with blank stares. My uncle did not seem surprised. "You perhaps knew him as Y, or possibly even K. Ring a bell?"

Wu shifted uneasily. He didn't like public airing of dirty MSS laundry; he liked even less the batting around of cryptonyms, even the most obscure, in front of the unwashed. Besides Wu's unease, I sensed something else in the room, a muffled spark of recognition, but it was snuffed out before I could catch the source. I glanced at my uncle to see if he'd been quicker than I was, but his attention seemed to be on other things, Miss Du's dress for one.

"Very good." My uncle closed his eyes and leaned back in his chair. "The man's real name was Lu Xin. His death, as I said, was not pleasant. You wouldn't want to shuffle off the mortal coil in that fashion, believe me."

Madame Fang paled noticeably and drew a quick breath, though I couldn't say her bosom heaved. Gao pursed his lips and attempted nonchalantly to scratch his neck. Miss Du uncrossed her legs and crossed them again, this time facing Ping Man-ho, who was otherwise occupied in swallowing.

"Anyone want to say a nice word about Lu Xin? Or should we leave the dead in peace?" My uncle waited. A piglet squealed from down the alley, but no one in the library blinked an eye. Finally, Ping Man-ho raised his hand.

"I have a question." He turned to address Miss Du. "I take it this session is primarily your idea."

"Not at all," she replied coolly.

That cinched it. They knew each other. This was not a woman who replied coolly to strangers. She scratched their eyes out.

"I don't know about the rest of you, but I could use some context," Ping Man-ho continued. "Perhaps we should ask Inspector O to give us a few minutes of background, as much as he can, of course. If he is working for you"—again he turned to Miss Du—"there are no doubt limits as to what he can say about a client. Am I right, Inspector?"

"Let's get something straight." My uncle pointed at Ping, then at Gao, then at Miss Du, and finally at Madame Fang. "I'll decide who gets context, how much, and when."

Madame Fang shivered again.

"To continue, Lu Xin—and I already know that each of you had a connection with him, so I am disappointed but not surprised that none of you spoke up to mourn his passing—died in Mongolia."

"I didn't kill him, OK? What the hell is this about?" Gao looked suspiciously around the room. "At least two people here, OK, owe me a lot of money. Why don't we talk about that, OK?"

"And you owe money to several others, as you perfectly well know." My uncle wagged his finger at Gao. "I think Mr. Wu may want a word or two with you when we're through here."

Gao craned his head around to get a good look at Wu. He didn't appear happy with what met his eyes. Wu took a small notebook out of his pocket and held it up for Gao to see. That seemed to make Gao even unhappier.

My uncle rapped the desk. "As long as you're paying attention, Gao, have you ever been to Mongolia?"

"Me?" Gao turned around on his stool and faced the front. "Are you crazy? Why would I want to go to Mongolia?" He was so stupefied that his normal verbal tic dropped away for a moment. "Mongolia? You kidding?"

"I don't mean recently. Recently you've tended your business here in Yanji, is that right? Still, a career path is long and winding. Perhaps yours wound through Ulan Bator?"

"Yeah, sure, OK, this is my home, OK. So it's not a fancy place, OK, like some people have." His eyes darted around the room. "But I don't bother anyone. And I wasn't ever in Outer Mongolia."

"What about Inner Mongolia?"

"I was in the army, OK?"

"You were mostly in the stockade, from what I've learned."

"I was in the army in Inner Mongolia. There's nothing there. Nothing. It drove people crazy, OK? Some guys took up with sheep. I took up gambling, developed a skill for myself, OK? I wasn't going to fix jeeps my whole life. I don't bother anyone."

No," my uncle said, "I suppose you don't, unless they happen to owe you money."

Gao shrugged, as if bothering people who owed him was as normal as rain.

"You said a couple of people in this room are in your debt. Who are they?"

I thought someone would jump up to protest, so I leaned forward, prepared to move quickly, but nothing happened. Silence descended. There must have been a shortage of piglets, because no sound came from the outside either.

Finally, Miss Du squeezed out a tear. "You've probably already checked. All right, yes, I owe him some money."

"Some!" The word half lifted Gao off the stool. "Some! She owes—"

"Be quiet, Gao, or I'll have Major Bing put some of this special tape on your mouth." My uncle opened his drawer and retrieved a roll of black tape. "Please, Miss Du, go ahead."

"Lots of people go to Gao's. At home, I know where the skunks are, but I'm not from around here so I didn't know what a racket he was running. Someone asked me to go along with them to Gao's, so I went. If I'd known, I wouldn't have gone."

"Nothing wrong with owing money, dear, as long as you owe it to the right sort of people," Madame Fang said evenly. "Of course, it's always better if they owe you." She patted Miss Du's hand, which I thought for sure would start World War III. Instead, Miss Du put her arms around Madame Fang's neck and began to sob loudly.

"Wouldn't have bet on that, would you, Bingo?" Gao turned

and grinned quickly at me. "Anyone mind if I smoke?" He took a Cleopatra from his shirt pocket, sniffed the tobacco with satisfaction, and stuck the cigarette in his mouth.

"No smoking in here or in the lavatories." My uncle motioned for me to relieve Gao of his cigarettes. "Someone get Miss Du a handkerchief. Ah, thank you, Ping Man-ho."

Ping Man-ho had handed Miss Du a sparkling clean, perfectly folded, white linen handkerchief. She blew her nose and handed it back.

"Miss Du, if you feel up to it, can we proceed? I didn't inquire how much you owed, I merely asked to whom. We now know Gao holds some of your IOUs. Do you owe anyone else?"

Miss Du's expression suggested she was considering her response. "Do you mean anyone else in this room, or just anyone else?"

"I think that will do as an answer." My uncle rested his eyes on Ping Man-ho. "You had something to add?"

Ping shook his head. "Nothing, Inspector."

"Can we take a break? I think it's time for a break." Madame Fang made a grab for control. "Coffee and cookies would be nice, if you have any. Also, I wouldn't mind going to see a man about a dog."

Wu grumbled, "No one leaves this house."

"What?" Gao swiveled around again to look at Wu. "We're not under arrest. You can't arrest me."

"As it happens, we don't have coffee, but we do have some tea, very fine tea from Yunnan. It arrived at our door this morning." My uncle reached on the shelf behind him for a small box. "Miss Du, since you are from Kunming, would you do me the honor?"

Miss Du took the box gingerly. She examined the sides and looked closely at the ribbon that held the lid on. "Why don't you save this for later?"

"No, please. It's my pleasure to serve our guests only the finest things, isn't that so, Major?" I wasn't sure if I was supposed to chime in, but I figured it couldn't hurt.

"Sure, only the finest."

Miss Du tugged reluctantly at the ribbon. It came undone more easily than she had anticipated. The lid slipped off, and the contents of the box spilled onto her dress. She looked in horror at the object sitting on her lap. Before anyone could move, she screamed, threw the object at my uncle, and fainted.

2

It took a few minutes to bring Miss Du around. Wu went to the kitchen for a glass of cold water to splash on her face.

I motioned my uncle to join me in the hall. "What the hell was in the box?"

"A damp squib. I may have miscalculated," he said.

"May have? She might have had a heart attack. What was it, and don't tell me it was a shell-like ear with a gold filigree earring attached."

"An ear? No, it was a piglet trotter. It looks a little like a human finger, several fingers actually, if you don't examine it too closely. It was all I could come up with in a pinch. I didn't realize she was quite so high-strung. I figured the sight of it would shock her into saying something unguarded. It nearly did. She's very anxious for such a rich person."

"You think she's guilty of something but you don't know what. You can't just hurl pig parts at a person on a hunch."

"It's not exactly a violation of human rights, or due process, or whatever the hell is the lecture of the day. All I did was throw a little scare into her. Do I think she's capable of murder? No, not murder, but everything short of that. Underneath that lace exterior, she's as ruthless as they come. In this case, she's motivated as well."

"Don't tell me you think she murdered Lu Xin. She wasn't anywhere near that clinic."

"You know that, do you?"

"It would be easy enough to establish."

"When I told you there were a hundred arrows in the air aimed at Lu Xin, I wasn't thinking hers was one of them. I still don't think she would pull back the bowstring herself, but she might contract to have it done."

There was a small scream from the library, then a string of curses, very Yunnan in content.

"Good, she's back in form," my uncle said. "When I give you the signal, you follow my lead. Tell Wu to be ready, too."

He stepped back into the library and was making his way to the desk before I had a chance to ask what he meant.

"I hope you have recovered, Miss Du," he said as he sat down. "Would you like a sip of whiskey to calm your nerves?"

"Why don't you lay off her, Inspector?" Ping Man-ho looked ready to pop out of his seat. I almost jumped in to restrain him, but I didn't want to move too soon. "You're bullying her for no reason."

"You have been acting gallant all afternoon, Mr. Ping. It would be edifying to see a man come to the aid of a perfect stranger, except you two know each other, have known each other for quite a while."

"That's your theory, Inspector. You're welcome to your theory."

"No, it's more than a theory. You are the one who invited Miss Du to Gao's; you are the one who watched her lose a fortune, more money than you'd ever seen in your life. You didn't gamble much yourself; MSS didn't give you much compensation."

I figured Ping would lunge, and was about to move in when my uncle gave me a look that held me in place. Ping's body tensed, but then he sat back in his chair. I wished I had frisked him when he came in.

"Should I go on, Mr. Ping, or do you want to say something?"

Ping looked at Miss Du. "It's over," he said.

That was all he uttered before Miss Du whipped out a small

pistol and shot him twice in the chest. From that point on, things happened fast. My uncle threw the piglet trotter and knocked the gun from Miss Du's hand; Madame Fang pushed her to the ground, and Gao, in the excitement, kicked her in the head with his cast, which knocked her out cold.

I retrieved the pistol from under one of the chairs because having a weapon lying around in that sort of situation usually isn't helpful. Meanwhile, Wu rushed up to check Ping Man-ho.

"Double damn," he said. "Dead."

3

That night, after a dinner of noodles and dumplings that we ordered out from a pretty reliable restaurant on Jinxue Street, my uncle sat at his desk, reading. Wu was relaxing in the red velvet chair, chewing on a toothpick and holding a glass of whiskey. I'd asked him to stay for dinner and then to hang around. He knew plenty, and maybe he'd help us find our way through the maze as we pulled on the loose threads. My theory had been mostly shot to hell by events earlier in the day, although a few fragments still appeared intact.

"Did you know," my uncle said, not looking up from the book, "that trees can sense earthquakes coming days in advance?"

"I didn't know it, and the reason I didn't is because it's not true. What are you reading?" The last thing we needed was to get off on the wrong track.

My uncle closed the book. "A lot of foolishness. Where do you get books like this, anyway? What about you, Wu, read anything good lately?"

Wu shook his head. "I never read anything but files. Better than fiction." He moved the toothpick from one side of his mouth to the other. "Out of curiosity, Inspector, how did you figure out that Handout was Ping Man-ho? Even I didn't know his identity, and I've been working night and day on that problem for weeks. Major

Bing didn't know either, and Handout was supposed to be his agent."

"You have to give Lu Xin some credit; he did everything necessary to make sure no one realized Ping and Handout were one and the same. I'll bet Handout's personnel dossier is incomplete in all the wrong places."

"You been showing him files he has no business seeing?" Wu grinned at me and took a sip of whiskey.

"Wait a minute," I said. "The Third Bureau must have known who Handout was. Fu Bin was running him for years."

Wu growled like an old dog. "The Third Bureau can't find its way to the toilet in the middle of the day. Your man Fu never met Handout. They were supposed to have face-to-face meetings, but when we checked, we found out that Handout always left his reports in a tree."

My uncle perked up. "What sort of tree?"

Wu shrugged. "The sort that has leaves."

"That's strange," I said to Wu. "You told me you didn't know who Fu Bin was."

"I lie now and then. Shocking, isn't it? How about you, Inspector? Are you going to tell me how you knew about Ping, or are you going to make something up?"

"It's not how did I know about Ping Man-ho, but when," my uncle said. "It's when that's important. I should have realized it sooner. Instead, I was rummaging around in the wrong bag of hypotheses."

"Blue Sparrow, here we come," I muttered.

Wu started to say something, but my uncle kept talking. "If I'd realized it sooner, I would have taken more precautions, Ping would still be alive, and we might figure out exactly what Miss Du had done. She won't talk, I guarantee you."

"That's no problem." Wu seemed more relaxed at how things had turned out than I would have imagined. The whiskey seemed to be helping.

"Oh? You have a theory?" My uncle closed his eyes and let his head lean against the back of his chair.

"Better than that. I have something I can tie up in a neat little package and send off to Headquarters. They know this is too much of a cock-up on their part to complain that I've left gaps."

"Go ahead, you have my undivided attention."

"Understand, I have nothing to do with the planning, and I don't play in external operations. I just clean up afterward. But I need to know a certain amount in order to do my job. Some of this tracks with what the major ran by me yesterday, but you had gaps."

"More whiskey, Wu?" My uncle opened his eyes and looked squarely at me. "Nephew, top his glass off."

Wu held his glass out, and I poured several weeks' salary's worth of expensive whiskey into it.

"No more for me, Major," he said when the glass was nearly full. "I'll sit with this for the rest of the evening. Where was I?"

"Your job," my uncle said. "I think you indicated it gives you access."

"Yeah." Wu put the toothpick in his pocket and gave himself a mouthful of whiskey. Another couple of those, I thought, and he'll end up unconscious on the floor. He was already getting a little extra color in his face. "When Beijing learned that the South Koreans were going to Mongolia to sign deals on rare earth and so forth, people decided they had to move quickly. Outbidding the Koreans isn't possible; bullying the Mongolians is possible, but people would rather hold off on that for now. The best idea, as I heard it, was to discredit the South Koreans in the eyes of the Mongolians, and what better way to do that than to convince Ulan Bator that dealing with Seoul meant getting mixed up in the messy, unending business of inter-Korean confrontation."

I almost said that we'd already figured out as much, but my uncle scooted in ahead of me. "Fascinating," he said. "So why did Miss Du kill Handout?"

"Because she owed a pile of money to Dr. Mike, more than she could possibly pay. She lost a lot at Gao's, but Gao only gets to keep what comes from the small fish. Mike gets the big losers, and he squeezes the life out of them by collecting interest on interest, hourly from what I hear. Gao gets a percentage of a percentage, a few scraps."

"In that case, why not shoot Mike?"

"There's a nice thought. I wish she had. Maybe she would have if she could have found him, but Mike doesn't show up in public very often, as the major knows, and he's smart enough to stay away from people who owe him money and thus don't wish him well."

"Back to the original question. Why Handout?"

"I'm getting to that. Before they had a falling-out, Miss Du and Ping Man-ho had the hots for each other. We weren't watching him, but we were keeping track of her. They were ripping each other's clothes off every night for a few months, but then something happened. She got tired of him, told him to get lost, but he kept finding his way back to her. By that time she was deep in debt, and Ping figured if he helped her fix her problem with Mike, she'd fall in love with him again. What is it with these lovelorn types?"

"Sappy bastard. Always the weak link in these things." My uncle sounded disgusted.

"Yeah, well, he died for his sins. Anyway, here we have to switch gears. Ping was panting after Miss Du, and in the meantime, thanks to Lu Xin but unbeknownst to us thanks to a big hole in our network, Handout wriggled himself in the middle of the counterfeit state seal gambit. Beijing dreamed up this complicated operation to use the seal to discredit the South Koreans. But Lu Xin had his own game. He decided to use the Chinese game as cover for his return home. As a first step, he had to get word to us that he planned to redefect. Word got back, I never figured out how."

"Always gaps," said my uncle. "Minor detail."

Wu might have given my uncle a suspicious look, but his eyes were starting to have a little trouble focusing. I topped off his glass.

"Yeah, details," Wu said. "The operation was already going two directions at once, and then Handout decided to use the seal to win back the heart of Miss Du."

"Beijing didn't get wind of any of this?"

"Hell, no. It never occurred to Beijing that a little germ like Handout would play such a big game. I doubt if Lu Xin knew either. If he had, he probably would have tried to stop it because it could end up compromising his own efforts to screw with Beijing. This is normal. This is why I run cleanup teams every day of the year. Always something going wrong."

"Dismal." My uncle shook his head.

"You said it. This one was over the cliff before it even got moving, total failure on all counts. I had planned a vacation right about then, but Beijing could tell it was starting to rain shit, so they canceled my leave. I was about to get on a plane when the courier came running up with orders to pull a travel team together in a hurry." He turned to me. "You know, those special orders wrapped in that fucking tape. I hate that tape." He took a healthy swallow from his glass. "That's why I ended up in your office at 2:00 A.M. Don't think it was my idea. It wasn't."

By this time I was settled in the chair behind my desk. No one needed my two cents.

Wu picked up the story. "From here on out I do a little creative thinking. I don't know this for sure, but I like the flow."

"I'm with you," my uncle said.

"Once Miss Du learns about the plan for the counterfeit seal—"

"She learned of the plan?" My uncle had it down to a fine science, exactly when to break into a narrative. "How?"

Wu smiled a crooked smile. "I figure it was Ping. Maybe not, but my money goes on Ping. There was a leak somewhere. Anyway, Miss Du pleads with her father to offer his services in crafting the state seal for Mike. She doesn't give a damn about the Chinese plans, and she doesn't know anything about Lu Xin's game. She just wants to get out from under her debt, and the best way to do that is to have her father offer to make the seal for Mike for next to nothing if he'll promise to let his daughter off the hook. This is fine with Mike because a world-class counterfeiter like Du charges plenty. You know how much plenty?" He gazed unsteadily at my uncle.

"No, how much?"

Wu examined his glass, searching for an exact figure. "A hell of a lot. If that expense goes away, Mike gets more for himself, more than enough to compensate for giving up what Miss Du owes him. So what do you think Mike does?"

My uncle yawned and looked at his watch. "I don't know, what does he do? Are we near the end of this tale yet?"

"Almost. You want to see it tied up with a pretty bow, or don't you?"

"Don't worry about me, I can live with uncertainty in these things. The world exists mostly in a palette of grays. Very soothing if you know how to adjust to it. "

"Good for you, good for all of you Koreans. Life's uncertain, that's for sure." He raised his glass to my uncle and then to me. "Come on, aren't you going to drink with me? The Kazakh lady complained you wouldn't drink."

The room suddenly fell into a profound silence. The color drained from Wu's face. He put down his drink and looked at my uncle. "Nice," he said finally. "You pulled me into that so I didn't even see it coming. What next?"

Since my uncle didn't say anything, I figured it was my turn to throw in a few words. "Keep talking. You're doing fine." I held up the bottle. "Want to finish this? It might ease the pain."

Wu shook his head. "Let me get to the end. Then I'll drink the rest and to hell with everything." He took a deep breath. "Beijing was going to work Du into the plan anyway. This phony state seal had to be perfect, and no one but Du could do that. When his daughter jumped in and got Du involved before it could be done according to the script, Beijing got a little nervous. You probably don't realize how nervous Beijing gets when it isn't holding all of the reins."

My uncle started tidying the top of his desk. "No, I didn't realize that."

"Du is a master, we know that, but sometimes he's too meticulous. He fell behind on the timeline Mike had been handed as his part of the deal. Mike didn't know for sure who he was working for. He thought it might be the North Koreans, but the offer came to him through a chain of cutouts and he didn't have time to trace it all out. Anyway, it was nearly a million U.S. in advance to take the deal, and another million if he delivered according to the schedule, which was tight. There was a bonus of two million if the South Koreans accepted the seal without sneezing and used it in Mongolia to ratify the mining deals, though Mike was simply told the bonus came 'if subsequent performance was satisfactory.' The lawyers insisted on that language. Mike didn't really care where the offer came from; he just wanted to get the work done and out the door. But like I said, Du was meticulous; he told Mike a job like this couldn't be hurried. Mike screamed at Du if it wasn't completed on time, he wouldn't be doing any finger painting in the future. These triad guys cut off their own fingers all the time. I guess Mike didn't think twice about waving the threat around. But it rattled Du. We heard he freaked out, couldn't get anything done for weeks because his hands were shaking so much. Mike started sending packages to Miss Du in hopes she would encourage her father to get to work."

My uncle scoffed. "I knew it, I knew those weren't Du's fingers."

"We'll never really know, unless we find Du. Mike was the type who might cut off someone's nose to spite his face."

"What about all that fancy DNA testing I hear about?"

"Forget it. This is an MSS operation that everyone wants buried. Beijing doesn't want to know what happened to Du. Better for them if he really is in pieces. Why, do you care what happened to him?"

"Not especially. Although there is one thing I would like to know."

Even with his brain half submerged in alcohol, Wu knew what was coming. His fingers tightened around the arms of the chair.

My uncle leaned into the question. "Who did you hire to kill Lu Xin at that clinic?"

I've seen men sober up quickly before, but never as fast as Wu did. He had himself under complete control when he answered. "You don't want to ask me that, Inspector. First of all, I don't know. Second of all, simply asking the question puts you in a lot of danger."

"That's friendly advice?"

"Beijing already thinks you never retired. Some people in MSS are sure you're an enemy agent. Didn't the major tell you?"

My uncle slowly drummed his fingers on the desk for what seemed a lifetime. I hate whiskey, but I never wanted a drink so bad in my life.

"What Major Bing and I discuss is not for you or anyone else to know." It was not what I expected my uncle to say. I could tell it wasn't what Wu expected either. "As to what Beijing thinks, I don't give a rat's ass. I've been through plenty in my life; there's nothing left that can scare me. I think we all understand each other, and I think from this point on we're all sort of in this together. So let's put the remaining pieces of the puzzle on the table and see if we can make them fit, shall we?"

Wu knew it was useless to argue or even to bluff. "Sure, you can try to make the pieces fit. The problem is, just when they look like they will, they won't. And you know why? Because Mike got greedy again, like he did in New York. He decided that if the seal was so valuable, he could keep it for himself, to forge South Korean government documents that would get him as much money as he wanted, even political access. Who needs a lousy few million? Mike tells everyone how much he hates it here in the northeast. He must have figured the seal could be his ticket up and out to better things."

"Touching tale of social mobility." My uncle looked at his watch. "End of story."

"No, that was the easy part. From here on it gets complicated. I'll summarize. Beijing dropped the operation when it pulled on a string and discovered that the seal had gone missing. From somewhere—if you ask me, it was from Lu Xin stirring the pot—the story started circulating that the North Koreans might have it. A report came in via Handout that the seal was on its way to Mongolia. This news arrived like a rocket from hell in the special MSS section running the operation. A hasty decision was made to send you, Inspector, and the major here to Mongolia to retrieve the seal, and once you did that, to get rid of both of you. That's what Ding does for a living."

I poured myself the rest of the whiskey.

My uncle excused himself. "It's getting late," he said. "Good night, Wu. Come by again some time for noodles."

Wu stood up. "I'll do that the next time I'm up here in the northeast, Inspector." They shook hands, and my uncle, after a brief nod in my direction, stepped into the hall. A moment later, the side door to his workshop opened and slammed shut.

Wu drained the last drop from his glass. "Amazing man," he said. "Well, that's it for me, Major. We have a lot to do tomorrow. We'd both better get some sleep. I'll see you in your office bright and early. How do you people in Jilin do it?"

"Do what?"

"Drink all the time. I guess there's nothing else to do in winter."

"It's almost June."

He looked at the empty whiskey bottle. "Must be something about this part of the country. Thanks for dinner, Major. I think I can find my way out."

Once Wu was gone, I went back to the library and sat in the dark. I needed the chance to go over things in my head. Some of what happened over the past few weeks was clear, no nuance. Li Xun didn't make it home; the counterfeit seal was in Mike's pocket somewhere between my sector and South Korea. I'd never see Tuya again, and on my desk there was the same pile of unpaid bills.

The rest wasn't so stark. Li Bo-ting had been loyal and reliable, only there was something in him I hadn't seen. The doctor in the clinic in Mongolia knew more about suffering than he let on, but he was still the kindest man I'd ever meet. Madame Fang? Where she fit I would never know. A lot of loose threads, and I was too tired to pull on them.

Walking down the hall to my bedroom, I stopped to open the door to the courtyard for a breath of air. A light was on in the workshop, and I could hear snatches of a melancholy Korean folk song. The voice quavered, and then all was still.

Somewhere I'd read that the human eye can distinguish 500 shades of gray. Or, in the case of my uncle, 501.

Ulan Bator
July 2009